Praise for Angela Knight's paranormal romances

"A terrific paranormal romantic suspense thriller that never slows down . . . The action-packed story line moves at a fast clip."
—*Midwest Book Review*

"Suspense and erotic romance . . . intense and compelling."
—*The Romance Reader*

"[A] paranormal with lots of imagination and plenty of sensual moments . . . one powerfully intriguing book . . . one of the hottest books out [there]."
—*The Romance Reader's Connection*

"A powerful romantic suspense and sensuous tale all rolled into one alluring and explosive package . . . Twists and turns, fairies, vampires, and sex hot enough to burn, *Master of the Night* delivers them all."
—*Romance Reviews Today*

MASTER
of
WOLVES

ANGELA KNIGHT

BERKLEY SENSATION, NEW YORK

THE BERKLEY PUBLISHING GROUP
Published by the Penguin Group
Penguin Group (USA) Inc.
375 Hudson Street, New York, New York 10014, USA
Penguin Group (Canada), 90 Eglinton Avenue East, Suite 700, Toronto, Ontario M4P 2Y3, Canada
(a division of Pearson Penguin Canada Inc.)
Penguin Books Ltd., 80 Strand, London WC2R 0RL, England
Penguin Group Ireland, 25 St. Stephen's Green, Dublin 2, Ireland (a division of Penguin Books Ltd.)
Penguin Group (Australia), 250 Camberwell Road, Camberwell, Victoria 3124, Australia
(a division of Pearson Australia Group Pty. Ltd.)
Penguin Books India Pvt. Ltd., 11 Community Centre, Panchsheel Park, New Delhi—110 017, India
Penguin Group (NZ), Cnr. Airborne and Rosedale Roads, Albany, Auckland 1310, New Zealand
(a division of Pearson New Zealand Ltd.)
Penguin Books (South Africa) (Pty.) Ltd., 24 Sturdee Avenue, Rosebank, Johannesburg 2196,
South Africa

Penguin Books Ltd., Registered Offices: 80 Strand, London WC2R 0RL, England

This is a work of fiction. Names, characters, places, and incidents either are the product of the author's imagination or are used fictitiously, and any resemblance to actual persons, living or dead, business establishments, events, or locales is entirely coincidental. The publisher does not have any control over and does not assume any responsibility for author or third-party websites or their content.

MASTER OF WOLVES

A Berkley Sensation Book / published by arrangement with the author

PRINTING HISTORY
Berkley Sensation edition / April 2006

ISBN: 0-425-20743-9

BERKLEY SENSATION®
Berkley Sensation Books are published by The Berkley Publishing Group,
a division of Penguin Group (USA) Inc.,
375 Hudson Street, New York, New York 10014.
BERKLEY SENSATION is a registered trademark of Penguin Group (USA) Inc.
The "B" design is a trademark belonging to Penguin Group (USA) Inc.

PRINTED IN THE UNITED STATES OF AMERICA

10 9 8 7 6 5 4 3 2 1

This book is dedicated to the men and women of law enforcement. Day in and day out, they risk their lives for little money and less respect, retaining their integrity despite all the temptations and stresses the job has to offer.

I would like to thank two of those officers for consulting on this book. The first is K-9 Officer Susan Millard of the Dallas Police Department, who offered several helpful ideas I incorporated.

But my greatest thanks go to K-9 officer Doug Jones of the Woodruff Police Department in South Carolina, who took time from his busy schedule to talk to me at length about what it's like to work with police drug dogs. My interviews with Doug and fellow Woodruff K-9 cop Todd Hendrix inspired *Master of Wolves* and the previous book, *Master of the Moon*. Officers like Doug, Todd, and Susan share a special bond of love with their dogs, and they do fantastic work.

I'd also like to thank those who gave me so much help with *Master of Wolves*. My agent, Roberta Brown, helped me pinpoint a maddening problem with an earlier draft. My test readers Morgan Hawke, Virginia Ettel, Martha Punches, Linda Kusiolek, and Katherine Lazo helped me track down and kill many other goofs. Those that remain are my fault.

And as ever, I would like to thank my wonderful critique partner, Diane Whiteside, for much hand-holding, brainstorming, and patient reassurance that "No, this book does not suck."

Last but certainly not least, I would like to express my deep gratitude to my editor, Cindy Hwang, who waited so patiently while I ripped it apart and started over. Twice.

I hope you, my reader, find that our efforts have been worth it.

PROLOGUE

Jim London walked down the hospital corridor, Mary Shay's arm in his. Her thin hand gripped his forearm with a strength that was almost painful. Concerned, he looked at her. Her face was expressionless, but agony lay over her blue eyes like a layer of frost. She was only in her fifties, the age of his own mother, but she looked much older today, her normal trim prettiness withered by grief. She had dressed with an almost painful care in a gray jacket and skirt that contrasted with her perfectly styled blond hair. The modest neckline of her silk blouse framed a single strand of pearls. It was less an outfit than a silent demand for respect. *Don't lie to me.*

A memory flashed through his mind, sharp and vivid.

The kids had sat together around the campfire, toasting marshmallows on green branches gathered from the surrounding woods. Jim was trying to burn his to gooey perfection when he heard his sister squeal.

On the other side of the campfire, Diana jumped to her feet, twisting and squirming as she tried to get at the frog his best friend had just dropped down her shirt. "Tony Shay, you rat!" Scooping the frog from under her hem, she dropped it on her nemesis.

Tony collapsed in giggles and caught the frog as it tumbled off his red-haired head.

Jim pulled his burning marshmallow from the campfire and blew out the tongue of flame. The treat was seared almost black, which in his experience meant creamy perfection inside. Popping the marshmallow into his mouth, he sighed at the gooey sweetness and licked his fingers. "Why do you keep picking on Di, Tony? You got a crush on her, or what?"

"Oooo!" Steve Carson hooted, his hazel eyes lighting with mischief. A short, thin boy, he loved nothing more than egging somebody else into a good fight. "Tony and Diana, sittin' in a tree, K-I-S-S-I-N—"

"Oh, gross!" Diana wrinkled her pert nose. "What a disgusting concept."

Hurt flashed across Tony's freckled face, only to instantly vanish into a tough-guy glower. "Like I'd want anything to do with you, you skinny, ugly little—"

"Hey!" Prodded, Jim sat up and glared at him. "Watch how you talk about my sister, jackass."

Tony balled his fists and sneered. "And what are you going to do about it?"

"Nothing," Mary Shay said firmly, stepping into the circle of firelight, slim and pretty in shorts and a pink knit shirt. She pointed a stern finger at her son. "No fighting, young man."

"He started it!" Tony protested.

"You insulted Di!"

"I can take care of myself," Diana snapped, glaring at her foe.

"Yeah, right," he sneered. "You're just a girl."

"I'll show you who's a girl!" Diana lunged for him. Jim jumped to his feet, ready to defend his sister even against his best buddy.

"Fight!" Steve crowed, jumping up and bouncing on his sneakered toes.

But as Tony tried to catch Diana's swinging fists and Jim barreled around the fire, magic rose in a hair-ruffling wave.

With a growl, Mary Shay Changed, her body growing, muscle and bone twisting and elongating into something much, much bigger. A wave of magic rolled over her body, replacing her knit outfit with a thick, lupine coat of blond fur.

A heartbeat later, she towered over the children, seven feet of fangs and lean muscle. Eyes cold with displeasure, she surveyed the scene above a long wolf muzzle before reaching down with huge clawed hands.

Diana and Tony yelped as she jerked them into the air by their collars and gave them a light shake. "I told you, no fighting," Mary said, her voice a deep growl.

Hanging in his mother's grip like a puppy, Tony glowered at Diana with sullen longing. "I wasn't going to hurt her—much."

"You weren't going to hurt me at all," Diana retorted, but her attention was fixed on Mary with naked hero worship. She sighed. "Man, I can't wait until I can do that."

The Dire Wolf's long muzzle curled into a smile that looked a little grim. "Give it time, child. It'll come."

It had, Jim remembered, listening to the measured click of Mary's heels at his side. Five years later, when they'd turned seventeen, he, Tony, and Steve had gone up to the mountains with his uncle Raymond to attempt their first Change.

It had been a pretty night, with the moon riding full over the wooded mountainside, serenaded by a chorus of frogs and crickets. Jim, Tony, and Steve were gathered around yet another campfire, breathing the cool mountain air for what might be the last time.

This was the night they'd all been dreading since they'd

found out about Merlin's Curse. Not that they feared becoming werewolves. Over the years, they'd come to see their first transformation as a rite of adulthood that brought fantastic power.

No, it was the alternative to that transformation that had even Tony looking unusually pale.

Jim watched Steve pull another Bud from the six-pack from the cooler and down it in one desperate swallow. "You sure that's a good idea?" His head was already buzzing pleasantly from the one beer he'd had. Or maybe that was the approaching Change.

Steve shrugged. "Probably not, but what the fuck. Did I tell you I finally nailed Bonnie?"

"No kidding!" Tony grinned around his own bottle. He'd grown into a tall, lean kid, just beginning to bulk up. "You've only been chasing her since junior high." He offered his hand for a high-five.

Steve slapped it. "Gotta love those pheromones."

"Friend to werewolf boys everywhere." Jim offered his own palm for a slap. Direkind teens produced such powerful sex hormones as they approached their first Change, even humans responded. A fact Jim had taken shameless advantage of over the past week.

"Look at that shit-eating grin," Tony said, laughing. "London got lucky. Was it Allie, Jo, or Karla?"

He tried to conceal his smug smile. "A gentleman's not supposed to tell."

"Oh, spill, already," Steve said. "You may not get another chance."

"'Fraid you boys have run out of time." Ray Johnston stepped from out of the woods, silent as smoke, in jeans and a camouflage jacket. He was not a tall man, but he had a wiry strength and steely will that won respect from much larger weres. As Jim's uncle, he'd agreed to serve as Wolfmaster for the three boys, guiding them through their first transformation.

"I left your parents waiting down the mountain," he

said. "They're sweating bullets. Let's get this done so we can go back and tell 'em everybody's safe."

Jim felt himself pale, swallowing hard as the beer he'd just drunk threatened to abandon ship.

"Hey, buck up," Ray said kindly, no doubt scenting their collective fear. "There are three of you. The odds are in your favor."

"One in five is just an average," Steve pointed out, then managed a sickly grin. "And I've got a feeling being one of the twenty percent would really suck."

"Think positive, kid." The older were sighed. "I'll start." His magic rose in a spill of tingling heat.

Jim had witnessed countless Direkind transformations over the years, but this time was different. Ray's magic surged into him, smelling of deep forests, tasting of endless nights running beneath the moon. Calling to him.

For the very first time, he felt the power jolt up from his guts, sizzling along his nervous system, jerking bone and muscle into new shapes with agonizing force.

Somebody began to scream.

For a moment of raw panic, Jim thought the voice was his own. His eyes popped open.

Steve glowed like a star beside him.

His friend writhed, screaming as magical fire licked across his skin, devouring him in shades of incandescent blue. Jim met Steve's pleading, horrified eyes through the unearthly flames, but there was nothing he could do except gag on the smell of magic and burning skin.

Until, mercifully, Steve winked out. Vanished. Gone as if he'd never been.

Ray began to swear in a roll of weary profanity, his big hands hanging helplessly at his sides.

"Steve," Jim said, his eyes going hot. "Oh, man . . ." Steve's mother . . . God, they were going to have to tell Steve's mother. She was somewhere at the base of the mountain with the other parents, waiting in miserable suspense to learn if her son had survived his first transformation.

Unable to face the empty air any longer, Jim turned away, his gaze falling on the tall, thin, red-furred werewolf standing across the campfire. It took him a moment to recognize those blue eyes.

Tony.

Mechanically, Jim looked down at himself, already knowing what he'd see. His own body was covered in thick black fur.

He'd survived.

He dropped to his knees and puked, distantly aware Tony was doing the same.

The loss of Steve had drawn Jim and Tony even closer together, their friendship solidifying as they moved into adulthood. As men, they'd continued to back one another up whenever either needed the other's help. Their last shared escapade had been only a few months ago.

It was the kind of neighborhood that frowned on strangers, particularly two big guys in body armor. The houses were run-down, with cracked and peeling paint and yards littered with broken malt liquor bottles. Here a car sat rusting on cinder blocks in a driveway; there a dog barked with feral hopelessness, straining at the end of a chain tied to a tree.

Cigars glowed from porches where old men sat, drinking beer and bitching about wives and girlfriends. Nobody looked twice at a German shepherd and a brawny red Doberman trotting down the middle of the street.

Which was why he and Tony had assumed dog form in the first place.

Jim had his long muzzle to the pavement, breathing in the scent of the bad guy they were tracking—an accused drug trafficker who'd skipped out on a fifty-thousand-dollar bond.

It seemed the tip from Tony's source was good. Billy Joe Arnold had strolled through the area just an hour before with several buddies. None of whom was nearly as fond of soap and water as he should be.

The scent trail led them to a shotgun shack even more ramshackle than its neighbors. Silent as a pair of wolves, Jim and Tony slipped into the overgrown bushes to change into something with hands.

Human again, Jim glanced at his friend. Tony was a tall man, broad-shouldered and muscular, and the bulletproof vest he wore made him look even bigger. The words "Bail Enforcement Agent" were printed across the front in big white letters. Jim's vest matched it.

"You know they're probably armed to the teeth," Jim said in a voice too low for an ordinary human to hear. He looked up at the house's sagging porch. "I hate getting shot."

His friend gave him a white, lunatic grin. "Oh, bullshit. You love a good adrenalin rush as much as I do. Besides, if they shoot you, you'll just heal."

"Depends on where they shoot me." But Jim found himself grinning back. His blood was singing hot in his veins, and he had to admit Tony was right. There was just something about kicking in some asshole's door and dragging him off to jail. As much as he loved painting, art just didn't carry the same hot, physical rush.

He straightened just long enough to steal a look in through the window. Five men sat in the living room, attention on the big-screen TV that was probably worth more than the house. Four of them were armed with pistols stashed in various places, and an automatic rifle lay on the floor next to the fifth.

"Pretty serious armament for watching a basketball game," he observed, ducking back down. "This is going to be fun."

Tony grinned at him and rose to stride toward the front door. "Always is, buddy." Without breaking step, he kicked the door in with one crashing thrust of a big, booted foot. "Billy Joe Arnold, you're going back to Atlanta to stand trial!"

Jim charged in behind him just in time to see the men going for their guns. Tony grabbed one thug off the couch and body slammed him to the floor, while Jim drove his fist into another's jaw before he could fire. He followed that up with a roundhouse kick that put a third man down and out. Tony gave the fourth guy a casual cuff that, delivered with Dire Wolf strength, sent him flying like a swatted bug.

"I ain't going to jail!" Billy Joe sprinted for the door, but Jim grabbed him and rammed him into the wall. Drywall cracked around the dealer's body, plaster dust flying like snow.

"Now, Billy Joe, your mama put her house up as surety for that bail." Whipping his captive around, Jim bared his teeth. "If you don't stand trial, she's gonna end up homeless." A pile-driver punch smacked the dealer into the wall again. Billy Joe's eyes rolled back in his head, and he collapsed. Jim caught him. "A man just doesn't do that to his mama."

With Tony's skillful help, Jim searched their unconscious prisoner, then cuffed him and tossed him across a shoulder in an effortless fireman's carry. As he turned to carry the man out, Jim met his friend's glittering eyes.

"Now," Tony said, "wasn't that more fun than daubing paint on a canvas?"

"Wasn't bad." Jim grinned, shaking one stinging hand. That last punch had split the skin over his knuckles. "Wasn't bad at all."

That had only been three months ago, Jim thought, escorting Tony's mother down the hospital corridor. Such a short amount of time for everything to go to hell.

Clarkston police chief George Ayers stepped out into the hallway to meet them, his expression solemn. "Mrs. Shay." He moved to shake her hand. Jim didn't offer his. The chief looked nonplused a moment before returning his attention to Mary. "I'm afraid Mr. Jones was called away on a traffic accident. I told him I'd help you."

Ayers was a good-looking man, with a tall, athletic build and artfully graying dark hair. He wore an American flag pin in the lapel of his charcoal gray suit and his chief's badge on his belt.

He also smelled, ever so slightly, of magic and rot. The scent made Jim ache to hit him.

"If you'll come this way," he said, opening the door for them and standing back to allow them to enter. Beside Jim, Mary began to tremble. He folded his free hand over hers. Her fingers felt like sticks of ice, thin, brittle, and cold.

"You sure you're up to this?" Jim whispered, concerned.

"I want to see." There was a faint growl in her voice that made him glance sharply at her.

"Hang on, Mary." *Don't Change in front of him.*

She looked at him, and the magic faded from her gaze. "I'll be fine." Drawing her hand from his, she straightened her shoulders and strode through the door.

Tony lay on a metal table covered by a sheet, his once-ruddy skin gray in death. Jim caught Mary's elbow as she swayed. "It's him," he said shortly.

Mary pulled free and walked forward, simultaneously frail and courageous. Jim followed, his heart twisting into a sick knot of grief. *Dammit, Tony, I wish I'd been there. I should have had your back.*

Together he and Mary stood looking down at the emptied husk that had been Tony Shay. Testing, Jim inhaled.

Magic and rot. His hands knotted into fists.

The scent of rot intensified. "I want to assure you, Mrs. Shay, we're going to do everything in our power to catch the people who did this," Ayers said.

Mary reached for the sheet over her son's chest. Ayers reached out to grab her wrist. "You don't want to see that."

She looked at him, her blue gaze so cold and steady, his hand fell away. "The papers said they cut out my boy's heart." She flipped the sheet back.

Mary made a choked sound at what she saw. Then, face grim with effort, she drew in a breath. Scenting. Her gaze met Jim's, and he knew she'd smelled the same thing he did.

Magic and rot.

Ayers was babbling. "I'm trying to find out who leaked that information to the press. I want to assure you that despite the speculation of irresponsible journalists, this was not some kind of Satanist thing. Not in my town. It may have been drug related, but—"

"My son was not involved in drugs," Mary gritted.

Ayers hesitated. "Mrs. Shay, Tony was thirty-two years old. He traveled frequently. You don't know what he was involved in."

Jim had heard as much of this as he intended to take. "I knew Tony well, and she's right. He was a bail enforcement agent."

Ayers curled a lip ever so slightly. "A bounty hunter."

"Yes, and he had nothing whatsoever to do with drugs." He glared at the chief, who had the grace to look uneasy. "He certainly wasn't some kind of trafficker. I don't know where you come off even making that kind of accusation in the paper. You admitted no drugs were found on him or in his SUV."

"You're lucky I don't sue," Mary rumbled.

Ayers looked uncomfortable. "Some drug cartels employ this kind of . . . mutilation in retaliatory killings against rivals. And Clarkston is located along I-85, a well-known cocaine corridor."

"I don't care." She glared at him, her eyes cold with grief and anger. "You don't make those kinds of accusations."

Ayers swallowed. "You're right, of course. I apologize." He shrugged. "It was only a supposition. As I told the reporter, it could have been the drunks he fought with the previous night. One way or another, we'll find out."

Yeah, right, Jim thought.

Frowning, he hovered at Mary's side while she signed the required paperwork to obtain her son's body for burial. His thoughts raced, wrestling with plans, calculating probabilities.

At last they were done. Jim escorted Mary from Ayers's maddening presence and out into the hall.

They walked down the echoing corridor until both were sure they were beyond human earshot. When Mary spoke, her voice was flat and cold. "Somebody worked death magic on my son. I could smell the stink of it."

"Yes."

She stopped and turned to face him. Her eyes burned hot in her gaunt, pale face. "You're not going to let them get away with this."

"No. No, I'm not. I'm going to find out who killed Tony, and I'm going to start with that police chief. He's involved in this up to his neck. The stench is all over him."

Concern flickered through the despairing rage in her eyes. "That may be, but he and his cops aren't going to talk to you."

Jim smiled without humor. "No, but I'll bet they'd talk *around* me."

She searched his face. "What have you got in mind?"

"There was another article in the Clarkston paper. Seems the chief is looking for a drug dog." Jim bared his teeth. "I'm going to make sure he gets one."

O N E

One Month Later

Faith Weston's new partner was big, muscular and covered in fur, and he didn't give her any crap. If the other males of her acquaintance would only follow his example, she'd be a happy woman.

Faith opened the back of her patrol car and leaned in to clip a leash on the German shepherd's collar. He tolerated the process, his eyes locked on the police department building behind her, as if eager to get to work.

"Come on, Rambo." Faith stepped back to allow the dog to leap from the car's rear compartment. "Time to catch some more bad guys."

"Nice bust last night, Weston."

She turned, recognizing Chief George Ayers's pleasant baritone. "Thanks, Chief."

He stood beside his blue unmarked Crown Vic, having just pulled in himself. Ayers wore another one of his end-less collection of suits, this one a gray pinstripe, accessorized by an American flag lapel pin and a tie clasp shaped like a pair of handcuffs. "A kilo of cocaine. That's one of the biggest drug busts we've had in years." He gave Rambo a genuine smile. "And that dog of yours found it?"

"Yes, sir. Rambo alerted on the wheel well of the guy's car. At first I didn't think there was anything there, but then I found a false compartment in the bottom, stuffed with drugs and ten thousand in cash."

"That's fantastic." The chief crouched to Rambo's eye level and patted him on the head, apparently not noticing the dog's stiff stance and raised hackles. Despite the outraged body language, the shepherd didn't growl. If she didn't know better, she'd think Rambo was practicing doggy diplomacy.

Ayers straightened to his full height, still wearing that pleased grin. "That money is going to come in handy for those dash cams I want to buy." Thanks to Federal law, police departments could keep a share of drug profits they seized.

"After the judge signs off on it." Faith shrugged. "When I was with the Atlanta P.D., it sometimes took months to work through all the red tape around a seizure."

"Not this time." The chief's gaze cooled. "Things are different in this county. Trust me, I'll see to it the judge doesn't drag his heels."

Which would be a neat trick. In Faith's experience, judges couldn't care less what cops wanted—especially the chief of a small town police department like George Ayers. She'd love to know why Ayers thought he had enough pull to make a Circuit Court judge dance to his tune.

Faith grimaced. *Then again, maybe ignorance is bliss.* A lot of things seemed to operate differently in Clarkston, South Carolina.

Ayers flashed her his best professional politician smile. "Keep getting me results like these, and the town council will wish they'd let us have a drug dog sooner."

"Well, tell them they got a bargain." She leaned down to

pat the shepherd's muscular ribs. "When I found out that
K-9 trainer was just going to give us a dog, I'll admit my
expectations weren't very high. But Rambo has turned out
to be hell on wheels. With his nose and his training, Ray
Johnston could have gotten five thousand for him even in
this area, and ten thousand in other parts of the country."
She shook her head. "Whoever arranged for Rambo's do-
nation to the department did us a big favor. We really
lucked out."

"Hey, I've always been a lucky man." The chief's smile
grew smug as they started across the parking lot. "Just
make good use of the opportunity."

She smiled down at Rambo as the dog trotted into the
department at her heels. "Oh, believe me, I intend to."

The redhead was tall, slim, and drop-dead gorgeous, a fact
she seemed blissfully unaware of. Her legs looked a mile
long in her black uniform pants, and her badge called attention to breasts that were pert and tempting. Police
equipment belts, with their holsters, gear, and pouches,
tended to make most women look dumpy, but Faith Weston
was tall enough to carry it all off.

Jim could have had worse partners.

He watched her as she stood in the Clarkston Police Department's break room, organizing the paperwork she'd
need for the coming shift. Jim had been with Faith a month
now while investigating Tony's murder, and he'd learned to
respect her intelligence and integrity. This department was
full of dirty cops, but Faith wasn't one of them.

She shifted her weight, drawing his attention to her firm
little butt in those snug black trousers. Over the past
month, he'd developed a definite thing for uniforms—or at
least, a recurring fantasy about getting Faith out of hers.

Unfortunately, he wasn't the only one with ideas in that
direction. As if on cue, a tall blond officer walked into the
break room, spotted her, and smiled with predatory inter-

est. Faith, Jim was pleased to note, eyed the cop almost as
warily as he did.

"Hi, there, Faith." The blond's grin was brilliant as he
sauntered over to join her. A whiff of rot accompanied him.
"I was wondering if I could buy you a beer after your shift."

How many times does she have to say no, dumbass? Jim
thought.

"Sorry, Dave." Her drawl was pure magnolias and
cream. "Like I told you before, I don't date coworkers." A
trace of pain flashed in her green eyes. "It can get ugly."

Just to make sure the cop didn't push the point, Jim
growled low in his throat.

Dave looked at him, surprised and a little wary, before
giving Faith a forced smile. "Well, if you change your
mind, you know where to find me."

He strode off, making a careful circle around Jim.

Faith dropped to one knee so she was eye-to-eye with
Jim, who lay under the break room table. "Well-timed
growl there, Rambo." She picked up his leash and gave his
furry head a pat. "Good dog."

Oh, baby, Jim thought, *I'd love to show you just how
good a dog I really am.*

With a last appreciative glance up at her endless legs, he
led the way outside.

Dave Green waved at Faith as she strode across the police
department parking lot, Rambo trotting along in front of
her on his leash. She nodded back, carefully professional.
The jerk just didn't want to take no for an answer.

"Hey, Faith," Green called. "Call me, okay? I'm serious."

She pretended not to hear. *When hell freezes solid.*

Opening the rear door of her unit, Faith stood back to let
Rambo jump in. "He's too damn good looking," she told
the dog, watching Green drive away. "Reminds me of Ron."

And after the job her ex-husband had done on her, she
had no intention of walking into the handsome-guy-buzz-

saw ever again. Men who looked like that couldn't be trusted. Women came too easily to them. Like kids in a candy store, there was never a shortage of goodies to catch their attention.

Faith had learned the hard way that she didn't have what it took to keep a man like that interested. Luckily, there were other things she excelled at.

She started the Ford Crown Victoria and pulled out of the parking lot, leaving the long, low brick building behind as she drove toward her patrol zone.

Clarkston worked hard at being a New South town, with its sprawling outlet mall and strip of chain restaurants running parallel to I-85. But for all its middle-class aspirations, the community still carried scars from the collapse of the textile industry. Faith's zone included the burned-out shell of a cotton mill and the surrounding neighborhood of Bomar, which had once served as the plant's employee housing. The residents had never been rich, not on textile wages, but they'd skidded even further down the economic ladder since the company closed. Few people had jobs, and those who did worked for minimum wage.

The only thriving business in Bomar was the drug trade. And, of course, police work.

In the past year, Faith had worked two murders, an arson, three convenience store robberies, and dozens of burglaries, not to mention countless domestics and drunken brawls. All of it in the same mile-long area. She never had to look very long before she found somebody breaking some law somewhere.

Today was no exception. Barely half an hour passed before she found herself a suspect.

Driving alongside the rattletrap Honda, Faith flicked its driver another assessing glance. After eight years as a cop, she knew a bad guy when she saw one.

He wore his blond hair in a greasy mullet, his face was long and homely, and he drove like a drug dealer. Not fast and recklessly, but five miles under the speed limit, a good fifteen miles slower than everything else on the road.

Both hands firmly on the wheel, he refused to look at her as she paced him. Most drivers eyed Faith whenever she drove up beside them in Clarkson traffic, whether it was a friendly *hello-officer* glance or a nervous *am-I-speeding* stare. This guy's body language was so throughly *I'm-not-doin'-nothing-Go-away,* he just had to be up to something.

"What do you think, 'Bo?" Faith murmured. "Kilo of coke in the trunk?"

A soft, deep woof sounded in her ear.

"My thoughts exactly. Let's see if Willie the Wonder Weasel will give us an excuse." Judges frowned on pulling people over just because they acted funny.

Some members of the legal profession had no imagination.

Faith slowed down and pulled into the lane behind her suspect. His head jerked nervously as he checked out his rearview mirror. She grinned toothily at him. "That's right, Willie, panic. Run away. I want to chase you."

But Willie was smarter than he looked—admittedly not difficult—and stayed right where he was, slowing down even more.

"Oh, yeah, you're carrying, you greasy little rat. What have we got here?" Faith checked out the back end of his car. No broken taillight. Too bad—that was one of her favorites. She scooped up the handset of her radio and called his tag number in to Tayanita County dispatch, hoping the car was stolen or registered to somebody with an outstanding warrant. As she waited for the dispatcher to tell her the results of the computer search, she checked out his car tag.

"Oh, look, 'Bo," she murmured, her attention narrowing on the small sticker on the corner of his license plate. The color and date were wrong for this time of year. "Our boy hasn't paid his county property tax this year. Sticker expired four months ago." Which meant the forty-day grace period had run out. "Come to mommy, weasel boy." Faith reached down to the box under her radio and flicked the switch to activate the car's lights and sirens.

Again, Willie didn't run. Instead, he drove into the parking lot of Bomar's sole Li'l Cricket convenience store, as demure as a grandma going to church. He was going to try to brazen it out.

"This'll be entertaining," Faith told Rambo as she pulled in behind his car. From long, cautious habit in this neighborhood, she parked a little to the left of his Honda, so their cars would block his shot if he suddenly opened fire.

She scooped up her handset again. "Tayanita, Clarkston 2-4. I'm out with a red 1992 Honda Accord, licence plate Lima Foxtrot Able 9-6-9."

The radio crackled at her. "Ten-four, Clarkston 2-4."

Grabbing her ticket book, she got out and closed the car door, eyeing the Honda. Her heart beating a little faster, she started toward it.

Contrary to popular belief, this was the moment when most officers got shot, which was why Faith wore a bullet-proof vest under her dark-blue uniform shirt. Her entire body sang with adrenalin by the time she approached the driver's window.

Willie rolled down his window. His eyes were a little too wide in his thin face. "I wasn't speeding, officer."

"Didn't say you were. License and registration, please." While he reached for his wallet, she asked pleasantly, "Did you know your tag has expired?"

An *oh-shit* expression crossed his face, out of proportion to the hundred-dollar fine for the offense. "Uh, no ma'am. I'll pay it tomorrow." He handed her his identification.

"Got any drugs in the car, Mr."—she glanced at the licence and read his name—"Cruise?"

Samuel Cruise stiffened and said the magic words. "Not to my knowledge."

Bingo. An innocent person would have given her a simple, surprised "No!" If there wasn't a kilo of coke in the trunk, she'd eat Rambo's badge.

"You sure about that? Step out of the car, please."

Which was evidently Cruise's cue to babble as he reluctantly obeyed. "I don't have no drugs in the car. Swear on a stack of Bibles, I ain't no drug dealer."

"Uh-huh." Every cop knew the minute a Southerner started swearing on Bibles, he was guilty as hell of something. Faith smiled, sweet as a mint julep. "Then you won't mind if I get my dog and check it out."

True alarm flashed over his face. "No! I mean, don't you got to have a warrant or—"

"A sniff is not a search, Mr. Cruise." She started back toward the car, glancing over her shoulder in case he bolted. He looked like he was seriously considering it until she got Rambo out of the back and clipped on the big animal's leash.

Cruise's eyes widened, and he went very, very still.

Faith didn't blame him. Most German shepherds weighed sixty or seventy pounds at most. Rambo was twice that, a hulking black beast who looked as if there was a pony somewhere in his family tree. She often joked if her Crown Vic ever broke down, she could saddle 'Bo.

Faith led him over to the suspect, who took a wary step back. "He won't bite," she told him. "Unless I tell him to."

Cruise gave both of them a wild-eyed look.

Rambo put his big head down and sniffed the man's grimy running shoes, then worked his way up ripped, dirty jeans to one pocket. He promptly plopped his fuzzy butt down on the pavement and gazed up at Faith with a rumble of satisfaction. 'Bo was a passive alert dog—the sit-down-and-look sequence meant he'd found something. Faith concealed a grin. *Let's hear it for puppy power.* "Please brace your hands on the hood of the car, sir."

There it was again, that flash of raw panic. "Officer—"

She caught him by one stringy forearm and turned him toward the car. "Hands on the hood, please. You got any needles in your pocket, Mr. Cruise?" The last thing she wanted was a needle stick from an AIDS-infected subject.

His expression was genuinely offended as he assumed the position with the ease of long practice. "Hell, no!"

Okay, that was sincere. She put her hand around and felt the pocket 'Bo had indicated, the dog watching with interest. A small, suspicious lump greeted her fingers, but no syringe-like tube. She reached in and pulled out a trio of dirty-brown pebbles wrapped in plastic. "Oh, Mr. Cruise, you disappoint me. You're under arrest for possession of crack cocaine." At least until she found whatever he was really nervous about. It wasn't three piddling crack rocks, that was for sure.

"That isn't mine!"

She looked up at him, amused. "They were in your pants."

His eyes shifted. "These aren't my pants!"

"Okay, I'll bite. Whose pants are they?"

"A friend's. I was staying at his house, and—"

"So you're telling me these are the communal pants? Those your skivvies, or did you borrow them, too?" He opened his mouth, but she'd hit her limit for stupid. "Bzzzz! Wrong answer, dude. You're going to jail. Do not pass go, we'll collect your two hundred dollars in the morning."

Then, for the first time that night, he surprised her. "Don't take me to the city jail. I'm begging you." His hazel eyes went wide with panicked pleading. "Take me to the county jail."

"Cruise, I'm a city cop. You're going to the city jail. That's the way it works."

"No!" Whirling around, he hit her square in the face.

Stunned, Faith reeled back, wiping at the blood that had splattered into her eyes from her busted lip. Cruise took off running, Rambo in furious, barking pursuit. The little rat didn't get far. Before Faith could even shake off the sucker punch, the dog caught the hem of his jeans and braced his forelegs. Cruise fell flat on his face.

"Oh, you're going to regret that!" Ignoring her swollen lip, Faith ran over and pounced. Just as she straddled his butt and grabbed his wrist, Cruise went wild. One swinging elbow caught her in the cheek. Pain detonated in the side of her face.

"Okay, that does it!" Faith snatched her Asp baton from her belt and telescoped it to full length with a flick of her wrist. She was seriously tempted to clock him in the skull with it, but head shots were a no-no. Instead, she tried to hook one skinny arm so she could lever his wrist into position for handcuffs.

Cruise twisted onto his side, grabbed her arm, and threw her onto her back. Face twisted in fear and desperation, he reared over her, fist drawn back.

This time he wasn't fast enough. Faith blocked the shot with the Asp and popped him in the nose with her left fist. His head snapped back with the force of the blow.

Damn, she thought with a snarling grin, *that felt good.*

Cruise yowled and started to scramble off her. Before he could make it all the way to his feet, Rambo reared up and smashed into his shoulders, knocking him sideways. The shepherd pounced, flattening him on the pavement.

Thoroughly pinned under the dog's weight, there wasn't much he could do when Rambo planted both big forepaws on the side of his head. With a happy growl of satisfaction, 'Bo thumped his butt down on the man's shoulder.

The suspect could only yowl. "Get him off me!"

"Nothing doing, jerk." Faith rammed a knee in the small of Cruise's spine, snatched her handcuffs from the pouch at her waist, and snapped them onto his flailing left hand. She used the cuff to drag it into position behind his back. "Give me your other hand!"

"Ahh! Lady, get your dog off me!"

"That's what you get for being a dumbass—a German shepherd sitting on your face. Give me your hand!"

"Don't take me to the city jail! I don't want to get my soul sucked out!"

Fighting to control his squirming, she panted, "What the hell are you talking about, you lunatic? Are you high?"

"Please!"

"If you don't give me your hand, you're going to the hospital, because I'm going to let Rambo *eat your head*!"

Right on cue, the dog began doing his Cujo imitation, barking until saliva flew. Cruise yowled even louder. "Ahhh! Get him off, get him off!"

"Give me your hand, or I swear to God, I'll tell Rambo you're a Scooby snack."

"All right, all right!" He thrust his right hand down, and she snapped on the cuffs. "Just don't let him eat me!"

Fighting her laughter, she looked at Rambo, who stood with both paws mashing down on Cruise's face. She'd never seen a dog look more thoroughly smug. "Get off the man's head, 'Bo. What are you, a hat?"

An hour later, she was considerably less amused as she stalked over to the police car where Cruise sat waiting. Since the backseat of her unit had been removed to make room for Rambo, she'd had to call another officer to transport her prisoner. With George Williams keeping an eye on Cruise, she and Rambo had conducted a thorough search of that rattletrap Honda.

Now she swung the rear door open so she could glare down at the man. "All that for three flipping crack rocks? Are you nuts? The way you were carrying on, I thought you had a kilo of coke or a body in the trunk."

He hunched his shoulders, pale and miserable. There were red scratches on the side of his face from Rambo's claws, and she'd given him a black eye. Faith didn't feel sorry for the little weasel though, because her own eye was swelling, and her uniform was ripped and bloody. Assorted scrapes and bruises had already begun to sting.

"I just don't wanna go to the city jail," he whined. "People go to that jail, they come out with their soul sucked out. Some of 'em get eaten by the monster."

"Monster? Oh, give me a break." She'd thought she'd at least get a decent bust out of this. Instead she'd ripped the knee out of her brand-new uniform pants. "You'll be out on bond before I finish writing the police report. You've got one simple possession prior. You wouldn't even get time, except I'm going to add assaulting a police officer to the charges. Public defender'll have a hell of a time getting you out of that."

Cruise moaned like a condemned man. "I'm gonna die. I just know it! I don't deserve to die for no crack rocks!"

Faith looked up at her fellow officer. "Do you know what this idiot is talking about?"

Williams shrugged his broad bull shoulders. "Bet you ten bucks he huffs on top of the crack. His brain probably has more holes than a chunk of deli Swiss." Huffers—people who inhaled paint—were notorious for brain damage.

"I don't huff!" Cruise looked offended. "Everybody knows you go to that jail, the witch gets you. And I don't wanna die!"

"Witch?" Faith straightened, disgusted. "Ah, shit. Yeah, he's high. I sure didn't hit him that hard."

"Told you. A huffer. I can always spot 'em." Williams rolled his eyes and closed the door on his prisoner. "I'll take him in."

"Do that. I'll start the paperwork." Disgusted, she stomped back to her own unit, where Rambo waited patiently in the back. "Witches. The gene pool in this town is in serious need of a dose of Clorox."

Biting back a groan of pain as her sore muscles protested, Faith peeled off her uniform shirt. She dropped it and sat gingerly on the edge of the bed to work on her slacks. The pants knee that wasn't ripped stuck to her skin. She cursed drug addicted weasels everywhere, knowing she must have skinned it.

The wound stung enthusiastically as Faith pulled the fabric free. Tossing the bloodied pants on top of her shirt, she got up and hobbled to the full-length mirror on the back of her closet door.

With a groan of effort as stiff muscles protested, Faith pulled her sore body upright and assessed the damages. A constellation of scrapes and darkening bruises marked her skin, half of which she couldn't remember getting.

God, she hated wrestling idiots on pavement. Depending on the idiot, asphalt could do more damage than swinging fists.

In this case, though, Cruise had definitely gotten the worst of the encounter. She grinned, remembering the way he'd looked with Rambo standing on his face. Where the hell had the dog learned that trick?

But then, Faith had realized weeks ago that Rambo was not your average pooch, even among K-9s. He was the most intelligent dog she'd ever worked with, including her beloved Sherlock. She never had to give him a command twice, and when she talked to him, he acted as if he understood what she was saying.

Which was more than she could say for her ex-husband. *"I just wanted to be with a woman for once."*

She flinched at the memory of Ron's snarl the night she'd caught him with the dispatcher. The girl had been a good six inches shorter than Faith, a perky, curvy blonde no more than twenty-two. A marked contrast to Ron Pettit's dark, smouldering masculinity.

The betrayal had wrecked Faith, especially coming less than a week after Sherlock had been shot by a drug dealer. She and the dog had worked together for five years, and his loss had been personally and professionally devastating.

To make matters worse, Faith soon realized she was the

only person on the Atlanta police force who hadn't known Ron was running around on her.

Under the circumstances, there was no way she could remain with the APD, so she started looking for another job.

She found it when she learned Clarkston Police Chief George Ayers wanted to add a K-9 officer to his roster. Though Clarkston didn't have a dog yet, Ayers was working on it, and Faith wasn't in a position to quibble. She turned her back on Atlanta and moved to South Carolina.

Unfortunately, Clarkston's highly conservative city council was reluctant to pay for a dog. It took more than a year before an anonymous benefactor and a Greenville K-9 trainer donated Rambo to the department. The shepherd had a fantastic nose and a great work ethic, and with his help, she'd started making major drug cases. Last night's big coke bust was only the latest in the string.

Her leg stung fiercely. Looking down, Faith realized blood ran down her shin. With a grumbled curse, she headed for the bathroom to clean up.

Then she grinned despite the pain, remembering the way Rambo had looked sitting on Cruise's head.

Who *had* taught him that trick?

An hour later, Faith sat on the long leather couch in her living room, a glass of white zin in her hand and Rambo's big head on her knee. She stroked him absently between the ears and sipped her wine, frowning.

It was two o'clock in the morning, but she was far too wound up to sleep. She couldn't get the brawl with Cruise out of her mind.

"Everybody knows you go to that jail, the witch gets you." Witch. Yeah, right.

Except the fear in his eyes had seemed genuine.

"He was higher than a kite, 'Bo," she told the dog, who shifted to look up at her. "He was paranoid and cracked up."

And yet . . .

"*. . . the witch gets you.*"

Something about the way he'd said it made her remember Tony Shay.

Shay had been a big, strapping redhead with a charming, smartass grin. Faith would have found him handsome if she hadn't been so busy trying to wrestle him to the ground.

The nearest they'd been able to figure out later, Shay was just passing through Clarkston when he stopped at the Silver Bullet for a beer and a ham sandwich. Somebody who'd had a little too much to drink decided to start a fight, and Shay elected to finish it.

Unfortunately for Shay, the drunk in question had a lot of friends. Before long, everybody in the bar was trying to kick the stranger's ass. That had proven a lot harder than it looked. Shay knew how to use those ham-sized fists, and he had enough muscle packed on his six-two frame to back up his skill.

Faith had been one of the six cops called to the bar to try to break up the fight. Four of them ended up wrestling with Shay, who by then was royally pissed off. They'd been losing the fight until Faith gave him a face full of Capstun. Some people were barely affected by the pepper spray, but it had put Shay down hard, choking and blinded.

While her fellow officers hauled the big man off to jail, Faith got a call about a domestic dispute. An hour later, she was escorting the offending husband to a cell when she spotted a woman she didn't recognize.

The city jail was housed at the police department, in a back section not designated for visitors. Yet there the woman stood in the hallway, leaning seductively against the bars of Shay's cell, flirting with him. He stood a little back from the door, watching her with a smart-ass grin and wary eyes.

It was hard to see a reason for the wariness. The woman certainly didn't look dangerous, being a full head shorter than the brawny prisoner. Slim and willowy, she was dressed in tight leather pants and a red sweater that displayed her lush body to advantage. Her hair tumbled halfway to her butt, its crow black a stark contrast to her creamy skin. Her lipstick matched the sweater, a deep crimson that looked even more theatrical against her pale, heart-shaped face.

Faith would have questioned her about what she was doing in that part of the jail, but the idiot wife beater suddenly decided he wasn't going into his cell. By the time she'd wrestled him inside and locked him up, the woman was gone.

The next day, a bartender found Tony Shay's body behind the Bullet. Apparently he'd been ambushed when he'd returned to pick up his car after making bail.

Whoever it was had cut out his heart with what the coroner had described as "surgical precision." The local weekly newspaper had a field day with that little detail. The article they'd run two days later speculated about Satanism and black magic rites in breathless terms, based on no evidence whatsoever.

Except they never did find that heart.

Faith, meanwhile, described the woman she'd seen to the detective investigating the case. He blew her off.

"You saying a chick did all that to *that* guy? Not likely. It was somebody from the bar fight." Gordon Taylor's beefy middle-aged face had gone closed and chill. "I doubt we'll ever solve it."

"Everybody knows you go to that jail, the witch gets you."

Faith felt the hair stand up along her arms. "Bullshit," she told Rambo. "And on that note, I'm going to bed."

TWO

Jim waited an hour to make sure Faith had dropped off. Lifting his muzzle off his paws, he rose from the rug beside her bed to peer over the edge of the mattress.

She was deeply asleep, moonlight spilling across the side of her face. Even with the bruises, he saw elegance in the rise of her high cheekbones and sensuality in her lush, full lips.

God, he'd love to kiss that mouth.

Sighing in regret, Jim sat back on his haunches and let the magic spill. It rolled over his skin, ruffling the black fur with waves of raw, tingling power. He suppressed a whine of pain as his muscles twisted around his distorting bones. The magic pulled him onto his back legs, stretching him upward as his body flowed like wax.

When the magic winked out, Jim rolled his shoulders to loosen them. It was good to be human again.

More or less.

He turned his attention to his pretty, unwitting hostess. Faith had kicked off the covers as usual, and the red T-shirt she wore was twisted up around her waist, baring a silken belly and tiny white panties. Her long legs were sprawled apart, and he could plainly see the tight points of her nipples under the shirt.

He'd wanted her from the day she'd come to collect "Rambo" from his trainer—none other than Jim's uncle, Ray Johnston. Ray's lucrative business as a K-9 trainer was what had given Jim the idea of going undercover as a Clarkston drug dog in the first place.

One look at Faith had inspired dreams of a far more intimate partnership. Among other things, he badly wanted to paint her pretty face, with its wide, intelligent green eyes and lust-inspiring mouth. Even her hair challenged him with its thousand shades of fiery copper. Normally tamed into a tightly coiled braid, it tumbled around her shoulders in a mass of curling silk whenever she took it down. He wanted to paint her like that, wild mane hanging loose around her face, her elegant body deliciously nude, all its lean, beautiful curves on display.

But there was a lot more to Faith than looks. She was a complete professional, cool under fire, with a good eye and sure instincts. She was also neck deep in a magical mess she didn't recognize and was totally unequipped to deal with.

He only hoped he could save her.

Sighing, Jim turned and slipped from the room with the surefooted ease of a man who could see in the dark. It was time to report in. Charlie was probably ready to chew nails by now.

Faith's house was a rented three-bedroom brick ranch just inside the city limits. It was scarcely bigger than a double-wide, furnished mostly in hand-me-downs from relatives. The rest was early American Wal-Mart, which was all Faith could afford on a cop's salary. The only decorations were photos and a few framed newspaper clippings, all of which seemed to feature cops and firefighters who were relatives of hers.

Through shameless eavesdropping, Jim had learned law enforcement was a Weston family tradition. Faith's father was a police chief, two of her brothers were Georgia state troopers, and the third was an FBI agent. The baby of the family was a firefighter and arson investigator just as intent on solving crimes as the rest.

Jim once heard her tell another cop that she'd been a hell-raising tomboy as a child. He figured it was probably in sheer self-defense against rampaging brotherly testosterone.

Pushing open the kitchen door, he stepped out into the carport and fished in a pocket for his cell phone.

For reasons no one clearly understood, when a werewolf shifted form, his clothes shifted, too. Once he resumed being human, the original clothing came back, along with whatever he happened to have in his pockets—car keys, phones, even guns. It was one of those Direkind mysteries Tony Shay used to call PFM—Pure Fucking Magic.

At the memory of his friend, a little needle of pain slid into Jim's heart. His lips tightened.

Closing the carport door behind him, Jim paused on the step to scan his surroundings, every sense alert.

It was three o'clock in the morning, and the neighborhood was still bathed in moonlight. Rows of brick ranches just like Faith's lined the narrow street, as alike as cookies, except for the color of the trim and shutters. Somewhere a dog barked, the sound carrying clearly in the chill night air. Inhaling, Jim scented the object of the animal's attention: a possum, waddling across the street in search of garbage cans to pillage.

Reassured that nobody was watching, he walked around Faith's police car and flipped the cell open. With his thumb, he punched the button combination to encrypt the call, then tapped out the number he'd memorized the month before.

Charlie Myers picked up on the second ring. "You're

late," the High Chieftain of the Southern States growled in
his smoker's rasp.

"She couldn't sleep."

"You should have scratched to be let out. I've got to go
to work in the morning." He ran a dry cleaning business in
Charlotte, North Carolina.

Jim suppressed a snort. "Faith isn't about to let Rambo
roam through the neighborhood alone, scaring small children and eating the neighbors' cats."

"You eat the neighbors' cats?"

"No, but she doesn't know that."

Charlie grunted. "Actually, I kind of like Siamese. I
stay away from Persians, though. The bastards give me
hairballs."

"Yeah, a little pussy can be a dangerous thing."

"Smartass. I didn't stay up 'til three A.M. to chat. What
have you got?"

He sat down on the low brick wall around the carport.
"In the past week, three more officers have been put under
that spell. Apparently sometime during the night, because
they were okay when I saw them the previous day. Now almost all the cops smell of black magic."

"So this witch, or vampire, or whatever the hell she is—"

"Vampire. Scent's too far off human for her to be anything else."

"Whatever. Point is, she's got the cops under her control. Has Weston noticed anything?"

"No. Most of 'em don't act that blatant around her."

"I don't understand why the vamp is going to all this trouble." The chieftain sounded frustrated. "If all she wanted was
to cover up Shay's murder, why not just put a spell on the investigating detective? Why the whole department?"

That was the question that had been gnawing at Jim since
he'd arrived last month. "I think she's figured out a spell to
let her draw on the cops' life force to power her magic. She's
got to be doing something. That vamp my sister fought last

month was murdering people every couple of days. This one has killed Tony and maybe a couple of others, but nothing like that. Which is why we're not neck-deep in media."

"But she hasn't tried to put a spell on Weston?"

"Not yet. When she does, she's going to get the surprise of her life." The bitch was not laying a hand on Faith.

Charlie hesitated, chewing that one over. "Could they be on to you? All this vamp has to do is get one good whiff, and she's going to know you're magic."

"Yeah, but I haven't seen the vamp. She's been leaving scent trails all over the department, though, so I figure she's coming in during one of the other shifts. I can't be sure, since Faith leaves me in the car a lot."

"It's a wonder you don't suffocate, wearing that much fur."

"She always leaves the air conditioning running." He shrugged. "Ray warned me that was standard procedure. Seems K-9 officers can't take reports and deal with their dogs at the same time."

"What about this rogue werewolf you smelled? Could he have scented *your* trail?"

"Oh, definitely, but he may not realize what he's smelling." In dog form, Jim smelled pretty much like a dog. The scent of Direkind magic wasn't that strong— unless you knew what to look for. "Which I doubt he does, since he's a rogue."

Charlie mulled that over a minute. "I don't like this, London."

"Me neither, but if they'd known what I was, they'd have jumped me by now. So they must not know."

"Or they're playing games." After another brooding silence, the chieftain swore. "I can't believe Tony Shay gave that bastard Merlin's Curse. He knew how to avoid creating rogues. That's the first thing any of us learns. Now we've got to worry about that idiot Turning the entire fucking department into werewolves. If Tony wasn't already dead, I'd kill his ass."

Stung, Jim glowered. His friend had been a hell-raiser, but he wasn't irresponsible. "Look, if Tony could have helped it, he wouldn't have bitten the guy. Autopsy said he was probably still alive when his heart was cut out. Bet you ten bucks he just lost control and chomped on one of the bastards who were holding him down."

"But why did he let one piddling vampire and a bunch of rogue cops get the jump on him? In Dire Wolf form, he could have chewed them all up and spit them out."

"Unless the witch came up with some new kind of spell."

Charlie made a disgusted sound, half snort, half growl. "Give me a break, London. The only magic that can touch one of us is our own. That's the way Merlin designed the Curse. Spells just roll off us."

Irritated, Jim glared out at the night. "Look, I've known Tony since we were kids. We grew up together. Hell, we went through our first Change together. I don't know why he gave that guy the Curse, but I'll tell you right now, it was something he couldn't help."

"You know what, London? I don't care. It doesn't matter why he infected the rogue—your job is to fix it. Find out who the bastard is and kill him. His little vampire bitch, too. Preferably before they start infecting cops with the Curse and we get a real mess on our hands."

"Charlie, believe me—the minute I spot him, he's a dead man. He helped that bitch cut out Tony's heart while he was still alive. They're going to pay."

"Good." A deadly little silence fell before the chieftain spoke again. "What are you going to do about Weston? If you have to Turn to Dire Wolf to jump him, she's going to see too much. You'll have to take her out, too."

Jim stiffened as his every instinct howled in rejection. "No."

"London . . ."

"If I have to, I'll Turn her."

"The idea is to keep the bad guys from creating a bunch of werewolf cops, not to start Turning them ourselves."

"She won't be a rogue. I'll be her Wolfmaster."

Charlie snorted, the sound cynical. "I'm sure your dick'll love that."

Jim forced himself to bite back several of the choicer replies he had in mind. "My sex life is none of your business, Charlie."

"Look, I don't care who you ball. The only thing I give a rat's ass about is protecting our secret so we don't get King fucking Arthur down on our collective heads. All I'm saying is, don't get so wrapped up in this chick that you forget to keep an eye on business."

He tightened his slipping grip on his temper. Charlie was an asshole, but he could also pull Jim off this mission if he wasn't handled carefully. And God knew what would happen to Faith then. "If you're that worried about Arthur, let me call in Diana. Her husband could work a spell to locate the vamp and that rogue, and I could finish them both off without anybody knowing anything. Including Arthur and Faith."

"Forget it."

"Chief . . ."

"Your sister had no business marrying that fairy, London," Charlie said hotly. "She didn't even ask permission from the Council of Clans. Arthur is in and out of Llyr's palace all the time. You think he's not going to notice that the queen of the fucking Sidhe is a werewolf?"

Two months ago, Diana London met and fell in love with Llyr Galatyn during a hunt for one of the rogue vampires. Neither of them expected the relationship to go anywhere. After all, she was a mortal werewolf, while he was the immortal king of the Sidhe.

Yet love won out, thanks to the intervention of Cachamwri, the Dragon God—Jim was still a little fuzzy on the details of how *that* had come about. At any rate, Cachamwri had made Diana both immortal and cross fertile with her lover, though she still remained a werewolf.

The problem was that Llyr's closest ally was Arthur

Pendragon and his Magekind, who didn't know were-wolves existed.

What's more, they couldn't be allowed to find out. Merlin himself had made that very clear sixteen hundred years ago when he'd created the Direkind werewolves to keep an eye on his magical champions. If Arthur and his warriors ever overstepped their bounds, the Direkind were supposed to step in and deal with them.

But that would only be possible if the Magekind never discovered the existence of the werewolves, whom they might otherwise destroy. The Direkind had kept themselves hidden for sixteen hundred years.

Now, however, a werewolf was living in the court of Arthur's closest ally. Keeping her true nature secret was going to be tricky, and they all knew it. Fortunately, Diana and Llyr had come up with a cover story.

Jim took a deep breath and explained one more time. "Diana and Llyr told Arthur she's from the court of Llyr's brother. Since Ansgar Galatyn never had diplomatic relations with Arthur, he bought it. And since Ansgar's dead, he's not going to be telling anybody anything different."

"You telling me she's convinced Arthur and his entire court that she's Sidhe?"

"Diana's *good.*"

Charlie snorted. "Or Arthur's a lot dumber than I thought."

Jim ground his teeth and reached for patience. "Are you going to let me bring Llyr in on this?"

"No." The word was utterly flat, allowing no room for argument at all.

Jim argued anyway. "So instead we're going risk the entire Clarkston Police Department going rogue?"

"Dammit, London, we've existed in complete secrecy since Merlin created us sixteen hundred years ago. We ain't coming out of the closet on my watch. Especially not because of some little . . . twit who couldn't stay out of Llyr Galatyn's pants. I'd sanction her, except—"

"Llyr would declare war on the Direkind, and Arthur would damn well notice the Sidhe and the werewolves fighting it out in front of God and the international media." *And I'd rip your lungs out for ordering my sister's murder.*

"Basically." The chieftain sighed. "You've got to face facts, London. Diana had a choice between us and the Sidhe, and she picked the Sidhe. I don't want to risk any contact with her that would get Avalon's attention."

"Charlie . . ."

"Do you want me to pull you out of there and send in Jennings?"

"No." Don Jennings was the Southern Clans' chief enforcer, a cold-blooded bastard who would happily kill anybody who got in his way—including Faith. Trying to keep him out of this was the only reason Jim put up with Charlie's crap.

"All right then. You're just going to have to find the vamp and her pet werewolf on your own. Then kill 'em both and get rid of any inconvenient witnesses in whatever way you have to, short of ending up on the evening news. Got it?"

"Yeah," Jim growled.

"Great. I'm going to bed. I've got to be at work in five hours." Charlie hung up without saying good-bye.

"Asshole." He resisted the impulse to hurl his cell phone across the yard.

Agitated, needing to run, Jim shoved the cell back into his pocket and called the magic again. It rolled over him in that familiar burning wave, foaming and invisible.

When it was gone, he held another of his forms: a wolf—big, black, and lean.

With a low growl, Jim bounced over the low wall around the carport, leaped the high chain-link fence around the backyard and bolted across the neatly trimmed lawn. After clearing the rear fence with another bound, he shot into the woods beyond it, sending animals and birds into panicked flight.

There were times when refusing to risk anything could cost you everything, but Charlie was too stupid or stubborn to admit it. He'd rather just kill the witnesses.

Damned if Jim would touch a hair on Faith's pretty little head.

In retrospect, he wished he'd left Charlie out of the investigation altogether. Still, the chieftain did have valuable contacts, like the ones he'd used to rent a house in Clarkston for Jim's use. Charlie thought they might need a base of operations if things went bad. Jim wasn't about to turn the offer down.

Given the spell on the police chief, they'd both agreed the investigation needed to focus on the Clarkston PD. Unfortunately, Ayers knew Jim, which made conducting an investigation in human form highly problematic.

A police dog, on the other hand, could watch the cops from inside the department without being noticed until he found out what was going on. Jim's uncle had been more than willing to use his position as a K-9 trainer to help set it all up. Ray had contacted Chief George Ayers and told him that an anonymous benefactor had donated a drug dog earmarked for Clarkston. All they had to do was pick it up.

When Ayers and Faith came to collect the dog, Jim was waiting in his favorite German shepherd guise. He'd put on a good enough show with Ray to convince them Rambo was the drug dog of their dreams.

But if he'd had any delusions this mission was going to be easy, they were dashed the next day. Encountering the werewolf's scent trail in a department hallway, Jim immediately realized the situation was even more complicated than he'd thought.

It hadn't improved any since then. What was more, his gut told Jim things were only going to get worse.

He had to find that rogue werewolf before somebody else died.

* * *

Guinevere Pendragon's heels clicked on the marble floor past a Waterford crystal vase filled with vivid Mageverse roses. She'd redecorated last year at Arthur's urging, and she had to admit she liked the results better than some of his other design ideas. With its elegant antiques and soaring ceilings, their home now looked like one of the Hollywood mansions her husband admired on the E! channel. There'd been a memorable decade there when they'd lived in a dead ringer for Graceland.

Arthur liked to keep up with the times, whether it was through his T-shirt collection, his Elvis CDs, or his addiction to reruns of *Everybody Loves Raymond.* He said it was the only way they could understand the mortals who were their sworn responsibility.

Sixteen hundred years ago, an alien magician named Merlin had given deserving residents of Camelot sips from a magical grail. His spell had turned the king and his men into vampire warriors, while Guinevere and her ladies became powerful sorceresses called Majae. Merlin had christened them all the Magekind and charged them with the task of protecting mankind from itself.

For the past sixteen hundred years, the Magekind had worked to guide the planet to a stable, peaceful future. It was a difficult job that had become even tougher since a pack of evil vampires had declared war on them all.

Rounding the corner, Gwen heard Santana's bluesy guitar sobbing from the entertainment center she'd magicked for Arthur. She brightened, lengthening her strides. The music meant her husband was home and not off fighting vamps somewhere.

Apart from her relief that he was safe, she needed him tonight. Her head pounded with that particularly vicious beat that meant they'd been apart too long. Thanks to Merlin's magic, Gwen had to provide blood for her vampire husband on a regular basis, or her blood pressure would spike dangerously high. She could magically remove the excess and bottle it, of course, but tonight she wanted that personal touch.

Rounding the corner, she found Arthur standing in the living room, staring down into the fire blazing in the black marble fireplace. He looked big and tough in black jeans and a U2 T-shirt, his dark hair curling around his broad shoulders. He held a bottle of blood in one hand, but he had yet to draw its magical cork.

Good. He was probably still hungry. Her body warmed and tightened for him.

"It's bad, Gwen." Arthur looked up at her, his voice rasping with exhaustion. "I don't know how much longer we can keep this up. Those bastards are killing too many of our people." His handsome, boyish face was gray with fatigue, and there were dark circles under his eyes.

"You haven't been eating enough." She moved toward him, forgetting her own headache. He was right about the Magekind's losses, but he had always been her first concern. "You've got to eat, Arthur. Even if it's from a bottle."

His smile flashed against the dark background of his short, neat beard. "You know I prefer to drink from that pretty throat of yours." His smile faded. "Speaking of which, you're looking flushed. Have you . . . ?"

"I've got a headache," she admitted.

"Dammit, Gwen!" he exploded, stalking to meet her in that long, sexy stride that never failed to make her heart pound. "When you get to that point, bottle it! Do you want to drop dead?"

She sighed as he pulled her into the warm strength of his arms. "I just haven't had time." Despite the clamor of her blood, she let her forehead rest on his firm chest. "Morgana and I have been working hard on that spell. If we can pull it off, we'll be able to track down those Black Grails. Unfortunately, whoever has them is doing a damn good job of shielding them from detection."

"You'll get it." His strong arms tightened comfortingly.

"Then we'll destroy the grails and wipe those vampire bastards right off Mortal Earth."

"The sooner the better." She sighed, listening to his immortal heart pound. "Hunting them down one-by-one is like pulling teeth. I'm not sure we'd ever get rid of them all without destroying those grails."

It had been little more than three months since they learned of the existence of Geirolf, a demonic alien from the magical universe they called the Mageverse.

Merlin had captured the creature sixteen centuries before and imprisoned him in an enchanted cell on the Mageverse's alternate version of Earth. The cell had held the demon until he'd escaped last year.

By passing himself off as a god to gullible—and psychotic—mortals, Geirolf managed to hoodwink them into forming cults that made human sacrifices to him. The alien then fed off the life force of the victims.

To strengthen his hand still more, Geirolf had created three perverted versions of Merlin's Grail, then used these Black Grails to transform his cultists into a vampire army. He and his forces had almost managed to destroy the Magekind, but they'd trapped and killed him instead.

Unfortunately, that hadn't ended the threat. Geirolf's second in command had transferred the dying alien's powers to his vampire followers, then scattered them all over the planet. The Magekind had been hunting them ever since, trying to wipe them out before they did even more damage.

Now Geirolf's nasty little brood had started using the Black Grails to create yet more vampire followers. Fortunately, Galahad and his new wife, Caroline, had stumbled on a solution. When they'd destroyed one of the Black Grails, every vampire it had created was magically wiped out.

However, two more grails remained. Until they were found and destroyed, the ranks of Geirolf's killers would grow.

"The sooner they're all dead, the better," Arthur

growled. "Merlin created us to keep mankind from committing mass suicide. With this planet teetering on the edge of a religious civil war, we can't afford to waste so much time hunting monsters."

"Unfortunately, we don't have a choice," Gwen pointed out dryly. "These particular monsters are killing people."

"So are the terrorists."

"But the terrorists can't work *magic*." She sighed and rubbed her aching forehead across his chest. "If we don't get rid of these vamps, God knows how many people they'll murder. Their magic is powered by death, so they kill even when they're not hungry. And unlike you boys, they like to drain their victims instead of just nibbling."

Thoughtfully, Arthur stroked a big hand through her hair. "What do you think about asking Llyr's help with the spell?" he asked. "A little Sidhe magic could come in handy."

She sighed. "At this point, we can't afford ego. As long as we find those grails, I don't care whose spell does the job."

"I'll contact him, then." His hand dropped down to cup her backside. "After, that is, I take care of my wife. I feel the need for a little nibbling myself."

Guinevere laughed, her grim mood lightening. With a wave of her hand and a swirl of magic, she made their clothing disappear. As her husband bore her back on the fur rug she'd conjured on the floor, Gwen sighed in pleasure.

There were vampires, and then there were *vampires*.

It was close to midnight and shift change when Faith started yet another circuit through Bomar. It being Monday night, the Clarkston neighborhood was, for once, almost painfully quiet.

Behind her head, Rambo whined.

"Yeah, I'm bored, too." She instantly winced at her unthinking reply. "Great. Just great. Now I've cursed us."

Every officer knew simply thinking things were slow

was an invocation to the evil cop gods, who would promptly deliver a fifteen-car pileup or a serial-killing axe murderer. The last time Faith had complained about being bored, she'd found three dead bodies in an Atlanta convenience store not two hours later.

It never failed.

Sure enough, ten minutes later she glimpsed what looked like a man lying near the basketball hoop in the city park. Faith slowed the car for a closer look, frowning past the swing set and jungle gym.

The figure lay in the spill of light from one of the park's security lights. It looked oddly dark and mottled, as if covered in dirt.

Or blood.

Faith grabbed her mike and radioed dispatch that she was getting out for a safety check. Then, ignoring Rambo's questioning whine, she swung the car door open.

The leather of her belt creaking, she ducked through the wrought iron gate in the park fence.

Judging from the size, the victim was an adult male. He lay on his side in a twisted, contorted position, covered in dark patches that did indeed look like dried gore. As if to confirm that suspicion, the breeze shifted into her face as she approached, bringing the scent of blood and human waste. Faith gagged.

"Sir? Sir, are you all right?" No answer, not that she'd expected one. Not with that smell. Instinctively, she dropped her hand to her service weapon and looked around for his attacker.

She saw nothing but the spidery silhouettes of the park's play equipment. In the distance, a dog bayed, the sound faint and lonely. The swings swayed in the breeze, knocking against the legs of the swing set with a metallic ring.

Holding her breath as every hair on the back of her neck rose, Faith looked down at the body.

White male, early thirties. Shirtless. He lay on his back,

arms and legs spread wide. Something had scooped a big chunk out of his torso, leaving his belly a red, stinking ruin.

Faith swallowed against her heaving stomach, then dropped to one knee to lay two fingers against his throat. His skin was cold. He'd been dead a couple of hours at least.

Good, her inner coward whispered. *I sure as hell don't want to run into whoever did this to him.*

Her instincts concurred, strongly suggesting she get her butt back to the safety of the patrol car and Rambo. Ignoring both mental voices, Faith grabbed her radio handset off the clip on her shoulder. Glancing down at the body, she finally recognized him.

Samuel Cruise, the drug addict with a phobia of the city jail, was just as dead as he'd predicted he'd be.

But it was damn sure no witch that had killed him.

THREE

Half an hour later, the area was swarming with cops. Units were parked up and down the street, blue lights revolving slowly across the trees and neighboring houses to give the park an unearthly glow.

Faith watched Detective Gordon Taylor walk toward her. A heavyset man in a cheap, rumpled suit, he wore an expression of irritation. "Weston," he growled, as he stopped at her side and looked down at Cruise's body. "This your . . ." He broke off. His expression shifted into horror as he saw the man's ruined torso, then went carefully blank again. Looking over at Faith, he drawled, "You got me out of bed at midnight for a dead junkie?"

"Somehow I don't think it's an overdose, detective."

He grunted. "Looks like a dog attack to me. Bet whoever he buys his drugs from turned his pit bulls loose on the guy."

"Hell of a way treat a customer." Faith frowned down at the body, considering the theory. People figured out some pretty creative ways to commit murder, but she still wasn't sure she bought it. "You know, I've seen dog maulings before. This one . . ." She crouched and shone her flashlight into one of the wounds. "Look at the distance between those teeth. I've never seen a dog with a bite like that. Looks more like a bear or something."

Taylor eyed her. "Who died and made you *CSI?*"

Faith glowered up at him, stung by the insult. Cops in general did not have a high opinion of *CSI*. For one thing, most real crime scene techs didn't conduct criminal investigations—they just collected evidence and handed it over to detectives.

Despite his scorn, she straightened and faced him. "Detective, I arrested this guy last night. He literally begged me not to lock him up in the city jail because he said people who go to that jail die. He even claimed some of them get eaten."

Taylor stared at her. "You suggesting one of our jailers *ate* him?" His voice dripped incredulous contempt.

"I'm not suggesting anything, detective," she told him with elaborate patience. "I'm reporting what the man said."

"He was a junkie, Weston. He probably saw flying monkeys, too." He nodded down at Cruise's mangled corpse. "And it's a lot more likely monkeys did this than the jailers."

"Knowing the jailers, I've got to agree. I can't believe any of our guys would be involved in something like this. But—"

Taylor cut her off. "Where's the coroner?"

"En route. He lives on the other end of the county."

"Glad I'm not the only one to get hauled out of bed for this." He reached into his pocket and pulled out a pair of surgical gloves. "Help me roll him."

"We haven't taken pictures of the body yet. I was waiting for you."

He gave her a superior-officer-to-dimwit-subordinate sneer. "So go get a frigging camera already and snap a couple of shots."

Simmering, Faith stalked back toward her car to retrieve

the cheap digital she carried to record accidents. Clarkston didn't have the budget for a crime scene photographer.

Taylor watched her walk off. One of the other patrol officers stepped over to him.

"Weston asks way too many questions," the uniform said in a low voice.

Taylor grunted. "Yeah. We're going to have to do something about her. She's becoming a pain in the ass."

Over the past month, watching Faith work out in her home gym had become Jim's favorite guilty pleasure.

He lay on the carpet next to her weight bench with his head on his paws. His stomach growled, but he ignored it in favor of concentrating on his pretty partner. He'd learned to eat kibble, but his belly never stopped hoping for something more substantial.

At the moment, however, his focus was on Faith, though he knew good and damned well he was no more likely to sample her than he was a T-bone. At least, not any time soon.

Sweat gleamed on her long legs and arms as she did barbell presses in a series of smooth, controlled thrusts. Every time she forced the weight bar upward, her hips unconsciously rolled.

He'd love to paint her like this. The morning light spilled a golden shimmer across her sweating skin that he badly wanted to capture. Her arms weren't brawny by any means—certainly nothing like his own—but the flex of those working muscles fascinated him with their clean, elegant shapes.

During his twelve-year career as an professional artist, Jim had painted any number of people—mostly urban studies of the folks who inhabited Hot 'Lanta. His edgy, stylish pieces now commanded critical acclaim and large sums of money. But the painting he wanted to do of Faith would be something different.

Something private.

Faith finished the set and sat up on the bench, panting, her pretty breasts rising and falling under the thin blue T-shirt she wore. Absently, she picked up the towel that lay across the bench and wiped her sweating face. He loved the fierce, intent expression she wore when she was working hard, but he loved watching her when she was spent, too.

She sat back, unwittingly giving him an idea for another portrait in his Faith series: leaning against the wall, breathing hard, a heathy flush on her face, strands of red hair tumbling down around those high cheekbones.

Glancing over, she saw Jim watching and leaned down to give his head a pat. He almost growled.

The woman of his dreams thought he was a dog.

His timing sucked, and he knew it. He was supposed to be catching his best friend's murderer. But he hadn't realized that pretending to be Faith's K-9 partner would mean spending so much time with her. And he hadn't anticipated the effect she'd have on him, with her intelligence, stubborn courage, and commitment to justice.

At first, he'd tried to dismiss the attraction as simple lust, then as an inconvenient infatuation. Over the past few days, though, he'd come to suspect it was a lot more than that.

Unfortunately, it didn't much matter what it was, because he couldn't do a damn thing about it. Oh, he could wait until he'd caught Tony's killers, then pretend to meet her as a human. Maybe she'd fall for him.

But even if she did, humans and Dire Wolves weren't cross-fertile, and Direkind law forbid them from marrying. The only way he and Faith could be together is if he bit her and infected her with Merlin's Curse.

Unfortunately, a fifth of the Dire Kind didn't survive their first transformation. Like Steve, their own magic consumed them. Hell, sometimes even established Dire Wolves triggered a magical meltdown by trying to Turn too often.

It was not a chance Jim was willing to take, despite what he'd said to Charlie. Anyway, he couldn't stand the thought of sinking his fangs into Faith's delicate flesh, or watching her endure the pain that would follow. He sure as hell didn't want to watch her die.

Besides, even if she did survive the Change, she wouldn't thank him for making her a werewolf. Maybe he could get her to fall in love with him first and agree to make the Change, but what if she refused after he told her about the Direkind? She'd know too much. The standard procedure was to bite one's human lover and *then* tell him or her the facts of werewolf life. Again, not something Jim had any interest in doing to Faith.

Face it, London, he thought grimly, *you're screwed.*

The next day, Faith pushed open the door to the briefing room where roll call was held. The three cops sitting at the long table fell silent and looked up. Their expressions cooled when they saw it was her.

Suppressing a frown, she gave them a nod. "Hi, guys."

Two nodded stiffly in return. The other watched her with brooding hostility.

She pulled out a chair and sat down, eyeing the three men. "Is there a bug going around, or did you boys stay up all night working that murder? You look like hell."

"Mind your own—" Frank Granger began hotly, only to break off as if someone had kicked him under the table.

"That's right, Faith," Gary Morrow told her with a stiff smile. "The sergeant had us canvassing the neighborhood."

Eyeing them, she decided she didn't buy it. She'd lingered on the scene later than they had, and she didn't look anywhere near as wrecked. All three had dark circles under their eyes, and their skin looked gray, almost as if they were suffering from anemia.

Maybe there was a bug going around.

The door opened, and a fourth cop stumbled in to drop

into a chair, sloshing his coffee on the table. Andy Jones put down the paper cup and scrubbed both hands over his haggard face. His eyes were bloodshot, and he'd missed a strip of black stubble along his jawline when he'd shaved. He didn't even grunt a hello, just sat hunched over his cup, his expression troubled.

"Something wrong, Andy?"

Jones looked up at her and started to open his mouth, but Morrow cut him off before he could speak. "He's just tired, Weston. We all are."

She studied the other cop's placating smile. Granger was red with rage, but to her surprise he kept his mouth firmly shut. Faith found that almost as troubling as their unhealthy skin tone. Restraint wasn't exactly Frank's best quality.

She flicked a glance at the other two men. They didn't seem to be tracking the discussion at all.

What the hell was going on?

Sergeant Randy Young walked in, looking even more drawn than the others, his shirt loose over what had once been an impressive belly. He must have lost a good forty pounds in the last two months. Faith had complimented Young on his weight loss before, but now she wondered if something more sinister than a really good diet was responsible. But what else could it be?

And why haven't I noticed this before?

Of course, her attention had been firmly on Rambo for the last month. Getting the dog settled in and learning to work with him had taken all her attention.

Also, police work in general often involved running from crisis to crisis at breakneck speed. It was easy to overlook undercurrents among coworkers in the race to catch bad guys.

Young launched into his briefing as Faith gnawed over the problem. He stumbled three times just reading off the description of a guy who'd been seen breaking into garages in the Pecan Point neighborhood. The sergeant was normally razor-edged and sarcastic, but he was definitely off his game today.

When he finished, Faith voiced the question that was bothering her. "Sarge, have we heard anything on the murder victim I found dead in the park last night? What did the autopsy find?"

At that, the cops looked at her with a hostility so thick and unspoken, she sat back in her chair in surprise.

"He was a crack addict, Weston," Young said. "He probably tried to rob the wrong house, and somebody turned their rottweiler loose on him." The sergeant grinned without humor. "It's like I always say—it sucks to be a maggot."

"You think one of us had something to do with it?" Granger demanded, glaring at her.

Faith blinked. "Of course not."

"Could have fooled me." Young studied her coolly. "You told Taylor the junkie said things happened to people who go to the city jail. And since the only ones with access to the jail are cops and jailers . . ."

"And what the fuck do you care about a junkie, anyway?" Granger's face was flushed under his thinning red hair. "The world's better off without him. Hell, he took a swing at you day before yesterday. Nice shiner, by the way."

"I'm well aware of that, Frank." Faith blew out a breath, striving for patience. "Look, it's my job to report anything that might be relevant to a death. When two guys in six weeks end up dead after a night in the city jail, that's relevant."

"The first guy got cut up by drunks, Weston," the sergeant said. "That dumbass last night ran into somebody's dogs. Unless you know something we don't. I mean, considering you were the one who got in the fight with him to begin with, and you've got that big-ass K-9. . . ."

Stung by the implication, she glared. "Rambo sure as hell didn't eat him."

Young nodded, his gaze cold. "Then like I say, must have been rottweilers."

She glanced around the table at the tense, angry cops who surrounded her. "Yeah," she said finally. "Must have been."

Faith was still brooding as she walked out to the car. It was a cool night, so for once she hadn't left the engine running to provide air conditioning for Rambo. The open windows were enough to keep him from overheating.

The dog whined softly from the back as she got in. She closed the door and sat still a moment, frowning out the windshield at the gas station across the street.

"Something's badly wrong with this department, 'Bo. The question is, what am I going to do about it?" She started the car and drove out of the lot, turning up Main in the direction of her zone.

The usual procedure when a cop suspected fellow officers of corruption was to report the incident to his or her immediate superior. Unfortunately, Faith's immediate superior was Sergeant Young himself. She could go over his head to her lieutenant, but that was virtually guaranteed to piss off the entire second shift.

Faith was willing to take them all on if she had to, but only if she had some kind of solid evidence of something going on. So far all she had was a gut feeling.

The only thing to do, she decided, was keep her eyes open and see what happened.

Celestine Gentry stood in the ballroom of her plantation house, concentrating fiercely on the spell she was about to cast. A mistake now could be fatal. It had to be perfect.

"What are you waiting for?" the werewolf demanded, clenching his clawed hands as he all but bounced on long, inhuman feet. He was a towering figure, covered in sable fur that shimmered in the light of the chandeliers. Golden eyes all but glowed in his lupine skull, feral with excitement. "Let's go."

"Shut up," she gritted. Keith Reynolds was an adrenalin junkie; he viewed the possibility of getting killed with the enthusiasm of a coke addict surveying a line of pure Peruvian flake. "I have to get this spell right or they'll be all over us."

"Don't worry about the vamps. I'll take care of them."

"It's not that easy." Reynolds had no idea what it was like to be at the mercy of people who relished your suffering. Celeste, on the other hand, understood that kind of powerlessness all too well.

Obtaining Korbal's Grail would go a long way toward ensuring her safety, but to get it, she had to go up against Korbal himself. And he was one of the most powerful of Geirolf's cultists—so much so, he'd been one of the three priests chosen to transform them all into the demon's vampire army. The idea of confronting all that chilling power made sweat break out on Celestine's forehead.

Get over it, she told herself savagely. *You're either predator or you're prey, remember? And you sure as shit don't want to be prey.*

Celestine squared her shoulders, took a deep breath, and reached deep for the power she'd seized. She'd told Reynolds to take his time with Cruise, and she reaped the benefit of that magical murder now.

Stolen life force surged though her as she lifted her hands, preparing to cast the spell. Slowly, she began the chant, the ancient, alien words burning her tongue with their twisted syllables. Dark energy boiled up from her soul like a bloody fountain, rolling down her arms to blast from her shaking fingertips. She kept chanting, shaping the magic with every word, forcing it to her will, building a dimensional gate between her home and the lair of her enemies. But not just any gate—one even Korbal with all his powers would be unable to sense.

At last it hung there, shimmering, gleaming red walls visible beyond its swirling forces. But Celestine didn't drop her aching arms.

"Is that it?" Reynolds asked, his voice a low growl of excitement. His big body coiled as if eager to leap through the gate, no matter who or what was on the other side.

"Almost," she gritted. "Hold on. I've got to shield us first." Her voice growing hoarse from manipulating death magic, she started chanting again.

Another wave of energy foamed from her hands, coating her body and the werewolf's, forming an invisible shield around them. Glancing at Reynolds, she watched him grow transparent and finally vanish. With an exhausted sigh, she dropped her arms. They were now impossible to detect by sight or magic. Even their voices wouldn't carry to anyone other than each other.

As long as nothing went wrong, anyway.

"Now," Celestine said. "Let's go." With the werewolf at her heels, she stepped through the gate. Power pulsed over her skin as that single magical pace carried her hundreds of miles, from Clarkston to the heart of New York.

She and Reynolds emerged in a corridor built of blocks of crimson stone polished to a mirror gleam. Celestine gazed around them, reluctantly impressed. If the decor was any indication, Korbal was even more powerful than he'd been before.

When last she'd been in the New York temple, the building had looked like the rundown warehouse it was, with rusting steel I-beam supports and graffiti-splattered walls.

Korbal's death magic had transformed it into a cathedral supported by black columns with gleaming solid gold capitals. Eyeing the closest pillar, she saw it was carved with naked, writhing figures, entwined in sex or murder—it was hard to tell which.

"Bet this goes over real well with the locals," Reynolds whispered. "Looks like a whorehouse."

"Not from the outside, if I know Korbal," Celestine said absently as she started down the corridor. "Probably looks just like it did before."

". . . did you call us, priest?" a male voice demanded from somewhere down the corridor. "This had better be good."

"I suspect you'll find my reasoning more than compelling, Jarvis."

Celestine's mouth went dry at the sound of Richard Korbal's sonorous voice. For more than a year, she'd been a member of his New York Satanic Temple, until Geirolf had summoned them to destiny. Within hours, she'd drunk from the third grail and tasted true power as a vampire. She'd fought the Magekind as a member of Geirolf's unholy army, only to watch the demon god die. She'd have died, too, if Geirolf's lieutenant hadn't scattered his vampire army to the four winds.

The spell had dumped Celestine in the wilds of South Carolina. She hadn't even known where she was, or where she should go next. She only knew she wasn't interested in rejoining Korbal's flock.

She wanted a flock of her own.

A week later, Celestine had been driving through Clarkston on her way to Florida when Reynolds had pulled her over. It was then she'd realized she could create her own temple. Hungry for blood, she'd seduced him—had, in fact, meant to kill him. Then she'd realized he was a kindred spirit beneath his badge. What's more, many of the other cops of Clarkston were just as amenable to seduction.

The question was, what had Korbal discovered while she was laying the groundwork for her own power? There was one way to find out.

Celestine started toward the set of open double doors where she'd heard voices. Reynold's claws clicked faintly on the gleaming marble floor as he followed.

Rounding the corner, she stopped short in surprise. The room beyond was huge, an echoing space wrapped in gloom and theatrical splashes of torchlight.

It was also completely filled with robed vampires. The stench of death magic rolled over her in waves. To Celestine, the scent was as intoxicating as it was nauseating.

"Jesus," Reynolds breathed in her ear. "There must be two thousand people in here. I hope to hell you don't want to take them all on."

"Not likely. Listen!"

At the other end of the cathedral, Korbal stood on an elevated stage. He was a tall man, graying and handsome, with blue eyes that blazed with fanatical charisma. Behind him, a massive carving depicted Geirolf presiding over ranks of cultists lined up to drink from the three grails.

"We face a great threat, my children," he said, his voice rising and falling in the hypnotic cadences she knew so well, "one we must band together to defeat—"

"Under your leadership, I assume?" a man sneered from the crowd.

"Does it matter who leads," Korbal told him, "as long as we deal with the threat?"

Celestine suppressed a snort. No matter what kind of game the priest played, his ultimate goal was power.

"What threat?" a female voice demanded.

The priest drew himself up in in his embroidered black robes. "Three weeks ago, on March tenth, precisely at 11:34 P.M., half my army was wiped out in the blink of an eye."

Celestine's jaw dropped. She wasn't sure what was less likely—the possibility that it would happen, or that he would admit it if it had.

On the other hand, Korbal was entirely capable of inventing a crisis to stampede the gullible into following him.

A babble of voices rose. "What the hell are you talking about?" one demanded.

Korbal lifted his graying head in an angry gesture.

"Somehow Arthur destroyed them all, while leaving the rest of us untouched."

Mutters of protest and disbelief. "What? *Why?*"

Celestine frowned. He was suckering them, he had to be. And yet . . . perhaps he wasn't.

"A sneak attack, then?"

"A spell?"

"He lies! Korbal always lies."

"Go then," the priest snapped. "Go and die when Arthur's witches work their magic again. Die unable to defend yourself, between one breath and the next, while you are murdered from a dimension away."

The shouts subsided to a sullen murmur until another man spoke. "If you know something, priest, spit it out."

"We determined that all those who died had drunk from the second grail," Korbal announced in that beautiful, deceptive voice. "Those who drank from my grail lived, and so did those turned by the third grail. But the children of the second grail have been wiped from the face of the earth."

"He's lying!"

"No." Now a woman spoke. "We ran with Harry Kent's group. The same thing happened to us. Exactly at 11:32 P.M. on March tenth, Harry and sixty of our cult mates burst into magical flame and disappeared."

"Oh, bullshit!"

"Korbal's subverted her."

"No," a man shouted over the murmurs of disbelief. "She speaks the truth. I can sense it."

There was another wave of sound. Korbal gestured, and his voice thundered, magically amplified. "I believe that one of Arthur's witches has created a spell to destroy the grails—along with all the vampires who were created by them."

"But if that's the case . . ."

". . . We have no defense," Korbal finished. "You'd be dead before you knew what hit you. Our only chance is to band together to defend our grail."

"I knew it—he wants to gain control of us all!"

The priest shrugged his black-robed shoulders. "Perhaps. Or perhaps not. Can you run the risk either way?"

"And perhaps we'll tell you to go to hell!"

"You certainly have that option," he said. "But consider—I have the grail. My forces have been greatly depleted by the spell. If I can't defend the grail from Arthur's next attack, we will all die—including those of you who turn your backs on me now."

"And what if we take the grail from you, Korbal?"

He made a dismissive gesture of one long, elegant hand. "Then you will have to defend it against Arthur—without the assistance of my warriors."

A simmering silence fell as the group considered the obvious implications. Join forces with Korbal and defend the grail, or separate and risk being overwhelmed by Arthur and his men.

Luckily, it wasn't an issue Celestine had to worry about. She'd drunk from the third grail, but she had no idea where it was and couldn't do anything about it one way or another. Her only interest in Korbal's cup was using it to create a vampire army of her own.

She frowned. Unfortunately, this lot would be even less likely to let the grail out of their sight now that they knew their collective lives hung on its possession. And considering how many of them there were, Celestine's chance of taking the grail and keeping it were faint indeed.

Unless . . . Her eyes narrowed thoughtfully. It sounded as if Arthur would be searching for the grail, too, and he'd likely bring an army with him when he came after it.

Now *that* had real possibilities.

A plan taking shape in her mind, Celestine turned toward the doorway. "Come on, Reynolds," she murmured, and slipped out. In the corridor outside, she hesitated a moment, trying to decide which way to go. Then, feeling the mental sizzle from Korbal's grail, she turned left and descended a flight of curving stairs. The werewolf's claws clicked after her on the gleaming stone.

They went down four floors—magical, no doubt; the warehouse had never extended that far underground before. Celestine's fingers brushed over the marble as she descended, tracing across the carved shapes of demons, killing and fornicating with hapless humans.

At last they reached what she sensed was the proper level. But when they stepped out into the corridor beyond the door, Reynolds cursed. "How the hell are we going to get past them?"

No less than ten armed vampires stood in the corridor, plainly guarding a doorway. That, no doubt, was where the grail was hidden.

"They'd be idiots not to guard it, Keith—it's precious. Which is why I brought you." She turned toward the werewolf, gave him her best honeyed purr. "You're going to provide me with a distraction."

"What have you got in mind?" Even cloaked and invisible as they were, Celestine could sense his anticipation.

She told him.

Then she waited as he crept toward the robed guards, invisible and silent. At least until she dropped the spell around him.

He flashed into view, more than seven feet of werewolf. Just to make sure they got the point, he roared like a lion, a blast of sound that made the guards jump.

Before they could recover, Reynolds dove forward, ripping his claws across one of the guards' throats. He toppled in a fountain of blood, dead before he hit the ground.

The others shouted in confusion, drawing their swords. Too late. The werewolf attacked like a cat among pigeons, and the fight began in earnest.

FOUR

Celestine knew she had only seconds to act before the congregation upstairs heard the sounds of combat. Invisible, she slipped past the battling men, dodging sword thrusts and energy blasts, to aim a spell at the grail in its chamber. It wasn't the one she'd intended, but it would have to do.

She felt the magic take effect, then whirled to cast a magical doorway. The werewolf was still locked in combat with the guards. Footsteps clattered on the stairs—more of Korbal's men coming to join the fight.

"Reynolds!" she shouted, "Come on!" She dove through the vortex, the werewolf at her heels. The minute they were through, Celestine spun, planning to cast a spell that would erase her magical trail.

But even as she completed the complicated enchantment and collapsed her gate, a second portal opened. A magical blast lanced from it, tearing apart her invisibility spell.

"There you are, you little bitch!" A guard with a pentagram tattooed on his bald skull leaped through the portal.
Four of his fellow cultists followed him, swords in hand,
armor gleaming. "You're going to die for that."

Reynolds howled a battle cry and charged them, as Celestine gathered her own magic. Apparently the rest of the
guards was staying behind to guard the grail.

Good thing, too. They were going to have their hands
full as it was.

Faith was still driving around brooding at ten thirty when
she got the call from dispatch.

"Tayanita, Clarkston 2-4?" Her unit number was 24.

She picked up the handset and keyed it. "Clarkston 2-4,
Tayanita."

"Elderly caller reports somebody's in the woods behind
her house, fighting and setting off fireworks. She's afraid
they're going to burn down her house. Two-nine-nine Andrews Lane."

"Clarkston 2-4, en route." Faith put the handset back in
its clip on the side of the radio and hit the gas. She didn't
bother with lights and sirens, since it was hardly an emergency call. *Weird time of the year for fireworks, though.*
Probably kids. That kind of thing usually was.

Since setting off fireworks was against city ordinance,
she'd just go confiscate them and run the kids off. Once she
got done dealing with that, it would probably be time to
head back to the department for shift change.

Afterward, I'll drop by the jail for an head count, Faith
decided. *Make sure none of them end up dead in the morning.*

The house at 299 Andrews Lane was located on the outskirts of her patrol zone, next door to a heavily wooded lot.
As Faith pulled up in front of the neat white farmhouse, a

flash of red light went off in the depths of the trees, followed by a loud crack.

She frowned. Didn't really sound like fireworks, but it wasn't gunfire, either.

Faith pulled over and parked, then started to radio dispatch that she'd arrived. Before she could even pick up the handset, Rambo went out of his mind, barking hysterically right in her ear.

" 'Bo, be quiet!" she snapped, glaring over her shoulder at the furious animal. "What's wrong with you?"

The dog usually wasn't a barker, but he refused to shut up this time. After trying and failing to hush him, Faith finally yelled, "Clarkston 2-4, 10-8 at 299 Andrews Lane!"

She could barely hear the dispatcher's reply. "Ten-Four, Clarkston 2-4."

Disgusted, Faith tossed the handset down, swung open the car door, and got out, ignoring Rambo's deep-throated protests.

Grabbing her hat from the seat, she put it on and collected her heavy flashlight from its charger. Accompanied by the K-9's despairing barks, she flicked on the flash and started toward the woods.

Blue light flared in the woods, followed by a hollow boom. She frowned and picked up her pace. That definitely didn't sound like fireworks.

Seething with frustration, Jim watched another magical blast light up the woods as Faith strode blindly toward disaster.

A light show that intense had to mean they'd stumbled onto the vampire, who was doing battle with something just as powerful as she was. Which meant the woman Jim loved was about to get her pretty head handed to her.

And here he was without opposable thumbs to open the flipping car door.

Luckily the windows of K-9 units were tinted; Faith wouldn't have been able to see in even if it wasn't the dead of night. He called the magic and waited as it spilled over him in a wave of burning energy.

A moment later, he was human again, crouched in the rear of the car. Unfortunately, he'd already noticed they'd taken the interior handles off the rear doors. The only way out was the front, which meant he had to get through the metal gate between the seats.

Cursing his partner and the vampire equally, Jim dragged the gate open and started trying to worm his way between the car's front seats. To his horror, he realized his shoulders wouldn't fit through the gate's narrow opening, no matter how he twisted.

Hell.

He glanced through the window. Faith had already vanished into the woods.

He had to get to her. Fast.

Jim seriously considered Turning into the Dire Wolf and ripping a car door off, but he wasn't sure the back compartment was big enough. He didn't know what would happen if he tried to Change in a space that was too small for his seven-foot-six-inch Dire Wolf body, and he didn't want to find out.

Growling, he transformed back into shepherd form and began trying to work his way through the gate. It was a painfully tight fit. Hooking his forepaws over the seat, he dug his rear toes into the carpet and pushed with all his strength. As he struggled, Jim glared at the car's digital clock.

Another minute ticked by.

Cursing under her breath, Faith skirted a briar bush her flashlight picked out. It was pitch black under the trees, and she couldn't see a damn thing. She wished the light was better, because it sounded as if people were trying to kill each other out here.

It was painfully clear from the sound effects that this was not just a couple of kids tossing fireworks in the dark. Voices chanted, grunted, and swore, and heavy bodies crashed around in the brush just ahead. Colored flashes lit up the trees, punctuated by rolling booms.

All of which sounded like Faith's cue to call for backup. She lifted the shoulder mike of her belt radio. "Tayanita, Clarkston 2-4 requesting assistance at 299 Andrews Lane. Sounds like several males and at least one female in an altercation in the woods. Weapons unknown." She paused, debating whether to wait for her backup to arrive or go on in and try to mediate.

A man screamed.

Hell with it. "Sounds like somebody's hurt. I'm going to proceed."

Without waiting to hear the reply, she clipped the mike back on her shoulder and pushed through the brush, ignoring the unseen branches that slapped her in the face. As she moved, she drew her weapon.

The crawling sensation on the back of her neck told her she was going to need it.

The bars dug savagely into Jim's ribs, but he kept struggling with every ounce of his considerable strength. He had to get to Faith. Luckily, magical creature that he was, he was stronger than a normal dog. The bars began to bend, and he popped through at last, tumbling into the passenger seat.

Still no opposable thumbs. He had to transform again.

This time the magic burned when it came, an acid reminder of the risk he was running. If a werewolf tried to change form too many times in too short a period, he ran the risk of the magic escaping his control. He'd burn like Steve had, consumed by his own power.

Human again, Jim jerked the door open and threw himself from the car. He almost fell on his face as his depleted body protested the changes he'd forced on it.

Jim caught himself, realizing with a stab of fear he was pushing far too close to the edge. He couldn't fight the vampire and her pet werewolf as a human, but if he tried to transform again, the magic might turn on him.

Then he remembered the shimmer of sunlight on Faith's skin, the flash of her smile. If the rogue got to Faith, he'd rip her apart.

Teeth gritted, Jim called the power for the fourth time— and screamed as pain seared his cells. For a terrifying instant, he thought his magic had gone bad.

But at last his body began to grow again as energy from the Mageverse flooded into it, stretching upward and outward as fur rolled across his skin in an itching wave.

When the transformation ended, his knees gave under him, dumping him onto the pavement beside the car. Helpless, blind, and shaking with pain, Jim crouched there, fighting not to vomit.

Get your ass in gear, London. Faith is out there alone.

Reeling to his full seven-and-a-half feet of Dire Wolf height, Jim stumbled toward the woods.

He had to get to Faith. Saving her was all that mattered.

Standing behind the dubious cover of a pine tree, Faith wondered if somebody had slipped her an LSD mickey.

A few feet away, a woman crouched, tight leather pants hugging her long legs, her breasts barely concealed by a red silk top. But what held Faith's attention was her hands, which glowed a ghostly blue as if she'd dipped them in something phosphorescent. The otherworldly shimmer threw strange shadows over her pretty heart-shaped face. Her long black hair whipped around her head, as though blown by a wind Faith couldn't feel.

It was the same woman Faith had seen talking to Tony Shay at the jail.

A body lay at her feet, twisted in a pose of agony like a burn victim, though there was no sign of any fire in the clearing. In the light from the woman's glowing hands, Faith saw two more corpses, both covered in the dark, wet gleam of blood.

Guess Cruise hadn't been high when he'd babbled about witches after all, Faith thought. *Now what the hell do I do?*

The woman was faced off against a tall, muscular man dressed in scarlet armor. He, too, had glowing hands, not to mention an upside down pentagram tattooed on his shaved head. It shone bright red.

So did his eyes.

"Did you really think you could just sneak into our temple and steal our grail?" He laughed, the sound ringing with contempt. The glow intensified. "Sorry, you're not that good. And now that Davidson's taken care of the were-wolf, I'm going to make sure you never have the chance to get better."

"'Fraid not, lamb chop." Something black bounded from the woods to slam into the armored man. He bellowed in surprise and went down under his attacker's weight.

"I heal quick." The newcomer laughed, the sound chilling as he reared over the fallen man. "A lot quicker than Davidson, anyway."

"Fucker!" Blue light blazed, accompanied by a sonic boom that shook the trees and made Faith duck. When it winked out, she was left completely night-blind.

"Like I told you before, magic doesn't work on me, asshole."

The robed man howled in agony. Another salvo of flashing explosions.

Dammit, where was her backup? Faith hesitated, knowing she shouldn't rush in without at least a dozen cops at her back.

Unfortunately, it sounded as if the robed man was being ripped apart just like his fellows, so she didn't have that luxury.

Like her daddy always said, you didn't stand around with your thumb up your butt when somebody was dying.

Heart pounding, Faith stepped out from behind the tree and leveled her gun at the trio as another flash illuminated them. The armored man was down on the ground, rolling around with the black thing on top of him. "Clarkston Police Department!" Faith shouted. "Everybody get away from everybody else—now!" Even as the words left her mouth, she thought, *This is really dumb.*

In a stunning display of strength, the armored figure heaved his attacker through the air, straight toward Faith. She ducked aside as he hit the ground with a curse and snarl, skidding across the leaves until he managed to dig in and roll to his feet, towering over her like a giant.

Damn, he has to be over seven feet tall, she thought. Incredulous, she backed way, flicking her flashlight full into his face. "What the hell?" she gasped.

Flinging up a hand to shield his eyes, he snarled. He had a mouthful of teeth every bit as long and sharp as Rambo's. "Get that light out of my face!" he roared, his voice so deep and guttural it didn't sound human.

He looked even less so. His head was elongated, forming a long wolf muzzle, his ears rising to tufted triangular points. His huge hands were tipped with curving knife-point nails, while his body was covered in a shaggy coat of fur.

Why is this asshole wearing a dog suit? Faith wondered, her sense of unreality increasing.

Not that it mattered. "Back off!" She pointed a gun toward that threatening muzzle.

From the corner of one eye, she saw the armored man reel to his feet and square off with the woman again. They snarled curses and started hurling what looked like ball lightning at each other. Every blast stopped short, splashing through the air as if hitting invisible barriers.

Dog Face took another step toward her, the claws that tipped his furry hands glittering in the strobing light. Despite logic, her gut told her those weren't gloves. "You really should have stayed out of this, Weston."

What she should have done is wait for backup. She was in way over her head. She bared her teeth at him anyway. "If you take one more step, I'll shoot you dead."

Dog Face grinned, exposing terrifying fangs that looked all too real. "Go ahead. I won't die." He took another step.

"Okay, that's it," Faith growled. "I've had about as much of this mumbo jumbo crap as I can take."

She fired.

He jerked as the bullet thudded into his chest, but he didn't go down. *He must be wearing a bulletproof vest under that suit,* she thought. His fangs flashed again in a chilling grin. "Ouch."

Faith adjusted her aim for his head, but before she could shoot again, the perp lunged. One clawed fist closed around her gun hand, jerking it up toward the sky. The other hand grabbed the front of her uniform and snatched her off her feet.

"I warned you about this kind of shit, Weston." He shook her back and forth like a doll. "You're so fucking intent on proving you're as good a cop as a man, you go rushing in when any guy with a single functioning brain cell would wait for backup."

Faith gaped, recognizing the spiel. She'd heard it half a dozen times over the past year. And that phrase—*single functioning brain cell.* Only one man she knew used it. "Reynolds?"

It didn't compute. Sergeant Keith Reynolds had been her training officer for six weeks back when she'd first joined the department. "Jesus, Sarge, what are you doing wearing that suit?"

He rolled his lips back from his fangs. "It's not a suit, dumbass."

Looking into those white teeth, Faith knew he was telling the truth. "Put me down." She was vaguely proud that her voice didn't shake. She grabbed his clawed hand with her own, tried to dig in her fingers. "Put me down *now.*"

"'Fraid we're past that, Weston. You've been asking too

many questions, and you don't show the proper gratitude. I killed that bastard Cruise for giving you that shiner, and what thanks do I get? You immediately started trying to stir shit up. We can't afford that."

"What? Who's 'we'?" It just kept getting worse and worse. "You killed Cruise?"

He grinned and licked his lips with a long, curling, thoroughly inhuman tongue. "Oh, yeah."

With sick horror, she remembered the man's mangled corpse. Reynolds had practically eaten the poor bastard. "You son of a bitch!" She swung her legs up in a violent kick right at that long muzzle.

The werewolf let go of her gun hand and slapped her feet aside before they could hit him. His fist tightened in her shirt. "Now, that's no way to talk to a superior officer." Gaping jaws lunged for her throat.

Faith threw up an arm to protect herself. Fangs clamped into her forearm with the sensation of grinding bone and ripping flesh. She screamed in agony, shoved her gun against his chest, and fired.

He roared and dropped her. Faith hit the ground so hard she saw stars, but managed to scramble away anyhow. All her attention locked on Reynolds as he reeled backward with one hand clutching at his chest.

Well, he'd felt *that*, anyway. Good, the traitorous fuck. He'd betrayed the badge and murdered a man. She hoped she'd killed his ass.

No such luck. Snarling, Reynolds regained his balance and stalked toward her again. Faith reeled to her feet, her punctured arm jolting spikes of pain through her body as she moved. Blood rolled from the wounds in twin hot streams. At least the blood didn't jet; he hadn't hit an artery.

"You little bitch," Reynolds told her, his lips rolling back from bloodied fangs. "You're going to pay for that."

"Get away from her, you bastard!" A huge black figure barreled out of the night to slam into Reynolds, knocking him flying. As Faith scuttled back, clutching her arm, the two tumbled across the clearing. Accompanied by a chorus of vicious snarls, they ripped at each other like battling bears.

Reynolds's attacker was just as big as he was—and, Faith saw in the light from the other battle, just as furry. *Good God,* she thought, *there are two of them.*

Stunned, disoriented, she fell against a tree and braced herself there, panting. Her left arm blazed with pain, and the blood still poured. She had to stop it, or she'd bleed out. Somehow she'd managed to hold on to her gun with her right hand, so she holstered the weapon and clamped her fingers over the bleeding wounds. If she'd had any doubt, the holes confirmed it hadn't been rubber fangs that had ripped into her flesh.

Reynolds really was a werewolf. And so was whatever fought him.

To hell with this, Faith thought. *I'm out of here.* She turned and started to stagger away.

The woman—or whatever she was—had apparently bested her own opponent. The armored man lay blooded at her feet as she crouched over him, holding a long knife with a snaking blade.

Oh, hell, Faith thought with weary frustration. *I can't just run away and leave the poor bastard to die.* Ignoring the mental voice that told her to do just that, she drew her weapon and leveled it. "Get away from him!" The pain in her left arm flooded her eyes with involuntary tears, but she blinked them away and snarled, "You heard me, lady, leave the guy alone. Get off him! Now!"

Where was her backup? Assuming she survived this, Faith was going to rip every cop on the force a new asshole. And she was going down the neck to do it.

The woman turned to glower at her. "My boys were right—you really are annoying." Her hands began to glow again. In their shimmering light, her eyes narrowed with chilling determination. "Well, I'm just going to have to do something about that."

Shit, Faith thought. *First werewolves and now witches.*
She steadied her aim and fired.

The bullet hit something in the air and ricocheted away.
Didn't *that* just figure?

Batting aside the rogue's claws, Jim prepared to drive a
fist into his opponent's snarling muzzle. He bled from a
dozen bites and deep scratches, but he was so juiced on
adrenalin, he scarcely felt the pain.

From the corner of one eye, he glimpsed a blue glow
backlighting a familiar uniformed figure. Faith stood pointing her gun in the vampire's face as the bitch prepared to
fry her with what was no doubt a death spell.

"Dammit, Faith!" Jim roared, leaping off the rogue.
He'd never moved faster in his life.

Belatedly realizing she was in danger, Faith jerked
back. Jim sprang, clearing fifteen feet in one hard dive. His
arms snapped around her as he twisted in midair, protecting her with his body. The spell struck him in the back. She
yelped as he wrapped himself tighter around her and took
the brunt of their landing on his shoulders. They hit the
ground hard and rolled, Jim curling around her, trying to
protect her.

When they finally slid to a stop, he lifted his head. "Are
you all—"

She shoved her gun into his face. "Get the hell off me!"

"Faith, dammit . . ." Jim snatched the weapon out of her
hand before she could fire. "What the—Shit!" Glimpsing
light flaring out of the corner of his eye, he threw himself
over her again.

Another spell sizzled through his fur. Though most
magic rolled off his kind, this one had so much voltage,
even he hissed at the burn.

Huddled in the protection of his arms, Faith yelped at
the stinging nimbus.

"Hurts, huh? It would have killed you if it had hit dead on." Jim snatched her into his arms and rolled to his feet, still clutching the gun in one hand. "I'm trying to save your ass here. Work with me!"

That seemed to get through to her. "Who *are* you?"

"I'm—" Hearing a growl, Jim spotted the rogue charging toward him. He ducked aside, swearing as the Dire Wolf's claws raked across his shoulder.

But as he inhaled at the pain, Jim smelled the blood flowing from the bite on Faith's arm. The familiar copper tang was tinged with a scent that was all too familiar.

Werewolf magic.

Jim's heart sank. The bastard hadn't just bitten Faith. He'd infected her with Merlin's Curse.

Which meant Jim had just run out of time. Though he badly wanted to continue the fight, he had to get Faith to saftey. The last thing she needed was to become a Dire Wolf in the middle of a battle. Disoriented, shocked, she'd be easy pickings—assuming she even survived her first transformation.

"Watch it!" Faith yelled in his ear.

Glancing around, he saw the vampire about to launch another blast. Jim ducked. The flying energy ball splashed into a tree trunk, sending splinters flying.

Out of time, out of options, he ran for his life, Faith cradled against his chest.

"Stop!" she gasped as they plunged over brush and around trees. "Let me go, dammit! Where the hell are you taking me?"

"As far away from here as possible," he said grimly.

He figured he had an hour at most before Faith either became a Dire Wolf . . .

. . . or died, burning in a blaze of magic her body could not control.

* * *

Muscles jerking in spasms from a near brush with a death spell, Celestine Gentry watched the enemy werewolf race off with the cop in his arms.

Bloody hell. She wasn't up to chasing them, not with her nervous system half fried from the vampires' magical blasts. Besides, she needed to sacrifice the last remaining son of a bitch before he had time to die. If she was going to drink his power, she had to do it *now.* And she needed that magic to heal her injuries. The others had died too quickly to do her any good.

Licking her lips, Celestine knelt at the vampire's side with the ceremonial dagger in her hand. Like her, he was one of Geirolf's spawn, but she felt no hesitation about killing him. With the demon god dead, it was every vampire for herself.

The vamp was a mess—raked by Reynolds's claws, burned by her spells. Normally his armor would have protected him from sorcery, but the werewolf had bent and mangled the enchanted plate, leaving gaping openings her spell had been able to penetrate.

Now all she had to do was finish him off and enjoy all that lovely magical life force.

Despite the crusty feel of his burned skin, Celestine grabbed the guard by the chin and dragged his head back as she began to chant the spell. Her hand shook from one too many blasts, but she somehow managed to steady it long enough to cut his throat. Blood spurted right into her face. She gasped at the immediate slap of power.

The guard, seared and half-gutted, succumbed to her magical blade and died. His life force streamed into her in an orgasmic wash of pleasure. Celestine shuddered, basking in its sweet heat, until the pumping stopped and the magical transfer ended.

Now, she thought, sitting back on her heels with a sigh of relief. *That's much better.*

* * *

Jim plunged through the dark woods, Faith in his arms. Leaves crunched under his running feet, and he had to dodge trees and duck low-hanging limbs. He could smell her blood rolling from the arm she held against her chest. The scent of magic grew stronger with every step. So did his dread.

Would she survive? What should he tell her?

She had a one-in-five chance of dying. Though he'd prefer better odds, she'd probably make it.

Then what, genius? Jim asked himself savagely. *If she lives, I've got what I wanted—a chance to be with her. But I've got to be completely honest about everything. Faith isn't going to accept anything less.* Not after that lying bastard of an ex of hers.

But what the hell was he going to tell her? Facts streamed through his mind, but when he imagined putting them into words, they sounded ridiculous. A race of werewolves called the Dire Kind had been created by an alien wizard as a way to control King Arthur, who was actually an immortal vampire? Oh, yeah, that would go over real well. Faith would laugh in his furry face.

Unfortunately, the facts were the facts. He just had to lay them out and pray she'd buy them—and agree to the partnership he both wanted and desperately needed.

FIVE

Bright red knives of pain lanced remorselessly up Faith's arm. Each of the werewolf's running bounds only seemed to make the agony worse. She gritted her teeth and tried to think.

It was all so unbelievable. Witches throwing death spells, her sergeant turning into a monster and trying to kill her, another werewolf saving her life. She'd think she was dreaming, except her arm hurt too damn bad.

And what the hell was going on with the werewolf who'd rescued her? He'd saved her life at least twice, shielding her from magical blasts with his own body. But werewolves were supposed to be cannibalistic killers. Should she fight him or what?

Though considering all the blood running down her arm, she doubted she was capable of giving a kitten a fight over a ball of yarn.

Suddenly Wolfman skidded to a stop in a patch of moonlight that was painfully bright. She blinked the spots out of her eyes as he put her gently on her feet.

"We need to talk," he told her in a deep, rumbling voice.

"What I need is a trip to the emergency room." Faith grimaced as she cradled her wounded arm. "Damn, this hurts."

She turned her wrist to get a look at the bite, but she couldn't see anything for the blood streaming from it. "At least it's not spurting—the bastard missed all my favorite arteries. Still needs stitches, though."

"I'm afraid stitches aren't going to do it any good."

She looked up, then took an involuntary step back at his thoroughly alien face. He looked much more like a wolf than the vaguely apelike movie werewolves she'd seen. A chill stole over her. "What do you mean, stitches won't help?"

"Hey, calm down. I'm not going to hurt you." He spread his empty hands.

She eyed him. "That gesture would be a lot more convincing without the three-inch claws."

"How about this, then?" His eyes shimmered, sparks of energy surging out of them to swirl around his body like a swarm of frantic fireflies.

The next instant, the flare of light was gone. So was the towering werewolf.

He'd become a tall, broad-shouldered man, handsome as a film hero. "Is this any better?"

Even with her arm aching in a kettle drum beat, Faith was impressed. His face was long, with broad, angular cheekbones and beautiful silver eyes under thick black brows. His short dark hair was thick and curly, and his mouth was wide and sensual, with a full lower lip that suggested kissing was something he'd do well.

His body was just as tempting, solid and strong in a black polo shirt and black pants. Her cop's eye figured him for six-two in height and two hundred well-muscled pounds.

"Very nice," Faith murmured. "But what did you mean about those stitches? I . . . shit!" A shaft of pain ripped up her arm with such viciousness, her legs buckled.

A warm male hand caught her elbow. "Maybe you'd better sit down."

"Maybe I'd better get to the doctor." She licked dry lips and shivered, knowing even as she did that neither sensation was a good sign. "I need to put a tourniquet on this before I bleed to death. Can I use your belt?" So what if he was a werewolf—he'd saved her life, and at the moment she couldn't afford to be picky anyway.

Sympathy shone in those wolf-pale eyes. "It's not going to help, Faith. You're Changing."

She glowered at him. Great, her rescuer picked *now* to turn into a bastard. "Fine." One handed, she tried to open the plastic buckle on her weapon's belt.

He caught her hand. "Faith, listen to me. In about half an hour, either the wound will heal, or you'll be dead."

"What the hell are you talking about?" Another stab of pain shot up her arm. "Ahhh—damn, that hurts!"

"That's what I'm talking about—it's starting." This time he bent and picked her up like a child before depositing her in the leaves on her butt.

"Get off!" she snapped. "Who the hell are you, anyway? What are you talking about?"

"My name is Jim London," he told her, crouching next to her. "I'm a Dire Wolf. And unless you get really unlucky, you're going to be one, too." As she squinted at him, uncomprehending, he took her uninjured hand in his. "Most everything they say about werewolves is wrong, except for one thing. When you're bitten by a werewolf . . ."

"You become a werewolf." Two and two clicked together at last, and she stared at him in cold horror. "You're kidding me."

He sighed. "I wish."

Faith surged to her feet as panic rolled through her, even more ferocious than the pain of her wounds. "No. I'm hallucinating this. This is some kind of delusion."

He stood up with her and took her shoulders in gentle hands. "Faith, you're a cop. You know what's real and what's not. This is real, and you're going to have to deal with it."

"Oh, come on!" She curled her lip at him in scorn, trying to ignore the mental voice that told her he was right. "Werewolves? People throwing magic around? This whole evening has been one long acid trip. Somebody spiked my coffee at the Li'l Cricket." She tried to shrug free of his grip, but he didn't let go. Though gentle, he was stunningly strong.

And he certainly didn't feel like a delusion.

His silver gaze didn't waver. "I know how hard this is to believe, but you're just going to have to accept it." She pulled against his hold, but he held her still without any effort at all. "Or are you going to let them just get away with it?"

"Get away with what?"

"Murdering Tony Shay. And Samuel Cruise, and God knows who else. They're killing people, Faith, and we're the only ones who can stop it."

She stopped fighting his hold and frowned at him. Her arm hurt like a bitch, but suddenly that was less important than what he was saying. "These lunatics were involved with Shay's murder? And how do you know about that, anyway?"

"Shay was my best friend. I came here to investigate his murder."

She'd suspected the killings of Shay and Cruise were connected, no matter what the detective said. "So the werewolf killed Shay."

"No. Shay infected the werewolf."

Faith peered at him. The trees did a slow circuit around her head. She really had lost way too much blood to process this conversation. "What the hell are you talking about? And would you please let go!"

London released her. "Tony was like me, a werewolf. I believe he ran into our witch friend back there, and she cut his heart out as part of some kind of magical rite."

Which would explain why they'd never found that heart—Witchy had done God knew what with it. "But how did Reynolds get involved?"

"Reynolds?" He frowned down at her.

"He's the werewolf who bit me." As London's brows lifted, she explained, "Sergeant Keith Reynolds. He was my field training officer when I joined the Clarkston PD."

"How do you know he's the rogue?"

"Rogue?"

He shrugged. "Rogue werewolf. He's not one of us, so he's a rogue."

"Who's 'us?' Never mind, I doubt it would make sense anyway." Faith shook her head. "One way or another, it's definitely Reynolds. He admitted it to me. But how did he get bitten?"

"I figure he was helping hold Shay down while the witch cut out his heart. Normally we can control who we infect, but given the circumstances, Shay must have lost it and bit him."

"And now Reynolds has bitten me." Faith swallowed hard, fighting down the fear. She had to keep thinking if she was going to make it out of this mess. "So the next full moon—"

"No," London interrupted. "In about twenty minutes. The moon thing is one of those myths. The bite takes effect within an hour."

"Shit." Feeling numb, Faith crossed to the nearest tree and sat down against its trunk, holding her aching arm. "How? How can it happen so fast?" She looked up at him as he stood over her, silhouetted against the moon. "Hell, how can it happen at all?"

London crouched in front of her. "That's a very long story, but what it all comes down to is magic."

"Magic. Shit." She let her head fall back against the tree. Its bark felt rough against the back of her skull as she stared up through its branches. The stars beyond them whirled in a slow, dizzy circle. "What the hell am I going to do?"

"What you have to do," he told her gently. "Survive and adjust."

"What am I going to tell the chief?" she asked numbly.

"Not a fucking thing."

Startled by the anger in his tone, Faith blinked at him.

London's mouth pulled into a cold, hard line. "Your chief is involved in this thing up to his neck. He stinks of black magic."

"How do you know the chief?" Faith's eyes narrowed. "Come to think of it, how do you know my first name? I sure as hell didn't introduce myself."

He dropped his eyes and ran a hand through his hair. "Well, we've, ah . . . been working together for a while."

She stared. "I don't think so."

London lifted his head and met her eyes evenly. "You've been calling me Rambo."

"No." Her jaw dropped. He was the dog? She laughed, then stopped when she heard the hysteria in her own voice. "You're lying."

He shrugged. "I'd transform and show you, but we don't have that much time, and that many transformations would be pushing it anyway."

Faith struggled to rise, but her legs wouldn't cooperate. Catching herself against the tree trunk, she glared at him. "Oh, that's convenient!"

"Faith, you just saw me as a seven-and-a-half foot Dire Wolf," he told her patiently. "Why can't you believe I can become a German shepherd? Why would I lie?"

He was right. Feeling numb, she propped herself there and watched him dust his hands and stand. "Why in the hell would you pose as my dog?"

"I told you, I'm investigating Tony's death." London reached down and steadied her, helping her regain her feet again. "I knew the chief was involved because I could smell the magic on him when I brought Tony's mother to Clarkston to view his body. And I knew the only way I could investigate dirty cops was from inside the department, so—"

"The K-9 trainer," Faith interrupted, as the pieces came together. "Is he a werewolf, too?"

"Yeah. My uncle."

Suddenly a lot of little details made sense. "I thought that dog seemed to understand what I was saying." She started to drag her good hand through her hair, then spotted the drying blood on it and grimaced. "So now I'm going to be like you." A short, painful laugh escaped her. "A K-9 handler, turning into a dog. How ironic is that?"

He stepped closer and touched her gently on the cheek. "You'll get through this, Faith. I'll help you."

"I'm going to need it. So how does this . . ."

Faith broke off. There was pain and regret in his eyes. "What?" she asked, alarmed.

"I'm . . . just sorry." He caught her under the chin and tilted her head up as he leaned in close. To her surprise, she realized he was about to kiss her.

Normally she would have stepped away, but she suddenly realized that, bloody and shocky though she was, she needed that kiss. She found herself rising onto her toes.

His lips brushed hers, warm and gently questioning. They felt so good, she let her own part.

London sighed against her mouth and slipped his tongue between her teeth in a slow stroke. He tasted like the deep woods after a rain, dark and wild and clean.

When he finally broke the kiss and stepped back, she had to fight the desire to pursue him. "I had to do that," he told her, sadness in his smile.

"What aren't you telling me?" The bite was shooting spikes of pain through her body now with steadily increasing speed. Whatever it was that was about to happen, it wouldn't be long.

His eyes shifted fractionally. Faith went on alert with a cop's sure instinct for when someone was hiding something. "Okay, London, what do you not want to tell me?"

He sighed. "Twenty percent of those attempting their first Change don't make it."

"What, like they get hung halfway?"

"They burn." His voice sounded hoarse. He cleared his throat. "The magic runs rogue and kills them."

"Damn." She cradled her injured arm closer. The fire in the bite was intensifying. "Is there anything I can do?"

"No. I can transform first—they say it helps to have someone lead the way." He shook his head. "I shouldn't have told you."

"No." Faith squared her shoulders. "I want to have all the facts. And I appreciate your honesty."

He nodded tightly, then offered, "The odds are in your favor, Faith. You should make it."

She eyed him. There was something haunted in his eyes. "But you've seen it go the other way, haven't you?"

London hesitated a long moment. "When I was a teenager. First time I attempted to transform. The victim and Tony Shay were my best friends. We'd grown up together. Steve . . . burned."

She decided she really didn't want to know the details. The ache in her arm was making it hard to concentrate anyway. A particularly savage stab made her eyes tear. Fiercely, she blinked them away. She didn't want him to think she was crying with fear. Why that was important, she didn't know. "Don't sweat it, London. I'll get through it."

His gaze was intense. "*We'll* get through it."

Oddly enough, something in the way he said "we" took the edge off her fear.

Faith straightened her shoulders and met his gaze. Her heart was pounding with vicious strength. So was the bite in her arm—long, rolling pulses that made her feel light-headed and sick. "So what happens now?"

"When I scent the change coming, I'll transform first. That'll guide you over into Dire Wolf form. And then I'll show you how to return to human form."

"Oh, good." Faith cradled her wounded arm in her hand

and blinked. Black spots were dancing in front of her eyes. She fought to concentrate. "So I won't have to wait for daybreak or something?"

"No, other than this first time, you'll be able to transform at will."

"Will it hurt?" She forced a smile that was more grimace than anything else. "Not that it isn't hurting now."

Jim laid a careful hand on her uninjured shoulder and gently rubbed it up and down. "The first time is usually a little rough. But the good news is, the transformation will heal that bite. It'll be gone when you become human again."

"Well, that's something." A wave of cold rolled across her skin, and she shivered. Her head was spinning. "How much longer? I feel like I'm going to black out."

London lowered his head toward her and inhaled, scenting her. "Not long." He slid a hand under her elbow, bracing her on her feet. "Just try to stay on your feet for a few more minutes, and the worst will be over."

She had the distinct feeling he was jollying her along. "If I live through this, I swear to God, I'm going to kill Reynolds."

"Sounds like a plan." His smile looked strained.

He's afraid for me, Faith realized suddenly. Surprisingly, that made her feel a little less alone. "If I don't make it . . ." She broke off, a dozen messages crowding her tongue. She finally contented herself with, "Tell my family I love them. My Dad lives in Columbia. Richard Weston. He's in the book."

"I'll call him." He cupped her face in one big, warm palm. "One way or another, Faith, I'm going to get Reynolds and the witch. They're not going to get away with this."

Touched, she smiled at him. "I appreciate that. You—" Before she could get the rest of the sentence out of her mouth, pain detonated in her arm. The ferocity of it bent her double. London caught her, lowering her to the leaves as she writhed in his arms. "Shit!" she gasped. "That hurts!"

"I know, baby." He tightened his hold as her muscles knotted and shook. "Hang on, Faith. It'll be okay."

Her only possible response was a strangled yell. Fire spread from her arm and up her shoulder, racing through her veins like a river of acid. A scream tore its way past her control.

He pulled her close, stilling her thrashing body. "Hang on, Faith, it's almost here. A little longer—"

"I don't like this!" she gritted out.

"I know, baby. You can make it." He inhaled again, this time more sharply. "Okay, it's time. Here we go!"

No! Her mind howled a panicked denial, but it was too late. The magic spilled from his eyes again, rolling over his body and leaping to hers. She screamed as the pain in her arm blazed, engulfing her consciousness in flame. It felt as though a vise gripped her, twisting and jerking muscle and bone until they stretched like taffy. Her skin seemed to swell, heating as though she were cooking from the inside.

I'm dying! The thought howled through her. The magic was going rogue.

Faith whimpered helplessly as the fire built, hotter and hotter, jerking and knotting her body until she flailed helplessly, like a manic rag doll. She found herself praying to die quickly.

And then . . .

. . . the fire winked out.

A whip-poor-will called somewhere over her head in sad liquid notes. Faith froze, panting, not quite daring to open her eyes.

The pain in her arm had vanished as if it had never been.

Gradually, her stunned and violated senses began to report in. Something firm and covered with fur pressed against her back. She felt warm, almost hot, though a breeze blew across her face, ruffling her hair.

"Faith?" The voice was so deep and rumbling it barely sounded like Jim at all.

Cautiously, she opened her eyes. London's dark silhouette loomed over her. He still held her across his lap. She blinked, and her eyes began to adjust.

He tilted his head, and she saw the long shape of his muzzle in the moonlight. "You okay?"

"Yeah." Her voice sounded strange—almost as deep as his. She cleared her throat, but she still sounded hoarse when she asked, "I made it?"

He stroked a hand over her shoulder. "Yeah. You made it."

Faith sucked in a relieved breath and tried to sit up. He helped her, pulling her upright. Automatically, she glanced at her hands.

Her skin was covered with thick red fur the same color as her hair. Her hands were much bigger than they should be, tipped with three-inch claws that gleamed in the moonlight, their points sharp as knives. "Damn," she muttered, staring at them blankly. "I can't believe any of this." When she tried to stand, her quivering legs refused to cooperate.

"I know." London shifted her off his lap and rose easily to his feet. "But you'll adjust, Faith. You're strong." He reached down to help her up.

Automatically, she put a hand in his. Their palms, unlike the rest of their bodies, were bare of fur. She looked at their joined fingers. Red fur gleamed against black. "I'm going to kick Keith Reynolds's ass."

London laughed, his deep voice booming. "I'll help." With an easy tug, he pulled her to her feet.

Faith looked up at him, taking in his wolflike face. She knew her own must look just as inhuman. "I should wake up right about now."

His big head tilted. " 'Fraid not. You really are a were-wolf. Sorry."

She sighed and released him. Experimenting, she took a step away from him. Her too-long legs shook, and she felt as awkward and weak as a newborn colt. "That's what I

figured. How do I turn back? Not that I'm looking forward
to going through *that* again."

"Wait a few minutes," he told her. "It's not a good idea
to Change too many times in too short a period. The magic
can get away from you."

Faith grimaced. "Wouldn't want that." Cautiously, she
reached up and explored her head. Her ears were triangular
points thrusting up from the mass of her hair, which fell
around her shoulders in a thick, surprisingly soft mane.
Probing warily, she discovered no tangles. Even the twigs
she knew she'd collected in their flight through the woods
had vanished. "So what do we do in the meantime?"

"Breathe."

Faith glanced up at him. "Ha. Funny."

"No, I'm serious." He stepped closer to her, staring into
her eyes. She suddenly realized she could see him as
clearly as if it were twilight instead of past midnight. "Your
senses are more acute now than they've ever been. Just take
a moment and feel that. Breathe." He inhaled sharply,
demonstrating. Almost hypnotized by his intensity, Faith
did the same.

He was right. She'd been so focused on the crisis that
she hadn't realized just how rich and intense the air
smelled. The crisp, sharply green scent of pine needles, the
turpentine reek of sap, the rich, dark aroma of loam and
dead leaves. The night breeze carried the imprint of those
scents so vividly, she could almost see them, taste them in
her mouth, vivid as wine.

Then the breeze shifted, blowing Jim's scent into her
face—clean, wild, richly masculine. Faith swallowed, staring at him wide-eyed.

The werewolf didn't seem aware of her fascination as
he turned to pace the clearing in long, muscular strides. He
didn't speak, seeming lost in thought as if he struggled to
put something important into words.

Moonlight silvered his fur, making it shimmer as muscle rippled beneath it. The effect was heightened by the

fluid power that gave a spring to his every step. He moved more like a tiger than a wolf.

Why, he's beautiful, Faith thought, startled. It wasn't the conventional male beauty of a *GQ* model—he was too fierce and elemental for that, too animal. Yet even as lupine as he was, something about him brought her body to quivering awareness.

Jim stopped and turned back to her. She watched, hypnotized, as he strode back toward her as if he'd decided how to approach a difficult subject. His shoulders looked impossibly wide.

"Don't look at this as turning into some kind of monster, Faith." His pale eyes gazed down into hers, intense and earnest. "I realize that's an easy, almost natural conclusion to draw, but it shortchanges the experience."

Faith started to lick her lips, then stopped. Her mouth felt so damned alien, long and narrow. She wondered what it looked like. "How should I see it, then?"

He took her hand in his, long fingers curling around hers. "Tonight you've become magic. You could rip the doors off a Hummer if you wanted. You can run faster than a horse. You can see in the dark. As time goes on and your body adjusts, your senses will become even more acute." A smile curved his mouth. "Tonight you were born to a new life."

Standing this close, his scent flooded her senses. Her body responded, nipples peaking beneath the fur that covered her body. She had the embarrassing suspicion she was getting wet.

For God's sake, Faith, he's not human, she told herself, shaken by the sudden, fierce rise of hunger.

Neither am I, something dark and hidden replied.

"It's a lot to take in." She spoke more for something to say than anything else. Her voice sounded tight and hoarse.

Jim's gaze didn't shift from hers. "I know. Remember, no matter how difficult all this is for you, I'm here. I'll help."

Faith dropped her eyes, unable to deal with the sheer emotional intensity of the moment. She'd learned the hard way that vulnerability could have painful consequences. "I . . . I . . . When can I turn back?" Human again. She needed to be human again, with dull human senses she understood.

He sighed, then seemed to accept her reaction. "Just close your eyes and listen to the dark, Faith."

She was more than happy to obey.

But as she stood there, Faith suddenly grew aware of Something. It was huge and restless and powerful, that Something, coiled and waiting on the edges of her consciousness. A vast, glowing Thing that seemed to sense her in return. It stirred.

Moved toward her.

A chill rolled over her. "What the hell is *that*?"

"What?"

"There's this . . . thing out there. A huge, glowing thing." She opened her eyes wide to stare at him.

"That's the Mageverse."

"The what?"

"The Mageverse." He shrugged impossibly broad shoulders. "I guess you could call it an alternate universe. It lies alongside our own—it even has its own version of Earth and its own version of humanity."

Faith remembered countless science fiction novels she'd devoured as a child. "Like another dimension?"

"Something like that. Only in the Mageverse, magic is one of the elemental forces of the universe. Kind of like magnetism and gravity here. That's the power we draw on to Change."

She blinked, returning her attention to the Thing. "Wow. I'm supposed to use all that? How?"

"Picture yourself as if you're looking into a mirror. Then you open your mind to the magic and let it work through you."

"That's it?" She felt her lips quirk up. "I don't have to chant some magic spell or something?"

"No. Just give the magic room to come to you."

Faith frowned, really thinking about the idea. "I didn't do that when I changed the first time."

He shook his big head. Moonlight silvered his pointed ears. "That was different. That was Merlin's magic. This is yours."

"Merlin?" Surprised, she stared at him. "Like King Arthur? That Merlin? What does he have to do with this?"

"Long story, I'll explain later. Just"—he made a fanning gesture with his clawed hands—"open yourself to the magic."

It all sounded a little too mumbo jumbo to Faith. But then, none of the rest of this made sense, either. Closing her eyes, she pictured looking into the mirror that morning. She saw her own face, narrow and foxy, with its stubborn chin and red hair, tightly braided to her head.

The Something stirred, massive and glowing. Her lips parted. A chill rolled over her in blended surprise and fear.

The power rushed toward her in a hot, bright wave. She sucked in a breath.

And it slammed into her, burning and foaming, dragging at her body, twisting it . . . an endless instant later, it was over. She stood on shaking legs and lifted her hands in front of her eyes. The skin was pale and hairless. She was human once more.

Well, as human as she'd ever be again, anyway.

S I X

———

George Ayers stalked through the woods, his belly churning. He could feel the witch up ahead. His very blood and balls responded to her seductive tug.

In his moments of clarity, the chief knew Celestine Gentry was going to destroy him, along with every other man in his department. The only chance any of them had was to kill her.

Yet when he was in her presence, all he could think about was fucking her and feeling her fangs sink into his throat. He hated himself for that weakness, but her magical grip was too strong.

God, he wanted to find a way out of this trap.

The only thing that kept him from doing something really stupid—like, say, planting a bomb somewhere she was going to be—was the thought that she really could deliver on her promises. In his more reckless moments, he thought that was a chance worth taking.

He walked into the clearing just as Celestine's pet were-wolf shifted form.

Sergeant Keith Reynolds turned toward him with that smug quirk to his lips that never failed to make George want to hit him. Reynolds was barely thirty, a tall, good-looking brunet who'd been a hotdogging glory hound even before he'd become a werewolf. The chief blamed him as much as Celestine for dragging them all into this mess. If Reynolds hadn't pulled the little bitch over as she'd speeded through town, she might have kept right on going.

Then Reynolds had compounded the problem by getting himself bitten by that damn werewolf. Not only had he become a furry Superman, he was now Celestine's favorite. The vampire seemed to like screwing and feeding on him more than the rest of them.

"Where's Weston?" George eyed Celestine, who sat beside the body of a man sprawled in the leaves. More bodies lay around her, variously burned and gutted. *Shit, the vamp's murdered half a dozen people,* the chief thought, appalled. *How the hell are we going to cover* this *up?* "I know she was here. Her unit is sitting by the side of the road with the door open."

George had been listening to his radio at home when Weston had called for assistance. He immediately radioed in and canceled the request as a false alarm, only to learn a county deputy was already on the way. He'd driven to the scene barely in time to intercept the man.

Unfortunately, the deputy had been determined to investigate such an obviously urgent cry for help from another officer. George had finally ordered him from the scene. Luckily the other cop had been cowed by his chief's badge, because he had no authority to order a sheriff's deputy to do anything.

Now Weston was missing. George hoped they hadn't killed her, too. He'd have a hell of a time talking his way around that one.

Celestine looked at him, indifferent. "I don't know where the little bitch went, and I don't much care."

These idiots were going to get them all killed. "You let her get away?"

"She had help." Reynolds's voice held a distinct rumble of frustration. "Another werewolf. Fucker was tough. He grabbed her and ran off."

George stiffened. "Another werewolf? What do you mean, another werewolf? What other werewolf?"

Reynolds shrugged and moved to help Celestine to her feet. She swayed slightly, wincing. Apparently one of her opponents had managed to hurt her. "Who knows? I've never seen him before."

"He must be connected to Shay. Looking for payback." George frowned thoughtfully. "Maybe the guy that showed up with Shay's mother. What was his name . . . ?" He snapped his fingers. "Jim London! I knew there was something off about that bastard."

Reynolds shrugged. "Don't know, but this guy did mention Shay when we were fighting. Something about making me pay."

"Great!" George threw up his hands. "Just fucking fantastic! And you let him get away?"

"He'll be back." Celestine dismissed his concerns with an infuriating little wave. She turned to Reynolds. "You bit Weston, didn't you?"

Reynolds looked uneasy. "Yes, ma'am. I'm sorry about that. Situation got away from me."

"You bit her?" George was horrified. "Does that mean she's going to become a werewolf, too? What the fuck did you do that for?"

The sergeant shrugged. "I was going for her throat. She got an arm up. Before I could finish her off, the other wolf slammed into me, and I got a little busy."

Celestine patted him on one brawny shoulder. "It's all right, darling. I'll make good use of them."

"What are you talking about, Celestine?" George demanded.

"If this woman has been infected, she's magical now," Celestine explained. "I can sacrifice her and this other were and feed on them." With a gesture, the vampire created a gateway in the air. Through the glowing opening, the chief could see a wavering image of her mansion's bedroom. "She'll report in, won't she?"

George stared at her uneasily. She wanted to sacrifice Weston? "Even after becoming a werewolf? Hell, Celestine, I don't know."

"Well, if she does, bring her to me."

"How? If she's a werewolf—"

"Don't be dense, George. Do the same thing you did to Tony. That worked well enough." She turned toward Reynolds, hooking his forearm with one hand. "Come, love. I need you."

"Oh, yeah." His eyes lighting with eager lust, Reynolds started to follow her through the gate.

"Wait!" the chief protested. "What if we need his help? We've got two werewolves loose here!"

"You'll just have to manage." Celestine tightened her grip on Reynolds's arm. "The fight with our friend there took a lot out of me. I need Keith."

George threw an appalled look at the corpses that littered the clearing. "Don't forget the bodies."

She waved a dismissive hand. "You deal with them."

"Celestine!"

"Dig a hole and throw them in, George. I'm not spending my power on them." As the two stepped through the gateway, Reynolds threw him a smug look over his shoulder that made him grit his teeth.

Prick.

The gate winked out. With a muttered curse, George turned on his heel and stalked back toward his car. He was going to need reinforcements.

With shovels.

* * *

The night was so intensely bright, Faith could see each leaf and blade of grass. Small animals and birds rustled and scuttled in the woods around her, and the breeze rattled the leaves over her head like a windstorm. And the smells . . . She took a deep breath. Leaf mold, fresh dirt, something a little rank that was probably an animal, and . . .

Masculinity. Clean, dark, seductive.

Faith looked around at London. He was human again, and even more breathtakingly handsome than she'd thought. She could see the clean lines of his face so much more clearly now—the strong angles of cheekbones, the sensual line of a seductive upper lip, the hooded shimmer of his eyes.

Faith wanted to kiss him again. The strength of her growing desire was shocking. It had hit her hard the moment she'd become human again, a ferocious craving that made her hands shake and her mouth go dry.

She wanted to peel that knit shirt up so she could touch the hard flesh of his chest. Run her hands over his abdominals and thumb his flat male nipples. Take him inside her in long, grinding thrusts . . .

"Faith." London sounded hoarse. His nostrils flared, scenting her, and he took a step toward her. He cleared his throat. "You look . . . better."

"I feel better." She licked her dry lips, trying to ignore the ringing ferocity of her desire. "But for a while there, I didn't think I was going to make it at all."

"Yeah, I was worried, too." He dropped his eyes to her right wrist. "But here you are, all healed up."

She glanced down. The skin Reynolds had savaged was unbroken now, pale and healthy in the moonlight. "Yeah, just like you said. If I didn't know better, I'd think I dreamed the whole thing."

"But you didn't." There was tension in the set of Jim's shoulders, hunger in his eyes. She knew he wanted her as badly as she wanted him. Stepping in close, he looked down at her for a long, thrumming moment. "It did happen, and you survived." He brushed his warm knuckles across her cheekbone. "You were very brave. But then, you always are."

"I feel strange." Swallowing, she rested her hands on his chest through the soft, skin-warmed cotton. "Hot."

"It's the Burning Moon." A muscle worked in his jaw, and she sensed he was holding himself fiercely in control. "When you changed that second time, it kicked in."

"What the heck is the Burning Moon?" Faith traced her fingertips over the fabric-covered muscles of his pecs. It seemed she could feel each tiny thread in the fabric. The scent of him rolled up through the material, sensual and intoxicating. She breathed in, savoring it.

"You know how animals go into heat?" His gaze rested on the rise of her breasts through her uniform shirt. "It's like that. Your body is producing all these hormones and pheromones. Urging you to . . ."

"Have sex." She should probably be outraged at the idea, but all she felt was fierce, burning desire. "And you feel it, too."

"Yes." When he drew her into his arms, Faith knew she should step away. She didn't. He lowered his head and took her mouth.

Cupping her face in one broad, warm hand, he savored her, licking her lips, teasing and kissing. The taste of him exploded in her senses, a hot male feast of lips and tongue and wicked skill. She groaned at the lush pleasure. He growled back, a deep sound that vibrated with feral masculine need.

His free hand settled on her backside, dragged her closer. She felt his erection against her belly, thick and rock hard, a blunt statement of his lust.

Faith's senses spun. How long had it been since she'd made love? A year? Eighteen months? She couldn't remember. Too long. After Ron, she hadn't wanted to risk it.

She shouldn't want to risk it now. London was even better looking than her faithless ex, the kind of man women threw themselves at. The kind of man all too willing to take anything he was given.

But when he kissed her like this, her body didn't care. Whether it was this Burning Moon or deprivation or simple crazed euphoria from surviving a close call, she wanted him.

Desperate to touch his bare skin, Faith grabbed the bottom of his shirt and dragged it up. Her hands slid beneath the knit and found firm flesh dusted with hair. He groaned against her mouth. She growled back. The sound was surprisingly throaty and deep, more animal than human.

Just like her.

He wasn't Ron. She didn't love him. But she did need him. She knew the score now, where she hadn't before. Why couldn't she take what she needed, as long as she kept her eyes open and her heart guarded?

In the back of her mind, Faith knew there were good arguments against it, but her clamoring body wasn't interested. She could feel herself skidding out of control.

And she didn't care. She wanted to touch that hard cock pressing against her zipper, wanted to feel it spill into her hands. Needed it.

Faith didn't give a damn about anything else.

Mouth open against hers, Jim gulped in her scent. Every swallow brought the taste of building arousal, rich with salt and musk and Faith. His entire body vibrated like a tuning fork with hunger.

It wasn't just the Burning Moon. It was Faith herself. She'd scared the shit out of him so many times tonight, relief alone would have had him all over her.

In her case, though, it was all chemical, and he knew it. Wary and wounded as she was, she never would have come anywhere near him had it not been for the demands of her body.

Jim had every intention of taking advantage of the situation anyway. Those hormones of hers had breached her formidable emotional walls, and he meant to make the most of the opportunity. He wanted her for his own, and he was by God going to have her.

She could have died a dozen times tonight, but she hadn't, in part because of him.

He rolled his hips against hers and felt her grind back. Some deep, atavistic part of him growled, *Mine!*

Jim wasn't in the mood to argue with it.

Dragging his mouth away from Faith's, he gently nibbled his way to the corner of her jaw. The hand in her hair tightened, pulling her head back. His mouth found her banging pulse. With exquisite care, he closed his teeth over it, just hard enough to sting. She made a shocked sound of arousal and arched. He smiled against her throat.

Wrapping his arms around her, he pulled her off her feet and lowered her to the leaves. She coiled her long legs around his hips, one heel digging into his ass in silent demand. Hands dragged at clothing. He fought the impulse to rip her uniform open.

His collar dragged at his neck with the ragged sound of tearing fabric. "Sorry," Faith growled.

Jim grinned as he wrestled with her shirt. "No, you're not." Then, frustrated, he demanded, "Why are your buttons so damn small?"

She laughed, the sound throaty with arousal. "Let me do that."

The black fabric parted, revealing more black fabric. "Fucking bulletproof vest." He peeled the shirt off her and attacked the velcro straps. They yielded with a protesting rip. More fabric. "Jesus, what are you wearing?"

"T-shirt."

"Fuck that." Riiiiiiip. Scraps of black fabric went flying.

Finally, the gleam of white lace in the moonlight. Her bra. With a growl of satisfaction, he jerked the soft cups up, revealing what he'd been dying to see for weeks.

Sitting back on his heels, Jim looked down at her, drinking in the sight. Her breasts were pretty cream mounds in the moonlight, tipped with tight nipples. Reverently, he brushed his fingertips over them.

Soft skin, damp from being trapped under too many layers of uniform. The scent of her rolled up, pure, intoxicating Faith, spiked with potent pheromones. His cock hardened still more, bucking against his zipper.

Jim throttled back on his desperate lust. He had to take his time, make sure she found the same pleasure he did. Gently, he cupped her, thumbed a nipple. Listened as she inhaled in need.

Dying to sample her, he lowered his head and took the nearest taut peak into his mouth. The taste of her exploded in his senses, making him shudder at the stark pleasure. His dick jerked again. Ignoring it, he licked her tenderly, teasing out a soft gasp. God, she tasted so good. Felt so good.

When he cupped her other breast, his hand shook.

Despite the savage need to plunge into her, he concentrated all his attention on making her as hot as he could. Closing his teeth over a hard nipple, he raked the tiny peak gently, savoring the way she squirmed under his hands. Both her hands fisted in his hair, demanding more. Jim gave it to her gladly, stroking and teasing.

Until finally he decided it was time to reach for her zipper.

Mindless with the most intense desire she'd ever known, Faith squirmed as Jim nibbled his way down her belly. He stopped at her navel, swirling his hot tongue around it, dipping suggestively into the little hollow, then ringing it with soft little bites.

"You're making me crazy!" she gasped.

"Good. You've been making me crazy for weeks."

But he'd been a dog. . . . She lost the thought as he nuzzled the open V of her zipper. Big hands slid into her waistband, pushed her uniform pants down her hips. With a sudden, hungry growl, he sat up, stripped his shirt off in an impatient jerk, and threw it aside.

Then he went to work on her pants.

Dazed, she watched him, admiring the way all the gleaming muscle of his shoulders shifted and worked in the moonlight. His body was truly beautiful, sculpted and tight, dusted in soft hair.

He growled in frustration, but her stubborn pants were caught around her thighs and refused to come off.

"Shoes," she reminded him breathlessly, then sat up to dispense with them herself.

With a triumphant rumble, Jim stripped her pants off at last, leaving her in nothing but socks and panties. The panties quickly fell victim to his warm, demanding hands as he settled between her thighs. She rolled her hips upward, pleading.

His tongue flicked out, licked at her outer lips. She groaned. "God, London . . ."

"Jim," he growled, and spread her with two fingers.

She almost catapulted off the leaves when he found her most delicate flesh and began to feast, licking, flicking, sucking. Driving her sweetly insane. One finger discovered her opening and delved inside, feeling thick and impossibly carnal.

"God," she whimpered.

"Tight." Anticipation roughened the word. He locked his mouth over her clit and suckled. Pleasure shot through her in spikes.

She shouted. "Yeah, oh, yeah! Jim!"

His only answer came in long, luscious suckles and tempting little bites, creating a storm of hot sensation that soon had her writhing.

The climax took her by surprise. She'd always taken so long with her ex-husband, but Jim drove her to her peak with merciless speed. Her hips rocked as she arched in the leaves, crying out, flying.

* * *

When the storm of pleasure passed, Faith collapsed, panting and sated, her muscles twitching in the aftermath of the ferocious pleasure.

Breathing hard, Jim sat up between her thighs. His zipper hissed, and leaves rustled as he wrestled off his pants. His scent filled her senses, feral and delicious.

She looked down to watch him as he sat up and ripped open a foil packet. "Where'd you get that?"

"Your bathroom. Put it in a pocket." His grin flashed, hot with triumph and anticipation. "I'm an optimistic kind of guy."

Then he covered her, his eyes blazing under the dark shelf of his brows. His mouth was wet with her juices.

She lifted her head to look down their bodies. His cock was deliciously long, its width impressive as he aimed it for her hungry core.

His entry tore a shout of pleasure from her mouth. Throwing her head back, she curled her legs around his bare, muscular ass as he worked his way inside, inch by silken inch. "God," Jim growled. "You feel so damned good."

"So do you," she groaned, grinding upward to get more of that amazing shaft. It filled her so perfectly, satin and steel, the solid embodiment of pleasure.

Ron had never felt anything like that.

He braced his powerful arms on either side of her head and began to thrust in slow, deep pumps that made her eyes roll back in her head.

"Faith," he chanted. "Faith, Faith, God. Merlin's beard . . ."

Dazed, she watched him tilt his head up toward the moon, eyes closed. She couldn't remember Ron ever looking that joyous when they'd made love.

She forced her attention away from those unwelcome memories to concentrated on the raw sensations that thick cock created as Jim rocked in and out, circling his hips to grind deliciously down on her clit.

"Good," she whimpered. "So good. So hard . . ."

"Yeah!" He picked up the pace, lunging hard against her, each powerful stroke sending bursts of white-hot pleasure up her spine. "You feel so tight!"

Just like that, she tilted over into fire. Faith cried out, writhing.

Jim bucked against her hard, grinding deep in merciless plunges that ground her back into the leaves. She didn't care, too lost in the endless pulses of her climax.

Until he stiffened with a roar, throwing his handsome head back. Limp with pleasure, she watched his orgasm blind him, moonlight painting the perfect masculine angles of his face.

No, Ron had never looked like that.

His arms shaking, Jim collapsed over Faith, then rolled onto his back, pulling her atop his chest. His heart thundered with the aftermath of the brain-storming pleasure she'd given him. Sweating, panting, he scarcely felt the leaves prickling his bare back. All his senses were focused on her—the sweet weight of her body, the luscious female musk of her skin, the damp red silk of her hair tickling his chest.

Damn, he loved her. If he'd had any doubts, they were gone now.

But he still hadn't won her.

On the other hand, he'd taken the first step. That was enough, at least for tonight.

The rest—including rogue werewolves and psychotic vampires—he'd deal with later. All Jim wanted for now was to be with her.

They lay still, wrapped in one another's arms as they regained their breath. All too soon, Faith stirred in his arms and lifted her head. "Man." She blinked down at him, discomfort flickering in her eyes. It had probably hit her she'd made love to a man she didn't even know.

So much for basking in the afterglow, Jim thought, resigned. He really wasn't surprised, though. Faith never did anything the easy way.

"We'd . . . better get back." Her gaze shifted from his. "We've got bad guys to deal with . . . shit!" She sat up and started looking around for her uniform. "That bald guy. The bitch probably killed him just like the others."

"Probably." Jim sat up and rolled onto his side, bracing on an elbow as he watched her search the clearing. "Faith, he had an upside down pentagram tattooed on his forehead. It's safe to say he wasn't on the side of the angels. And neither were his buddies."

"That's not the point." She found her panties and paused to pick the leaves off them before putting them on. "Even assholes don't deserve to be murdered."

"Yeah, but there wasn't much we could do about it. Most of them were dead when we got there, and then we were under fire. Besides which, you did get bitten trying to save him. I think you've done your part for justice."

"Not yet. Not until Reynolds and the bitch are behind bars." She pulled her underwear on, then dragged her bra down to cover her pretty breasts. "What did you do with my T-shirt?"

He winced and picked up a scrap of black fabric—all that remained of it. "'Fraid that's a lost cause."

Faith grimaced at the rag. "Okay, guess I'll wear the vest without it." She looked around for her body armor.

Jim found it lying under his left knee and handed it over. He helped her strap it on, then started putting himself back in order as she put on her uniform shirt. "So what do you have in mind for a next move?"

"Get back to the scene. Call it in." Faith picked up her holster and buckled it around her slim hips. "Then figure out what to tell that asshole detective. Who, I don't doubt, is going to be just as obstructionist as he's been every other time."

Jim zipped his pants. She wasn't going to like what he had to tell her next. "You do know there's a reason for that, right?"

She frowned at him. "You think he's involved?"

"Yeah, actually, but that's beside the point." Jim found his shoes and slid his feet into them. "Faith, the woman is a witch. You saw the way she was throwing magic around. Do you really think the city jail is going to hold her?"

She braced her fists on her hips and glowered at him. "What do you suggest?"

"What I had in mind all along. I'm going to kill her."

"Just like that?"

"Just like that." He buckled his belt with a jerk and glanced at her. He bit back a curse. She looked as if he'd slapped her. "Faith, we're not dealing with an ordinary human being here. She's a *vampire*. Reynolds is a werewolf. The system is not equipped to deal with either of them."

Faith dragged a leaf out of her hair and frowned at it absently. "I thought you said she was a witch."

"She is. She's also a vampire. Which makes her about ten times stronger than a human being, even aside from her ability to throw death spells. You don't put *that* in jail."

She threw the leaf aside and braced her fists on her hips, glowering at him. "So you're saying we should just murder her in cold blood?"

"I seriously doubt it's going to be that damned easy. We'll be lucky if we can get her before she gets us."

"There's got to be some alternative to . . ." Faith's hand fell to her holster. She swore, finding it empty. "Where's my weapon?"

"Good question. I think I had it." Jim looked around and spotted it in the pile of leaves where he'd dropped it after he'd put Faith down. He retrieved it and handed it over.

"Thank you." Faith holstered it, snapped the strap across it, then turned on her heel to stalk off. She stopped to shoot him a glittering look over her shoulder, frustration boiling off her in waves that were almost visible. "Which way did we come?"

He sighed and stepped past her. "Come on."

Leading the way through the woods, Jim tried to decide

how to break the really bad news to her—that most of the police department was involved. Trouble was, there was no easy way to tell her except to just come out with it. He turned to her. "Faith, I've got something to tell you."

SEVEN

Faith listened in growing horror as he laid out accusation after accusation against the Clarkston police department. Finally she could take no more. "No. I don't believe it."

"Look, I know how hard this is for you to accept, but—"

"London, you're off base. Period. I could believe Reynolds, even the chief—he's always seemed oily to me—but the whole department? Impossible. All those cops can't be dirty."

Jim stopped walking and turned to face her. His gaze was level with certainty. "They're under some kind of spell, Faith. I can smell it on them. It's very distinctive— smells like something rotting."

"So if there's a spell, we break it. *If.* I don't think there is." But even as she denied the possibility, something in the back of her mind whispered that maybe he was right.

There'd been something off about the way Detective Taylor had blown off her report about the woman near Shay's cell. Then there was his insistence that drug dealers had turned a rottweiler loose on Cruise, a theory that had seemed far-fetched from the first. Admittedly, it was a more believable idea than the truth—a seven-foot were-wolf with a grudge—but still.

Then there was the attitude she'd been getting from the men on her shift. Their increasing hostility had made her feel like an outsider for weeks now, though they'd welcomed her when she'd first joined the department.

"What kind of 'spell' are we talking about?" Faith grimaced as she said it. Spells, werewolves, witches—her life had dived straight into the Twilight Zone. She'd always prided herself on being a hardheaded, practical cop. All this stuff made her cringe.

She could just imagine what her dad and brothers would say. She'd never hear the end of it—assuming she was ever stupid enough to tell them. What was she going to say? *"Hi, Dad. I was bitten by a werewolf, and now I'm seven feet tall and fuzzy."*

She didn't think so.

Jim shrugged. "I have no idea what kind of spell she's using." He sounded so damn casual about it all, too, as if magic and witches were as routine to him as speeding tickets and drunk drivers. "I'm pretty sure she's feeding on them, but she could have warped their thinking, too."

"Feeding on them? As in drinking their blood?" Faith remembered how gray everyone had looked during roll call. "I'd thought the guys on my shift looked a little anemic. Do you think she—?"

He lifted his head. "Shh."

She stilled and listened. The wind shifted, bringing the sound of male voices from somewhere up ahead.

Magic ruffled across her skin as Jim transformed into his Dire Wolf form. He jerked his head in a "follow me" gesture and slunk off through the woods toward the voices.

Faith hesitated, wondering if she should change, too, then decided against it. Better not attempt something that tricky in the middle of a potentially dangerous situation.

She hurried after him, trying to move as quietly as she could.

". . . not comfortable with this, chief," one man said. "Are you sure this is necessary?"

Faith frowned and craned her neck, trying to see through the screening trees. That sounded like Gary Morrow.

"Celestine told me to pick her up and bring her in," Chief Ayers replied, his voice carrying plainly on the wind. "And considering that Reynolds just bit her, we need all the firepower we can get."

"You think she's already turned into a werewolf?" Sergeant Randy Young asked. He sounded nerved up and jumpy at the very idea.

"Reynolds Changed within an hour of Shay's biting him."

At that confirmation of his suspicions, Jim shot her a grim look over his shoulder.

Detective Taylor grunted. "Scared the shit out of me."

The chief laughed, the sound a bit nasty. "Scared Celestine, too, considering she was fucking him at the time."

Faith frowned. Celestine must be the witch. Wait— she'd banged Reynolds with Frank and the chief watching?

Jim sank into a crouch and worked his way closer to the roadside, moving with surprising silence for somebody that big. Faith hunkered low and slipped after him, placing her feet carefully. Good thing her brothers had insisted on taking her hunting so often when she was a kid. She'd learned how to move quietly in the woods before she'd even hit puberty. This wasn't the first time in her law enforcement career the skill had come in handy.

They rounded a strand of trees to see the group standing by the side of the road. Faith's brows lifted.

The chief was apparently treating this like a major operation. Patrol cars were parked up and down the street, and she counted thirty cops standing around in body armor. Every man in the department was in on the hunt. It looked like London was right. They were all involved.

Faith felt sick.

Ahead of her, Jim slipped toward the group like a cat creeping up on a flock of pigeons. Faith sank lower as she moved after him. It helped that they were downwind of the bastards. The breeze would help carry the sound away.

A branch snapped behind them.

Jim whirled, snarling—and jerked, his back arching, arms flying wide, before toppling with a crash like a furry seven-foot tree. Faith whirled to see Frank Granger standing behind them, a TASER in his hand.

It had been a trap, she realized. Even as they'd crept up on the cops from downwind, Granger had been sneaking up on them. The breeze had carried away both his scent and the sound of his passage.

"You really should have kept your nose out of this, Weston," he told her with a tight, cold smile. He lifted his voice. "I got the male!"

Faith snarled, going for her gun as bodies started crashing through the brush behind them. "You son of a—"

Before the weapon cleared her holster, something stung her neck. *Oh, hell,* she thought, recognizing the bite of TASER probes.

Lightning struck with a searing wash of pain. Every muscle in her body spasmed as she went down hard, unable to scream, unable to breathe. Her body wouldn't obey, caught in the searing electric shock.

Her gaze darkened, and the Something she'd sensed winked out. *Magic's gone,* she realized in despair. *I've lost it . . .*

Jim tried to reel to his feet, only to jerk as dozens of wires hissed through the air, their hooks catching in fur and flesh. He went down as if somebody had smashed him in the head with a baseball bat. Every cop in the mob must have TASERed him. Even big as he was, he wouldn't be getting up anytime soon.

Paralyzed, her body still twitching helplessly, Faith could only concentrate on breathing as booted feet surrounded her. From the corner of one eye, she saw Jim's dark-furred arm shimmer pale again. He'd returned to human form as his magic was disrupted.

"Guess she's not a werewolf after all," Taylor said.

"This one is." There was a thud and muffled grunt as somebody kicked Jim in the ribs. "As many times as we hit him, he won't be able to change back until it's too damn late to do him any good."

"What about Weston?" Morrow asked, sounding uneasy.

"What about her?" Ayers demanded, cold as an ice cube and twice as hard.

"It's one thing to give the witch some junkie or out-of-town asshole, but Weston is one of us."

Like hell, Faith thought, furious. *I want nothing to do with you bastards.*

"Not anymore. Look, I don't like it, either, but we don't have a choice. You think she's going to turn a blind eye to this, especially after this one turns up with his heart cut out? She's too noble." Scorn dripped from the last word.

"Fuck you," Faith croaked. Not smart, but at least her vocal chords were working again.

"Juice her again," Ayers snapped.

Another silent, agonizing jolt surged through her body.

"Dammit, Taylor, cut it out," Morrow growled. To Ayers he added, "Are we really going to let Celestine sacrifice a cop?"

"Don't be an idiot, Morrow." The chief's voice rang with impatience. "Think about what we stand to gain. If Celestine gets her hands on that grail, she'll make us all immortal. We'll never have to worry about getting sick or dying, and neither will our wives. Or our kids when they grow up. And we'll be able to keep this town clean of drug dealers and killers. No more worrying about pussy judges and stupid juries. Everybody'll be better off."

Except anybody you don't like, Faith thought bitterly. *Or anybody you want to give to your witch as a human sacrifice. Prick.*

She spotted the glitter of a TASER probe on her arm.

The hook was buried in her skin. If she could just pull it out, they wouldn't be able to juice her again with the remaining probe, since it took two to carry the current. Good thing only Taylor had shot her.

"But we'll be vampires, Chief," Morrow said. "Not to mention accessories to a cop's murder. I—"

"Look, Gary, you're either with us, or you're against us. Pick one."

There was a long, uneasy pause. "I'm on board, Frank." Morrow's voice shook. "I'm one of y'all."

Ayers cursed. "The werewolf is moving! Light him up again."

Jim grunted in pain.

Faith winced, fingers twitching. Spotting the motion, she felt a little burst of hope. She could move again! Evidently being a werewolf gave her a faster recovery time along with everything else.

Cautiously, she grabbed the TASER lead and jerked it out of her skin. Her lip curled into a snarl. These assholes were in for a surprise.

"All right, he's done," the chief said. "Get him cuffed and let's call Reynolds. I want to get this over with."

She was running out of time. She had to act now, or both of them were going to end up with their hearts cut out.

But what the fuck was she going to *do*? There were twenty cops around her. She didn't have a prayer.

Except . . .

She could sense the Something again. Her magic was back. If she could only Change, maybe she could get Jim to safety, too. Trouble was, she'd never tried to transform to Dire Wolf form before. She only had one chance to get this right.

Taylor bent over her and flipped her onto her belly. "Okay, Weston, don't give me any trouble now." A hand grabbed her wrist. "I don't want to have to hurt you."

"Fuck you!" she snarled, and reached for the magic, picturing Jim's Dire Wolf form. If she failed . . .

But the magic surged at her call, filling her body in a hot white wave, muscle and bone twisting and growing. The detective let her go and leaped back with a startled yelp.

Faith surged to her feet as the men scattered with shouts of fear.

"Damn! The bitch is a werewolf!"

"TASER her!"

"Chief, the guns are out of juice!"

Faith spotted Jim lying on the ground and jumped for him. Somebody grabbed for her arm, and she swung her fist. The cop went flying like a ping pong ball.

She really *was* strong.

A bullet whined past her head as Faith grabbed Jim by one arm. He jerked toward her as if he weighed no more than a rag doll. TASER leads tore free in a shower of blood drops. Not daring to stop, she slung him across her shoulder, whirled, and shoved past five cops trying to work up the guts to tackle her.

They scattered, shouting and cursing. A gun boomed. Faith ducked and ran faster. More gunfire. Something stung her back, but she kept going. An engine roared, and blue lights flashed.

"Weston, you bitch!" Ayers howled. "You're a dead woman!"

"Gotta catch me first, asshole." Faith lengthened her stride, bounding for the woods in desperate leaps. She might be fast, but she knew damn well she couldn't outrun a patrol car. Diving between the trees, she ducked low-hanging limbs and dodged through the thick brush with all the speed she could manage. The cops crashed after her, but she quickly left them behind.

Well, she thought grimly, protecting Jim's head with one hand as she ran. *Guess I'm going to need another job.*

But first I'm going to make these bastards pay.

* * *

Jim hung limp in her hold, concentrating on breathing as he jarred up and down on her shoulder. His skin stung from all the TASER probes Faith had torn free, but he wasn't about to complain.

At least his muscles had finally started to obey his commands. He'd been gathering his strength and waiting for his magic to return when Faith had transformed and grabbed him. Thinking about it, he supposed it was a good thing the bastards had shot him so many times. They'd used all their weapons' charges on him, so they'd been unable to do anything to stop Faith.

Unfortunately, the mass blast had stripped his magic away even as it paralyzed him.

Guess we know how they overcame Tony now. If they'd shocked him like they had Jim, it was no wonder he'd accidently infected Reynolds with Merlin's Curse. The electricity disrupted voluntary muscle control. If they'd jolted him while he was biting Reynolds . . .

Faith slid to a stop and carefully lowered him to the ground. "You okay?"

He shrugged, then grimaced as his sore muscles protested. Even talking hurt. "More or less. Good job on getting us out of there."

Faith shrugged. "They underestimated me. Made it easier." Twisting around, she put a hand to the small of her back, then withdrew her fingers. Blood gleamed against the fur. "I can't believe this—the bastards *shot* me."

He frowned and sat up. "Turn back. It'll heal your injuries."

Faith nodded shortly and closed her eyes, tensing with effort. Magic shimmered around her, and she shrank back into human form. She opened her eyes again, her expression wary, then sighed in relief. "You're right. The pain's gone." She crouched beside him, her expression concerned. "How about you? Can you transform yet?"

Jim frowned and concentrated, but the magic refused to

respond. "No. But then, the chief said I wouldn't be able to use my magic until it was 'too late to do me any good.' Whatever that means."

"Nothing you'd enjoy, apparently." She sat down beside him and drew her knees close to her chest, her expression brooding. "Seems I owe you an apology. They're all just as dirty as you said. And I'm not sure it's all spell, either."

Jim sighed. "Believe me, I wish I was wrong."

"The question is, what are we going to do about it?" Her frown deepened. "And where are we going to go? We don't dare return home. It's the first place the bastards will look for us." She stroked a thumb across her lower lip. "Ditto for the motels in town."

Jim got to his feet and stretched his aching muscles, then delved into a pocket to pull out a set of keys. He dangled them with a crooked smile. "Luckily, I thought I might need a place to stay—as a human, I mean. My chieftain leased a safe house in town, and I parked my car there."

"Chieftain of what?"

He shrugged. "The local werewolf clans."

"Okaaaay." She sighed. "At least we have a place to stay."

"Now all we have to do is get there without getting caught."

They slipped through the darkened streets together, alert to the sound of approaching cars, police or otherwise. Given Faith's dirty, bloody uniform, she wouldn't exactly pass close scrutiny. All they needed was for some yahoo to call 911 and get the whole mob after them again.

Jim's back was still stinging, but he hadn't attempted a transformation yet and wasn't interested in another fight.

At least he had the most important pieces of the puzzle of Tony's murder: who the rogue was, and why the entire Clarkston Police Department had gone bad. He even knew how they'd immobilized Tony and why he'd bitten the rogue.

Unfortunately, new questions had arisen to replace them. What was this "grail" the cops had mentioned, and how did Celestine intend to use it to make them vampires? Jim decided it was time to consult Diana, despite Charlie's paranoia. Being queen of the Sidhe, Jim's sister would either know what was going on or would be able to find out.

Of course, Diana lived in the Mageverse, which meant he couldn't exactly pick up the phone and give her a call. Fortunately, she'd asked her husband to give Jim a way to contact her. Llyr had put a communication spell on Diana's old key chain, then given him instructions on how to use it. All he needed was a few uninterrupted minutes.

Right now, though, what most concerned Jim was Faith herself. She'd taken a series of very hard blows in close succession.

Even so, she'd handled the cops' murderous plot with restraint and skill. Given that the Burning Moon made any new were's temper more explosive, she could have easily killed the entire lot of them. Instead she'd controlled her anger and gotten herself and Jim to safety.

He wasn't surprised. Faith's strength was one of the things that had attracted him to her from the start.

At the moment, she was also really, really pissed off. Every time Jim took a breath, her scent communicated her stinging rage. He studied her in the moonlight as they walked, taking in the stony set of her delicate jaw, the tight line of her mouth. "Want to talk?"

Faith stopped abruptly and turned to face him.

He realized he'd actually underestimated her sizzling anger. Those green eyes burned with rage. Her hair had tumbled from its usual neatly braided bun, leaving silken strands hanging around her dirt-smeared face. "They played me for a fucking *fool*!" she exploded. "They were going to hand me to that bitch to get my heart cut out!" Both fists clenched, she whirled away to pace. "Everybody's been playing me. Hell, my fucking dog has been lying to me for a month. My dog!"

He winced. "Uh, Faith—"

"What am I, the world's biggest idiot?" She blinked hard, eyes shining with angry tears. "First Ron, banging that bitch dispatcher. But you expect that. Men are bastards. But cops . . . cops don't do this to each other. Reynolds tried to *eat* me, Jim! And the rest of them—you saw what that witch did to Tony. But they were just going to hand us over to her, knowing—*knowing*—what she'd do!"

"Ah, Faith." He sighed and moved to take her into his arms.

She stepped back. "Don't touch me. I'm tired of being betrayed."

Jim recoiled, then gave her his best cool, expressionless stare. "I realize you're just blowing off steam, but I'm not going to betray you. And I don't appreciate the suggestion that I would."

Breathing hard, Faith glared at him for a long, angry moment before she looked away. "Okay, you're right. That was a cheap shot. It's just . . ." She started pacing again. "All my life, I've played by the rules when nobody else did. I was faithful while my husband screwed everything in sight. I backed up my brother officers whenever they needed it."

"I know," Jim said quietly. "I've seen you do it."

Faith didn't seem to hear. "Hell, when Reynolds was getting his ass kicked trying to arrest Shay in that bar fight, I was the first one on the pile." she smiled bitterly. "Damn near got my nose broken for it, too. You'd think the son of a bitch would maybe hesitate half a second before trying to rip out my throat, but no. He turned me into a fucking *monster*, and my entire life has gone to shit."

"We're not monsters, Faith."

"And now my own chief is plotting to deliver me to a psychotic vampire who'd cut out my heart and eat me like a Happy Meal." Grabbing her badge, she ripped it from her shirt and whirled, arm drawn back.

Jim caught her wrist before she could hurl it into the night. "Don't," he said quietly. "You're the only one in the entire department who really deserves to wear that badge."

Faith curled her lip. He could smell her rage. "What difference does that make?"

"It makes a hell of a difference to the people of Clarkston. Remember them? The ones you took a vow to protect? Who are, by the way, the same people Ayers and Celestine and Reynolds are preying on. You're all they've got, Faith."

As he watched, some of the fury died in her eyes. "You play dirty, London."

"When I have to."

She tugged her hand from his grip and opened her fingers, looking down at her badge. Slowly, she rubbed her thumb over its engraved surface. "You're right." The last of the anger drained away, leaving only a weary determination. "I took an oath, and I'm going to keep it."

The knotted muscles in his back relaxed fractionally. "Good."

Faith tucked the badge into her pocket, meeting his gaze. "But I'm through being stupid. I'm not going to play by the rules anymore. And I'm going to make those assholes pay."

Jim ventured a tight smile. "And I'll help you."

"I know you will." She squared her shoulders. "So where's this house of yours?"

The safe house was located in a neighborhood of century-old Victorians and aging colonials that dated back to the heyday of the town's textile industry, when the original owners had been company officials. Oaks towered in front yards, their thick, snaking roots cracking sections of the sidewalk. Acorns crunched underfoot, keeping the squirrels busy collecting them.

The house Jim had rented was a charming white Victorian, its wrap-around porch festooned with gingerbread. His black Jaguar convertible looked distinctly out of place parked in the concrete driveway, acorns scattered across the hood.

Faith stopped to look at the car, frowning. "If they do a tag search—"

"They won't find it registered to me," Jim told her. "I switched tags with another were."

She nodded. "Good. I'd rather stay under the radar for a while."

They found the house fully furnished but aging, smelling of mothballs, cedar chips, and lingering Windsong perfume. It reminded Faith of one of her elderly great-aunts.

Standing in the living room, Jim looked as out of place as his Jag, broad-shouldered and intensely masculine against the fussy lace curtains. Unable to resist, Faith inhaled, breathing in his dark forest-after-a-rain scent. Her libido purred in approval.

Unfortunately, the rest of her was aching and tired, and her stomach emitted a demanding growl. "I'm starving." She eyed a door that looked as if it might lead to the kitchen. "I don't suppose you've got something to eat here?"

"As a matter of fact, I think I stashed a bunch of steaks in the freezer." Jim circled an armchair festooned with lace doilies on his way through the door. "Changing always makes me hungry."

She followed and leaned a shoulder on the doorframe. The kitchen looked just as fussy and old-fashioned as the rest of the house, right down to the harvest gold appliances.

Jim swung open the freezer door and contemplated the contents. Faith eyed his back with Burning Moon approval.

The long, powerful line of his body from broad shoulders to narrow waist to tightly muscled ass was enough to make her mood lift.

Maybe being a werewolf wasn't so bad.

EIGHT

Faith watched as Jim pulled a couple of steaks out of the freezer, then popped them into the small microwave to thaw. "So," she said, "The question I have is—I get were-wolves, and I get the vampire witch, but where the hell does Merlin fit into all this? You keep mentioning him."

"That's . . . complicated." He raked a hand through his dark hair. Biceps flexed and rippled temptingly.

She eyed them with muted longing. "That's okay. We seem to have plenty of time."

"Good point." He leaned a narrow hip against the counter, folding those delicious arms. "First off, about ninety percent of the legends about Merlin and Arthur and the Knights of the Round Table are bullshit."

"Not surprising. They seem to have gotten most of the werewolf stuff wrong, too."

"You noticed, huh?" Jim grinned. Faith really wanted to nibble that sensual lower lip. "The legends describe Merlin as Camelot's resident wizard, but he was really an alien."

"Merlin was an *alien*?" The microwave dinged. As Jim

popped open the microwave, Faith crouched to rattle through a cabinet full of ancient cast-iron frying pans and copper boilers. Hauling out a broiling pan, she asked, "Are we talking a little green man kind of alien?"

"Something like that. Merlin's people, the Fey, are a highly advanced race that originated on another planet in the Mageverse."

She frowned and started opening drawers, searching for the silverware. "The Mageverse is that alternative universe we draw the magic from, right?"

He pulled open a drawer, got a fork out, and handed it to her, then watched as she transferred the defrosted T-bones. "Right. The Fey discovered that most intelligent races destroy themselves before they ever get into space. So they decided to create guardians among each species that would work behind the scenes to keep them from committing mass suicide."

"That was nice of them."

"I thought so." He turned and started opening cabinets. As he stretched his arms upward to lift out a couple of glasses, Faith's gaze dropped down his broad back to his tight, muscular ass. It really was a very nice backside. "So about sixteen hundred years ago, Merlin and his lover Nimue came to Earth—"

Focus, Weston. "How? I mean, by UFO, or what?"

"No, they open magical dimensional gates that let you travel instantly between worlds."

She contemplated the concept. "Now, *that* would be a time-saver."

"Apparently." He got out a couple of plates edged with tiny blue flowers. "Merlin and Nimue started testing warriors all over the planet. Arthur and his knights were among those who were allowed to drink from Merlin's Grail."

"As in the Holy Grail?" Faith opened the oven to turn the steaks. "How did Merlin get the cup Jesus used at the Last Supper?"

"The grail didn't have anything to do with Jesus." He got a couple of beers out of the refrigerator, handed her one, and popped his own open. "Medieval storytellers added that bit in later. What the grail did do was genetically alter the people who drank from it."

Faith lifted her brows. "Genetically? How the hell did a cup do that?"

He grinned. "P.F.M."

"Which is?"

"Pure Fucking Magic. It turned the men into vampires, and the women became witches. Actually, the politically correct term for a vamp is a *Magus*, while you'd call one of their witches a Maja. Collectively they're the Magekind."

"Wait a minute—the chick that wants to sacrifice us is connected to King Arthur?" Faith opened her beer and took a sip.

"Hell, no. Different bunch of vampires altogether. She's one of the bad vamps. Arthur and his bunch are the good vamps who are trying to catch them."

"And we're werewolves." She rolled her eyes. "Do you ever have trouble believing all this shit?"

He lifted one broad shoulder in a shrug. "It doesn't matter whether we believe it or not. It's happening, and we've got to deal with it."

Faith found a package of napkins and carried them and the silverware to the Formica-topped table. "But why create vampires and witches to begin with?"

"Merlin figured the guardians needed magic and muscle to do the job." Jim took a contemplative sip of his beer. "Besides, the Fey themselves were magic-using vampires. They based their champions on what they were familiar with."

The timer dinged. Faith stepped over to the oven to prod the steaks. Deciding they were done, she got two plates and transferred the meat to them. "How do all these lunatics hide? Why isn't CNN camped out on their doorstep?"

"Because the Magekind don't live here." Together he and Faith sat down at the table to attack the food. "After

Merlin left, they built a headquarters for themselves on Mageverse Earth, where they could remain safely hidden between missions on *our* Earth."

"Let me guess—Camelot?"

"Actually, I think they call it Avalon." He cut himself a bite of steak and closed his eyes with a sensual purr of approval. The sound made something low in her belly tighten—and it wasn't her stomach. "God, that's good. Anyway, ever since then, they've been busy behind the scenes trying to keep human kind from exterminating itself."

Faith grunted. "Judging from recent events, I'm not impressed."

"Actually, considering we've survived a couple of World Wars and sixty years with an atomic bomb we've only used twice, I think they're doing pretty good."

"Okay, I'll grant that. So just how does this secret society operate, anyway?"

Jim took another bite of his steak. "Mostly by working in deep secret with officials from various governments. Lots of politics, lots of playing both ends against the middle based on whatever vision some witch had."

"Sounds like a conspiracy theorist's wet dream." Faith swallowed another bite of steak and closed her eyes in sheer pleasure at the taste. The flavor seemed so much more intense than it ever had before. She swallowed and asked, "What happened to Merlin and Nimue?"

"They created us." He cut another bite and chewed.

She found herself watching his mouth a bit too intently, and forced herself to look away. "What the heck for?"

"Insurance. Apparently one group of their champions on some other world went nuts and established a magical dictatorship."

"Not exactly what the Fey had in mind."

"Not really, no. So without telling Arthur what he was doing, Merlin chose a second group of champions and gave them what we call Merlin's Curse, making them werewolves. Super strong, resistant to magic, practically invulnerable. In short, he made sure that we could take on the Magekind and win."

Faith considered the idea. "Now that would be an interesting and unpleasant fight."

"Yeah, and we'd have the advantage. The Magekind can only increase its numbers the way other humans do—by old-fashioned reproduction." Was it her imagination, or did he add a purr to that last word? "We, on the other hand, can create new werewolves just by biting people. In theory, if the Magekind ever go off the deep end, we could create an army to oppose them in a matter of weeks."

She stopped eating to stare at him, as a new and troubling thought occurred to her. "Does that mean Reynolds could create an entire army for Vampire Bitch?"

He nodded grimly. "That's about the size of it."

"Oh, shit."

"Exactly."

"But the chief was talking about becoming a vampire, right? He said something about a grail. Did they get Merlin's, or what?"

"I don't know, but I'm going to find out."

"So what about this Celestine?" She sipped her beer.

"From what I gather, she's one of a new group of vampires who were created earlier this year by some kind of demon."

Faith stared. "Tell me you're kidding."

"'Fraid not." She listened with growing horror as Jim explained Geirolf's creation of a magic-using army of evil vampires.

"And the cops of Clarkston want to become part of *that*?" she said when he was finished.

"Apparently." He sighed. "We really need to find out about this grail of theirs. Luckily, I've got somebody I can call, but she doesn't exactly have phone service."

"Where does she live—Tibet?"

"No, the Mageverse." He gave her a crooked, charming grin. "My sister is queen of the Fairies."

She lifted her brows. "Just how many times *did* they TASER you?"

"Not that many." He laughed and reached into his pocket, pulling out his keys. From the ring dangled a small object that looked like a tiny blond woman with wings. "Diana gave me a magical charm I can use to contact her at the palace."

Faith eyed it. "That's a Tinkerbell key chain."

Jim looked at it. "Yeah, my brother-in-law made it. He's got a twisted sense of humor."

"You're pulling my leg, right?"

"Nope." Jim glanced at his watch and frowned. "I need to call my boss, too, but it's four in the morning. He's not expecting me to phone, so he wouldn't appreciate it." He grimaced. "Plus, I'm not exactly looking forward to this conversation."

Grimly, Faith imagined a conversation or two she'd like to have with Ayers. "Yeah, there's nothing like a boss from hell."

By the time they finished doing the dishes together—he washed, she dried—Faith was stumbling with fatigue. Even his delicious scent couldn't get a rise out of her. "I hope there's a bed in here somewhere," she told him. "Or I'm just going to curl up on the floor."

"Not only is there a bed, there's two." His tired smile took on a wolfish edge. "Which, given your Burning Moon, is a good thing. Otherwise neither of us would get any rest."

The bedroom he led her to was small and fussy, with yellowed lace curtains and a spindly bed she was almost too tall for. Faith didn't care. After locating a set of clean sheets in the hall linen closet, she made the bed, then stripped naked, and collapsed across it with a groan of exhaustion.

Given the circumstances, she expected to have trouble getting to sleep, but seconds after her head hit the pillow, she was out like a blown candle flame.

Keith Reynolds's back was a mangled mess, blood oozing from it as he hung in his bonds, panting in shallow gasps of pain.

Admiring his wounds, Celestine dropped her whip. Its metal-tipped lashes rattled on the marble floor. Hunger curling through her, she stepped forward and bent to lick one of the oozing welts. The taste of magical blood made her shudder in pleasure. Reynolds's deep groan spoke of lust as much as pain, as she fastened her mouth over the wound and drank.

"Please," Reynolds groaned, rolling his hips against the column he was bound to. She smiled around the hot flow of his life and pressed closer, knowing it would madden him.

The mix of lust, shame, and pain he felt was as intoxicating as his blood. He was the reason she didn't have to kill as often as most of Geirolf's vampires did. She could gorge herself on his blood and lust, and he only had to change form to heal any damage she chose to do.

He'd Changed twice tonight following her feedings. Dawn pressed close, and with it the need to take cover in her lair, but Celestine was reluctant to give him up.

The only thing that would have been more delicious was killing him.

She shivered, remembering the ecstasy she'd felt when she'd sacrificed Tony Shay. It would be stupid to kill Reynolds, of course—he was too valuable an ally and food source—but she would love to get her hands on another werewolf.

With any luck, he'd infected Weston, and her boys would be able to deliver the little bitch into Celestine's hands.

Celestine smiled, anticipating the power that sacrifice would give her.

Plus, it would be a hell of a lot of fun.

By the time Celestine had finished drinking, she could feel the leaden press of daylight beyond the shuttered windows. She drew away, ignoring the hungry quiver of Reynolds's big body.

"Let me come," he rasped, twisting his head to meet her eyes. The desperate need in his gaze filled her with a sense of power just as real as the taste of his blood.

She pretended to consider his plea, then curled a contemptuous lip. "No. And you'd best not touch that dick of yours, you perverted little bastard."

Perverted little bitch. It was what her grandfather had called her every time he'd . . .

Banishing the memory, Celestine turned her back on the werewolf, freeing him of his bonds with an offhand flick of magic. "Have they found Weston yet?"

Frustration burned in his gaze. She hid a smile. Reluctantly, Reynolds moved toward his discarded uniform. "I'll call the chief and ask."

As he clicked open his flip phone, Celestine glanced around her home with idle satisfaction. She'd employed the magic she'd stolen from Shay to turn a half-burned plantation house into a dead ringer for Tara, complete with sweeping staircases, lush antiques, and a ballroom hung with gilded mirrors. Marble columns supported the soaring ceiling—and served as whipping posts to tie her victims to.

There was something delightful in using a symbol of the old South to commit her acts of magical heresy. Her parents would have had a stroke, assuming she hadn't already killed them.

"Shit."

Reynolds's low hiss had her whirling in instinctive alarm. "Geirolf's balls, what now?"

"Weston and the werewolf got away."

"What?" She stared at him in growing rage. "How?"

He shrugged. "The men ambushed them and TASERed her and the werewolf. But because Weston was in human form, they assumed she hadn't been affected by my bite, so they only hit her a couple of times."

Celestine swore vilely. "So she was able to transform and help the werewolf escape. Those *stupid* fuckers!"

"That's about the size of it."

"Were any of the men hurt?" Though it would probably serve the morons right, she needed all of them intact for her plan to work.

"No." He shrugged. "They got lucky. Apparently Weston's primary objective was getting the hell away, and the werewolf was still stunned."

Her pleasant fantasies of blood sacrifice vanished. The idea of a magic-resistant werewolf on the loose was terrifying. And *two* of them. "Find her, Keith. Find them both and bring them to me."

He straightened his bloody shoulders. "It's done."

"It had better be." Throwing a look at the shutters— fingers of sunlight were stabbing between the slats—she gestured, creating a magical gate to her lair deep beneath the plantation. Without a backward glance, she stepped into the blessed dark.

Faith woke to a house full of magic, male voices, and alien scents. Alarmed, she rolled out of bed, bare feet hitting the worn rug with a muted thump. A quick glance out the window told her it was early afternoon.

She hastily jerked on her uniform, grimacing in disgust at its stains. Even as she reached for her gun belt, she realized she needed a hell of a lot more firepower than any nine millimeter could give her.

Closing her eyes, Faith summoned her magic. Given the circumstances, the pain of transformation felt oddly comforting.

When she opened her eyes again, something red and

looming stared back at her. Startled, Faith jerked away. The monstrous wolf-headed thing did the same. Belatedly, she realized it was her reflection in the bureau mirror.

Staring into her own glowing green eyes, Faith straightened to her full height. She wasn't as broad and thickly muscled as Jim in Dire Wolf form. Her body was smaller, with curves beneath the red fur that was the same color as her human hair.

But if she was smaller than Jim, the claws tipping her fingers were just as sharp as his. And so, she saw, opening her jaws, were her long white teeth. *I'd scare the shit out of an armed robber,* she thought, oddly pleased. *Hell, I'd scare the shit out of Charles Manson.*

It was a comforting realization for a woman used to being the weakest person in any fight. Her fear retreating, Faith headed downstairs to help Jim deal with their "guests."

Silent as a cat on her bare feet, Faith reached the landing to find a man standing with his back to the stairs. One glance told her it wasn't Jim, but it wasn't a cop either. Not only was he wearing a tailored blue suit, that pink waistlength hair definitely didn't belong to anybody she knew. And he smelled like magic—clean, bright, and wild.

"Who the hell are you?" she growled.

The man whirled. His metallic silver eyes widened as he caught sight of her. She felt the rush and tingle of magic swirling through the air. In an instant, the blue suit became gleaming armor, and a long sword shimmered into existence in his hand.

Faith took a wary step back on the landing, not sure whether to attack or run like hell. Was this one of those knights Jim had mentioned?

The pink-haired man started up the stairs toward her, his silver eyes cold with murderous intent. She lifted her clawed hands in a gesture of warning. "Back off, Pinky."

"Hey," a female voice called from the foot of the stairs. "Don't eat my guards. Lairgnen, stand down!"

"It's okay, Faith, he's a friend," Jim added.

Faith looked past Pinky to see a tall, slender woman standing at Jim's side. The resemblance was so striking, the two had to be related. Though the woman wore peach slacks and a knit top rather than royal robes, the conclusion was obvious. "You must be the queen of the Fairies."

"And you must be . . ." The woman's gaze slid toward Jim. ". . . Faith. Nice to meet you. Lairgnen, let her pass."

Pinky moved aside grudgingly, his silver gaze wary. Magic burst around him, and his armor became exquisite tailoring again.

But the sword remained firmly in his hand.

As Faith slipped past, she noticed that his ears formed elegant points thrusting through his silken fall of pastel hair. His face was just as astonishingly gorgeous and every bit as alien.

Looking down at Jim and the queen, Faith saw a group of men had joined them, all dressed in similar suits, all with long hair in rainbow shades. And every one of them glowered with identical expressions of incandescent hostility as she came down the stairs.

Of course, Faith realized. *They must be the queen's bodyguards, and I'm a seven-foot werewolf. No wonder they're jumpy.*

Pausing on the stairs, she closed her eyes to call the magic and return to human form. When she opened them again, all the men looked much happier.

And . . . surprisingly interested.

"Thanks," the queen murmured to her with a dry smile. "They'll jerk a lot less." She offered a hand as Faith descended the last of the stairs. "Diana Galatyn."

"Faith Weston." Shaking Diana's hand, she found the queen's grip was warm and strong, and she smelled . . . interesting. There was the same magic and evergreen scent that surrounded Jim, but under that was something Faith didn't quite recognize, something that reminded her, oddly, of fresh milk and baby powder. Catching Diana's amused expression, Faith realized she was sniffing.

"I'm pregnant," the queen said softly. "That's what you smell."

Heat bloomed across her face. Good God, she'd been sniffing the woman like an inquisitive poodle. "I beg your pardon!"

"Oh, cut it out." The queen patted her shoulder. "You're practically family."

Faith blinked. What had led her to *that* conclusion? Unless she meant "family" as in werewolf kind in general.

Jim gave her a comforting smile and turned to lead the way into the living room. "My sister isn't big on ceremony."

Faith cleared her throat as her sense of mortification retreated. "I gather you used your magic Tinkerbell key chain."

"And I was glad to get the call. Arthur and his crowd were driving me nuts." Diana flung herself down in an overstuffed armchair and stretched out her long legs. Catching Faith's questioning look, she explained, "Arthur decided to ask my husband for help searching for those Black Grails of his, and I suddenly found myself hip-deep in the Round Table. Those knights may be decorative, but they're a pain in the ass."

"Black Grails?" Faith said, glancing at Jim. "Like the grail the chief mentioned?"

"Apparently," Jim said.

"Everybody's after those damn things." Diana launched into a long and truly appalling account of Geirolf's creation of the Black Grails and how they were being used to create more vampires.

None of it was good news. "So if Arthur and his lot can find and destroy the two remaining Black Grails, the entire problem goes away," Diana concluded, accepting the glass of Coke Faith handed her. She took a sip and sighed in pleasure. "God, I've missed this stuff. Anyway, whoever has the grails are doing a very good job of shielding them, and Arthur is at the end of his rope. He and assorted witches and knights showed up at our palace last night, asking my husband to help them break through the shields around the grails."

"Which is a problem for Diana," Jim explained, a beer propped on his knee. "Because the knights have evidently realized she's not Sidhe, but they're not sure what she is."

"So every time I turn around, I'm tripping over them," Diana finished, grimacing. "There's this one, Gawain—he's just scary."

"Gawain," Faith said, remembering a favored childhood story as she sipped her own Coke. Attempts to serve drinks to the bodyguards had been gently rebuffed. "Didn't he fight the Green Knight?"

"Yeah, only he's not nearly as cuddly as the guy in the story," Diana said. "He's got this stone killer thing going that makes my entire guard quiver like bird dogs."

"You are in no danger from him, Your Majesty," one of the guards told her with stiff dignity. "We will protect you with our last breath."

"Yeah, yeah, I know." She waved a hand. "So anyway, I'm more than happy to get away from the palace for a while and hunt vampires. Where do we start?"

It was almost comical, the way identical expressions of alarm flashed across the faces of her brother and bodyguards.

"I don't think that's a good idea . . ." Jim began.

"Your Majesty, you can't be serious," a silver-haired guard protested. "You carry the Heir to Heroes. You cannot personally involve yourself in a fight with this"—he grimaced—"vampire."

"Indeed not," Pinky agreed from where he stood at Faith's shoulder. "Some of us will assist your brother. You have no need to involve yourself."

"Oh, for God's sake," Diana growled. "I'm not made out of spun sugar, boys—I'm a Dire Wolf! I am more than capable of taking care of myself."

"And we have lost far too many queens," the silver-haired guard said with immense dignity. "We will not allow you to risk yourself."

"Llyr wouldn't like it," Jim agreed.

"Yeah, well, I don't like my brother fighting rogue werewolves without backup," Diana snapped.

"Then assign a detachment of us to assist him," Pinky said. Faith looked up to meet his gaze as he looked down at her. "I would be delighted to offer my services." There was a distinct purr in his voice.

Good God, Faith realized, *he's hitting on me.*

Every muscle in Jim's body coiled into furious knots at the look the pink-haired guard was giving Faith.

And he wasn't the only one, either. From the minute she'd returned to human form, the Sidhe had been watching her like cats eyeing a fluttering canary.

Faith hadn't seemed to notice, but it was obvious to Jim. They, too, were responding to her Burning Moon pheromones. *But she's my woman, dammit,* his inner Neanderthal growled.

"You need only say the word," the one with cotton candy hair told Diana. "We will be happy to slay this vampire for your brother."

"I can slay my own vampires," Jim told him.

Diana's gaze flicked from Faith's face to Cotton Candy's. "I understand your concern," she said delicately, "but does the expression, 'cutting off your nose to spite your face' mean anything?"

She had a point, but Jim was damned if he'd admit it. "You know Charlie. He'd have a stroke if he knew a bunch of Sidhe started hanging around me with Arthur in the middle of a vampire hunt."

Diana glowered. "I really don't give a rat's ass what Charlie Myers wants. He's a self-absorbed prick who's more interested in politics than his people's lives."

"Frankly, I agree with you." Jim spread his hands. "But I've got to live here, and if he decides to go after me, I've got a problem."

"No, you don't."

"Diana, he's threatened to sanction Mom and Dad if we blow the Direkind's cover."

Diana's eyes widened in shock. "That little prick!"

Faith frowned. "Does that mean what I think it does?"

"If you think it means sending an assassination team to murder our parents, then yeah. It does."

She looked at Diana. "You're right—Charlie is a prick."

Jim nodded. "That's putting it mildly. The only reason he hasn't already sent a team after Diana is he knows Llyr would declare war on the Direkind."

"*After* my darling husband told Arthur all about the werewolf facts of life." His sister's eyes glittered with a cold and growing fury. "You tell Charlie to keep his distance from Mom and Dad, Jim, or I'll go to Arthur myself. Swear to God." She rose from her seat, determination tightening her jaw. "On second thought, *I'll* deal with Charlie. I'm in the mood to kick a little fat ass. Lairgnen, I'll need a dimensional gate. Jim, what's Charlie's address?"

Alarmed, he rose and stepped into her path, knowing he'd better nip this in the bud as fast as possible. "Diana, I'm not sure that's a good idea. I think I've got Charlie cooled off right now, but if you get him stirred up again . . ."

For a moment she glared at him, rage simmering in those silver eyes so like his own. Then, thankfully, her fury drained away, and Diana sank back in her seat, glowering. "Oh, hell, maybe you're right. You and the rest of the family would end up catching the blowback."

Jim frowned. "I can take care of myself."

Diana smiled slightly, then rubbed her temples as though massaging a headache. "I suppose I should have listened to Dad and talked to the Council of Chiefs before I married Llyr. But I was damned if I was going to let a bunch of stuffed shirts dictate my private life."

"Particularly since they'd have said no, and then you'd have had to disobey them." Jim smiled dryly. "Given a choice between pissing off the Council and pissing off Cachamwri, I know who I'd choose."

"Good point. The Dragon God is not the kind of guy you want to irritate."

"Are you sure you don't want us to have a word with this"—Silver hair sneered—"Charlie, Your Majesty?"

"It's tempting, but no." Diana shook her head. "Jim's right. The last thing I need is a war between the Sidhe and the Direkind, with my family caught in the middle. Much as I hate to admit it, I'm going to have to stay out of this thing."

Cotton Candy looked disappointed. Jim felt the muscles in his shoulders relax.

"That may be for the best, Di," he said. "After all, it's one rogue and one vampire. I can take care of them."

Her expression was troubled. "I hope so, big brother. But if it breaks bad on you—"

"I know who to call."

But as he smiled at his sister, his gaze slid to Faith, surrounded by Sidhe warriors wearing calculating expressions. That's all he needed—the woman of his dreams courted by charming, horny fairies while she was in her Burning Moon.

Over his dead body.

NINE

Just before Jim's self-control shattered altogether, one of the guards created a dimensional gate back to the palace. Glowing energy swirled into being in the middle of the tiny living room. Through the magical shimmer, they could see the elegant white walls of the palace, set with gemstones and accented in pure gold.

Faith's green eyes looked even bigger than usual as she watched the guards step through the gate. A moment later, they signaled it was safe.

Cotton Candy bowed over her hand and stared seductively into her face. "If you decide you need magical aid after all, I will be delighted to assist you."

She smiled dryly. "I'll keep that in mind."

Jim growled.

His sister elbowed him gently. "Behave."

He curled his lip at her, in no mood for even false civility.

Diana caught Cotton Candy by the shoulder and nudged another eager warrior before he could work his way closer to Faith. "Come on, boys, I think it's time for a lesson in

Alpha Werewolf Etiquette 101." She steered them gently toward the portal.

Jim watched with a sense of relief as the whole lot disappeared through the gate. A moment later, the magical structure collapsed on itself, leaving the room dark and blessedly empty.

Except for the sweet, seductive scent of Faith.

He turned to face her. *Watch it, London,* he told himself, feeling his self-control rock.

"Was that a growl?" At the amusement in her voice, Jim's face heated.

"My sister said the Sidhe sense of smell is more acute than human," he mumbled. "They knew you were in your Burning Moon."

Her gaze flickered, but being Faith, she brazened it out. "So?"

"So that's why Cotton Candy was all over you like a rash."

Her gaze cooled. She lifted one red eyebrow. "Because raging hormones are obviously the only reason he'd be interested in me."

All Jim's experience with women warned him to back slowly away from this conversation, but he couldn't seem to keep his mouth shut. "Those guys are users."

"In my experience, good-looking men usually are."

There it was at last—the elephant in the living room. After heating all morning, his temper went into a slow boil. "I'm not your ex, Faith."

Those green eyes looked colder than emeralds and twice as hard. "Were we talking about you or my ex?"

"That's what you were driving at."

"So werewolves read minds, too?"

Which would have been a smart man's cue to shut the hell up. Unfortunately, it seemed he wasn't a smart man. "I just know the way you think."

"Whereas I spent the last month believing you were a dog."

It was definitely time to shut up. He just couldn't seem

to do it. "We've been over this. I was only trying to find out who killed Tony."

"And using me to do it." Her eyes narrowed into an icy glare. "There's that word again—*using*."

"I'm not trying to use you, dammit. I care about you!"

"Spare me." Her mobile mouth tightened. "Look, I understand all about the Burning Moon and pheromones. I understand blowing off tension with a little recreational sex. It's not necessary to bullshit me by pretending some emotional attachment that isn't there."

"You really think I'm some kind of asshole, don't you?"

The cool shield over her eyes cracked just slightly. "I don't think you're an asshole, Jim. I think you're a guy."

"Which you evidently consider a synonym for asshole."

She threw up her hands with an expression of disgust. "Why are we having this conversation?"

He bared his teeth. "Because you need to get laid."

At last, heat flooded those cool green eyes. "Okay, now *that* was being an asshole."

"Yeah, it was." He glared at her, frustrated and pissed. "It's those fucking pheromones of yours. They make everybody crazy."

"So this whole fight is my fault?"

"Pretty much."

"Kiss my ass." She started to whirl away, but he caught her wrist and spun her into his arms.

"I've got a better idea—*you* kiss *me*." He smirked into her eyes. "I dare you."

Faith bared her teeth. "You have a hell of a nerve."

"Yeah, and you're in your Burning Moon. All it would take is one kiss, and you'd go up in flames."

"In your dreams!"

"Let's find out. Kiss me."

She glared up at him for several seconds before rising up on her toes. He knew good and damn well what she intended, and it wasn't a kiss.

So he kissed *her*.

* * *

Faith should have bitten him anyway. She intended to. But his lips were soft against hers, and his mouth tasted of toothpaste, and something feral and delicious. Something that made her anger drain away. Trying to identify it, she slipped her tongue between his lips, wanting a taste.

Just a taste.

He rumbled a dark, approving sound against her mouth and angled his head, nibbling gently at her lower lip, then swirling his tongue over the little bite.

She drew back, breathing hard. "You know you can be a real sexist jerk, right?"

"Yeah. Kiss me again." His arms tightened, drawing her closer. Instinctively, she rested her hands against his chest. He felt big. And firm, with lots of fascinating ridges and hollows, his skin warm under her hands, his chest hair fine and surprisingly soft. She stroked him while he kissed her, sipping from her mouth as if she was fine champagne and he wanted to make her last.

"God," he breathed against her lips, "I've been hung up on you since the moment I saw you all buttoned up in that black uniform."

Faith laughed, instinctively rejecting the idea he might feel something more for her than Burning Moon lust. "Got a thing for badges, London?"

"I've got a thing for you." His hands left her back to cradle her face in long, warm fingers. Gently, he angled her head so he could lave his tongue over the corner of her lip, the jut of her chin. His fingers tangled in her hair, tugging her head back, giving him access to the underside of her jaw. Pressing delicate little bites against the tendons and soft flesh, he explored slowly until he reached her ear. His nibbling teeth on her lobe made her squirm.

To retaliate, she raked her blunt nails across his ribs. He caught his breath and twisted his brawny torso back out of range.

"Ticklish?" she purred.

Jim gave her a wolf grin. "Are you?"

"I asked you first." She strummed his flat nipples with her thumbs.

His eyes shuttered in pleasure. "Well, as long as we're doing that . . ." One hand tugged her uniform shirt out of her pants and stroked boldly upward. Skillful fingers tugged down her bra and captured the soft globe of a bare breast.

Faith gasped as he delicately tweaked the hard peak between thumb and forefinger. Pleasure shivered along her nerves until she had to bite back a moan.

"Like that?" Pale eyes watched her face, knowing and hot.

Her lips twitched. "Hate it."

He grinned. "Too bad."

Before she could protest—if she'd intended any such thing—he unbuttoned the neck of her shirt and whipped it off over her head. Reaching around her waist, he unfastened her bra and dropped it. Her breasts bounced in the golden light streaming through the living room windows.

All the humor fled his eyes, leaving them pale and intent with hunger. *"God."* He breathed the word, a prayer of thanksgiving or plea.

Then he dropped to his knees.

Faith swallowed as he took one nipple in his mouth, engulfing it in sweet, wet heat. He suckled it with delicate little tugs, then used his tongue to roll the peak against his teeth. Her head fell back as pleasure rolled over her in a warm, foaming wave.

Lost in delight, she barely felt him unzip her pants and tug them down her hips, stripping off panties and pants in one smooth pull.

He turned his attention to her other breast, raking and suckling by turns as he reached between her thighs. One long finger brushed gently over the rise of her mons, stirring the soft hair.

Dizzied by the pleasure, Faith looked down, her hands

instinctively cupping the back of his head as he licked and suckled each breast in turn.

He'd stripped her. Her pants lay around her feet in a little puddle, and she was naked under his skilled, determined hands. The morning light painted his muscled body in shades of gold. Unable to resist, Faith slid her hands down to rest on the broad planes of his shoulders.

One finger slipped between her lower lips and found her opening. She was so slick and ready for him, she gasped at the sensation.

Jim groaned. "God, you feel like every dream of pleasure I've ever had." He thrust a finger inside her in one sweet plunge.

She shivered. "I don't even have dreams this good."

"Let's see if I can expand your horizons." Jim sank down further, kneeling at her feet. He looked up at her. "Spread for me."

Faith licked her lips and edged her feet apart. "All right."

Slowly, luxuriously, he leaned closer and inhaled, breathing deeply. Scenting her the way a wolf scents its mate. He licked his lips and leaned even closer.

The first touch of his tongue made her jolt up onto her toes, seared by the raw power of the sensation. She would have stepped back, but his big hands snapped up, catching her buttocks in warm palms and holding her still. With a low, masculine growl, he nuzzled her, then stroked his tongue through her slick lips.

It was like being struck by an erotic lightning bolt. Pleasure sizzled right up her spine, shooting her onto her toes. "Jim!"

"Oh, yeah." There was a distinct note of satisfaction in his voice. She looked down to find him staring up at her, his pale eyes hot with lust.

He reached down and caught her right knee, steadying her with a hand on her left buttock. Before she could squirm free, he'd lifted her leg and draped it over his broad shoulder, opening her even more to his mouth. With a yelp, she grabbed for his head, steadying herself as he went to work with feral greed, sucking and licking, his tongue flickering over her clit and between her lips.

The force of her own hunger took her by surprise, as it suddenly flamed up in an erotic firestorm that soon had her grinding her groin against his face. He cupped her butt and licked harder.

Just as the pleasure started whipping itself along her nerves, Jim drove two fingers deep in her sex and started to pump. Faith stiffened as fiery delight pulsed through her consciousness in time to his strokes. With a shout, she came, convulsing in his arms.

The aftershocks hadn't even died when Jim tumbled Faith to the floor, stood, and unbuttoned his jeans with a single impatient flick of his fingers. Dry mouthed, she watched as he jerked down his zipper and tugged at his briefs to liberate his cock. It spilled out at her in a long, thick rush, eager and hard as a gun barrel. And every bit as impressive as that bulge had hinted.

He grabbed her behind both knees and . . .

Stopped, his eyes widening. "Condoms! Damn, where did I put the condoms? My bedroom . . ." Before she knew what he was up to, he snatched her off the floor and carried her toward the stairs.

She bit back a shout of laughter as he climbed them three at a time. Looping an arm around his brawny neck, she looked up at his intent face. "You he-man, you."

He slanted her an amused, feral grin. "Laugh now. Just wait until I get you into bed."

Carrying her around the corner into his room, he strode for the queen-sized bed and dropped her in the middle of the mattress.

Naked and breathless, she looked up at him. Just the sight of that big body would have been enough to overcome any scruples she had—tall, hard, and strong as an Olympic athlete, his handsome face tight with need.

Jim reached into a drawer in the bedside table and fished out a condom. He stopped barely long enough to sheathe himself, his silver eyes burning into hers.

She'd never seen a man that so embodied sex—rough, raw, and wild.

Jim hesitated a moment, staring down at Faith as she waited for him, heat and challenge in her green gaze. She looked hotter than any wet dream he'd ever had, leaning against a pile of pillows, glorious long legs sprawled in front of her. Her body was lithe and strong, curves of feminine muscle adding definition under the soft pale skin. Her breasts lay deliciously full on her narrow torso, capped with tight pink nipples that tasted of woman and magic. The scent of her Burning Moon heat damn near buckled his knees. His cock bucked as his lust leaped even higher.

"God," he breathed. "You're beautiful."

Discomfort flickered in her eyes, but she grinned at him. "Back atcha." Her tone was arch, a little flip, denying any possibility of vulnerability.

He'd deal with that later, he decided, taking one long step forward to catch her by the hips. She spread those pretty legs for him and wrapped her calves around his butt. The silken slide of her skin across his made him shudder with hunger.

Jim grabbed his latex-clad cock and aimed it for her sweet opening. Even as he started to push inside, he looked up to meet her eyes. He wanted to watch her face when he entered her.

Green eyes widened, and her mouth parted on a gratifying gasp. Jim groaned, sinking luxuriously into her deliciously slick, snug depths. She was so tight he had to work at it, even as wet as she was.

At last his belly touched the warm satin flesh of hers. He found himself panting as he braced his palms on the mattress, not from exertion, but from pure, driving need.

"Damn." Faith gave him a little smile. "I know we did this once already, but—wow."

Jim couldn't resist a cocky grin. "You ain't seen nothin' yet." He only hoped he could hold on.

Carefully, he drew back, his eyes closing at the intense pleasure of her snug, creamy clasp. Rolling his hips, he sank deep again. Her tiny interior muscles rippled around him. He shivered. "God, don't do that. I'll never be able to last."

She smiled wickedly. "I've got confidence in you."

His balls tightened as she milked him. He gritted his teeth and thrust again. He damn well was not going to come until she did.

But it wasn't going to be easy.

To distract himself, Jim looked into her face. Her green eyes were starting to look dazed over those sweet, parted lips. With a sigh of need, he leaned down and kissed her. He loved the way she tasted—toothpaste and woman and clean magic, like an evergreen forest after a rain. Stroking his tongue into her mouth, he slid his cock deep into her sex.

When he drew back, Jim breathed, "I had dreams about this, but doing it is even better."

She rolled her head back, spilling her long red hair over the pillow. "Dreams?"

"Yeah." Another mind-blowing thrust. "Lying on the rug next to your bed. In my dreams, I'd turn into a man, and . . ."

Her lips tilted up. "And here I thought you were chasing rabbits."

"Nope." He picked up the pace, grinding a little harder. "Just you."

She gasped. "You seem to have caught me."

"Oh, yeah." Another thrust, strong and sweet. "And I don't intend to let go."

Faith threw back her head and groaned. He thought she muttered, "They always let go."

His eyes narrowed in sudden, fierce determination. "Not me."

Faith gasped as Jim began to ride her hard, in long, deep plunges. She writhed, maddened by the deliciously brutal delight.

God, he made every other man she'd ever had feel like a toothpick. She didn't think she'd ever been hotter in her life, not even the first time they'd made love.

The raw sensations of sex had never felt so intense. It seemed that every nerve in her body was broadcasting at twice the volume. Just the rasp of his chest hair over her nipples was maddening.

And his cock . . . the way he angled his hips with every deep thrust hit her clit with just the right pressure at just the right angle. Her climax had gathered in a tight, pulsing knot right under her belly button, swelling like a heated balloon every time he sank inside her. Tighter . . .

Thrust.

Tighter . . .

Thrust.

Tighter!

Maddened by the building pressure, she twisted against him, rolling her hips mindlessly against him, trying to force it that last fraction. Responding to her desperation, Jim started hammering her with his width and heat, faster and faster and . . .

The ball of pleasure blew wide, showering burning sparks into her blood. Faith arched, screaming. Jim growled and slammed to his full length inside her.

And came, the tendons standing in hard relief along his muscular neck as he threw back his head and roared.

At last Jim collapsed over her, mantling her in his damp, sweating strength. Faith clung to him, panting, listening to their hearts hammer. The double thump seemed incredibly loud—probably another result of her transformation.

With a groan, he coiled his arms tighter around her. "Thank you."

She grinned and wrapped her own arms around his broad back. "Believe me, the pleasure was all mine."

Jim lifted his head to give her a teasing grin. "Well, not *all* yours." Slowly, he arched his hips, carefully pulling free. She groaned as his softened cock slid from her sex. He sat back and rose to take care of the condom.

Lax and sated with pleasure, she watched him bend to dispose of it in a bedside wastebasket. The long, bare curve of his back and the flexing muscles of his rump made her smile in lazy approval.

The smile slowly faded.

It was one thing to satisfy a mutual itch with him, but she couldn't afford to let it get any deeper than that. A man like him made a dandy partner in a fight or the bedroom, but falling for him would be nothing less than emotional Russian roulette.

And that was a game she had no intention of playing again.

Abruptly she rolled out of bed and padded toward the bathroom. "I'm going to take a shower."

He looked around at her and grinned. "I'll join you."

"I'd . . . rather you didn't." She started to walk into the bathroom, but his voice stopped her.

"Faith, what are you going to wear when you get out? You don't have any clothes."

She frowned. "Good point. I need to hit Wal-Mart or something."

"Not unless you want to have every cop in Clarkston down on your head." He reached into the bedside table and rummaged around for a pen and pad. Handing them to her, he said, "Why don't you give me a list of your sizes, and I'll pick up something for you."

She accepted the pad, frowning. "Didn't you Change in front of them last night? They may recognize you."

He shrugged. "Yeah, but it was dark, and they were busy trying to kill us. I doubt anybody got a good look. I should be safe."

Faith nodded and started to write in long, slashing strokes. "I hope you're right."

Folding the list a moment later, Jim watched as she retreated into the master bathroom and closed the door.

Give her time, he told himself. *She's had a lot thrown at her over the past twenty-four hours.*

Then again, so had he.

He'd fallen in love with her. If he'd had any doubt, it was gone now. Watching all that strength, intelligence, and passion in action had finished off his heart.

He'd finally met a woman he was actually willing to enter a Spirit Link with. At thirty-four, he'd almost given up hope of knowing the kind of complete union his parents had.

He could love Faith like that. And now that she was a Dire Wolf, she could love him—if she'd allow it.

Unfortunately, Faith Weston seemed incapable of doing anything the easy way. He was going to have to win her over, despite her ex-husband, despite her fears, despite Charlie.

Hell. Charlie. He let his head fall back with a silent groan. He needed to report in before he hit Wal-Mart. And wasn't that going to be fun?

With a sigh, he unplugged his cell phone, which he'd left charging by the bedside lamp, and went downstairs to make his call.

The chieftain picked up on the second ring. Without mincing words, Jim told him the whole thing, though he carefully left out the fact that Diana had told him most of it. No point in pouring gasoline on that particular situation.

"You're kidding me," Charlie said when he'd finished. "The cops actually *want* to become vamps? What the hell for?"

"Apparently they like the whole immortality thing. You've got to admit, living forever would be a pretty powerful lure."

Charlie grunted. "Those assholes'll be lucky to live a week if the Round Table starts gunning for them. And once they all start hunting the same Black Grail, it's bound to happen. You get somebody like Lancelot or Gawain pissed off, you'd better have your life insurance policy paid up."

"I don't think the cops have any idea what the Magekind is capable of. Celestine seems to have kept them in the dark about a lot."

"Well, you need to make sure that rogue gets dead before Arthur and the boys find out about *him*."

"That's the plan."

"Speaking of ugly realizations, how's Weston handling her new fur coat?"

An image flashed through Jim's mind: Faith, moaning in pleasure as he slowly thrust into her. He cleared his throat. "Pretty well, all things considered. I'm more concerned about Reynolds."

"Yeah, well, you keep an eye on the girl, too, London. Make sure she understands that we keep our secrets, period. If she looks like she's going to have a problem with that, teach her otherwise."

Jim opened his mouth to tell the chieftain what he thought of that order, but Charlie bulled on. "And don't give me any of your chivalry bullshit. She toes the line, or I'll send Don Jennings in to eliminate the problem."

Jim's temper went into a slow boil. He'd had about as much of Charlie's bloody-mindedness as he could take. "I wouldn't advise it."

There was a long pause before Charlie spoke, his voice dropping dangerously. "What did you say?"

"I'm Faith's Wolfmaster. I'll take care of her. You send anybody else down here, it had better be with sanction papers for both of us."

It sounded as if Charlie was speaking through his teeth. "London, you took an oath to obey the council."

"I also took an oath to protect civilians, women, and children," Jim snapped. "I'll make sure your precious secret stays kept, but I'm not going to allow the abuse of an innocent woman under my protection."

"Do I need to remind you I'm high chieftain of the Southern states?"

"Do I need to remind you that you took the same oath I did? Maybe you ought to think about that before you advocate killing everybody in sight."

Charlie was all but panting in sheer rage. "All I have to say is, you'd better not fuck this up. Or I swear to Merlin, I will sanction you—*and* your pet bitch."

The cell went dead.

"Asshole." With a growl, Jim clicked it off and shoved it into a pocket.

Charlie was going to be a problem.

TEN

When Celestine strutted into the ballroom, the cops came to attention with a combination of fear and desire. Thirty of them, some in uniform, some in civilian clothes, most young. Almost all healthy and well-built, though a month of satisfying her needs had taken a toll. She smiled a cat smile and swirled her diaphanous crimson skirts, watching their eyes glaze in lust.

Just the reaction she'd intended when she'd designed the gown to make the most of her considerable assets. The jeweled bustier lifted her full breasts until their nipples played peekaboo with the lace neckline, while the skirt's countless glittering scarves swirled around her legs, revealing as much as it hid. Normally she hated using magic unless she absolutely had to, but this particular outfit needed to be something special.

She had to bait her hook.

And it was working. Even the chief was all but drooling, and he normally thought far too much to suit her. Only Reynolds seemed to realize she was playing a part for them. He wore a faint, cynical smile as he leaned on the wall next to Gary Morrow. Celestine made a note to torture him a little later. He obviously needed to be taken down a peg.

"Hello, boys," she purred.

"Hello, Celestine," they chorused, polite as infatuated schoolboys greeting their teacher.

Ah, this was sweet. She never had liked cops.

A memory flashed through her mind: the sneer on the school resource officer's face when she'd tried to report her grandfather. "Lying little brat probably made the whole thing up, looking for attention."

She supposed she couldn't blame him. After all, her own mother hadn't believed her, even after Celestine showed her the bruises on her inner thighs.

Grandpa had been very, very rich and very, very powerful.

Celestine later spotted the cop driving a brand new Mustang convertible. Even at twelve, it hadn't surprised her.

She never forgot the lesson they'd all taught her that day—the powerful made their own rules. And enjoyed it.

When she'd gotten her new powers, she'd certainly enjoyed hunting the cop down and ripping out his throat. Almost as much as she'd enjoyed killing Granddad.

Now, of course, she had another errant cop to deal with. Anticipation sizzled through her at the thought. She struck a seductive pose and watched the men come to attention like bird dogs.

"I've got good news," Celestine announced with a flirtatious smile. Ayers, apparently recognizing it, paled. "I've located that grail I told you about. The problem is, it's heavily guarded, so I'm going to have to lay the groundwork before I can acquire it."

"What kind of groundwork?" the chief demanded, his gaze hard and suspicious. She reminded herself to keep an eye on him.

Celestine dropped her head, letting her black hair tumble to cover her face, then slowly tilted her chin to look at him with a sidelong smile. It was a move she'd practiced in mirrors from the time she'd hit sixteen. "The grail has thick magical shields around it to protect it from detection by Arthur and his witches. I had to create a spell to breach those barriers."

Ayers frowned. "But that risks Arthur getting his hands on it before we do."

She laughed lightly, concealing her anger. Who did the bastard think he was, questioning her? "Oh, that won't be a problem. There are a good two thousand vampires guarding that grail. Arthur will have his hands full with them— and vice versa. And while they're all busy . . ." She smiled slowly.

"You'll sweep in and steal it out from under their collective noses."

Celestine gave him a sunny smile. "Something like that." Ayers really was too smart for his own good. Fortunately for him, she suspected she might have a use for those brains down the line.

Otherwise she'd be tempted to spill them from his skull.

"And of course, once I have the grail, a whole new world will open up for all of us." She sauntered across the ballroom's gleaming floor. The men straightened with a heady combination of fear and eagerness.

Smiling, Celestine paused to trail her long nails across Frank Granger's jaw. His eyes flamed with sexual hunger, and she inhaled, feeding on the small emotional charge like a woman savoring a bon-bon.

"You have no idea of the world that will open up for you once you become lords of the night," she told them all. "Power such as you've never dreamed of. Blood. Sex. Magic."

Sweeping her gaze over them, she began to pace like a general whipping up the troops. With each step, she reinforced the spell she'd laid over them. Making them believe. Blunting their willingness to question or doubt. "And let's not forget immortality. Think of it, boys—living forever at the age you are now. Never growing old. Never getting so much as a head cold for the rest of your life. No threat of cancer or Alzheimer's. Never watching your life bleed away with every tick of the clock. Immortal and powerful. What a beautiful thought."

Power. Oh, yes, a very beautiful thought. Especially now that she'd finished designing the spell that would put them all completely under her control after they'd drunk from the grail. Unlike Korbal, she wouldn't have to worry about her followers turning on her once they had powers of their own. They'd be her loyal foot soldiers, willing to fight and die at her command.

All she had to do was cull out a few bad apples whose willpower was a little too strong.

"Any questions?" she asked, with deceptive mildness.

None of them answered. They didn't dare, which was encouraging. Either they were afraid of her or they were afraid of losing the chance at that rosy future she'd painted for them.

Unfortunately, there was still a worm of rebellion gnawing away at what she was trying to build. And it was past time to stomp it out.

"Gary?" She paused in front of Morrow. "Any questions?" Raising on tiptoe until her mouth was inches from his, she breathed, "Any doubts or fears I could lay to rest?"

He licked his lips as the terror he'd been fighting sprang to the fore of his mind. Celestine could smell the acrid stench of it. "No. No questions."

"Are you sure, Gary?" Shuttering her lids, she breathed in his fear, savoring it. God, this was power. Holding his life in her hands, and knowing Morrow knew it. "I realize I ask so much of you. Particularly when it involves other cops. You're such a moral man."

Sweat popped out on his forehead as his eyes widened. "No. I'm . . . I'm loyal, Celestine. I swear!"

"Well, of course you are. That's why you weren't comfortable with the idea of sacrificing a cop, even though your chief assured you it was necessary."

The whites showed all around his gray pupils, reminding her of a frightened horse. "I'm sorry, Celestine. It won't happen again."

She smiled slightly. "Of course it won't. Because you understand I needed the power from Weston's death to work my spell. Otherwise, I won't be able to acquire the grail and make you all immortal. You can see how important that is."

"Yeah. Oh yeah." He licked his dry lips, fear stench rolling from his body. "I'll go out and find her, Celestine. I'll bring her back for you."

"What a kind offer, Gary. I appreciate your team spirit." She slid an arm around him and smiled brightly up into his eyes. "But I'm afraid that's not good enough. Because I need that sacrifice right now."

The knife sparkled into existence in her free hand. He tried to jerk back, but she tightened her grip around his waist, holding him still as she drove the blade into his chest.

Gary's wide eyes met hers in agony and disbelief as she began to chant the spell to drain his spilling life force.

Guinevere nibbled on some unpronounceable Sidhe delicacy and tried to make conversation with King Llyr's new queen. Lithe and dark haired, Diana Galatyn seemed a nice enough girl, but there was a wariness in her silver eyes that had aroused Arthur's suspicions. Particularly since it was damn sure she wasn't Sidhe—or even Magekind. Gwen hoped to find out exactly what she was hiding and calm her husband's suspicions.

So far she'd determined Diana was (A) pregnant, (B) desperately in love with Llyr, who was equally devoted to her, and (C) surrounded by the a cadre of bodyguards who could give the Round Table a run for its money for sheer menacing paranoia.

Currently, the one with pink hair was exchanging glares

with Gawain, who stood behind Arthur's seat pretending to be a bodyguard.

Gwen glanced around the hall, appraising the crowd of glittering fairy nobles. She'd dined with the Sidhe king before, of course—thanks to Merlin, they'd been allies since the beginning. But something had changed here in the palace, and she thought it was for the better.

The decor was the same—glittering white marble, jeweled tiles on the floor, impossibly beautiful Sidhe artwork hanging on the walls or standing in niches. And court fashion hadn't changed in six hundred years. The women wore exquisite gowns shimmering with embroidery and gems, while velvet doublets and hose showcased the impressive physiques of the men. They were, without doubt, the most beautiful people Gwen had ever seen.

Yet the atmosphere had subtly changed. An air of grief had always hovered around Llyr Galatyn—no surprise, since his murderous brother had arranged the death of every wife and child he'd ever had.

But last month, Llyr had finally slain Ansgar—and she'd love to know how he'd pulled that one off—and acquired a new queen in the process. One the Sidhe seemed to view with something close to awe, an emotion that seemed even stronger because she was pregnant. Gwen gathered this particular child had some kind of religious significance to them. Given all that, it was really no surprise that Llyr and his guards were so protective of her.

Unfortunately, the bodyguards' icy paranoia was bringing out the worst in the Magekind knights. Even Arthur was unusually tense.

"I don't know about you," Gwen murmured to her hostess, "but I'm starting to get testosterone burns."

Diana chuckled, the sound rich and throaty. "They are laying it on a little thick, aren't they?" She sat back in her seat, toying absently with her golden fork. "Ansgar may be dead, but I'm afraid Llyr and his people are going to carry the psychic scars for a while. I keep telling them I'm more than capable of defending myself, but it doesn't seem to re-assure them."

"I'm curious." Gwen leaned her elbow on the arm of her chair. "Just exactly how *would* you defend yourself?"

Diana smiled wickedly. "I could tell you, but then I'd have to eat you."

Gwen blinked. Somehow she had the definite feeling Diana hadn't mangled that particular idiom by accident.

Maybe she was Dragonkind.

Well, Llyr had wanted a queen who could take care of herself. A shape-shifting dragon would definitely qualify.

The lighting dimmed. Gwen looked up automatically, only to see the ceiling darken overhead. As she watched, the elegant white marble melted into blood-red stone.

Gwen frowned. "What the . . . Diana, do you see . . ." She turned to her hostess only to realize she, too, had melted away, along with Arthur and the rest of the dinner guests.

Instead, everywhere Gwen looked, there was blood-red stone, supported by massive black columns. *A vision,* she realized belatedly. *I'm having a vision.*

But of what? Where was she?

Wherever it was, it wasn't good. The sense of evil that surrounded her was almost choking. And it was even stronger off to the left.

Driven by a compulsion she didn't even attempt to ana-lyze, Gwen followed the intensifying sense of menace. Passing one of the columns, she absently glanced at it. Fig-ures were worked into its gleaming black surface—men and women, some writhing in sexual congress, others at-tacking one another with swords or knives.

Repulsed, Gwen veered away from the column and kept walking. Rounding a corner, she saw a complement of heavily armed men and women standing guard over a doorway. Still driven by an inexplicable compulsion, she moved toward the group, her insubstantial body passing through their armored forms like smoke.

Looking through the doorway, she saw a cup sitting on a

blood-red pedestal. Made of solid gold, the goblet was heavily engraved in writhing figures.

It was one of the Black Grails. It couldn't be anything else.

Diana Galatyn took a sip of her Sidhe wine and turned to address another remark to Gwen. The delicate, ageless blonde sat next to her in an elaborate court gown that shimmered with magic, its blue silk a perfect complement for her pale hair.

Except . . . breathing in, Diana caught scent of the smell of rot so intense, she almost gagged. What the hell?

"Guinevere?" Blinking, she gazed into her guest's pretty face. The Maja's expression was blank, her eyes unfocused. And the smell of black magic surrounded her with such intensity, Diana wanted to vomit. "Bloody hell! Llyr!" She jumped from her place and started to reach for Gwen, then froze, her hand extended. What if touching the Maja would hurt her?

"What?" Arthur demanded from the other side of Gwen, turning to look at his wife. Alarm filled his voice as he, too, realized something was wrong. He jumped to his feet. "Gwen, what's wrong?"

"Don't touch her," Llyr snapped.

"To hell with that," Arthur growled, jerking his wife into his arms. "She's under some kind of spell. I can feel it through our Truebond. Gwen!"

"Arthur . . ." Guinevere moaned and stirred in her husband's arms. The scent of rot retreated, and Diana relaxed.

"What happened?" Arthur demanded. His face was white with anxiety.

"A vision." Guinevere wrapped her small fists in his velvet doublet. "I had a vision. I saw one of the Black Grails." Her vague gaze cleared and sharpened with excitement. "I know where it is!"

"Maybe." Diana studied her with narrowed eyes. "Or maybe you know where somebody wants you to think it is."

Arthur's dark, perceptive gaze met hers. "A trap?"

She shrugged. "Could be."

Guinevere frowned. "I don't think so. I saw it. I can feel it. If it was simply some kind of delusion, I'd know."

Arthur looked worried, apparently sensing something through the mental bond he shared with his wife. "It does feel real, but . . ."

Llyr moved around Arthur to Gwen's side. "If you'll allow me, perhaps I can determine whether what you sense actually exists."

The former high king looked at his wife, who nodded slightly. Her face was as white with strain as his was.

Diana watched as Llyr rested one big hand on Guinevere's forehead and closed his eyes. Through their own psychic bond, she sensed his magic rise and twine around the Maja, probing gently.

Finally her husband stepped back, concern on his handsome face. "She's definitely got some kind of link to one of the Black Grails."

"But that was vampire magic, Llyr." Diana frowned. "I recognize the smell."

Gawain moved to her side. He was a big man, with shoulder-length blond hair and a neat goatee. "Why would one of Geirolf's vampires show us where to find a Black Grail? It makes no sense." His nostrils flared, as if sensing rot. "It's got to be a trap."

"Or perhaps someone is trying to get rid of a rival," Arthur said, frowning heavily. "Either way, we have no choice except to follow up on this."

"I agree," Llyr said. "But we'd better be ready for anything. I have the distinct impression someone's playing a very dark game."

Celestine collapsed, sweat and blood streaking her naked body, plastering her black hair against her back. Her head ached like a kettle drum.

The Sidhe king had almost tracked her spell right back to her. She'd barely managed to block his probe.

Despite that scare, her plans were coming together. Earlier she'd punched a hole in the temple's thick shields during her little visit to Korbal's grail. Now, thanks to this new spell on Guinevere, Arthur and his forces had a fix on the cup's location. They'd attack soon, in the next day or so, unless she missed her guess.

Celestine smiled slightly.

All hell was about to break loose. And she meant to take advantage of it when it did.

Faith poured shampoo into her palm, then paused for a sniff. It smelled rich and delicious, the scent so intense she could almost taste crisp green apples on her tongue.

She breathed in, savoring the tangy odor, then started rubbing the shampoo into her hair. Everything seemed so much more sensual since her Change. Even her skin felt more sensitive, responding to the slightest touch. Her entire body tingled with energy and life.

No wonder she was in such a good mood.

Which, when she stopped to think about it, was pretty strange in itself. She'd become a werewolf. She'd lost her job, and her former coworkers had tried to kill her. She couldn't even return home to get her things for fear they'd jump her again. If Jim hadn't gone shopping for her, she'd have nothing to wear except a torn, bloody uniform. Any sane person would be depressed.

Yet Faith felt as if a huge weight had been lifted from her shoulders. And it wasn't difficult to figure out why.

In the back of her mind, she'd known for weeks something was going badly wrong in the Clarkston police department. All the signs were there—officers falling silent when she'd walked into the room, ugly sidelong glances that blended guilt and hostility.

Then there was Shay's death.

Weird murders weren't, in themselves, all that unusual. People killed each other in disgusting ways all the time, even in towns as small as Clarkston.

No, what had set off Faith's mental alarms was the department's attitude toward this particular killing. It had smelled far too much like a coverup, but she hadn't wanted to believe cops could be involved. For God's sake, they'd cut out Shay's heart.

Now that Faith knew the truth, everything was black and white. She didn't have to worry about being disloyal, because her fellow officers had shown absolutely no loyalty toward her or anyone else.

Oh, maybe they were under some kind of spell, but they could have resisted it. Gary Morrow had proven that when he'd questioned the plan to kill Faith. If they'd all fought like that, the witch might have been unable to control them. Judging from the chief's comments, they'd been persuaded to cooperate with promises of immortality and power, not to mention sheer peer pressure.

They were bad guys, and they had to be stopped. Period. In this particular case, there were no shades of gray. Which was pretty well the way she liked it.

Then there was Jim.

Faith smiled, her thoughts drifting to the night before as she stroked her soapy palms over her breasts. He'd made her feel cherished. Almost . . .

Loved.

Her smile faded. It was one thing to enjoy her new senses, but she couldn't afford to let them deceive her. Jim was a great guy, but a good chunk of his response to her was born of her body's pheromones. She couldn't afford to take what he said or did too seriously.

Maybe she should put on the brakes . . .

Yeah, right—if she was an idiot.

Jim definitely didn't find her lacking as a woman, and after Ron's rejection, that felt pretty damned good. Besides, fighting the Burning Moon was an exercise in futility. So she'd just roll with it. The sex was fun, and the partnership with Jim could obviously be very useful in stopping the witch.

But she couldn't afford to deceive herself about how either of them felt about the other. This wasn't love, it was sex. And it wasn't going to last forever.

As long as she kept that fact firmly in mind, she'd be okay.

Dressed in one of Jim's T-shirts and a ridiculously big pair of his nylon shorts, Faith headed downstairs to rustle up something to eat.

He still wasn't back from his shopping expedition, so she grabbed an apple and wandered into the living room. More for something to do than anything else, she switched on the ancient television and sat down to watch the noon news.

She was crunching into the apple when the perky blond anchorwoman assumed an uncharacteristically somber expression.

"A Clarkston police officer is dead, victim of a one-car accident when he lost control of his patrol car last night."

The image cut to a mangled police car wrapped around a tree, a blue tarp thrown over its driver's side to shield the body from cameras.

"According to an investigator with the Tayanita Coroner's Office, Officer Gary Morrow died instantly when he lost control of his Ford Crown Victoria. The car went off the road, hit a ditch, and went airborne before slamming into a tree."

"Chief George Ayers expressed sympathy for Morrow's family at a press conference this morning."

Ayers appeared, standing at a Plexiglas podium bearing the department's shield. A piece of black ribbon slashed across his gold badge in the traditional symbol of mourning for an officer's death. "Officer Morrow was a fine cop, and his loss will be keenly felt by all of us with the . . ."

"Shit," Faith breathed as the sick realization rolled over

her. "The bastards murdered him!" In the kitchen, the door creaked open. Jim's deep voice called, "Faith?"

She didn't look away from the television, both elbows planted on her knees as she leaned toward the screen. "Jim, they killed Morrow."

"What?" He walked into the living room, carrying a couple of plastic bags. His thick brows lowered with his frown.

"Morrow." She nodded at the screen, where the officer's picture had replaced Ayers. "They're saying he died in a one-car accident last night. Like hell."

Jim moved closer to the small set for a better look at the photo. "Isn't he the one who didn't want to hand you over to the vampire?"

"Exactly." She sat back on the couch. "And they killed him for it. But I don't understand why the coroner is going along with this. I'll bet money an autopsy would show Morrow was dead before that car hit the tree."

Jim walked over and handed her the bags. "Knowing the way this bunch operates, Celestine put a spell on the coroner. No autopsy will ever be done."

"And if the Highway Patrol's accident reconstruction team raises any red flags, she'll shut them up, too." Faith shook her head. "Poor bastard."

"Don't waste your pity," Jim told her. "Judging from the conversation the other night, he had some choice about going along with this mess. If he didn't, why bother to kill him?"

"Yeah, I was just thinking about that." Brooding, she absently reached into the bags and started pulling out the clothes Jim had bought for her. "But he had a wife and two little kids, too. They're completely innocent, and now their lives have been destroyed."

"If he had kids, he sure as hell should have stayed out of it."

Faith shrugged. "Maybe he didn't think there was a choice. Even aside from Celestine's spell, when the whole department went bad, fighting them could have gotten him killed."

Jim lifted a dark brow. "Hasn't stopped you."

"I've always been bullheaded." She pulled the last of his purchases from the bag. "Thanks for all this, by the way. I'll pay you back after I hit the bank for cash."

Jim had outfitted her from the skin out—underwear, jeans, knit shirts, even socks and a pair of running shoes. Picking up one of the shirts, she looked it over. It was a pretty peach that would compliment her hair color perfectly. Glancing at the rest of the selection, she saw a rainbow of shades, without one screaming red in the bunch. "You know, you've got good taste."

He grinned. "You sound surprised."

"Hey, sometimes even I buy stuff that clashes with my hair. If I'm not careful, I end up looking like Ronald McDonald."

"I seriously doubt that. Besides, I'm an artist—color is my job."

"When you're not hunting witches or eating bad guys." She sobered, thinking once again of Morrow. "I wonder how they really killed him."

"I doubt we'll ever know." His gaze sympathetic, he slapped her lightly on the shoulder. "Why don't you get dressed and we'll go work off a little stress."

She managed a flirtatious grin. "Why, whatever do you have in mind?"

"Werewolf combat training."

Faith gazed at him a beat. "Somehow that was not the answer I had in mind."

ELEVEN

Half an hour later, they zipped down the road in Jim's black Jag. They were far enough away from town that he'd decided it was safe to put the top down, and the wind whipped Faith's hair into a red froth. She tilted her head back, enjoying the sunlight on her face. "Why am I not surprised you own a convertible?"

He flashed her a white grin. "Let me guess—this is the setup for a joke about Rambo's love of hanging his head out car windows."

"First, sane people do not talk about themselves in the third person. And second . . . pbbbbbbbtttt!" She blew a loud, very juicy raspberry.

"I can't help it if you're predictable—and ever so slightly juvenile."

"Says the man I once caught licking his own balls."

"Hey, that was the closest I got to action all month."

Faith lifted her head to stare at him in mingled amusement and horror. "I was joking! You didn't really . . . ?"

Jim gave her a bland, slow blink. She snorted in disgust, realizing she'd been had. "Dog."

"Woof."

She settled back into the soft leather seat to watch trees whip by, sunlight lancing through the limbs in golden streamers. "So what's the point of today's little exercise?"

He shrugged, one big hand resting lightly on the steering wheel. "You need to learn how to manage your new strength in a fight. If you'd hit one of those cops in werewolf form the way you'd have hit him when you were human, you'd have taken his head off."

Faith winced, picturing the results. "That would have been bad."

"Not to mention really messy. Plus, you need to learn how to control the bite so you don't accidently turn some asshole into a werewolf."

"That, too, would be bad."

"Particularly for the asshole, since I'd have to kill him."

She started to laugh, then cut it off as his cold tone registered. "You're serious."

"We can't afford to give this kind of power to just anybody. It's too easy to misuse."

"I'd like to argue that, but after watching Reynolds at work . . ." She broke off and frowned as a new and unpleasant idea occurred to her. "Do I want to ask you what you'd have done if you felt *I* wasn't worthy?"

His mouth quirked up at the corner in a grim half-smile. "You are worthy, Faith."

She lifted a brow, not reassured. "Which is evidently a damn good thing for me."

Five minutes later they reached their destination, parked the car under a stand of trees, and strolled into the woods together. It was a pretty day under a cloudless sky, cooled by a breeze scented with spring flowers and pine.

They stopped in a clearing beside a creek. Water chuckled over stones, and a squirrel rustled through the leaves of the oak towering overhead. Perched on another limb, a bird poured out a liquid plea for love in a series of bright, high notes.

Jim glanced around them with satisfaction. "We should be far enough out. Nearest house is two miles away, neighborhood kids are in school. Good a place as any to Change."

"If you say so." Faith closed her eyes and opened herself to the power of the Mageverse. It surged through her in a long warm rush, and she caught her breath as it began to reshape her body. It hurt less this time, though the furious itch of growing fur was no better.

The bottom seemed to drop out of her stomach as she shot upward to her full Dire Wolf height. When she opened her eyes, she found Jim big and dark and feral, his silver eyes bright against his black fur. For such a thoroughly magical creature, he looked at home under the pines and oaks, a wolf in its natural habitat.

"Now," he said, "I teach you to fight."

Faith braced furry fists on her hips and eyed him. "Jim, I have four brothers. I learned how to fight before I hit puberty."

"You know how to fight as a human. A Dire Wolf is not just a really big guy." He waggled his clawed hands in a bring-it-on gesture. "Hit me."

She hesitated a moment, frowning. "How hard?"

"Hard."

"Jim, I don't know how strong I am. I don't know how much force to use."

He gave her an infuriating little smile. "Don't worry about it. Hit me."

The patronizing glint in his eye pissed her off. Faith threw the punch the way she'd been taught, straight at his head, driving her full body weight behind it.

A big hand snapped around her wrist, stopping her fist well before it struck the target. "Never punch a Dire Wolf in the face," Jim told her. "A human's face is just target, but a Dire Wolf's head houses his primary weapons." Opening his jaws, he caught her hand gently between his teeth.

"Hey!" Startled, she jerked back.

He let her go. "If I bit down, I could crush every bone in your hand and cripple you."

Faith frowned, considering the problem. "But wouldn't it heal when I shifted?"

Jim shrugged those impressive shoulders. "Yeah—when you shifted. Until then, you've got crippling pain and no use of that hand. And what are you going to change into?"

"Good point." She paused, thinking it through. "If I go human . . ."

"You're lunch if you don't shift back before I get you. Wolf is better, but you'd have no hands and not much in the way of claws. Again, if I get you, I eat you. Or, if I hurt you bad enough in enough forms, I can make you shift so fast, your own magic will destroy you."

"Ouch." Faith bit her lip absently. "What about a round-house?" She swung out in a slow-motion punch, coming at his head from the side.

He nodded, automatically blocking with a powerful forearm. "That's better. In fact, if you're not in a fight to the death, that's pretty well the way you want to do it. But you've got to be careful. In Dire Wolf form, you can put your fist through a car door, much less somebody's skull."

She rocked back on her heels and propped her hands on her hips as she studied him. "Okay, so how do you fight when you *are* in a fight to the death?"

"That pretty much depends on the form. As a wolf or dog, the teeth are our primary weapons. The claws, not so much. But Dire Wolves fight more like bears or big cats." Opening his hand, he mimed a swat with one hand.

Faith smiled dryly. "Basically, what my brothers called fighting like a girl."

"Your brothers never saw somebody get half his face

ripped off by a Dire Wolf." He extended his claws. They looked like curving three-inch knifepoints protruding from his furry fingertips.

She grimaced. "You know, it occurs to me this could get really ugly."

"In a heartbeat. It's a good thing that idiot Reynolds didn't know how to fight as a Dire Wolf." He flexed his claws and smiled grimly. "I'd have cleaned his clock if I hadn't had to keep one eye on you. Next time, though . . ."

"I'll be in the mix." She bared her teeth. "So show me what to do."

With claws retracted, he demonstrated the ins and outs of Dire Wolf combat. They spent the next hour practicing, grappling, and exchanging blows, with frequent pauses as he stopped to explain or critique.

And as each minute passed, Faith found herself more and more aware of him.

When he held her during their struggle, her body rose to his, nipples tingling, heat building between her thighs. She could smell the salty musk of her arousal.

Which meant he could, too.

That, perversely, turned her on even more.

Feeling something hard press against her belly as they struggled, she looked down. His dark, heavy length lay against her red-furred belly.

Suddenly the profound strangeness of the whole thing hit her, and she rolled away from him, throwing her hands in the air. "Okay, I'm done."

Leaning on one elbow in the leaves, dark and graceful as a panther—and just as unselfconscious—Jim raised a brow. "Well, you are in your Burning Moon."

"I know that. And it's one thing when we're in human form. But . . ." She shrugged and looked away, struggling with the blend of arousal and discomfort she felt.

He rolled over on his back and arched his spine. His cock described a long, dark arch of its own over the shining black fur of his belly. "Feeling a little too animal, sweetheart?" Lazily, he wrapped one big hand around the shaft and slowly stroked.

Faith realized she was staring and forced her gaze away. "Don't do that."

"Why?" He cupped his heavy balls. "It's just as much me in this form as it is when I'm human." His silver eyes shuttered. "And it's just as much you, too."

"Maybe, but it doesn't feel like it." She glowered as a new thought struck her. "And for the record, I don't care who Rambo is, I ain't doing him."

He shouted in laughter and released himself. "Darling, I wouldn't even dream of suggesting it." Magic swirled up from his eyes, and his body shifted and shrank. The next moment, he was human again, reclining in the leaves in his jeans and black T-shirt. He sprang to his feet, lithe as a gymnast. "Change to human form. I need to give you that lesson in bite control."

Faith lifted a brow. "As a human?"

"Well, I sure as hell don't want you biting me with *those* teeth."

"Good point."

As she prepared to Change, she tried to ignore the little voice that murmured she'd be happy to bite him in any form at all.

Once she was human again, they squared off. "The bite is a spell," Jim told her. "When you bite someone, your power is going to want to rise. Your job is to control it. It's basically calling the magic in reverse."

He moved around behind her and caught her in his arms, forearm pressing lightly against her neck. "Now, try to bite me."

"In this position, the logical move is a throw," Faith pointed out, grabbing his wrist as she got ready to flip him over her shoulder.

"Yeah, but we ain't practicing throws. We're practicing bites. Bite me." Deliberately, he tightened his arm against her throat.

She sighed, opened her mouth, and closed her teeth lightly on his muscled forearm. He tasted of salt and clean male skin—and just a hint of magic.

"That's not going to work, Faith." His breath blew lightly against her ear. "The magic isn't even going to try to rise if that's all you're doing. You've got to put a little more into it."

Frustrated, she threw a look over her shoulder at him. "Put a little more *what* into it? You mean chomp down? Or what?"

"It's not the force, it's the emotion." He tightened his hold on her hip, dragging her back.

Her eyes widened. If his erection had softened, it was back now. She could feel its thick bulk even through their jeans. "You're having a little too much fun back there, hoss."

"Not yet." He rolled his hips until the shaft stroked the length of her backside. "But I'm giving it serious thought."

She grinned. "Bad dog."

"Every chance I get," he breathed in her ear. The arm around her throat shifted until he could close long fingers around her breast. Slowly, teasingly, he squeezed.

Her nipple peaked against his palm. She licked her lips. "I thought we were practicing."

"We are practicing." He brushed his palm across the hard nubbin until it tightened even more.

"Practicing what?" His left hand left her hip to stroke down her belly. Two strong fingers slid between her thighs, brushing teasingly along the seam of her jeans. "Driving me nuts?"

He laughed against her ear, a low masculine rumble. "Yeah. How am I doing?"

She caught her breath. He'd found her clit. "Pretty good."

"Good." Ruthlessly, gently, he tormented nipple and sex through her clothing. Faith's panties dampened as her body heated under his skillful touch.

His fingers traced up her zipper, caught the tab, drew it

down. Traced up again, over the silk and lace, drawing a line of heat up her belly. She gasped. "Jim!"

"Mmm?" He sounded lazily amused as he ran his thumb along the elastic band of her underwear, slowly, as if considering dipping inside.

"Are we still practicing?" Her libido was definitely growling now.

"Practicing what?" His hand slid down her waistband. His palm felt deliciously warm. "Faith?" he prompted. "Practicing what?"

One finger stroked between her damp lips. "Practicing . . . Oh! . . . biting."

His fingertip circled her clit, almost touching it, but not quite. "Yes."

Pleasure spooled up her body in long, slick ribbons. "So we're not having sex?"

"Nope." The finger dipped into her slick core, then retreated again.

"Ummm. Feels like we're having sex."

He tugged her nipple through the fabric of her bra. "But we're not."

His cock felt like a steel rod against her ass. It was getting really difficult to concentrate. She licked her dry lips. "So what are we doing again?"

He raked her clit with a teasing thumbnail. "Pissing you off." He jerked his hand from her shorts.

As she gasped in outrage, he presented his forearm to her teeth. "Bite."

Frustrated—he was teasing her!—Faith sank her teeth into the tangy masculine flesh. She felt the magic boil up, surging out of the Mageverse. Belatedly, she remembered the idea was to block it and tried to force it back down again. It refused to obey, surging through her jaws and into the impressions left by her teeth.

She opened her jaws and studied the bite in dismay. "Shit. If you'd been human . . ."

"You'd have infected me." Jim released the breast he'd

been toying with, grabbed her T-shirt, and whipped it off over her head. Before she could squawk a protest, he attacked her bra. A moment later, he dropped it on top of the shirt.

"So you're just going to torture me until I get it right?" she demanded.

"Basically." He nuzzled her ear and gave it a taunting nibble.

"Forget that!" She squirmed, but despite her new powers, Jim was still bigger and stronger. He just laughed and cupped her, rolling the little peak between deliciously rough fingertips.

"Give me your arm," she growled. "I'm going to bite the living hell out of you."

"I don't think so." He thrust his other hand down her jeans and caught her belly to drag her back against his erection.

"Oh, yeah!" Faith glowered over her shoulder at him. "I'm going to bite you, and then I'm going to bang your furry little brains out. You're going to be the dumbest werewolf in South Carolina."

She grabbed his wrist in both hands, hauled it to her mouth, and bit down. The magic boiled up again, even faster than it had before. Desperately, Faith tried to block it and force it aside, but it came on too strong, fueled by the intensity of her emotions. She snarled as she felt it surge into her mouth.

"Sorry, kiddo." There was definitely laughter in his voice. "Close, but not quite."

He tried to pull away, but Faith had no intention of letting him. Dragging his arm forward, she shot her hip into his and let him roll.

He hit the ground with a startled woof. Faith pounced on him, jerked his head back, and bit down on the side of his neck. He yelped, more in surprise than pain, as the magic boiled up. Faith threw her will against it . . .

And it stopped. Seethed in her mouth for one long, trembling second.

Then seeped away.

She lifted her head and gave Jim a triumphant look. "I did it!"

"So you did." He smiled darkly at her. A set of red indentations marked where her teeth had pressed into his skin.

"Now I get my reward." Sitting up, she reached back and found the tab of his zipper. It slid down with a loud hiss. His erection pressed into the opening, covered with the thin white cotton of his briefs. Its bulk forced the zipper open still more.

Meeting his lazy, hungry stare, Faith reached down his briefs to find the thick satin head. A pearl of pre-cum greeted her fingers. She stroked over it, slicking the moisture across the warm shaft, which bucked in eager welcome. "Hello."

He rolled his hips upward, lifting her body with his strength. "Hello yourself."

She rose off him and began to slide her jeans and panties down her legs. Desire blazed up in his pale eyes as he watched her pull off every stitch.

Faith kicked her clothes away and showed her teeth. "Strip."

He showed his own. "The lady's wish is my command." Rolling to his feet, Jim dragged his shirt over his head. As he threw it aside, muscles rolled temptingly up and down his broad chest. The corner of his mouth kicked up in a rakish half-smile as he reached for the waistband of his jeans.

"Take it off!" She hummed a teasing bump and grind, crossing her bare legs as she leaned back on her elbows. A cool breeze blew across her nipples, teasing them to harder peaks.

He spun around like a stripper and rocked his hips teasingly. The movement made the muscle ripple in his tight backside.

Faith watched him work his snug jeans down those long, brawny legs. After kicking off his shoes, he stepped out of his pants with an artistic twitch of lean hips.

She grinned in pure admiration. "Has anyone ever told you that you have a truly outstanding ass?"

Jim pivoted smoothly to face her, revealing the long, arrogant jut of his cock. Hooding his eyes, he stroked the shaft teasingly. "Somebody may have said something about it."

She laughed. "You're a bad, bad boy, Jim London." She watched as he swaggered over to stand astride her bare feet. "You need to be spanked."

He lifted both arms and raked his big hands through his hair. The movement made his chest look the width of a wall. "Think you're up to it?"

Quick as a cat, she hooked the back of one of his ankles with her foot and pulled, tumbling him backward.

With a startled yelp, Jim hit the ground on his muscular backside. Faith pounced, straddling his thighs.

He braced on his elbows and lifted a dark brow, watching her prowl her way up his thighs. "Bit violent, aren't you?"

"Us werewolves are like that." Sliding her hands up his sleek thighs, she framed his cock between her hands and contemplated it, head cocked. "Merciless."

"Should I be worried?"

Faith lowered her head and blew a breath along the length of the smooth shaft. "Oh, yeah. Are you?"

He rolled his hips upward, making his cock bob. "Shaking."

"You should be." She caught the shaft in one hand and angled it upward. "Us merciless werewolves like to eat our prey."

"Oh, God, I hope so." His heartfelt moan made her laugh.

Eyeing him, she put out her tongue and gave his cock a long, slow lick.

He let his head drop back and groaned.

Enjoying his reaction, she opened her mouth and took

the shaft in, then suckled it teasingly. Finally, she let it escape with a soft pop. "Still scared?"

"Terrified."

She grinned. "Good."

Jim shivered in agonized delight as Faith proceeded to give him the blow job of his life. Her mouth felt wet and slick and impossibly delicious as she played slow, licking homage to his shaft, nibbling up and down its aching length. He could feel the orgasm gathering in his balls like a hot fist slowly tightening.

Just as he started to tell her to slow down before he came, she stopped. Dazed, he looked down his belly at her foxy face as she contemplated his hard-on. Several seconds ticked past, but she did nothing, just staring at his cock as if fascinated.

"Uh, Faith?"

"Ummm?"

"Going to do something with that?"

"Actually, I just thought I'd drive you crazy for a while." She looked up, lids dipping over green eyes. "That teasing thing works both ways."

He stared at her as his infuriated libido howled in outrage. "Ah, no."

"Ah, yes." She swirled her tongue over the tight, smooth head and smiled tauntingly.

"You do realize I'm bigger than you, right?"

"You do realize I've got your dick in my mouth?"

He watched her give him another tiny, teasing lick. It was all he could do not to beg. "You're the one that needs the spanking."

A haughty red brow lifted. "You and what army?"

"I don't need an army. I'm an Alpha Dire Wolf. I *am* an army." He gave her his best mock-ferocious glare.

"I'm aquiver." Another tiny lick.

"I'm really going to enjoy giving you that spanking."

She closed her teeth over the head of his cock, not quite biting.

"Or not."

"Smart man." Another lick.

"How long do you think I'm going to let you get away with that?"

"Dunno." Lick. "I thought I'd find out."

Jim managed to survive another set of tortuous licks before his control broke. Then, growling, he sat up, grabbed both her arms and flipped her off him and onto her belly. Before she could even squeak, he rolled between her thighs, pulled her taut little backside up, and drove his cock into her sex.

Her yelp of startled pleasure was gratifying. "Apparently—ah!—not long."

"Nope," he agreed, driving to his full length. "Not long at all."

With a feline purr of pleasure, she braced her legs apart as he started shafting her, slipping in and out in long, fierce digs. With every thrust, his hips slapped against her tight little backside. He shuttered his eyelids in pleasure and fought not to come.

Jesus, he felt good in this position. His cock seemed to reach all the way to her bellybutton, teasing her slick walls every time he drove in. Faith groaned and lifted her ass, thrusting back at him so hard her breasts danced.

God, she'd loved this. Loved teasing him like this until he lost control and jumped her. After all the shit Ron had put her through, it felt good having the upper hand for once.

Though, braced on her hands and knees while he rode her like a madman, she wasn't completely sure who had what. Then again, she wasn't sure she cared either.

Pleasure coiled and tightened in her belly, straining to break free. Another hard, delicious lunge, so deep and strong she felt his balls tap between her thighs. And then another, even harder, and a low growl from behind her, deliciously wild and animal. And another, and . . .

She came with a long yowl of pleasure as the fire closed

over her head. Behind her, he echoed the cry, his sounding distinctly triumphant.

They collapsed in the leaves in a sated pile, to watch the sun cut through the trees overhead. Two squirrels rattled through the branches, pursuing each other up and down the trunk like a couple of kids playing tag.

"You know," Jim said. "This is really nice. I could stay like this."

"Me too." She paused. "Except for the killer vampire and the rogue werewolf we've got to slay."

"Yeah," Jim said. "Except for them."

TWELVE

Keith Reynolds drove down a winding gravel road toward Celestine's reconstructed plantation house. Pines, oaks, and sweet gum trees crowded close to the narrow road, their gnarled limbs threatening in the moonlight. With every foot he drove, the knot in his gut tightened with a combination of dread and sick excitement.

Celestine was going to be pissed that they hadn't found Weston yet, and she was going to take it out on him. Reynolds wasn't sure which galled him more—that he feared her so much, or that he found her vicious attentions so seductive.

Men didn't crawl to a woman. Especially not a man who could turn into a seven-foot monster and disembowel with a swipe of his claws.

Yet nothing had ever aroused him like crawling to Celestine. The power that swirled around her fascinated him. Even the scent of rot that surrounded her when she worked her spells attracted him as much as it repelled.

Reynolds supposed it was the danger she represented

that drew him. He'd always been an adrenalin junkie; it was why he'd become a cop. Every time she lashed him to that pillar in her ballroom, he never knew whether this would be the time she killed him—or he killed her. It could go either way.

He wondered sometimes if she knew how many times he'd considered ripping out her sadistic, lying heart.

Tonight might be the night she finally drove him to do it.

Every cop on the Clarkston police department had spent the day looking for Weston. But though they'd staked out her house and combed the town, she was nowhere to be found. Ayers seriously considered a press conference ac cusing her of police misconduct. Unfortunately, they'd need the cooperation of the Solicitor's Office for something like that, and that office's head prosecutor was female. Which meant Celestine's usual sex-based spells wouldn't work. Too, going public meant media attention and questions from the State Law Enforcement Division, which investigated police misconduct. In the end, Ayers had reluctantly discarded the idea.

None of this was going to please Celestine, who would no doubt take her rage out on Reynolds.

Ahead of his car, the woods suddenly came to an end at a rolling expanse of lawn. The crunch of gravel turned to the smooth hiss of blacktop under the Crown Vic's wheels, as Reynolds drove up the circular drive to reach the plantation house.

It shown pale in the moonlight, three stories tall, with towering Doric columns and a porch wide enough to host a cotilion. He almost expected Scarlett O'Hara to sweep out through the double doors, surrounded by adoring beaus and miles of floral skirts.

It was all far different from the snake-infested wreck he'd remembered from boyhood. Five years ago, some teenaged arsonist had reduced the plantation house to a couple of listing brick chimneys and half-standing, smoke-blackened walls.

Until Reynolds had mentioned it to Celestine. The vampire had used the magic she'd gained from killing Tony Shay to recreate it as a shimmering Southern palace. It was probably far finer than it had ever been in real life, but at times Reynolds wished she'd left it to rot decently. Somehow that would have been preferable to turning it into a perverted version of itself.

He parked the Crown Vic at the foot of the sweeping stairs. To his shame, his hand trembled when he shut off the engine—whether from fear or anticipation, he didn't know.

He really should kill her, but he knew he wouldn't.

Grim-faced, he strode up the brick stairway to the arched double doors. Without bothering to knock, he pulled them open and was greeted by the unmistakable sounds of combat. Swords clashed, as voices screamed in pain over the boom and crackle of magic. Cold fear gripped him.

Someone was attacking Celestine!

Reynolds transformed and raced toward the ballroom, his clawed feet clicking on the marble. In the doorway to the huge room, he skidded to a halt, with a mix of irritation and relief.

Celestine wore a suit of gleaming iridescent plate armor as she stood before a hole in the air—one of those dimensional gates of hers. She'd evidently managed to make it invisible on the other side, because no one there seemed to notice it.

Then again, they might be too busy to care. Armored figures battled with swords or hurled bolts of shimmering energy at each other. Judging from the familiar red and black stone, they fought in the same magical temple he and Celestine had visited before.

"What the hell is going on?" Reynolds demanded.

Celestine looked around. Her eyes were almost glowing in her excitement. "Good, you're just in time. We need to go steal Korbal's Grail."

He relaxed fractionally. She'd planned all this after all.

Assuming they managed to pull off the theft, Celestine would be in such a good mood, not even the cops' failure to capture Weston would bother her. "Who's fighting?"

"Arthur and his knights have attacked Korbal, just as I intended. But they haven't found the grail yet." She clenched her fists, all but dancing on her armored feet. "This is our chance!"

Reynolds felt a feral grin twist his long muzzle. "Let's go get it then."

As she'd done before, Celestine cast another invisibility spell around them, then closed the dimensional gate and opened another.

They stepped through into a surprisingly empty corridor. They must be on one of the lower floors; Reynolds's acute werewolf hearing detected the clash and scream of battle somewhere overhead. "Where are we?" he murmured.

"My spell directed them to a point two floors above the grail chamber. It's going to take them time to find it."

Obeying her insistent tug, he followed the invisible vampire down the marble corridor until she stopped him with a short, sharp pull.

"What do . . . ?" he began, until a savage dig in his ribs shut him up.

The scent of magical decay rose as Celestine cast another spell, shimmering the air in front of him like a disturbed pool of water.

When the shimmer cleared, he was staring into the startled faces of ten vampire guards. They must have surrounded themselves with a cloaking spell of their own when Arthur's people attacked, but Celestine had just broken it.

Before anyone else could recover, Reynolds roared and struck out with his claws, ripping one vampire's face open from forehead to chin. The man fell with a shriek of agony, as Reynolds leaped to attack his comrades with claws and teeth.

They recovered fast and fought back with a flurry of

swinging swords and magical blasts. Celestine must have dropped the invisibility shield around him as a distraction, though she herself didn't appear. Reynolds was too busy fighting for his life to care.

Five bloody moments later, somebody grabbed his shoulder with invisible hands. "Come on!" Celestine's voice screamed. "This way!"

He whirled and charged after her, ignoring the stench and sting of death spells splashing against his furred back. A gateway opened in the air, and they leaped through, Celestine hurling a last spell of her own before it closed.

Panting, bleeding, he stood in the center of the ballroom, his knees shaking from adrenalin.

Suddenly Celeste appeared in front of him as she dropped her invisibility shield. A triumphant grin stretched across her face, and her eyes gleamed.

In her hand was a heavily engraved golden cup. "Look what I've got," she purred.

Jim cast a wary glance at Faith as she worked in the kitchen cooking up a couple of thick rib eyes. Her expression was fierce with a concentration that seemed to far exceed the demands of the task.

"Okay," he asked suspiciously, "What are you plotting?"

Faith blinked. "What?"

"That's your thinking-about-catching-bad-guys look. You've got something in mind. What?"

She gave him a look so wary, his instincts instantly howled. "Nothing you'll like."

"Yeah, I figured as much." Jim folded his arms. "Tell me anyway."

She sighed and opened the oven, then forked the steaks onto plates. "I've been thinking about these pheromones. They're pretty powerful, right? I mean, even the Sidhe reacted to them, and they're not even human."

"Right." He liked this less every time she opened her mouth.

"So why don't we use them to trap Reynolds?"

"Absolutely not."

Faith propped her fists on her hip, a stubborn expression on her pretty face. "Not so fast, think about it. Once he scents me, he's going to want to come after me."

"Along with half the Clarkston police department, all armed with TASERs."

"What if I was in dog form, though? What if he just smells me, and he thinks I'm alone? He's not going to want all those cops in on this if he's got sex in mind. He'll come after me all by himself. And then we could nail him."

Jim felt his hackles raise in primitive male outrage. "He'd have to be an idiot."

She gave him a long look. "Pheromones don't exactly encourage cool, logical thought. And Reynolds has never encountered them before, because he's never encountered a female werewolf. He's going to want to investigate. Plus, he's an arrogant bastard. He'll assume that even if it is a trap, he can turn the tables on me."

Jim frowned. "I don't like this, Faith. It sounds like a big risk."

"It's all a big risk. Besides, aren't you the one who said Reynolds didn't know how to fight like a werewolf?"

"Yeah, but—"

"Look, we need to take him out, right? We know he's on first shift, so we can be pretty sure he'll be leaving the department at 3 P.M. We can ambush him then, but if we tried to do that in human form, we'd be ass-deep in cops. But if we did it as dogs . . ."

"Or better yet, if I was a wolf . . ." Reluctantly, Jim considered the idea. He still didn't like it, but he saw how it could work.

"Everybody would simply think it was a dog fight. I don't think even the cops would realize something else was going on until it's too late."

Jim raked a hand through his hair as his alpha male protectiveness warred with his common sense. "All right," he said finally. "But you can be damned sure I'm going to be right there."

Faith gave him a warm smile. "I'm counting on it."

They made love with a hot, desperate ardor, fueled as much by fear of the future as the Burning Moon. Afterward, Jim pulled Faith into his arms and quickly drifted off to sleep.

Faith, on the other hand, lay wide awake, staring at the ceiling.

Tomorrow, if all went well, she'd kill another cop. And she'd just planned out the whole thing, cooly, logically. With what a prosecutor would have described as "malice aforethought."

True, it wasn't as if they'd be shooting Reynolds in the back. In fact, his death would probably look a lot like self-defense. But the fact was, they were setting him up.

Yet what choice did they have? Reynolds had been killing people, and would probably go right on killing people until he was stopped.

Still, Faith had the nagging feeling she'd crossed a significant line tonight. She'd stopped thinking like a cop to become what amounted to a vigilante.

And she very much feared there would be no going back.

Where the hell was the Black Grail?

Blinking blood from her eyes, Guinevere hurried down the corridor, her husband and four of his knights at her back. Her right arm was numb from shoulder to elbow from a death spell she'd barely managed to block, and Arthur himself was limping. She badly wanted to peel his armor off and check the wound she could feel throbbing through their psychic Truebond, but there wasn't time.

They had to find the grail and destroy it.

The six of them had managed to break away from the mob battling in the upper floors to search for the Black Grail, but time was running out. When dawn came, they'd have to break off the search. Mageverse magic barely worked on Mortal Earth during the day, and the vampires couldn't function at all once the sun came up.

At dawn, the Magekind would have to return to the Mageverse, while their enemies retreated to whatever burrows they could create.

"Do you think we've been suckered?" Gawain asked. The Dragon Sword shimmered in his hand, light rippling up and down its enchanted length. "Maybe the Black Grail isn't here."

"It's here," Gwen said grimly. "I sensed it, and Llyr confirmed its presence. I doubt any spell could have fooled us both." Still, it should have been on the floor they'd gated to. Apparently they had been diverted, which raised all kinds of uncomfortable questions.

"Hold." Arthur threw up a mailed fist even as the knights tensed and stopped.

"Something's dead up there," Kay said, scenting the air like a wolf.

He was right. The reek of spilled blood was obvious even to Guinevere, whose sense of smell was no better than that of a human.

Arthur nodded, his expression tense, and gently pushed her behind him with one hand. Her husband in the lead, the six of them moved up the corridor, silent as tigers in their enchanted armor. But when they rounded the corner, they found a scene even more gruesome than they'd expected.

The hallway was stacked with gutted, dismembered bodies.

"Merlin's beard," Gawain breathed. "What the hell did that?"

Exchanging a hard look, the other knights started searching the corridor and adjoining rooms for the killer.

Gwen barely noticed as she and her husband concentrated on the bodies. They were obviously Geirolf's vampires, but they hadn't been the victims of a Magekind attack. "No sword did that," she told Arthur quietly, pointing at a ragged, gaping wound.

He frowned, crouching over the corpse. "Looks like an animal attack. I don't understand—Geirolf's vampires are like us. They heal any wound not inflicted by a magical blade."

Guinevere leaned over the body and sent a quick probing spell into it. An image flashed through her mind—a horrific wolflike creature lunging for her throat, knifelike teeth gleaming. It had been the last thing the vampire had seen. She shrank back in horror. "Merlin's beard!"

"What?"

Shaken, she looked up at him. "Some kind of magical creature attacked him. I almost hesitate to say it, but it looked like a werewolf."

Arthur frowned and stroked his dark beard with an armored hand. "I've lived on Mageverse Earth for sixteen hundred years, but I've never seen anything like that."

"Perhaps it's some kind of alien demon, like Geirolf."

Gawain stepped back out into the hall, having finished his search of a nearby room. His expression was grim. "Well, whatever it was, I think it took the Black Grail. There's a pedestal like the one you described in one of the rooms ahead, but there's nothing on it."

Arthur growled a quiet curse. He and Gwen followed Gawain back into the room he'd just emerged from.

Just as Gawain said, there was the red stone pedestal she'd seen in her dream, but it was indeed empty. The golden cup was gone.

With her Maja senses, Gwen detected the lingering black glitter of death magic. "Somebody gated out of here not fifteen minutes ago," she told Arthur, moving toward the altar.

He cursed. "What do you want to bet it was the same person who sent you that vision?"

She turned toward him as everything became far too clear. "They used us as a distraction. While we were fighting the cultists, they gated in and took the grail."

"Can you track them?"

"I can try." But when she sent a magical probe into the lingering energy from the gate, it led nowhere. The vampire that had created it had done a very good job of erasing his tracks. Silently, Gwen caught Arthur's gaze and shook her head.

"Perfect," he snarled, throwing up his hands. "Just perfect!"

"Don't give up just yet." Narrow-eyed, she studied the fading glitter. "Our friend may have outsmarted himself."

A slow smile spread across her husband's face. "What do you have in mind?"

"He gave me a link with the grail to lure us here. Maybe I can use it."

Gawain shook his head. "He'll block your probes."

"Oh, yes." She gave them all a feral smile. "And death magic is very strong. Luckily it doesn't have a lot of staying power. I'll wager that if I pour enough Mageverse magic at it, it'll pop like a balloon."

A wolfish grin spread over Arthur's face. "We'll see how our furry friend likes having a thousand or so of Avalon's best leaping down his throat."

"Unfortunately, a spell like that is going to take time, and dawn is much too close," she told him. "I won't have time to work it before the sun's radiation begins blocking my magic."

A prickle of Mageverse fire spread over her skin, warring with the building weight of the sun as it began to beat on the earth overhead. Gwen looked up. "Our people are beginning to gate out. We'd better go."

Arthur frowned, looking unhappy. "At least the Geirolf

vampires will have to den up, too. I only hope they don't get to the thief before we do."

As the afternoon sunlight streamed over downtown Clarkston, Faith and Jim drove into town. The convertible's top was firmly up, and she wore a ball cap and sunglasses with her red hair down around her shoulders instead of tied up in its usual bun. Even so, her instincts howled as they cruised past the Clarkston police department. Dread clenched her belly in a cold fist, just as it had since she'd woken that morning.

Her dreams had been bloody and confused—nightmares of Reynolds jerking her off her feet and ripping into her with claws and teeth. After fidgeting her way through the afternoon, all she wanted now was to get it over with.

Jim seemed to share her tension. He'd been quiet all morning, but it reminded her of the silence of a volcano on the verge of eruption.

They drove up and down Main Street until they found a parking place a block from the station. A convenient alley stood nearby with a dumpster that looked as if it would provide good cover for a shape-shift. Turning off the engine, Jim studied her, his pale gaze searching. "You sure you're up to this?"

Faith shrugged, despite the sickly fist kneading her belly. "Doesn't matter whether I am or not. It's got to be done."

"No, actually, it doesn't. I could play decoy just as well."

"Not when it comes to pheromone production. He'd be expecting a fight the minute he got a whiff of you. With me . . ." She shrugged. "Hopefully his big head won't be doing the thinking."

"That's what worries me." A muscle flexed in Jim's jaw.

Despite her own tension, something about his obvious worry made Faith feel oddly warmed. "Hey, you'll be right

there, right? Knowing you, you're not going to let him anywhere close."

Some of the worry lifted from his eyes, replaced by
pleasure at her confidence in him. He smiled. "You've got
that right."

"Damn straight." She reached for the door and swung it
open. "Now let's go do this thing."

Reynolds watched as Ayers stared out the window at the
afternoon sunlight. "So you think it'll be tonight?"

He shrugged. "With Celestine, you never know. But I'd
think so. She wants that army of vampires pretty badly, so
I'd imagine she'll trot the grail out for you boys as soon as
she can get her hands on a sacrifice to power the spell."

A speculative light flared in Ayers's eyes. "That brings up
an interesting point. The grail won't work on you, will it?"

"Magic in general doesn't seem to do much to me, other
than my own. So I guess not."

Ayers leaned a hip on his desk. "So what are you going
to do once we're all vampires?" His eyes glinted with a hint
of malice. "Sounds like you'll be outnumbered."

Reynolds stiffened. "I can take care of myself, Chief."
He bared his teeth. "Believe me."

The chief looked at him for a long, cool moment. Then
he smiled easily. "Of course."

Bastard!

Reynolds stormed from the building and across the parking lot toward his patrol car. With every stride, he found
himself struggling with an unaccustomed emotion: worry.

Once the entire department had vampire powers, where
would that leave him? Over the past couple of months, he'd
grown to enjoy the authority he wielded as Celestine's
right-hand man. Just as heady was the physical intimida-
tion he could command as a werewolf.

But once all the other cops were vampires, much of that advantage would be gone. He . . .

Sex!

Reynolds stopped dead as the scent filled his nose. Blinking in surprise, he drew in a deep, astonished breath. The smell of raw eroticism surrounded him, so intense and overwhelming his dick instantly hardened.

What the hell was that? Cautiously he inhaled again, but the smell hadn't faded. There was something familiar about it, a scent he knew . . .

Weston.

He sniffed again, surprised. She'd been hanging around his police car. Just recently, too. But why? What the fuck was she up to?

And when had she turned into sex on the hoof?

Unable to resist the temptation, he dropped to one knee, the better to breathe in her deliciously tempting scent. He'd always thought she was reasonably hot, but this was something else again. It was as if somebody had dipped her in raw sex.

He wanted her. Even Celestine had never turned him on like this, even with her all magic and perverse sexuality.

Reynolds took a deeper sniff, drinking in the impossibly tempting aroma. He frowned, noticing a strong canine overlay.

Weston must be in dog form, he realized. Which made sense, considering the entire department was gunning for her. Becoming a mutt would make a very effective disguise. Plus, he'd never be able to catch her on two legs, not without assuming werewolf form. Something he damned well wasn't going to do at three in the afternoon with half of Clarkston looking on. Celestine would kill him.

Reynolds licked his lips as a dark, tempting idea crossed his consciousness. Why not assume a canine form of his own? He'd have a lot better chance of catching her.

And when he caught her . . .

What would it be like doing it as a dog?

Damn, now there was a kinky thought. But tempting, very tempting. And after two months of being at Celestine's beck and call, it would be nice to be on top for once.

Reynolds glanced around cautiously, decided no one was watching, and called the magic, picturing the biggest, blackest rottweiler he could imagine.

A moment later, he put his muzzle to the pavement and started following Weston's scent trail.

Faith popped her Irish setter head around the corner of the police department just in time to see the enormous rottie trot from behind Reynolds's car. It was all she could do to suppress a yip of excitement.

The bastard had swallowed the bait hook, line, and sinker.

And there he came, nose to her scent trail, trotting across the parking lot like God's gift to *Animal Planet*.

All Faith had to do was lead him to Jim.

She turned tail and loped off, making straight for the Clarkston Fire Department, a big brick building that stood a block away. Where Jim waited, all two-hundred plus lupine pounds of him.

A menacing growl rumbled in the air. She threw a quick look back over her shoulder to see the rottweiler running in her wake, his massive jaws open.

Shit. Wouldn't do to let him catch her. With a yelp, she took off running, hoping she looked suitably panicked.

Her sensitive ears picked up Reynolds's triumphant growl as he shot in pursuit.

Oh, yeah. They had the bastard now.

Stretching out her long canine body, Faith flung herself into a dead run, dashing across the parking lot for the fire department building.

Reynolds's deep-throated bay of excitement echoed as he charged in her wake.

That's right, you son of a bitch, she thought grimly. *Come and get it.*

THIRTEEN

Reynolds galloped after Weston, almost drunk on the smell of sex and the trace of fear floating in her wake. He wasn't even running all out.

He wanted to enjoy the chase.

His lips pulled back from his teeth in anticipation. She'd fight him—Weston wasn't the type to give in. But he was bigger, and he'd been a werewolf longer. In the end, she wouldn't have a prayer.

After he had his fun, he'd hand her over to Celestine. Sacrificing the little bitch on top of acquiring the grail would make his mistress a very happy vampire. She'd no doubt reward him well.

He lengthened his stride, impatient to catch his tempting prey. The red flag of her Irish setter tail disappeared around the corner of the firehouse, and Reynolds sprinted after her.

The wind shifted, carrying a wild, feral scent. He lifted his head in alarm, but before he could even break stride, something big and black rammed into his side. It was like being hit by the Space Shuttle, a bone-grating impact that sent him tumbling in yipping astonishment.

The thing rolled with him, snarling like a chain saw, fangs snapping for his throat. *Shit*! Reynolds twisted, barely managing to kick free before the beast could get a good grip. *The other werewolf!*

As Reynolds scrambled back, he saw that a wolf was exactly what his foe was. The bastard was the biggest, blackest beast Reynolds had ever seen, easily two hundred pounds of hard muscle, with a mouthful of teeth that would put a crocodile's to shame. Reynolds hadn't even known they could assume wolf form; he'd only stumbled on the dog thing by accident.

He sure as hell didn't have time to figure it out now.

Jaws clamped down on his foreleg. With a howl of pain, he lunged for the nearest target—the wolf's left ear. His teeth clamped down. Blood flooded his mouth, so hot with magic it was like drinking white lightning.

Instincts he hadn't even known he had suddenly kicked in. With a baying howl, he went for the werewolf's throat.

Faith was no stranger to bloody fights, but she'd never seen anything like the way Jim and Reynolds ripped at one another. It was one thing to exchange punches or even knife swipes, but tearing at one another with claws and teeth . . .

It wasn't human, a voice in the back of her mind protested. *They* weren't human.

One endless heartbeat later, the two separated with a crimson splatter and began to circle. Blood dripped from Jim's wolf muzzle and one torn ear, while Reynolds limped on a wounded foreleg.

The rogue charged Jim, growling savagely. Her lover dodged, snaked his head forward, and sank his teeth into Reynolds's thick neck. The rottweiler didn't stop, plowing into him and forcing him over onto his back. Teeth snapped like castanets, punctuating snarls and growls.

And what the fuck was she doing, standing around do- ing nothing? So what if she was scared? Jim needed her.

Taking a deep breath, Faith called her magic, changed from Irish setter to wolf, and charged in. Without letting herself stop to think, she sank her teeth into Reynolds's thickly muscled shoulder. The taste of fur, dog, and magic flooded her mouth. Blood followed in a burning wave, the taste both revolting and so shockingly seductive, her first impulse was to let go. Conscious of Jim's danger, she bit deeper instead.

Faith heard a yip. Something clamped down on her cheek. She jerked away from the fiery pain, yelping as flesh tore. Her Burning Moon temper exploded, and she lunged for Reynolds, snapping at any part of him she could reach. He reared out of range of her teeth, then drove his weight against her chest, rolling her over on her back. Fangs clamped into her throat, cutting off her breath.

Gasping, Faith struggled, trying to kick her way free. She heard Jim's deep-throated roar of rage. Teeth snapped. Snarls. Blood splattered across her face. Reynolds yelped and let go. She scrambled clear, panting.

Jim had his fangs buried in Reynolds's muzzle as the rottie jerked back and forth, trying to tear away from him. Yeah! They had him! She plunged in and clamped her jaws into the rogue's haunch.

With a howl, her foe heaved his body upward, jerking away in a shower of blood. He whirled and ran. Baying like all the hounds of hell, Jim shot after him. Faith raced to catch up.

Reynolds flew across the road, his bobbed tail tucked against his butt as he ran in desperate bounds. Jim charged after him.

Right into the path of a pickup truck. Faith screamed a warning, but the words emerged as a strangled howl.

She saw Jim's head turn, as he registered the danger and threw himself into a desperate leap . . . too late. The truck's bumper clipped his rear haunch, spinning his body through the air. He hit the curb and flipped across the sidewalk, then tumbled down the embankment beyond it. The truck's brakes screeched.

Frantic, terrified, Faith shot across the street after him, dodging around the truck and narrowly avoiding an oncoming Honda. Leaping the sidewalk, she galloped down the embankment.

If he was hurt too badly to Change, he'd die.

A still, black-furred body lay in a heap at the bottom of the embankment, smeared with blood, barely breathing. His eyes were closed. Faith's heart crammed its way into her throat as she skidded to his side. Without considering who might be watching—not even caring—she Changed to human form.

"Jim!" Half afraid to touch him, she laid a shaking hand on his bloodied shoulder. He didn't move. "Jim, wake up! Please!"

Nothing.

"Jim!"

Finally, a whimper. The bloody shoulder under her hand twitched. Silver eyes opened, dazed.

"Jim, Change!" Faith stroked his matted fur. She felt sick, her eyes dry and burning. "Please! You've got to Change!"

He blinked and whined softly, the sound tight with pain.

Desperate, she blinked away the tears and hardened her tone to an authoritative snap. "Jim London, you shift right this minute!" Was it too late?

He closed his eyes and shuddered with effort. Magic boiled around him, shimmering to her werewolf senses.

Then he was blessedly human again, whole and unharmed in his jeans and T-shirt. Silver eyes opened and looked up at her, still a little dazed.

Faith sagged in relief. "Thank God!" She found herself stroking his handsome, unmarked face. "Didn't your mother teach you to look both ways before you cross the street?"

Jim sat up with a groan, rubbing both hands over his eyes like a man waking up from a nightmare. "Yeah, that was stupid. I was so focused on catching that bastard. He *hurt* you."

"Well, that truck hurt you." She gave him a light slap across one brawny shoulder, having recovered enough to get pissed off. "You scared the crap out of me, London."

To her bemused surprise, he actually grinned, pleased. "Yeah?"

Disgusted, she rose to her feet. "You're an idiot."

He stood. Faith automatically reached to steady him, but he stretched his big body, obviously none the worse for his adventure. "I know. I guess the bastard got away."

"Well, I was a little focused on making sure you weren't bumper pâte." They started up the hill together. Faith felt almost giddy in her relief.

"Where's the wolf?"

Startled, they looked up. A thin, elderly black man stood on the bank above them, his long face confused. "What?" Faith asked.

"I could have sworn I hit a wolf." He scanned the length of the bank in concern, gnarled fists braced on his hips. "Didn't even think there was any in these parts."

Faith glanced at Jim, then back at the bewildered driver. "In the middle of Clarkston? I don't think so."

The driver scratched his head. "Guess not. Thought maybe it had escaped from a zoo or something. I could have sworn . . ." Shaking his head, he turned and trudged back up the embankment, his red checkered shirt cheery against the blue sky.

"Let's get the hell out of here," Jim murmured to Faith.

Together, they scrambled up the embankment. As they reached the sidewalk, Faith recognized the city's animal control officer standing in front of the fire department. She tensed. If he recognized her . . . Luckily, she was wearing her hair down, something she never did on duty. That, combined with her blue jeans and T-shirt, provided something of a disguise from people used to seeing her in uniform. At least from a distance. She hoped.

"Did you see any stray dogs around here?" he called, showing no sign of recognition. "I got a report three of them were fighting out in front of the department."

Jim jerked a thumb over his shoulder in the direction Reynolds had gone. "I think I saw one run that way."

The officer sighed and started back toward the police department and his animal control truck. A gust of wind carried his scent into her face. It was free of magical rot. "He's probably long gone, but I'd better take a look."

Afraid he'd recognize her voice, Faith made no answer as she and Jim hurried up the sidewalk toward his car.

It was the longest block she'd ever walked.

With a sense of relief, she closed the car door and fell back into the Jag's glove-soft leather seat. "I'd love to see Reynolds talk his way out of that one."

Jim grunted. "He'd probably just eat the poor guy."

"Good point. Let's hope our friend back there isn't too good at his job."

But as Jim waited for an opening in the afternoon Clarkston traffic, Faith's giddy mood quickly darkened.

He'd almost gotten killed.

The memory of Jim carooming off that bumper kept running through Faith's mind like a news clip on CNN, an endless loop of terror and disaster that made her stomach knot all over again. When she reached up to tuck a lock of hair behind her ear, her hand shook.

Involuntarily, Faith glanced over at him. He met her gaze, his eyes brooding and hot.

"I'm sorry," he said abruptly. "I almost got you killed. I should have told you to stay out of it, but I was so intent on killing that bastard."

Indignation punctured her funk. "I hope you realize by now that I'm not going to just stand back and wring my hands when you're fighting for your life. What do I look like, the heroine of some sixties cop show? Give me a break."

"Forgot who I was talking to." His lips quirked. "Nobody could ever mistake you for a coward."

Faith frowned, remembering the taste of Reynolds's blood in her mouth. "Though having said that, I've got to admit there's a big difference between throwing punches and ripping into somebody with your teeth. It's really . . ." She broke off, unable to put it into words.

"Primal."

"Not to mention a little disgusting. And when he had me by the throat . . ." She shook her head. "I thought I was scared when he tried to kill me the first time. This was actually worse."

"It's because you didn't have hands." His voice seemed to rumble, deep and dark. "You had to do your fighting with your teeth, which is a hell of a lot more intimate."

"Yeah, that's it exactly. I felt like an animal." She looked over at him and caught her breath. For an instant, their gazes met. His was hot with male awareness. Inhaling in surprise, she scented the delicious musk of his desire.

In a heated flash, all her leftover adrenalin and fear found a new focus. Faith swallowed and looked away, battling the effect. After what they'd just been through, neither of them should be in the mood for sex.

Except it was precisely because of the close call with death that they felt so turned on.

Faith was familiar with the effect—she'd experienced it before. She and Ron once had the best sex of their marriage after a daylong firefight with a barricaded subject. But even then she hadn't felt anything like this sudden, clawing lust.

"During a fight, you're more in touch with your body." Jim's voice dropped even more, taking on a dark velvet note of seduction. "The scent of things, the taste of things. It . . . affects you. Strongly."

Unable to resist, she looked at him just as he darted a hungry look at her breasts. Her nipples tightened behind the scratchy lace of her bra. "I noticed."

Involuntarily, her gaze dropped to his lap. The muscles of his thighs flexed under the fabric of his pants. He had an erection. "I want you." The words were blunt, a deep male rumble of demand.

"I noticed that, too." Faith dragged her eyes away. "But in the middle of Clarkston at four o'clock in the afternoon is not the best place to jump each other."

"Then we'll just have to find someplace else to do it." He hit the gas.

She clenched her teeth as the Jag responded with a primal roar that seemed to echo her own need. *I can hang on until we get home.*

Despite his obvious lust, Jim drove with ruthless control, his big hands steady on the wheel, his gaze locked on the road as he maneuvered the powerful sports car through traffic.

His lap drew Faith's fascinated gaze like a magnet. His cock pressed against the fly of his jeans, so hard and thick she ached to free it.

"Where can we pull over?"

"What?" Startled, she lifted her gaze to his face.

"I'm not going to make it home. Where?"

"Not here, for God's sake! The cops'll be all over us."

His eyes glittered. "Then you'd better tell me somewhere close."

Faith could smell her own desire, just as rich with musk as his. "Make a left."

He obeyed, turning the convertible toward the outskirts of town a couple of blocks away.

She licked her lips and tried for a joke. "Those Burning Moon pheromones are a bitch."

"Yeah, but it's not just pheromones. I have to touch you." His voice dropped to a low, rumbling register. "He *hurt* you, dammit."

Now, that she could understand. When she'd seen him go airborne off the bumper of that truck, she'd felt the impact in her own heart. It made no sense—she barely knew him—and yet the reaction was too powerful to deny.

They had to slow down when they hit the elementary school's traffic, but at last they left it and the outskirts of Clarkston behind. The road wound through thick trees, leaves so green with early spring they almost glowed. The dogwoods were in bloom, their petals shimmering white against the green.

Spotting the dirt road she was looking for, Faith directed him down it. The sports car jolted over bumps and rocks as it followed the deeply rutted road past sweet gum, oaks, and spindly southern pines.

Finally they broke from the woods to see a lake spreading before them, glittering in the afternoon sunlight. Faith scanned it cautiously, but there was no one around.

Jim parked under a stand of trees, then got out without a word. His door slammed, the sound shouting his impatience. As she slid out her side, she felt wet heat between her thighs.

When they met in front of the car's nose, he dragged her into his arms. His mouth crushed down on hers in a kiss of hunger and desperation. Faith wrapped herself around him, savoring the feeling of his hard muscled body under her hands.

The memory of him flying off that bumper made her curl her nails into his skin. His tongue thrust into her mouth in strong, mating digs. Faith answered his desire with a hard roll of her hips. His erection felt like a length of solid steel against her belly.

Jim dragged his mouth away from hers and began kissing and biting down her chin to her neck. His strong hands found the hem of her T-shirt and jerked it upward so he could delve beneath.

"You scared the hell out of me," she said hoarsely. "Running in front of that truck like that."

"He had you by the throat," he growled back, one hand sliding under her shirt to discover bare, aching skin. "All I was thinking about was killing the son of a bitch."

"He's a sociopath," she agreed.

Impatient, he caught the hem of her shirt and jerked it up and over her head, revealing the lace bra cupping her breasts. "You wear too damn many clothes," Jim growled, and grabbed the cups of her bra in both hands. He jerked, and it tore.

For a moment he just looked down at her hard pink nipples, gilded by the afternoon sun. Then, with a low growl, he fastened his mouth over one and began to suck. Groaning in pleasure, Faith threaded her hands into his thick curling hair and abandoned herself to the stroke and swirl of his tongue.

Finally Jim drew back and gazed hungrily at her half-clad body. "Oh, man."

Faith grinned at the dazed lechery on his face. "Pervert."

"Only where you're concerned." He cupped one bare breast, rolling its nipple between skillful fingertips. With a groan of raw pleasure, she arched her back and shuttered her eyes.

Then he stepped against her, his hands closing over her backside. With easy strength, he boosted her onto the hood of the car. Instinctively, she grabbed at the knit fabric of his shirt as he shifted his grip to her waist and bent her backward. His mouth closed over the other nipple, suckling with honeyed greed.

Faith moaned as his tongue danced over the sensitive flesh, teasing her with shimmering waves of pleasure. Skillfully, he shaped her breast in his fingers, forcing the tip into an imploring peak he tormented with raking teeth. She fisted both hands in his hair and let her head tilt back, enjoying the hard suction.

As he teased her with delicious little bites and suckles, his free hand went to work on the zipper of her jeans.

Needing to touch him, Faith managed to grab a handful of his shirt and drag it up over his flat belly. He stepped back just long enough to let her pull it over his head. Tossing it aside, she looked at him.

He stood with his legs braced apart, his broad muscled chest heaving as he stared hot-eyed into her face. She breathed in and shuddered at his scent. He smelled like sex distilled in human form. He looked like some pagan god of passion, come to Earth to work his wiles on some hapless mortal girl.

"Is this just chemical?" Faith met his blazing eyes. "Is this just pheromones?"

"No." He stepped forward and unbuttoned her pants, then dragged them and her panties ruthlessly down her legs. "I've wanted you for weeks."

"We don't even know each other," she protested as he tossed her clothes aside and unbuttoned his pants.

"Yes, we do." He jerked down the waistband of his briefs and let his cock spill free. As she stared hungrily at its smooth, long width, he grabbed her by the waist, lifted her off the car hood, and turned her in his arms. Her hands hit the hood as he bent her over it and kicked her feet wide. "You know exactly who I am," he growled.

The thick, smooth head of his cock brushed the wet petals of her sex. "God!" Stiffening, she gasped as he began forcing himself inside. He felt huge in this position.

"We've fought side by side. We dared death together," he rumbled, working still more of the big shaft into her. "I've listened to your dreams and your fears and your pain."

"Jim . . ." she moaned.

He just kept coming, more and more of him sliding deeper and deeper as his relentless voice continued. "You're mine, and you know it. That's why it scared the shit out of you when you thought I'd been killed by that truck." He pulled out, silk and heat sliding endlessly through slick flesh. "And that's why I damn near died when that bastard grabbed you by the throat."

The words carried a powerful resonance, like the tolling of church bells. "No," she moaned. "It's just the Burning Moon."

"No." Jim dragged his cock out, then rammed it back in, ripping a cry of savage pleasure out of her mouth. "I'm not your ex, Faith." Another withdrawal, followed by another driving inward thrust. "I'm your Wolfmaster, and I'm your partner, and that's got nothing to do with hormones."

Faith, feeling the pleasure coiling in tight, glittering spirals in her sex, could only moan.

The slick velvet clamp of her sex around Jim's cock was the hottest thing he'd ever known in his life. He threaded one hand through her red hair and curled it into a fist. Drawing her head up and back, he leaned close, hunching hard, stroking his cock as deep in her heat as he could.

"Mine," he breathed in her ear, rolling his hips. "You're mine."

"God, you feel so thick," she moaned.

He smiled, more a baring of the teeth than anything else. "You make me that way." He rammed in another thrust and felt her writhe against him. Sliding one hand under her torso, he found her nipple, tugged it, twisted, and pounded in another thrust.

She cried out, convulsing. Coming.

Jim grinned savagely and started shafting her in long, relentless strokes that gave her no mercy. Her delicate inner sheathe rippled around him, milking hot surges of pleasure from his cock.

Until the orgasm he'd been seeking exploded through him in sweet, hot jets of fire. He bellowed, surging against her one last time. Coming. "Mine!" he roared, knowing it was true whether she was ready to admit it or not.

He could feel it in his bones.

Limping, bloodied, Reynolds finally decided it was safe to stop running.

He spotted a likely looking house and staggered behind it. He felt so drained, for a panicked moment he wasn't sure he could call the magic. Then, at last, it answered him, slowly at first, then in a white-hot surge that twisted and transformed.

Returning him to human form.

Wearily, he staggered to the steps of the house and sat down, letting his head hang. Despite the Change, he felt exhausted—and more than a little terrified.

He'd royally fucked that one up. Weston and the werewolf had suckered him, pure and simple, and he'd fallen for it.

Celestine was going to have his ass.

Uneasily, Reynolds considered the implications. The vampire had her grail, which meant she'd probably want to start turning the cops tonight. She'd need a death to work that spell.

And he damned well didn't want it to be his.

Fear gripped him with cold and sickly fingers. After he'd become a werewolf, Reynolds had felt like a furry superman.

Hell, that's damn near what he was. He'd even taken on Celestine's vampire enemies and handed them their collective asses. It had felt as though nothing could stand against him.

Until this afternoon.

Fighting other werewolves was a whole 'nother can of worms. They were just as fast as he was, just as strong, and every bit as nasty. It was galling, particularly considering that one of those weres was a woman. If they came after him again—and they would—he wasn't sure he'd be able to beat them off again.

Unless . . . Reynolds's eyes narrowed as a sudden idea pierced his sense of failure.

What if he had werewolf reinforcements, too?

Cautiously, then with growing enthusiasm, Reynolds considered the idea. All he had to do was bite a few cops. True, they probably wouldn't be happy about it, especially since it would mean they'd lose the chance to become immortal magic-using vampires, but tough shit. He needed them.

And once they were all in it together, they'd have no

choice except to embrace his leadership. Reynolds, after all, was the only one who knew how to be a werewolf.

Then he and his team could hunt Weston and her werewolf buddy down, and Celestine would have her sacrifices.

Yeah. That would work.

Pleased, he rose from the stoop and started the walk back toward the police department.

Somebody was about to get the surprise of his life.

Feeling sated, almost boneless, Faith relaxed back into the leather of the convertible's seat as Jim drove them home. She glanced at him, admiring the pure male line of his profile, the mussed lock of dark hair falling onto his forehead.

"Mine!" Remembering his possessive roar, she smiled. It felt a little smug.

Except . . .

The whole incident had been a product of the Burning Moon, mixed with a healthy dose of adrenalin from a painfully close call.

Faith frowned, some of her lush lassitude draining away. She couldn't afford to let herself forget that none of this rosy emotion was real.

Particularly not since it would be all too easy to fall in love with Jim London. Losing him would hurt a hell of a lot more than catching Ron with that dispatcher ever had.

And she really didn't want to go there.

FOURTEEN

George Ayers sat at his desk, lost in a pleasant dream of
immortality and power. Tonight Celestine would begin
changing them all, and he fully expected to be the first to
drink from Korbal's Grail.

Of course, there'd be a price to pay. He'd be a vampire,
which meant no more leisurely Sunday steak dinners. On the
face of it, drinking blood seemed fairly revolting, but God
knew Celestine seemed to enjoy it. And there was something
erotically wicked about the idea of entrancing young women
into letting him do whatever he wanted to them.

His wife would probably feel differently.

He'd originally intended to let Lucy drink from the
grail, too, but thinking about it, he wasn't sure he wanted to
spend his immortality with her. She could be a bit of a
bitch. Besides, it was for damn sure there would be no seduction of pretty young things if Lucy had a vampire's
powers.

Brooding, he stared at her portrait, which sat on his
desk next to those of their two children. An elegant, cool

blonde, she'd taken care of herself over their twenty-five-year marriage, weighing scarcely more than she had the day they'd married. Still, it was a fact that things were no longer so firm and tight as they'd once been.

Maybe he should just put a spell on her to make her give him a divorce. And forget alimony. No way in hell was he giving up half his salary. He didn't make enough as it was.

His gaze shifted to his children's pictures. Fifteen-year-old Bonnie and twelve-year-old Rich resembled their mother more than they did him, and their constant bickering drove him nuts. He wouldn't mind seeing them only every other weekend or so.

Sitting back in his chair, he tried to decide whether to pay child support.

Oh, hell, it would do them all good to get jobs.

His office door swung open, startling him into a guilty jump. Reynolds stepped in, looking surprisingly white and nervy for a man who'd acquired a distinct swagger since becoming a werewolf. "Dammit, Reynolds, don't come in my office without knocking," George snapped, annoyed.

Yesterday he would have hesitated to say anything to the bastard, but by tonight, he'd be a vampire. Then he'd be the one on top again, and the werewolf would be kissing his ass.

Reynolds shrugged his shoulders. "Sorry." But he didn't look even remotely repentant as he closed the door. His expression was tight, his gaze glittering with an odd blend of determination and excitement.

George eyed him. "What the hell are you doing back, anyway?" Reynolds's shift had ended an hour ago. "I thought you were going over to Celestine's."

"There's something we need to talk about." He moved around the desk, a tight, ugly smile on his face.

Something about the calculating look in his eyes made George rest a wary hand on the butt of his gun. "Yeah? What?"

"This." Between one step and the next, Reynolds Changed, his body suddenly going massive, filling the small room with fur, claws, and the feral musk of magic. His jaws gaped, tongue lolling between white, knife-edged fangs.

With a startled shout, George lunged up and out of his seat, drawing his weapon as the werewolf dove at him. The desk chair crashed backward behind him. He stumbled over it and fell flat on his back with a yell. His gun went flying. He rolled, scrabbling desperately for the weapon. Before he could recover it, an enormous clawed hand grabbed the back of his jacket, jerking him upright toward Reynolds's gaping jaws. Bones grated, as the werewolf bit down on George's shoulder.

Bellowing in pain, he kicked furiously at his captor. The werewolf dropped him, watching as he scrambled away. *He doesn't even look pissed off,* George thought, stunned, one hand clamped to his bleeding shoulder. "What the hell did you do that for?"

"Chief!" Footsteps running in the hall—other cops racing to the rescue. Too fucking late.

Frank Granger shoved open the door. "Chief, are you . . . ?" He barely had time for a yelp as Reynolds cleared George's desk and plowed into him. The pair crashed against the opposite hallway wall. Frank screamed. A gun went off amid curses and thumps.

George didn't move, staring numbly at the bright-red blood spilling down the blue wool sleeve of his suit.

"Keith, what the fuck are you doing?" Sergeant Young bellowed. More running footsteps, accompanied by male shouts, curses, and questions. George dimly remembered the sergeant had called a meeting of the second-shift cops.

A woman screamed—the new clerk, Doris Miller, a pretty little thing George had earmarked as the first girl he'd want to bite as a vampire.

Heavy thuds as Reynolds plowed down the hall in werewolf form. Shouts. More gunfire. The girl screamed like a fire siren. George wished she'd shut the fuck up. It was too late for them all anyway.

I'm going to be a werewolf.

Faith was being too damned quiet.

Jim threw another look at her as they sat in the living room. CNN was detailing its usual litany of disasters, but though her eyes were fixed on the ancient television, she didn't seem to be registering anything. Her expression was brooding, and her scent made it clear what she was brooding about. There was the lingering odor of sexual arousal, of course, but overlaying that was a hint of anxiety.

He'd freaked her out with that "Mine" of his.

Frowning, he turned his own attention to the set, though he wasn't registering much, either. In retrospect, he probably should have kept that bellow to himself.

But it was true, dammit. They belonged together, if Faith could just look past her own emotional scars long enough to see it.

Though, come to think of it, there was one way to reassure her.

The Spirit Link.

Jim went still, startled by the thought. Normally werewolf couples formed a Link only after they married, but there was no reason he and Faith couldn't do it now. It would even carry a number of tactical advantages.

But more importantly, once they were Linked, she'd be able to see into his soul to the man he really was. She'd realize he loved her, and her doubts and fears would be put to rest. Ron would no longer stand between them.

Still, it was a big step.

Restlessly, he rose from his seat and looked at her. "I'm getting a beer. Want one?"

Faith muttered a refusal. He stalked into the kitchen and opened the fridge. For a moment he stood there, not really seeing its contents.

If they Linked, they'd be bound together on such a deep level, if one died, the other would follow soon after. That was one reason the Direkind didn't enter into such unions lightly.

Jim grabbed a beer and walked back into the living room as he opened it. Brooding, he looked over at her.

Faith sat with those long legs stretched out in front of her, crossed at the ankle, her tough, graceful hands laced over her flat belly. Even given her troubled expression, her profile was beautiful, from high forehead to stubborn little chin. Her lower lip pouted slightly, tempting as a fresh peach. He wanted to suckle it.

Yeah, he realized. He wanted a Spirit Link with her.

The next time he yelled "Mine!" he wanted to hear her yell it right back.

George hurt all over. His shoulder ached like a bad tooth, and sweat poured off him as he stood with his six co-victims.

After the attack, Reynolds had forced them into the department's van and driven them all out here, to a burned-out textile mill on the worst side of town. Now, as the sunlight of late afternoon threw the mill stack's shadow across the ground like a long, bony finger, they all stood bleeding and resentful.

For a moment there following the attack, it had been a toss-up whether they'd go with him or try to shoot him again. But since everybody knew shooting him was pretty much a waste of time—he'd just heal and hurt them some more—they'd finally gotten in the van.

Besides George himself, the victims included five second-shift cops: Frank Granger, Sergeant Randy Young, Tim Morrison, Detective Gordon Taylor, and Dave Green, who'd replaced Weston on the second shift. Last was twenty-four-year-old Doris Miller, the part-time records clerk Reynolds had evidently bitten solely because she was about to call 911.

Now the girl stood huddled, hugging her bleeding hand with tears rolling silently down her cheeks.

It was a damn good thing Hazel Shelly had taken the afternoon off to go to the dentist, or she'd probably be getting ready to turn fuzzy with the rest of them.

"I can't believe you did this to us, you bastard," George snarled at Reynolds. "What the fuck possessed you?"

The werewolf shrugged his shoulders. He'd resumed human form. Unlike the rest of them, he looked regulation neat in his dark blue uniform, without a bite or bullet wound to be seen. "Hey, you were planning to become vampires anyway. I figure one monster's as good as another."

At that, Doris sobbed loudly before covering her mouth and giving them all a wide-eyed, panicked stare. Reynolds stared back, wearing an unpleasant expression of speculation.

"We were going to be fucking immortal," Frank snarled, pain evidently making him reckless. "We were going to be able to cast fucking spells and get all the women we wanted! Now we're going to be *furry!*"

"You'll also be the strongest, meanest bastards on the planet—other than me," Reynolds told him coldly. "Quit bitching, you pussy."

"You—"

"Frank, shut up," Ayers snapped, glaring the other to silence. "Now isn't the time."

But once they'd all changed, he promised himself, they'd gang up on the furry psycho and rip him apart. Reynolds was, by God, going to pay for this.

Doris edged away from them, horror in her eyes, as blood dripped from her mangled hand.

George glowered at her, stung by that *you're all monsters* stare. Idiot. Reynolds was the fucking monster. "Where do you think you're going?"

Her pale mouth worked as tears ran down her face. "I just—I need to call my mom. And my hand hurts."

He wasn't in the mood to listen to her whine. "Join the club. As for calling Mommy, I don't think so. Like it or not, you're in this with the rest of us."

Her big hazel eyes flicked from one to the other. "In what?" Her voice was so faint, he could barely hear her.

Nobody answered.

"How long is this going to take, anyway?" Frank demanded coldly.

Reynolds shrugged. "Took me about an hour before the bite kicked in. But that was me."

"Did it hurt?" The question came from Tim Morrison, a rookie who'd joined the force the year before. His face was almost as white as Doris's.

The werewolf curled a malicious lip. "Yeah."

"Asshole," Frank muttered.

Reynolds straightened away from the fender of the car he leaned against, the movement so sudden Doris flinched. "We need to get a couple of things straight before anybody gets any bright ideas." His gaze locked on George's, cold as an ice pick. "I'm going to be the leader of this little pack, got that? You do what I say."

The bite seemed to be pouring acid through George's blood. Pissed and reckless, he sneered. "Says who?"

"Says Celestine."

That thought pierced even the pain with its ugly implications. "You're full of shit. You saying she authorized this?"

Reynolds didn't so much as flicker an eyelash. "She needs more werewolf muscle."

It was just the kind of double-cross Celestine was more than capable of pulling, too. Which meant they didn't dare jump him. If they killed the vampire's pet when he was acting on her orders, she'd gut the lot of them. George frowned, feeling cheated. Like it or not, they'd better keep their collective hands off until they knew for sure.

"Shit!" Suddenly Tim bent double, his face contorted in a spasm of pain.

Taylor grunted, his beefy face paling as he grabbed his bitten thigh. Others groaned or shouted. George gritted his teeth as the pain intensified to a raking, burning blaze.

"It hurts!" Doris moaned. "God, it hurts! What's happening? Somebody get a doctor!"

A broad, unpleasant grin spread across Reynolds's face, as he watched the girl drop writhing to the debris-littered ground. "And on that note, I think it'd be wise to get furry myself. Show you how it's done." George figured the bastard was probably afraid of being caught human when they all changed.

With that, Reynolds transformed, his body growing to its full towering werewolf height, sable fur spreading over his skin in a silken wave. This time George actually saw it happening—for about half a second before fire roared up from his own guts.

The pain ripped a scream from him before he could drag it back. George bent double, vaguely aware of the others dropping to the ground to writhe in agonized convulsions.

Doris started shrieking, her voice high with agony. Light blazed across the clearing.

Before the chief could tell her to shut the hell up, Something came barreling out of nowhere and slammed into him—something not physical, yet huge and glowing with power. It closed clawed fists in his guts, ripped, twisted his arms and legs like taffy, pulling him mercilessly. He burned, vomited, pissed himself at the agony.

And then . . .

Like a light going out, the pain was gone.

George collapsed, shocked and shaking, bracing himself on hands and knees as he fought to get his bearings.

That idiot Doris was still screaming, and the whole area was lit up with blazing blue light. Alarmed, George turned toward her.

The clerk was burning like a witch at the stake. Ghostly blue flames leaped from her eyes and mouth as she screeched. "Help me! Somebody help me!" Her mouth twisted into an animal howl. "Hel . . ."

Then she was gone. Vanished. All that was left was tiny

blue sparks, floating on the breeze like the remnants of a campfire.

"Shit," George breathed. His voice sounded all wrong, a deep, growling rasp. Startled, he looked down at himself.

His body was huge, covered in black and gray fur.

Staring wildly around, he realized he was surrounded by werewolves—two blondes he thought were Tim and Dave, a couple of heavyset ones that might be Young and Taylor, a red-furred one that had to be Granger. And Reynolds, who stood staring at the spot where Doris had disappeared. "Huh," the werewolf said. "Wonder what the fuck happened to her?"

"We need to talk," Jim said.

In the middle of fixing sandwiches for them both, Faith looked around. Her heart sank at the expression of determination on his handsome face. Something told her this wasn't a conversation she was going to enjoy.

She hid her alarm and turned to put the sandwiches on two plates with chips and pickle spears. "About what?"

He got a couple of beers out of the fridge. "Us."

Oh, great. Just great. "You want to have sex again?" She carried the sandwiches to the table.

A grin flashed across that handsome face. "Yeah, actually. But first I want to talk."

"So, talk." Faith sat, watching as he did the same.

"There's this werewolf thing." He picked up his BLT and took a healthy bite.

Her lips twitched. "Another one?" She crunched into her sandwich, the wolf in her growling in approval at the taste of the crispy meat.

" 'Fraid so. But this one could actually work to our advantage. And right now, we need all the advantages we can get."

"Granted." She picked up her beer, took a sip. "What kind of 'werewolf thing' are we talking about here?"

He hesitated. "It's a little complicated."

"Jim, it's been my experience that all werewolf things are complicated." She licked mayo off her lips and tried to ignore the heated glance he gave her mouth.

"Good point." He went silent and applied himself to his sandwich, obviously working up to whatever he was about to say. Oh, peachy. Anything that required that much buildup was probably bad news.

"My people have something called the Spirit Link," Jim announced after several meditative bites. "It's a bond couples can form—another one of those magical gifts Merlin gave us. Magekind couples have the Truebond, which lets them read each other's thoughts, but ours is more spiritual and less invasive."

"Couples?" *As in married couples?* She put her beer down with a thump. "Jim. . . ."

He just charged right over her interruption as if reluctant to give her an opening. "We don't read each other's minds like Truebonded Magekind.

"A Spirit Linked couple senses each other's emotions and intentions—you just instinctively know what your partner is going to do."

Curious despite herself, Faith asked, "Just how do you go about forming one of these things?"

He shrugged. "As I understand it, you just kind of transform together, calling your power while touching. Then you just sort of . . . blend your magic, and the Link forms. People have been known to Spirit Link during combat." Jim gave her a grim smile. "It's supposed to come in handy."

"Yeah," she drawled, "I can see where it would."

Jim cleared his throat and put down his sandwich. He actually looked more nervous than he had when he'd told her about the bite. Then he'd been afraid for her, but now he was visibly worried about her reaction. "It carries physical advantage in a fight, too. You basically blend your magic during the moment you transform, and it strengthens

you both. You don't have to worry about losing control of
the magic, either. My dad says you steady each other—"

"Are you asking me to marry you?"

To her amazement, he actually blushed. Then he tilted
up that strong chin and gave her a defiant look. "Yeah."

Ron had proposed on one knee, flipping open a little
velvet box that had probably cost him two months' salary.
Of course, it had meant exactly nothing, so the cost of the
ring scarcely mattered.

"You can't be serious," Faith told him with a growing
sense of panic, pushing her sandwich aside. "We've known
each other less than a week. You can't just—"

"I'm in love with you."

The bald words took her breath. She stared at him for a
helpless moment before she managed to speak. "The Burning Moon."

His steady, demanding gaze didn't even shift. "I started
falling for you the first time I saw you."

"At Johnson's Kennel? Jim, you were a dog."

"No matter how many legs I happen to have, I'm always
a man." He sighed as she stood and started clearing off the
table. "Look, I know it's a big step. Dire Wolves mate for
life. And when one member of a Spirit Linked couple dies,
the other usually follows soon after."

"Well, now that's comforting!"

"I realize you need to think about this."

With an effort, she softened her tone. "Actually, I'm
pretty sure I don't."

His silver gaze bored into hers. "Then consider this.
You would never have to wonder if I was deceiving you.
Even if I was the kind of bastard Ron was, you'd know my
emotions. You'd feel what I feel."

"Jim, that's what I'm afraid of."

The werewolves howled as Sergeant Randy Young swaggered up to a pine tree, wrapped his furry arms around it,

and heaved. Wood groaned as if the pine were protesting. Roots popped and cracked. With a triumphant roar, Young ripped the tree out of the ground and let it fall with a thunderous crash.

The heavyset were laughed, his jaws gapping as the others clapped their big clawed hands. As Reynolds had expected, they had begun to see the possibilities in being werewolves.

Immortality would be nice, but being Supermen didn't exactly suck either.

"All this," Reynolds called over their shouts, "and you can still enjoy a good steak—without bursting into flames when the sun comes up."

Frank's laughter cut off. Reynolds concealed his rising tension. He'd expected problems from that one—Frank was a hothead.

Ayers's calculating stare was no surprise, either. The chief was looking for a weakness. Reynolds had to make sure he didn't find any.

"That's all well and good." Frank stalked across the ruins toward him. He stopped muzzle to muzzle with Reynolds and peeled his lips back from his fangs. "But you didn't fucking ask. You just jumped us!"

Reynolds smiled faintly, coldly.

Then he popped his claws and punched them right into Frank's gut. The werewolf bent double with a strangled cry of agony and collapsed in a heap.

"Jesus!" Taylor gasped.

Coolly, Reynolds knelt and rolled Frank over on his back. Panting, the were looked down in horror at the deep, bleeding rips in his belly. "What's wrong with you, you fucking psycho!"

"What did you expect, dumbass? You challenged me." Reynolds gave him a deliberately chilling smile. "I figure you're gonna bleed out in half an hour tops."

Frank stared up at him in shock. "You bastard!"

"The good news is, if you Change right now, you'll survive." He grinned. "Oh, wait—you don't know how, do you?"

The werewolf threw back his head and whined in pain. "Shit, Keith. What the fuck do you want?"

Reynolds bared his teeth. "Obedience." He looked up at the horrified weres standing around them. "From now on, I'm in charge."

"Yeah. Whatever, man. How do I Change?"

Point made, Reynolds told him.

Jim had offered Faith his very soul, and she'd kicked him in the teeth.

Anger buzzed through him like a high voltage electric line, snarling and popping. Almost steaming with it, he channel surfed on the ancient TV, but there was nothing on except crap. Stupid crap. Depressing crap.

He hit an image of Bogart in a tux, brooding over a glass of whiskey. "Of all the gin joints in all the world . . ."

"Sap," he snarled at the screen, and changed the channel.

"Want a beer?" Faith called from the kitchen doorway, looking guilty.

"No." The growl sounded distinctly basso. It occurred to him he was a little too close to Changing, but he didn't give a shit.

Something jangled cheerfully from his pants pocket. He knew from the ring it was the encrypted cell Charlie had given him.

Great. Just great. He dug it out of his pocket. "London."

"Why the hell haven't you reported in? I was starting to wonder if the fucking rogue had eaten you."

Charlie sounded almost as foul tempered as he felt. Perfect. "That pussy? Not likely."

"Is he dead?"

"Almost got him today. Had him on the ropes, but he rabbited."

"Why the hell did you let him do that? You should have chased him."

"I did. Got hit by a car."

Charlie started cursing with considerable verve and vulgarity. "Screw it. I'm sending Jennings."

"Dammit, I said I'd take care of him!"

"Then do it! Or are you waiting for him to die of old age?" The phone went dead.

"Asshole." Jim stuffed it in his pocket and looked up to find Faith watching him warily. "I'm tired of fucking around with Reynolds. Any ideas how we can find him?"

"I don't . . ." She broke off, frowning. "I seem to recall that he likes to get a beer and a sandwich at the Silver Bullet."

"The bar where Tony got into that brawl?"

"Yeah." She shrugged. "The owner lets cops eat free. And there's a woman he sees there—Sheri Miller. Waitress, about five-six, blond." She held her hands out in front of her, cupping large, imaginary tits. "Gets very big tips."

Jim indulged in a cynical snort. "And he loves her for her mind. Sounds like just the woman I need to talk to." He got up and headed for the door.

"Wait a minute—I'm not going to the Bullet in shorts." Faith made for the stairs, obviously intending to change.

He didn't break step. "You're not going at all. They know you there, remember?"

"Now, wait just one minute!" Hurrying after him, she caught him by one shoulder and turned him around. There was outrage and worry in her eyes. He felt just petty enough to enjoy it. "You're not going after him alone."

"Aren't I? I'm the Alpha, Faith. I'm more than capable of handling him with no assistance whatsoever."

"I don't care." She folded her arms and glowered at him. "There's no way in hell I'm letting you go against Reynolds without backup. Any rookie cop would know better."

"I'm your Wolfmaster, Faith. You don't 'let' me do anything." He stalked out the front door and slammed it behind him, then bounded down the porch steps. He didn't look around when he heard the door open, instead striding toward the convertible.

As he vaulted over the driver's door, a flash of red leaped into the opposite seat.

Faith, in Irish setter form, curled a defiant lip.

"If you shed on those seats, you're vacuuming it up." He started the car with a violent twist of his wrist.

FIFTEEN

Korbal stood in the hallway, staring down at the mangled bodies of the grail guards. They looked as if they'd been ripped apart by wild animals.

A sensation of sick dread spread over him, not for the guards' deaths—the incompetent bastards had failed him—but for what he knew he'd find inside the grail chamber.

It was the end of everything.

Mechanically, he stepped over the bodies of his men and looked through the chamber's open double doors. As he'd known it would be, the grail was gone.

His knees went weak, and he sagged against the door-frame.

The battle for the grail had broken off at dawn. Korbal and his men had fought the Magekind to the last possible second, until the sun weighed on him like a lead coat as its radiation ate into his magic.

At last Arthur and his men had fled. Even their witches had gone with them just before the sunlight rendered them all powerless. With bare seconds to spare, Korbal had conjured a lair behind the nearest wall and transported himself into it.

But the battle had been only a distraction. While Arthur's men kept him busy, Arthur's pet monster had taken the grail and killed his men.

The last time the creature had attacked, five of his best guards had gated after it. They'd never returned, and his attempts to follow their magical trail had been blocked by their killer.

Two had survived, only because they'd stayed behind to watch the grail. They had described an assault by a wolf-like monster who had appeared out of thin air to slaughter two men before gating away.

Whatever it was, the creature had not been one of Geirolf's creations. Its lingering scent trail smelled of the Mageverse, not the demon's dark magic. Logically, it had to be one of Arthur's.

Korbal had no doubt the creature had been responsible for the theft of the grail. The same overwhelming scent of wolf and Mageverse filled the corridor, mixing with the blood reek from his murdered men.

The only question was, why weren't Korbal and all his people dead? The Magekind should have destroyed the grail the moment they had it in their possession. Why were they holding off?

A gasp of horror drew his attention. Glancing over his shoulder, he met the eyes of the female vampire who stood in the corridor.

"The grail?" she asked, her voice high with fear.

"Gone." He lifted one hand in a complicated gesture, sending out a spell to the minds of his people. "Arm and armor yourselves. We meet in the Sanctuary."

The wind whipped Faith's long ears and combed cool fingers through her Irish setter fur, but she was too focused on Jim to pay it much attention.

Just like a man, she told herself. He hadn't gotten his way, and now he was acting all pissy.

Except she kept seeing that flash of hurt in those pale eyes when she'd turned him down. That wasn't just wounded ego.

Oh, some of it was, she decided, watching a fine muscle flex in his handsome jaw. And she really couldn't blame him. After all, Jim had asked her to share something more intimate than marriage, and she'd blown him off.

Brooding, she rested her chin on the window and watched the night zoom by.

Jim had offered to Link himself to her so thoroughly, he wouldn't survive her death. If any other man had made an offer like that, she'd think he was nuts.

But Jim meant it. He'd decided it was the right thing to do, and he seemed to feel no doubt at all.

Then again, he rarely seemed to doubt himself. He just determined what to do and did it, no second thoughts. No wavering. Which was fine as long as he was right, but what if he was wrong?

Faith lifted her head and turned to watch his big hands on the wheel as he took a curve with easy skill. He was so damned good, she felt no hesitancy about putting her life into his hands. He was one of those rare leaders she'd follow through any door he cared to kick down.

But love was different. As much as she hated to admit it, she'd loved Ron with a blind, hot passion. Just the way he looked at her in those first days made her feel good about herself. For a woman who'd always felt too tall and just slightly too masculine, there'd been something highly seductive about feeling so feminine.

Come to think of it, she wasn't sure which she'd really loved—Ron or the way he made her feel.

Either way, it hadn't lasted. Ron had the attention span of an amorous hamster, and soon he was off to other conquests. Subconsciously, she'd felt him slipping away even before she'd known it for sure.

Of course, Jim was a lot more man than Ron had ever been, in virtually every way. Maybe that was what scared her. Nobody could have held Ron for long—that was just the way he was wired. But Jim . . . If she lost Jim, that would say something about her, wouldn't it? Something she really didn't want to know.

So okay, she'd been really clumsy in her refusal. He'd caught her off guard. But that didn't mean she'd been wrong.

The thing to do was keep it light and professional, Faith decided. Gently make it clear to him that she wasn't interested in anything more permanent than a little passion and catching bad guys—without stomping his ego. She could do that.

How hard could it be?

Korbal looked out over the angry, fearful faces of his congregation. "Arthur's monster has taken the grail. We must go to Avalon and recover it, or we die."

The group burst into appalled shouts.

"Avalon?" one bellowed over the din. "You want us to follow Arthur to his very stronghold? Are you insane?"

"What other choice do we have?" Korbal demanded coldly. "They have obviously not yet destroyed the grail— we'd all be dead if they had. As long as we live, there is some chance we can track and recover it."

"You don't know they took it to Avalon. You don't know they took it at all!"

"Don't be more stupid than you can help," Korbal snarled. "They attacked us. While we were distracted, a creature that smelled of the Mageverse took our grail. Do you think this is coincidence?"

"But—Avalon!" a female vampire whined. "Even Geirolf himself did not dare attack Arthur's capital!"

"I assure you, he'd have attacked it if he'd faced what we do—immediate destruction if we don't." Korbal's hands curled into fists as he considered incinerating the twit where she stood. Unfortunately, they needed every fighter they had, even fools. "Would you rather stand here dithering while they destroy the grail and wipe us all out? Or would you rather fight and seize the chance to survive?"

"It's not much of a chance," another woman said dryly.

"It's better than nothing!" This was a man, lifting his voice in a shout. "Korbal is right. I'd rather die fighting than wringing my hands. But we've got to move now!"

The crowd went silent, and Korbal saw his chance to seize control again. "Unit leaders, start generating your gates. We march on Avalon!" He raised his voice in his congregation's battle cry. "Geirolf lives in us!"

"We live in Geirolf!" they shouted back. Korbal hid his relief.

He had them again.

The Silver Bullet was a long, low white cinder block building with flashing neon signs hanging in the windows. Across one side, a bad mural depicted a cowboy riding a bucking bronco in chalky, gaudy florescent paint. It was lit by three floodlights, one of which was either broken or had burned out. Knowing the Bullet's clientele, it was probably busted.

In the patch of darkness left by the absent spot, a woman stood smoking a cigarette. From past experience, Faith knew Sheri Miller got off shift about this time. She'd said once that she liked to have a smoke to steady her nerves after a night spent dealing with amorous drunks.

Sheri was a pretty woman, so petite and generously curved Faith always felt like an Amazon standing beside her. She and Reynolds had gone together hot and heavy for most of the year Faith had been in Clarkston. He was nowhere to be seen now, though.

Faith waited for Jim to park the convertible, then hopped over the door and trotted across the parking lot.

Sheri loved dogs; she'd never failed to give Rambo a pat. With any luck, she'd react the same way to Faith's Irish setter, giving Jim a conversation opener.

"Oh, aren't you the gorgeous thing!" As she'd hoped, Sheri tossed aside her cigarette and dropped to her knees to give the dog a good ear rub. "You're beautiful! Yes, you are!"

Faith froze, feeling a little uncomfortable as the woman stroked her ears and rubbed her head. It felt . . . surprisingly good, if deeply weird.

"Better watch out," Jim said, strolling up. "She's a heartbreaker."

Sheri looked up with a moment's wariness at the strange male voice, then blinked as she registered Jim's stunning looks. A hint of calculation entered her smile. "She yours?"

"Or I'm hers. We're still working that part out." He gave Sheri that lazily seductive grin of his.

She rose to her feet with one more absent pat for Faith and offered Jim her hand. "Sheri Miller."

"Jim Galloway." The last being a cover identity. He turned to look out across the parking lot, where the moon was just beginning to rise. "Pretty night."

"Yeah. Better enjoy it now—it'll be hotter than blazes in a couple of weeks." She studied him with dazzled eyes, scanning from his handsome face to broad shoulders and down his narrow hips. "You're not from around here." Her tone said she'd have noticed him by now if he had been.

"Nope. New in town." He leaned a shoulder against the wall, his torso bending in an easy masculine curve. "I don't know a single soul."

Sheri took the opening and ran with it, giving him an eager smile. "You know me."

"I'd certainly like to." He hooded those seductive eyes and purred, "But a pretty girl like you probably has a boyfriend."

The laughter vanished from her face. "I did, but not anymore. He dumped me for this witch." She tossed her blond hair. "Probably just as well, considering some of the shit they're into." Despite the defiant tone, there was pain in her blue eyes.

"Drugs?"

"Nah, he's a cop. That's what makes it so bad." She forced a flirtatious smile. "But you wouldn't be interested in that."

"Actually, I am." He crossed one muscular ankle over the other, the picture of indolent power. "I'm a reporter for the *Atlanta Mirror*. I'm here looking into Tony Shay's death."

Faith's head whipped up, but fortunately Sheri didn't seem to notice.

"A reporter?" The waitress looked uneasy. "Shay— that's the guy they found dead behind the Bullet."

"The cops say some of your customers did it. But the paper here said it was Satanists. What do you think?"

"Look, I don't want to talk about any of that. I need to get home." She turned to walk off.

"I won't use your name." He reached out and touched her shoulder, a light graze of the fingers that stopped her in her tracks. Uncertain, Sheri looked back at him, and he gave her that warm, seductive smile again. "I just want to talk to you. You know Keith Reynolds, and you know he's involved in this up to his neck."

A car pulled into the parking lot, tires crunching on the gravel. Sheri's head whipped toward it. Nervously, she licked her lips. "I don't want to be seen talking to no reporter."

"We can go somewhere else. Your place. Or we can get a cup of coffee."

She shifted from foot to sneakered foot, trying to make up her mind. "You got ID?"

Shit, Faith thought. *That blows that.*

"Sure." He straightened away from the wall and started toward the Jag, the two of them at his heals. Faith noticed Sheri's gaze dropping to his backside and lingering. Apparently Faith wasn't the only one who thought Jim had an outstanding ass.

They reached the car and waited while Jim slid in and opened the glove compartment, pulling out a laminated card on a neck chain.

Where had he acquired *that*?

He handed the card to Sheri, who looked it over and handed it back. She hesitated a moment. "I guess we can go to my house."

Jim nodded. "Sounds good. Want to take my car?"

She looked back at the Bullet's door nervously. "No. I'll take my own."

"Great. I'll follow you."

A moment later, they were driving through Clarkston, following the taillights of Sheri's battered Toyota.

Faith sat in the front, her head buzzing with a frustrating set of questions and no way to voice them in dog form. She didn't dare transform, either, because Sheri might look back and catch her.

"My cousin works at the *Atlanta Mirror*," Jim said, apparently reading her mind, "He made me a set of credentials, just in case I needed them. And since reporters can ask all the nosy questions they want without raising any eyebrows . . ." He shrugged. "I'd considered using the reporter thing as my cover to begin with, but the chief knows me, so that was out."

Up ahead, the Toyota's taillights took the turn into a trailer park. Jim followed, driving down the narrow road between the mobile homes. Most were single-wides, aging and dingy, surrounded by abandoned children's toys, battered cars, and bicycles lying on their sides. Lights glowed from narrow windows, as voices rose in shouts, arguments, and laughter.

Sheri stopped in front of a blue and white double-wide. After pulling in behind her, Jim and Faith followed her to the trailer's cinder block steps. As Sheri dug for her keys, a frantic, high-pitched barking sounded from inside the mobile home.

Sheri gave them an apologetic look. "That's Snowball, my poodle. Your dog won't go after her?"

Jim reached down to give Faith an infuriating pat on the head. "Red's too well-mannered to eat her hostess, aren't you, Red?"

Depends. The attempted sarcasm emerged as a soft woof.

But when Sheri got the door open, Snowball spotted Faith and Jim through the screen. Her doggy brown eyes widened. She whirled and fled, yelping, painted pink toenails clicking on the vinyl floor, her white puffball of a tail tucked firmly against her woolly butt. Apparently Snowball knew a couple of werewolves when she smelled them.

"Wow." Sheri frowned after her. "She never did that before. I've seen her try to jump a Doberman."

Jim shot Faith a significant look. Faith laughed, though it ended up sounding like another woof.

She was still grinning when she followed Jim and Sheri inside. "Want a beer?" Sheri asked her handsome guest. "Or I've got Jack Daniels."

Faith narrowed her eyes. What was the waitress planning to do—get him drunk and take advantage of him? She suppressed a growl.

"Beer's fine." Jim gave Sheri an easy smile and sauntered into the narrow living room.

The trailer looked like every other mobile home Faith had ever been in over the course of her law enforcement career. The kitchen was cramped, with avocado appliances and green vinyl flooring that was peeling in places.

The long, narrow living room held a brown plaid couch and a couple of worn armchairs, one of them patched with silver duct tape. The carpet was a gold shag in desperate need of a good cleaning. Faith lay down on it cautiously, trying not to inhale the sour smell from an old spill.

Jim and Sheri exchanged chitchat while the waitress opened a couple of Buds. Finally they settled down on the couch together. Sheri's knee brushed Jim's. Faith suppressed a growl.

"So what can you tell me about what happened to Shay?" he asked.

Sheri drew back and took a sip of her beer as if buying time to think. "It wasn't our customers that killed that guy, no matter what the chief says."

"So who was it?" He looked at her, his silver gaze steady and honest.

Sheri was no more immune to it than Faith herself. She cleared her throat. "Maybe the paper was right."

"About what?"

She licked her lips, her gaze anxious. "About it being magic."

Jim said nothing, letting the silence build with a skill Faith had to admire. He might be an artist by profession, but he knew how to work a witness like a cop.

Sheri finally gave in to the need to fill the silence. "I'm hearing stuff that ain't natural. Crazy stuff. Like about the guy they found with his guts ripped out."

"What about him?"

"They're saying he was killed by a werewolf. People say they saw it. Big fucker. Head like a wolf. And claws. Running through town in the moonlight." There was something haunted in her eyes that suggested she wasn't just reporting a rumor. She forced a laugh and looked away. "Like I said, crazy stuff."

"Maybe it's not as crazy as it sounds." Jim's voice was calm and quiet, and his gaze was sympathetic.

Sheri studied him a wary moment before she went on, talking faster and faster as she gained confidence that he wouldn't laugh at her. "And there's other stuff, too. Like rumors about people being fine one day, and the next they're walking around like zombies with their souls sucked out."

"I heard something about that."

Sheri looked down at the beer in her lap and began to nervously peel the label away with her long red fingernails. The polish was cracking. "I did see something one night. Something . . . weird."

He waited patiently, his gaze encouraging.

Finally she worked up the courage to finish her story. "There's this old house outside town. It was some kind of plantation or something. They say it goes all the way back to the Revolution. Burned down five, six years ago. Some kid arsonist." She raked the label down the center with a nail. "I heard it was whole again. Between one week and the next, it just reappeared. But it wasn't like somebody rebuilt it. This guy I know, he said it was magic. And he said the cops was over there all the time. I told him he was nuts, but I wanted to find Keith, so I went over one night to take a look."

"What did you find?"

She looked up, her eyes wide in a pale face. "I went to that place once when I was a kid on a dare. It always looked rundown and haunted as all hell. But now . . . now it looks like something out of an old movie. There was red stained glass windows with light shinin' out. Looked like fires burnin'. And . . ." Sheri broke off.

"And what?"

"I heard screams."

Despite her thick fur, Faith felt a chill roll over her skin. She knew the house Sheri was talking about. Keith had taken her out there one evening, apparently in an attempt to spook the rookie. As the waitress said, it was widely reputed to be haunted. It was easy to see why, with the boarded-up windows and sagging porch barely visible through the briars and overgrown bushes that surrounded it.

If she'd been a vampire, she could think of nowhere better to hole up during the day than a haunted house.

"I don't think I want to talk about all that anymore." Sheri had eased over next to Jim. Giving him a seductive smile, she ran a long red nail across his wrist. "That's the kind of thing that gives me nightmares, you know?"

He studied her, his gaze compassionate rather than lustful. "I can see how that would be a problem."

"Yeah, it gets right lonely here all by myself." She looked up at him through the screen of her eyelashes.

"I know." He leaned over and pressed a gentle kiss to her cheek. Faith's werewolf hearing picked up what he breathed in her ear. "But I'm afraid I've misled you. I'm spoken for."

Anger flashed through the waitress's eyes, to be replaced by resignation. "Yeah. You would be."

He rose to his feet with easy masculine grace. "We'd better be getting home." Faith stood and headed for the door, eager to escape the role of doggy companion.

"Are you sure?" Sheri said, a hint of a whine in her voice as she followed them to the door. "Your girlfriend doesn't have to know."

"But I would."

The waitress sighed heavily and opened the door, letting Faith slip past them and down the trailer's cement steps. "Yeah, guys like you are always spoken for."

Jim paused, then pulled a notebook out of his pocket and scrawled a number on it. "Look, this is my cell. If Reynolds comes back and starts giving you a hard time, give me a call, okay?"

Sheri took the paper, but her expression was bitter. "I doubt he'll ever be back. I hear he's taken up with somebody else."

"Yeah," Jim said. "But just in case."

Faith remained a dog all the way home, mostly because she was in no mood to talk. Knowing she couldn't continue to stall, she transformed once he closed the door behind them.

"I know what house she was talking about. Sounds like a good, solid lead."

"It also sounds like the place is going to be swarming with cops," Jim said, tossing his keys onto the coffee table and dropping onto the couch. "I suggest we follow the tradition of great vampire hunters everywhere and hit the bitch after the sun comes up. Once we kill her off, we can pick off the rogue and figure out what to do about the cops."

Faith considered the idea a moment, then nodded slowly. "Yeah, that makes sense."

"Good." His silver gaze narrowed, his expression going cold. "In the meantime, I think we need to get a couple of things straight."

Oh, great, she thought. *Here we go again.* "Like what?"

Jim crossed those brawny, powerful arms and rocked back on his heels. "For example, Ron was a self-serving asshole, and it offends the hell out of me when you persist in seeing me in the same light."

Faith stiffened. "When did I accuse you of being anything like Ron? Sure hasn't been tonight, considering I've been a dog for the past three hours."

"I could tell by the look on your face what you were thinking. I flirted with that girl to get the information we needed, Faith. For no other reason."

"And you were very good at it." She was proud of her cool tone. "You almost fooled me, and I knew the truth."

"Yes, I'm good at it." His gaze didn't shift from hers. "I've had a lot of practice deceiving people. My parents are werewolves living in a small Southern town. I grew up lying to protect them. After I Changed the first time, I started lying to protect myself." His voice lowered to a deep, angry rumble. "But that does not make me an immoral, cheating son of a bitch."

"I never said it did."

"No, you think just having a dick makes me an immoral, cheating son of a bitch. Makes me wonder about your brothers."

She gaped at him before hot outrage steamed through her astonishment. "You wait just one minute!"

"No, you wait!" He pointed a stiff finger at her chest. "I was raised to be an Alpha. I realize that doesn't mean anything to you, but—"

"Frankly, I don't care." She spun toward the hallway.

"But I do." A strong hand grabbed her shoulders and spun her back around. Her Burning Moon temper sparked, and she tried to jerk away. Strong as she was though, she couldn't break his seemingly gentle grip. "An Alpha protects his mate and his children—"

"Let go of me!"

". . . as well as the elders of his family. He does not hurt them. Hell, since a Linked Alpha shares his mate's emotions, any pain he inflicts on her, he feels himself."

She bared her teeth. "You're about to feel some serious pain if you don't let go of me!"

Ignoring her rage, he continued coolly, "My father lived by those principles, and so did both my grandfathers. They taught me."

"So you're a third generation sexist jerk." Too furious to think about the consequences, she hooked an ankle behind his and threw her weight against him, meaning to throw him and stalk past.

Instead he twisted like the wolf he was and dragged her down with him, taking the brunt of their fall on his shoulders before rolling on top of her.

The next thing she knew, Faith lay wrapped in those long, powerful arms. She jerked and fought, but he didn't let go. For a furious moment, she glared into his eyes, tempted to Change.

"Don't," he said in a low, deep voice.

She inhaled, about to tell him exactly what she thought of him. But as she breathed in, his scent filled her senses, potent and male. Faith froze, suddenly aware of him with disconcerting intensity.

He felt so big and hard beneath her body, his arms strong around her. Her Burning Moon anger twisted neatly into desire.

Awareness flamed in his eyes.

"Forget it," she snapped, knowing exactly what he was thinking. "We're so not doing this."

"You keep telling yourself that. But unless I miss my

guess, your body has other ideas." As Faith battled conflicting desires to throw him off her and pull him closer, he settled between her thighs.

She felt his erection harden against her belly with a rush. Apparently, her body wasn't the only one with other ideas.

SIXTEEN

Bracing his weight on his arms, Jim let his aching hard-on grind between Faith's long legs. Even in human form, she was strong enough that there was no danger of crushing her, and he wanted her aware of him.

Judging from the furious blend of heat and anger in her eyes, it was working. "What are you going to do now?" she jeered. "Force me?"

That she could even ask such a question pissed him off even more. "I don't have to." Tauntingly, he grinned into her face. "You're going to beg me."

She spat a curse that had his brows rising. He still didn't budge. He was tired of paying for Ron's sins.

He'd much rather pay for his own.

As Jim stared into her angry face, breathed in the sweet hot musk of the Burning Moon, his own hunger began to steam. He remembered what she felt like when he thrust into the tight clasp of her sex. He could almost taste her skin, rich satin against his tongue, nipples deliciously hard as they filled his mouth. His cock swelled behind his zipper.

He started to lower his head, and triumph flared in her eyes.

He stopped.

No, dammit. She was going to admit she wanted him—*needed* him—as much as he did her. Holding tight to her wrists, Jim stared into the angry green of Faith's eyes and prepared to endure.

He lay over her, hard, strong, heavy and thoroughly pissed off. Faith had no idea why he felt so good.

His erection pressed against her belly, promising in its heat. His metallic eyes glared into hers, narrow and demanding. Helplessly, her attention dropped to his mouth. His lower lip seemed to be beg for her teeth.

Her nipples peaked as his chest pressed against them. Faith could feel herself growing damp.

"It's not going to work," she told him defiantly. "I'm not going to beg for a damn thing, Burning Moon or not."

He curled his lip. "Then this is going to be a very uncomfortable night, because I'm not getting off you."

"Wanna bet?" She bucked, seeking to throw him. He calmly wrapped his long legs around hers and held on.

Jeez, he was strong. It was easy to see why, too—he was built like a brick wall. She could feel every ridge, hollow, and ripple of his hard strength.

And it was insanely tempting.

An image flashed through her mind—lying beneath him as he stroked that thick cock in and out of her in luscious digs. His head, lowering to lick and suckle her aching nipples, sending sweet streamers of pleasure through her body.

She realized she was panting and tried to stop.

Her gaze locked on his mouth. She remembered how his lips felt moving over hers, surprisingly soft and possessive.

God, she wanted to taste him.

Without really intending to, Faith lifted her head to seek his mouth. He lowered his, and her heart began to pound even harder.

Then, so close his lips brushed hers, he breathed, "Beg me."

She pulled back and snarled, furious. "Bite me!"

His eyes narrowed. "No."

But he'd miscalculated. Though she couldn't quite reach his mouth, his neck was still accessible. She lifted her head and raked her teeth gently over one of the cords of his throat. He drew back even farther with a low growl of hunger. Faith smiled and licked the hollow of his throat, then nibbled at his Adam's apple.

Another delicious rumble. Strong fingers wrapped around her jaw, tilted up her face. His mouth crushed down over hers in a slow, famished kiss that made a tingle of pleasure roll over her body. His tongue slid into her mouth in a lazy swirl. Her nipples hardened still more. She rolled her hips against his and knew the gesture held more than a hint of pleading. She didn't much care.

He was breathing harder, too, as he licked and bit at her lips.

Faith ached between her legs, the sensation growing increasingly desperate. She untangled her thighs from his and put her feet flat on the floor for more leverage. But grinding her hips against the thick, teasing promise of his erection only made her ache more intense.

She wanted his hands on her nipples. "Touch me, dammit," she panted against his mouth.

Faith half expected him to refuse in the name of making her beg, but he didn't. Instead he released her wrist to reach under the hem of her shirt and tug down one cup of her bra.

They both groaned when he palmed her bare breast.

With a low growl, he jerked the shirt up. For a moment he stared at her panting breasts as she waited for him to touch her in an agony of need. Then, at last, he lowered his head and took the aching point in his mouth.

That hot, skillful tongue teasing her nipple sent pulses of pleasure through Faith so potent, she threw her head back and groaned. "God, Jim . . ."

Silver eyes flicked up to look into hers. "That's right—Jim." He swirled his tongue around the peak, then raked it with his teeth. "Not Ron. I'm nothing like Ron. Say it."

That was for damn sure. Ron had never made her feel anything like this. "You're nothing like Ron." She whimpered, tormented by a strong suckling pull on her nipple.

"Damn right." He reached down and unsnapped her jeans. The whisper of the zipper sounded loud against their strained breathing. "And I'm going to make you love me like you never loved that lying son of a bitch."

He released her and sat back on his heels to drag her jeans down her legs and off. They sailed across the room as he turned his attention to her underwear. Removing her jeans had worked the panties down onto her thighs, but Jim didn't even bother to pull them the rest of the way off. A ruthless tug was followed by a loud rip.

Faith blinked at him, caught between amusement and outrage. "Did you just tear my panties off?"

"Yeah," he growled. "Got a problem with that?"

She found herself laughing. "Not really."

"Good, 'cause I don't much care if you do." He settled down between her thighs and spread her knees wide, then spread her nether lips with two fingers.

Faith caught her breath as he nuzzled her sex, blew tenderly across her flesh. Licked. Her sex clenched in anticipation.

His tongue flicked out, traced slowly and lovingly across her clit, then circled it in teasing little flicks. Faith squirmed and panted.

"You taste good," he murmured, and turned his head to nibble at the taut flesh of her thigh.

She laughed at the ticklish sensation. "You feel good."

"I do try." Jim slid one finger into her opening, thrust deep. Lapped slowly, as if she were a particularly delicious ice-cream cone.

A second finger pumped inside her, slowly delving. He

locked his mouth around her clit and suckled until she whimpered at the storm of pleasure.

Faith threaded her fingers through his hair as he teased her slowly. He reached up her body with his free hand, found one breast, stroked and petted. Teased her aching nipples while he feasted.

Desire stormed through her, driving her to roll her hips. "God, Jim," she moaned. "You make me insane."

"Good." Pulling away from her, he caught her by the hips and flipped her over onto her belly. Dazed, she lifted her head as he pulled her up onto her hands and knees.

Ready to be mounted.

Excitement surged through her as she braced her trembling knees apart. His thumb stroked over and around her clit, sending another set of blazing jolts through her. At the same time, he slid two fingers deep again. Pumped slowly. "Very nice," he said in that low rumble of his. "Soooo hot. So ready."

He twisted his wrist, screwing his fingers into her with a total lack of mercy. Faith whimpered as the motion teased her clinging sex.

"*Are* you ready?"

"God, yes!" she gritted, throwing her head back and her hips up, wordlessly begging for his cock.

"Good." She heard his zipper hiss and twisted her head around to watch his cock spill free, violently hard. He took the thick shaft and aimed it for her core. His hand trembled slightly with the intensity of his lust.

She caught her breath at the seductive sensation of his width slowly impaling her.

He worked his way inside another hot fraction. "We belong like this." His voice was rough with hunger. "Mated. Linked."

More and more of him, deeper and deeper. Faith closed her eyes and shivered.

At last he was in to the balls. Jim stopped there as if

basking in the sensation. Or perhaps, giving her a chance to experience what it was like to be stuffed so very full of him.

"You never loved him." He spoke in a fierce growl. "Never."

Before she could even remember who he was talking about, Jim caught her backside in his hands and started pumping—grinding the strokes in, rolling his hips until she writhed at the pleasure.

"But you're going to love me," he rumbled a burning eternity later. "And nothing he did will mean anything to you anymore." He slammed all the way in, ruthlessly hard.

Fire exploded through her, tearing a scream from her throat.

Faith's silken sheath clamped around Jim, milking him with every thrust. Her smooth ass slapped against his hips, round and warm in his hands. He watched the fiery red of her hair fly as she tossed her head in pleasure.

Every time he stroked deep, heat surged, sweet and fierce, until it exploded in a supernova of a climax that made him roar. He felt his balls empty in endless hot pulses, and he shuddered like a palsy victim, blinded by the stark delight.

For a long moment afterward, they crouched there like survivors of a storm, panting. Jim's thighs shook, and she trembled under his hands.

"Ummm," Faith said finally. "Wow."

"That about sums it up." He hesitated, knowing he should withdraw from her, but oddly reluctant.

"You know, maybe you could . . ." She let the words trail off.

"I was just thinking I like it in here."

Faith looked over her shoulder at him with amusement in her eyes. "I hate to point this out, but as a lifestyle choice, this ain't going to work."

"Too bad, too." He laughed and withdrew, groaning a little at the sensation. Suddenly concerned for her, he asked, "Are you sore?"

She sat back on her haunches and rolled her slender back from side to side, stretching her muscles. "Little bit. But it's a good sore."

He smiled. "Me, too. And yes, it is a very good sore."

Faith's bra and T-shirt were twisted up over the pretty mounds of her breasts. He reached out and tugged them back into place.

She looked him over, a smile teasing her mouth. "Do you know, you're still dressed. Basically."

Jim looked down and realized it was true. He'd pulled down his jeans only enough to free himself. "I was in a hurry."

"Apparently." She glanced around. "Where are my pants?"

He found them under the coffee table and handed them to her. Instead of putting them on, though, she sauntered out of the living room carrying them. He followed her, watching her backside with deep appreciation as she climbed the stairs. "You know, you've got an ass like a peach."

She looked back at him and tucked her tongue in her cheek. "You silver-tongued romantic, you."

Jim shrugged. "Hey, I'm male."

"Now there's a point I'm not going to argue."

They took a shower together, stroking soap over each other, enjoying the sensation of flesh sliding on flesh. One thing soon led to another, and the shower ended with them shivering as they escaped its icy spray.

"The hot water heater's not the best," Jim said, toweling her off.

"No." Faith was frowning, her thoughts apparently drifting back to something he'd said when they'd made love. "You don't think I loved Ron?"

Jim blinked at the abrupt conversational switch. "No, I really don't. I think he was a good-looking bastard who made all the right noises, so you wanted to be in love with him."

"And you know this how?"

It belatedly occurred to him that it might be a good idea to step carefully. He bulled on anyway. "There were an awful lot of midnight patrols there when nothing was going on. You liked to kill time by talking to Rambo."

"And?" She faced him, chin lifted in challenge, long skeins of wet, red hair draping her slim shoulders.

He looked her in the eye. "When you talked about catching Ron with that dispatcher, you didn't focus on being hurt that he'd cheated. What really pissed you off was that you were a cop, and you never noticed the signs he was betraying you."

"So?"

"So if you'd really loved him, it wouldn't have been your observational skills that you were worried about." He caught her by her shoulders and turned her to face him. "There was more grief in your voice when you talked about the drug dog those gang members killed."

"Sherlock was a really good dog," Faith told him dryly. "Ron was just a hound."

"Exactly. And despite the fact that I sometimes run around on four legs, I'm not."

"Give me one good reason I shouldn't kill you right now!" Celestine snarled, as death magic gathered around her shaking hands.

Reynolds glanced down at the cold glow. There was not even a trace of fear on his face. Belatedly she remembered her most powerful spell wouldn't work on the son of a bitch.

It only pissed her off even more.

She conjured a blade instead and eyed him, trying to decide where to strike. Something in her face finally sent a flicker of alarm through his eyes, and he took a wary step back.

"Calm down, Celestine. Think about this," he said, lifting his hands as he eyed the knife. "Given the games you're playing with Korbal and Arthur, you may end up with them both on your ass. And nobody kills vampires the way I do."

"Well, thanks to you, I now have *seven* werewolves," Celestine spat. "What's one less?"

She'd say one thing for him, Reynolds didn't lack courage. "I have a feeling that before it's all over, you'll be glad of every werewolf you can get."

Some of her fury faded as she realized he could be right. Reynolds had butchered those grail guards like a cat loosed in a pigeon coop.

"Seven of us," he murmured seductively, as if reading her thoughts. "Just imagine what we could do. That's why I bit them, Celestine. I knew you needed them."

"It wasn't your decision to make!" With a flick of her wrist, Celestine transformed the knife into a razor-tipped cat o' nine tails. "*I* decide what forces I need, not you. Overstep your bounds again, and you'll bleed for it!"

Quick as a snake, she sent the lashes snapping out. They wrapped around his shoulder, ripping through the thin fabric of his uniform and tearing into his skin. Caught off guard, Reynolds bellowed in pain. He glared at her as if considering striking back. Luckily, he didn't quite dare.

Celestine inhaled at the heady burst of emotion, drinking it in hungrily. The scent of his blood filled the air, and she shuddered, tempted to fall on him and whip the very flesh from his bones.

But no. There was too much to accomplish before dawn.

Instead she stepped up to him and lowered her voice to a deadly hiss. "You'd better damn well keep your new pack in line, Keith. If they give me any shit, you're the one who's going to pay the price."

He nodded tightly, sullen resentment in the set of his mouth. "Understood."

Her attention fell on the blood staining his uniform shirt, and she licked her lips. "In fact, plan to stay until dawn. I'm sure I'm going to work up quite an appetite tonight. Got that?"

"Yeah." Even as he glared at her, a hint of sick excitement flashed through the depths of his eyes.

Celestine turned on one spiked heel and stalked away, satisfied. She had more than one kind of magic at her command. As long as Reynolds remained addicted to the other one, she could control him. And through him, the rest of his pack.

Her anger began to fade into speculation. This might work out after all.

Faith lay curled against Jim's broad back, listening to his deep, even breathing. What he'd said kept running through her mind.

Had she ever loved Ron? She'd certainly thought so at the time.

Yet looking back on the way she'd felt when she'd discovered his betrayal, she realized Jim had called it exactly right. She'd been more angry at her own blindness than his lack of morality.

She'd always known Ron played fast and loose with the rules, from hitting a suspect a little too hard to accepting the free meals cops weren't supposed to take.

Faith had been equally aware of his low opinion of women, whether they were crime victims or other cops. Ron's attitudes had troubled her, but whenever she'd tried to bring them to his attention, he'd dismissed her as oversensitive or humorless. He'd never actually used the word *nag*, but it had definitely been implied.

In retrospect, she could kick herself for putting up with that kind of behavior. But Ron had seemed to know just where the line was. Just as she got ready to cut him loose for good, he'd do something sweet or seductive, and somehow she found herself giving him yet another chance.

At least until the dispatcher incident.

Brooding, Faith stared at the opposite wall, listening to Jim's even breathing as he slept. A memory flashed through her mind of the hour after Reynolds had bitten her.

Jim had known there was a chance she could die. He was, in fact, deeply afraid for her. He'd also known there was nothing either of them could do about it.

Yet when she'd asked him what her chances were, he'd been completely honest with her.

Jim had been equally honest about the Spirit Link. He could easily have avoided telling her that if they Linked, his death might kill her, too. He must have known the admission would hurt his chances of talking her into it, but he'd told her the truth anyway.

All of which indicated a man very different from Ron—one who respected her strengths as much as he enjoyed her body.

Jim London was the kind of man you could trust.

The question was, what was she going to do about it? This Spirit Link he'd talked about was basically a proposal of marriage. If she accepted, not only would there be no possibility of divorce, but the death of one of them would doom the other. Even if the Link did convey some kind of combat benefits, she wasn't sure she wanted to make a commitment that profound to a man she barely knew.

Even one who made her feel like nobody ever had.

Sometimes I think my armor has fused itself to my skin," Guinevere murmured to Morgana Le Fay as they met in the Great Hall to tackle the problem of finding the missing Black Grail.

"I know," Arthur's half-sister replied with a grimace. She appeared a bit pale, the effect enhanced by the stark contrast of her black hair framing her face with an intricate coil of braids. She looked stern and beautiful in her magical armor. Guinevere only felt hot and untidy in hers.

The comfort spell on it probably needed a little more juice. Gwen sent a short magical jolt into the featherweight plate and instantly felt cooler.

"So we go to hunt this grail thief," Morgana said, leaning one fist on the Round Table's gleaming, intricately carved wood. "Are you sure you can punch through his shields?"

Guinevere sank into her customary seat. "Well, he—or she—did send me that vision of its location. I still feel the echo. If you can give me a boost, I should be able to track it back to him or her."

Morgana nodded and moved to sit beside her. "We've boosted one another often enough before. Where's Arthur? We're going to need some vampire muscle if we locate it."

"He's gathering a team to . . ." She broke off as an alien sensation crawled over her skin, triggering a sense of danger so acute, her every cell seemed to recoil in revolt.

Morgana must have felt it, too, because she glanced at Gwen in horror. "Someone's using death magic in Avalon!"

Springing from their seats, the two Majae raced across the Great Hall and down the endless corridor beyond it. With every step they took, the sense of evil increased.

Voices shouted, the sound carrying through the heavy doors of the hall. Steel clashed with the distinctive ring of enchanted blades. With a gesture, Morgana sent the double doors flying wide. Beyond them was a scene that froze them both in cold horror.

The central square of Avalon was a seething mass of battling vampires. Magic flashed and boomed, splashing against hastily conjured shields or enchanted plate. Swords rose and fell, crashing against one another with the vicious ring of mortal combat.

And over it all rang a horrifying chant. "Geirolf lives in us! We live in Geirolf!"

For just and instant, Guinevere met Morgana's horrified gaze. "Merlin's beard," Gwen breathed. "Avalon has been invaded."

* * *

The cops waited for Celestine in the ballroom, including Reynolds's new werewolf recruits, who stood in a group looking variously anxious, pissed, or swaggering, depending on their respective personalities.

"I want to talk to you!" Ayers, not surprisingly, was one of the pissed. His face was red with rage as he strode across the ballroom. He probably thought the werewolf had been acting on her orders. Celestine wouldn't put it past Reynolds to tell his victims she'd double-crossed them.

Still, the sullen fury on the chief's face was not an attitude she had any intention of tolerating. Celestine stalked toward him, letting the lashes of her whip rattle across the marble tiles.

"So it seems you won't be immortal after all," she said coolly.

"You promised—"

"Too bad," she interrupted. "I need you as you are."

Ignoring his infuriated sputter, Celestine began to pace in front of the weres, flicking her whip on each turn like a cat swishing its tail. "Arthur and Korbal may decide to move against me before I have my forces assembled. In that case I'll need shock troops." She flicked a glance across them. "You will do very nicely."

"If you think we're going to be your cannon fodder—" Ayers began furiously.

Celestine whirled and struck out with her whip, hitting him hard across the face. Blood flew, and Ayers fell back with a shout, one hand clamped to his injured cheekbone. "Silence!" she raged. "I will not tolerate insubordination or disobedience!"

Shocked, the chief stared into her eyes, holding his wounded face. She knew perfectly well that if he transformed, he could rip her apart. She didn't let even a hint of unease show.

Everything depended on the next few seconds. He was

paramilitary. If he accepted her authority now, she had him. If not, she'd loose it all.

"You will obey," Celestine gritted, calling her magic to snap and spark in her eyes, "or you will pay the price. Is that clear?"

Ayers blinked hard at the magical shimmer. She saw the exact moment his nerve broke. "Yes ma'am."

Celestine nodded shortly, then turned to the others. They stared at her like birds at a cobra. Good. "How about the rest of you?"

"Yes, ma'am." The chorus was ragged, but fervent.

Some of the sick anxiety lifted from her belly, and she nodded curtly. "Good."

Turning toward the rest of her men, she raised her voice. "Let's get started, gentlemen. There's much to do and damned little time to do it. Have you got the sacrifices?"

"Here." One of the cops stepped from the crowd, dragging a thin, terrified man in shackles with him. Bruises mottled the sacrifice's face, and he shook in racking shivers. Behind them, Celestine spotted another man lying unconscious on the floor, also bruised and handcuffed. She could smell the alcohol reek all the way across the ballroom.

"Emptied the drunk tank for me again, I see." She wrinkled her nose. "I do wish you could find sacrifices that smell a little better. Where's the third? You'll need one to feed from."

A female voice made a thin, high-pitched sound of terror and despair.

Interested, Celestine started toward the sound. "Who's this?"

The men stepped aside, revealed a bound, gagged blonde with impressive tits. "It's the barmaid from the Silver Bullet," one of the cops explained. He shrugged. "I always thought she was hot, so I went by and picked her up."

"Sheri?" Reynolds said. He'd transformed to werewolf form, either to heal his whip injury or to assume his usual role in the sacrifice. "You grabbed Sheri Miller?"

The cop looked uneasy. "I thought you'd lost interest. I saw some guy coming out of her trailer tonight, so I assumed you two were definitely over."

Reynolds looked mildly interested. "Who?"

"Never saw him before. Had this big Irish setter with him though, which I thought was a little odd for a guy taking a pussy break, but . . ."

"An Irish setter?" Reynolds's eyes widened and lit with sudden, ferocious interest.

SEVENTEEN

Keith Reynolds had turned into a monster.

Sheri stared at her former lover as he leaned one hairy arm against the back of her chair. He towered over her, seven feet tall, his eyes shining yellow against the sable backdrop of his fur. She felt so sick with terror she wanted to vomit.

When he spoke, he bared teeth like knives. "Who was he?"

She didn't dare lie. "A . . . a reporter."

Behind them, another of the cops drank from the gold cup the witch held. He screamed in agony and fell on the ground, writhing.

Sheri swallowed and tried not to watch. They'd slit the two drunks' throats and filled the cup from their gushing blood while the witch chanted some kind of spell.

It was like a nightmare.

"What was this reporter's name, Sheri?" Reynolds asked with elaborate patience.

She licked her lips. "Jim. He said his name was Jim

Galloway." Her mind spun frantically, trying to come up with anything that might save her. "He gave me his cell phone number."

Reynolds's yellow eyes narrowed. "Where?"

"It's in my pocket." Sheri had shoved it in her jeans when the cop drove up and told her she was under arrest. Confused, but thinking it must be some kind of mistake, she'd gone with him.

Dumbass.

Feeling numb, the waitress watched Reynolds fish the slip of paper out of her pocket.

In the ballroom, another cop screamed.

Faith had barely dropped off to sleep when a shrill jangling jolted her awake. She lifted her head blearily as Jim stirred, cursed, and rolled out of bed.

"If that's Charlie, I'm going to rip his head off." He snatched up his pants and fumbled in the pocket until he found the ringing cell. Flipping it open, he snapped, "London."

With Faith's werewolf hearing, she heard the woman's terrified sobs. "Jim? I need help!"

He looked at Faith, frowning. "Who is this?"

"Sheri Miller." She sobbed again. "From the Silver Bullet? We talked? You said to call if Keith . . . he. . . ." Her breath hitched, then exploded in a torrent of terrified words. "They're after me! Please, you've got to help! They showed up at my trailer. I got away, but—"

"Where are you?"

"I'm hiding. Lockwood Road. There's some trees . . ."

"You know where that is?" Jim asked Faith, who was already out of bed and getting dressed.

"Not far from the trailer park." She jerked a T-shirt on over her head, then picked up Jim's pants and tossed them to him.

"Okay." To Sheri he added, "Find some brush and stay hidden. Put your cell on vibrate—you're on a cell, right?"

Another watery sob. "Yeah."

"We'll call you when we get close. Just hold on." He clicked the phone off and sat down to jerk the pants up his legs.

Faith dragged her hair back into a ponytail and popped a rubber band around it. "Think it's a trap?"

He nodded grimly and scooped up the knit shirt he'd left draped over the arm of a chair. "No way in hell would she be able to lose Reynolds. But unless she's got an Oscar stashed away we don't know about, she's scared out of her mind. We've got to rescue her."

Faith stuffed her feet into her sneakers. "Maybe you should use that key chain of yours and call us in some Fairy reinforcements. We could use a couple of big guys with swords right about now."

"Good idea." Jim dug it out of a pocket as they headed for the stairs. "Hey, Diana," he said to it. The key chain began to glow. "I need some help here, kiddo. I've got bad guys getting pissy."

The key chain glowed brighter and brighter, as if trying to punch through some kind of interference. Jim frowned. The last time he'd used it, his sister had responded right away. "Diana?" They reached the bottom of the stairs and strode out the front door. "Diana?"

The key chain abruptly stopped glowing.

"Shit. They must be off hunting vampires with Arthur." He met Faith's worried gaze. "Looks like we're on our own."

Diana Galatyn paced her chamber like the wolf she was. "This sucks," she snarled to her guard.

"Yes, Your Majesty." Lairgnen didn't even flick a pink brow.

"Do sit down, dear." The Dowager Queen Oriana conjured yet another elaborate gown for her coming great-grandson. "You're making me nervous."

"*You're* nervous?" Diana whirled, both fists clenched. "Your grandson is off fighting evil vampires by himself, and we're stuck here! You should be nervous!"

Oriana looked up, her gaze patient. Though she was well over four thousand years old, she looked barely forty, a trim, dark-haired woman. Her gown was worked with exquisite magical embroidery—peacock feathers that shimmered and fluttered as if alive every time she moved. "Llyr can draw on the power of the Dragon god. He is more than capable of defending himself without your help."

"And I am more than capable of defending myself without the Fairy patrol!" She waved an infuriated hand at her guard, who stood around the chamber looking tense. Given the current alert, all ten of them wore full armor, gleaming and beautifully embossed. Diana was half-tempted to start a fight with them just for something to do.

"Of course you are, Your Majesty," Lairgnen said soothingly. "And once the heir is safely born, you may war all you like."

"What if Llyr gets hurt?" Diana aimed another frustrated glare at Oriana. "With the palace in magical lockdown, he won't be able to call."

The dowager queen sighed and gestured, conjuring another outfit. "Dear, you're not a magic user. There's nothing you could do about it anyway. We don't want the palace full of evil vampires now, do we? Besides, Llyr is surrounded by the Magekind and our own people. If he needs healing, someone will do it for him."

Diana flopped down in an armchair and glowered at the Sidhe. "Did I ever tell you the story of the big bad wolf and Little Red Riding Hood's grandma?"

* * *

Faith's stomach had tied itself into a solid knot of tension and adrenalin. Cop that she was, she ignored it. She knew she'd steady down when the fight started.

Drumming her fingers against her knee, she glanced at Jim's tight profile as he drove. The light from the dash painted a green gleam along his high cheekbones and stubborn chin. *God,* she thought out of nowhere, *he's so handsome.*

And that was only one of his endearing characteristics. There was also the courage and iron nobility. He hadn't questioned whether they should risk their necks for the girl, even knowing she was probably leading them into a trap.

It would be entirely too easy to fall in love with him. *If I'm not already . . .*

Which was not a thought Faith wanted to examine too closely, particularly right now. Restless, she glanced at the car's dashboard clock. Two A.M. She wished it was a little closer to dawn.

Spotting the green glow of a street sign, Faith gestured at it. "The next right will be Lockwood."

Instead of turning, he pulled over, sending the car bumping onto the grassy shoulder before he braked to a stop. Jim switched off the engine and turned to her. "We'll go in wolf form. Quicker and quieter that way."

Faith nodded. "Especially if we want to spot the rogue and the rest of the cops before they spot us." She opened her car door and lowered her voice. "They'll probably have those TASERs again."

Jim flashed her a grim smile. "Let's try not to get shot this time."

"Gotta admit, riding the lightning's not my idea of a great way to spend Saturday night." They got out, leaving the doors open to avoid the thunk of closing them.

Faith met Jim's silver gaze in the darkness in a silent message of determination and mutual support.

Then they transformed. She felt the power rise even

more quickly this time, a tingling flow that brought her transformation in a rush. When the magic drained away, she shook herself, settling her red wolf coat around her, and trotted off after the dark flag of Jim's tail.

The wind was blowing, and the air smelled of rain. There'd be a storm soon, she thought. Rotten timing. The rattle of the trees and the whip of the wind would make scenting their foes a tricky proposition.

Together, she and Jim ghosted silently through the brush, senses alert to the smell of magic. But all Faith's sensitive nose detected was the musky scent of deer and rabbit. Frogs croaked over the hiss of whipping leaves, while something shrill whined through the darkness. The sound puzzled Faith, until she spotted a black shape swooping past overhead. It was a bat, using its screeches like a sub's sonar to find prey. Its cries would have been too high-pitched to hear in human form.

Then the wind carried something else to her ears—a woman's sob.

Jim's eyes flashed silver as he looked back at Faith. He began to run. Faith raced after him, ears pricked, nose in the wind. She found what she was looking for when the breeze shifted, carrying the reek of fear, blood, and woman.

They found Sheri standing in the middle of the road, trembling and dazed, making no attempt to hide. Her clothes were torn and dirty, revealing bruises mottling her arms and legs. She had a black eye and a swollen lip, and she was crying.

The bastards had beaten her.

Faith started forward, only to break step when Jim nipped her gently on one ear. He shook his head at her and Changed. Human again, he crouched down at her side and murmured, "Go to Dire Wolf form. I don't smell anything, but that doesn't mean much in this wind."

Faith knew why he'd gone human—Sheri was trauma-tized enough as it was—but she wasn't sure doing so was particularly smart. Even so, she let the magic spill and suppressed her own whine of pain as her body stretched and grew. It was tougher going from wolf to Dire Wolf—the size difference was so much greater. Difficult or not, though, it was certainly safer than stopping as a human in between and risking too many transformations.

Jim didn't wait for her, instead working his way farther up the road at a crouch, probably not wanting to emerge from the woods too close to Faith's location. Finally he stopped behind some screening bushes. "Sheri?"

The waitress only stood there with her back to him, shaking. She evidently hadn't heard him. He rose from the brush. "Sheri?"

She whipped around with a muffled yelp. He held a finger to his lips. "Shh. It's Jim. You okay?"

Instead of throwing herself into his arms, as Faith would have expected, the woman held back. Her eyes were wide and white with fear. Her lips moved soundlessly, as if terror had stolen her voice.

The wind shifted, bringing the acrid reek of deer urine from off to the left. Faith wrinkled her nose, recognizing the smell from childhood hunting trips when her brothers used it to fool . . .

"Jim!" she shouted, springing aside just in time to dodge the TASER leads that shot hissing out of the darkness. "To your left!"

With a roar, the rogue exploded from the brush. Sheri shrieked as he slammed into Jim, knocking him off his feet and pinning him to the ground. Reynolds lifted a hand, claws glinting, a snarl of triumph on his face.

Faith leaped from cover and bounded toward them, frantic to get Reynolds off him long enough to give her lover a chance to Change.

She barreled into Reynolds with the full force of her body. They went flying, tumbling across the roadway in a windmilling knot of fur, fangs, and claws.

Spotting an opening, Faith sank her jaws into the back

of Reynolds's thick bull neck. Her mouth flooded with the taste of blood, hot copper, and wild magic. The rogue yowled and grabbed the back of her head, heaving her over his shoulder before she could get a good grip. Stars exploded in her head as she slammed into the ground.

Before the spots even cleared, something hit her hard in the muzzle with stunning force. Shaking off the impact, she lunged upward and bit. Bones crunched. Reynolds howled. She'd nailed his hand.

Faith bit down harder. He clouted her across the face, claws raking her muzzle. She lost her grip.

"Fucker," Jim snarled.

Suddenly Reynolds's weight was gone. Faith blinked the blood from her eyes and saw the two weres, both in Dire Wolf form, snarling and slashing at one another like biped tigers.

Faith wiped her face and rolled to her feet, intent on joining the fray.

And smelled deer urine.

Somebody grabbed her from behind and spun her around. "Why, hello, Weston." A huge Dire Wolf, his fur shot with black and gray, bared his fangs in her face. He had the chief's eyes. "You smell gooooood."

Faith hit him as Jim had taught her, in an open-handed clawed swat. He staggered back a pace, one hand clamped to the wound. "Bitch!"

"Asshole," she raged back. "You broke your oath, Ayers. What happened to serve and protect?"

He curled his lip. "I'm going to enjoy watching you die."

"You're not going to live that long." Too pissed off to care that he was bigger and stronger, she dove for him.

Only to go down hard as something slammed into her knees. She saw stars again, tasted blood. Somebody grabbed her mane and jerked her onto her feet. "You've needed your ass kicked for a long time, Weston," the hulking werewolf said. Something in the shape of his eyes told her it was Sergeant Young. "We're going to give it to you."

"Among other things." Ayers strode over and slapped her across the muzzle.

The roar of rage startled even Faith. Something plunged out of the sky, knocking the werewolves away from her. She jumped back, startled, as the attacking Dire Wolf tore into the two rogues. He must have leaped right over their heads to come down on top of them. God knew what he'd done to Reynolds. "Go on!" Jim roared over his shoulder at her. "Get the girl to safety!"

Every instinct rebelled. "I can't leave you!"

"Go!"

Just beyond him, Faith glimpsed Sheri. She was struggling with a uniformed cop, who was bent over her throat. White fangs glinted in his open mouth.

Shit, Faith thought, *Celestine must have gotten hold of that grail!* If she didn't save Sheri, the girl was dead.

With a growl, Faith raced toward the vampire as he buried his fangs in Sheri's neck. Without breaking step, she raked her claws down the vampire's back. He howled and dropped Sheri. Started to turn . . .

Claws spread, Faith hit him with all her strength right in the side of the head. Blood splattered. She didn't stop to see what she'd done to him, just grabbed the blonde, heaved her across her shoulder in a fireman's carry, and ran. Sheri shrieked in her ear.

"Shut up!" Faith bellowed. "I'm trying to save you!"

If she could just move fast enough, she could get the waitress to safety and get back to help Jim.

"There she goes!"

Faith looked back and saw two werewolves racing after her. One was a blonde, the other as red-furred as herself. She had no idea who they were. Shit, how many cops had Reynolds bitten, anyway?

It didn't matter. She didn't dare stop until she got the

waitress to safety. Otherwise the weres would kill Sheri, and all this would be for nothing.

Desperately, Faith put her head down and ran for her life, ignoring the waitress's terrified screams.

Surrounded by her new troops, Celestine watched from the shelter of the trees as five of her werewolves fought the one Ayers had identified as Jim London. Power poured off them in blazing waves of pain, magic, and rage. As fast as Celestine drank the energy in, it kept coming.

London was so skilled and strong that even outnumbered, he held his own.

"Shit," one of her new vampires breathed. "Man, feel that. All that power."

"Oh, yeah." Another fledgling swallowed hard. "Smell the blood. It's . . . God, I want some. Celestine, let us—"

"Not yet," she snapped. "I want this to go on a little longer." Her mind raced.

A fight like this with all seven werewolves would produce a staggering amount of power, far more than just sacrificing London the way she had Shay. Enough to provide her new fledglings with a significant magical charge.

Then they could feed on London after they got him down. A creature that size would have a great deal of blood.

Celestine frowned, watching Ayers stagger back from a particularly vicious claw swipe. The only problem was the risk that some of her own wolves might be killed in the process.

Then again, so what? It would just be more life force and more blood for the rest. If it came right down to it, she could always have the survivors create new were recruits.

On the other hand, the conditions could be controlled a little better. As it was now, London might decide to run for it.

"TASER him," she ordered. "I want to take him back to the house so we can do this properly."

They nodded eagerly and started forward, drawing their freshly charged weapons.

Once it was over, Celestine would have the power for another crucial spell, one that would draw the entire adult population of Clarkston to her. Since there were five thousand people in the town, she'd have the makings of a decent army.

The vampires closed in on the battling werewolves, TASERs in hand. The first set of probes flew, biting into London's shoulder just as he ripped out one of the weres' throats. He fell, convulsing. More probes flew.

Celestine smiled in satisfaction as the enemy were went down at last.

Rain pelted Faith in hard needles she felt even through her thick fur. She ignored the sting, concentrating on keeping a grip on Sheri's wet body as she bounded through the woods at full speed.

She could no longer hear the sounds of the rogues' pursuit, but she wasn't sure if she'd lost them or if the wind and rain simply drowned it out.

Breaking out of the trees, Faith spotted the dark silhouette of a house and darted for it. Taking refuge in a thick patch of shadow, she crouched to wait.

"What—?" Sheri began.

"Shh!" she snapped, peering back the way they'd come. For the past twenty endless minutes, she'd backtracked and dodged, her gut knotting tighter with each second. Too often, the scent and sound of her werewolf pursuers had driven her onward.

Now she listened hard, rain dripping from her muzzle and running down her back. Faith ignored it, staring intently into the trees.

Nothing. Not a shout, not a movement. Faith let herself sag in relief. She'd lost them.

Straightening, she turned to Sheri. "Do you still have that cell you used to call us?"

The blonde, soaked and shivering, stared up at her. "Us?"

"I'm that girlfriend Jim mentioned. Have you got the cell or not?"

She sniffed. "In my pocket. They gave it to me in case he called back."

"Good. Is there somebody you can call—not 911, obviously." Faith grimaced. "Last thing we need is another cop."

"My brother lives right outside Clarkston."

"Good. Call him." She rose and started toward the woods.

"Wait! You're just going to leave me?" Sheri called.

"If I don't get back to Jim, he's dead," Faith told her, and began to run.

Guinevere saw the vampire's hands glow as he gathered his magic for a blast. She threw up her shield just as he launched it. The energy splashed off her magical barrier in a shower of electric blue sparks, pulsing with death energy. She reinforced the shield until the sparks faded.

Knowing it would take her foe a couple of seconds to recharge, Gwen dropped it and blasted him with all her strength. But the vamp ducked. The spell shot harmlessly past his head as he charged, sword lifted, apparently meaning to kill her with pure muscle.

But before he could bring his weapon down, Arthur's familiar battle cry rang over the field. Excalibur's blazing magic lit up the vampire's face as he whirled to block the stroke. Arthur only hacked harder, trying for a head shot that would end the battle.

Magic flashed off to the right, and Gwen threw up a shield barely in time to deflect it from her husband. Even so, the blast almost punched through.

Merlin's beard, she thought in despair, *the bastards are getting more powerful!*

That was the problem with warring against an enemy that used death magic. Every fighter who went down—even their own—provided the Geirolfians with more and more death and pain to power their spells. That left the Majae at a disadvantage, since their magic came from the Mageverse itself. It didn't decrease, but it didn't increase either.

Gwen threw a desperate glance around Avalon's central square as magical blasts lit up the castles, mansions, and villas. Everywhere she looked, Magekind and Sidhe alike were locked in brutal combat with the Geirolfians. Technically, they had the enemy outnumbered, but with the bastards getting stronger with every death, that was fast becoming a moot point.

She turned toward her husband again just in time to witness the distinctive blaze of Excalibur's magic, followed by a spinning dark shape. Arthur had just sent the Geirolfian's head flying.

Panting, she met her husband's weary gaze through the slits in his helm. His armor was splashed with blood, some of which was his. Through their Truebond, she could feel the leaden weight of his exhaustion. She felt no better herself. "We can't keep this up," he told her. "We've got to get that grail!"

He was right. If they could just find and destroy the cultists' Black Grail, the resulting magical blast would wipe out most of the enemy. Whoever remained would be easy prey.

Gwen gathered herself and reached out her magical senses, struggling to concentrate despite the screams and clash of battle. Straining, she could just feel the grail's distant malevolence. "It's still out there."

"Can you do that location spell you mentioned before?"

"Yes, if I can get five minutes of quiet. We don't want any of these bastards following us to it."

He nodded. "I'll call some of my knights. We're going to need help."

A magical blast lit up the city, so bright they were forced to shield their eyes. "We'd better make it fast," Gwen told her husband. "Or there won't be an Avalon to come back to."

"You want us to do what?" George Ayers stared at Celestine in disbelief. He'd taken some nasty injuries at the hands of Weston and London. They'd healed as soon as he'd transformed, but they'd hurt like a son of a bitch. And now she wanted him and the other weres to fight the bastard again for no good reason?

"What's the matter, George?" Celestine asked in a contemptuous feline purr. "Afraid you can't take him?"

"Of course we can take him." Reynolds curled his lip. "There are six of us. We'll rip the pussy apart."

George eyed him. "That 'pussy' killed Dave Green."

He shrugged. "And I'm looking forward to giving him a little payback. Unless you're scared . . ."

He stiffened angrily. One thing no cop could tolerate was an accusation of cowardice. "I just don't see any reason to fight in some kind of pit with that bastard like something out of *Fight Club*."

Celestine's eyes narrowed. "I told you, I need the power for my spell."

"So rip out his heart. God knows you've done it before."

"Yes," she said on a note of silky threat. "I have, now that you mention it."

George flinched.

Then he remembered the damage he'd done with his claws. The bitch could hurt him, but he could hurt her, too. He lifted his chin. "So take care of him."

"My men are hungry," she said through gritted teeth. "They need to feed on a strong power source. One way or another, you're going to provide us with what we need."

George opened his mouth, ready to tell her exactly what to do with her power source.

Then he became conscious of the eyes on him, eyes hot

with bloodlust and growing anger. The eyes of men who had once obeyed his orders without question.

But they weren't really men anymore, and the orders they obeyed were no longer his.

Celestine was right, George realized with a chill. They were her men. And if she gave them the order, they'd tear him apart just as surely as they would London.

He swallowed. "Fine. We'll take him out."

A slow cat smile spread across Celestine's face, feral and terrifying. "I knew you'd see it my way."

EIGHTEEN

Jim pressed his muzzle against the airholes on one side of the metal crate. When he'd been in human form, he'd had to curl in a ball to fit between the box's narrow walls. He'd Changed to wolf the moment his powers returned. Becoming a Dire Wolf was out of the question. There was simply no room.

He'd still been stunned from the TASERing when the witch had conjured the box and ordered him stuffed inside before magically sealing it shut. Jim figured it wouldn't be long before they'd drag him out, TASER him again, and cut his heart from his chest. Sick fear gnawed at him, mixed with building claustrophobia from being in a box with no door.

But what really terrified him was the thought of Faith at the mercy of these lunatics. He knew good and damned well she was charging to the rescue even as he sat here. She was psychologically incapable of leaving him at the mercy of Celestine and her band of psychopaths.

The problem was there were just too fucking many of

them, and they were too powerful. There was no way Faith could fight them all. And since they'd taken both his cell phone and that useless key chain, she couldn't even call Charlie or Diana for reinforcements.

So like the suicidally heroic twit she was, she'd come alone. In the middle of her Burning Moon. To run right smack into a pack of werewolves and bloodthirsty vampires who'd delight in raping her and cutting out her heart.

Helpless rage surged through Jim. He wanted to scream. He wanted to kill somebody.

He had to do something, anything, no matter how pointless.

Bellowing curses that emerged in animal howls of fury, he flung himself against the sides of his enchanted cage, ramming his body against the metal walls over and over, ignoring the pain of the impacts. The cage didn't give, but that didn't stop him from trying again. And again.

And again.

Faith!

"Cut it out!" a male voice yelled. Something banged against the top of the cage. "Save your energy, London. You're going to need it."

Jim growled at his tormentor.

Suddenly the crate swung into the air. He lurched, then braced his legs apart as the metal box began to rock. They were carrying it somewhere. Jim tensed.

The moment they opened it, he was going to make somebody bleed.

"What do we do with it?" a voice asked.

"Throw it in," Celestine replied, excitement in her voice.

Shit! His stomach lurched as they swung the crate back, preparing to hurl it. His ass slapped into the rear panel as the box flew through the air and arched downward.

It hit with a stunning impact, tumbling over and over, rattling Jim around like dice in a cup. He bit his tongue and tasted blood.

Light flared as the cage disappeared from around him in a swirl of magic.

Finding himself free, Jim immediately called his own magic. It surged around him, but even as his body transformed to Dire Wolf form, he wondered why the hell they were allowing it.

Warily, Jim straightened to his full seven-six and took a cautious look around. Smooth black rock walls surrounded him, slick as glass. Light cascaded from above. He looked up and discovered he stood at the bottom of a thirty-foot pit.

High overhead, a crystal chandelier shimmered, hanging from what appeared to be a domed ceiling. Jim's gaze narrowed as he calculated whether he could—

Bodies plunged toward him.

With a startled growl, he leaped aside as the six Dire Wolves landed lightly on the stone floor.

Reynolds grinned. "Ready to die?" Claws clicked on the marble as they moved toward him in a feral, menacing slink.

Jim looked from him to the ring of vampires standing around the edge of the pit. "Who the fuck do I look like, Russell Crowe?"

With a roar, the werewolves charged.

The plantation house stood in the midst of a rolling two-acre manicured lawn, a towering, elegant structure with Doric columns and a broad, wraparound porch. The only discordant note was the red and yellow stained glass in the windows. Lit from within, the plantation reminded Faith of *The Amityville Horror* more than *Gone with the Wind.*

As if to confirm that negative impression, male shouts and laughter rolled across the lawn. Celestine's merry band was having far too good a time, which didn't bode well for Jim.

Was she too late? The thought made her sick.

Faith studied the house with burning eyes. So many police cars were parked on the lawn, it looked like a cop convention. Somebody had even brought one of the department's motorcycles.

She had to get to him, but she couldn't afford to just charge in like Bruce Willis. There'd be guards armed with TASERs, werewolves, vampires, and . . .

Jim in there getting his heart cut out.

Fuck it.

Running fast and low, she darted out of the woods, senses alert for any hint of human, vampire, or Dire Wolf. Moving in a rapid slink, she headed for one of the police cars and crouched behind its cover, nose flared, ears pricked.

Nothing.

Bursting through the front door seemed the height of stupidity. She needed a distraction, something that would draw at least a couple of the bad guys away from Jim.

Her gaze fell on the motorcycle. It was a hefty beast, one of those BMW had donated to local departments when the German manufacturer had taken up residence in nearby Greer.

She walked over to it and laid a clawed hand across its seat. Slowly, she rocked the cycle back and forth, testing the weight. It felt surprisingly light in her Dire Wolf form. Grabbing it by the handle bars and seat, Faith straightened, whirled, and hurled it like a discus.

The cycle spun through the air and landed on a group of parked Crown Vics with a crash.

Then she ran like hell.

Even over the snarls from the pit, Celestine heard the metallic crash. She turned, irritated. "What the fuck was that?"

The vampires around her shrugged, more interested in the bloodshed going on below. "You," she snapped, pointing at three of them at random. "Go check out that racket."

*　*　*

Faith found a long, low building attached to the rear of the house—probably a kitchen, if she knew her antebellum architecture. The lock on its screen door was hardly a match for Faith's Direkind strength. Twisting the knob off, she threw it away and slipped onto the porch.

A male voice shouted in pain. She hunkered down, heart pounding, then crossed the porch to the kitchen door beyond it. Another twist and shove forced it open. Faith stepped inside.

Breath held, she scanned the kitchen warily, spotting an industrial stove, a freezer, and . . .

The nude, gutted body of a man lying on the table.

Faith's heart stopped. A moaning whine of agony escaped her as she took one long stride to reach the corpse. The world spun around her, and she thought for a second she was going to faint for the first time in her life. She looked down, tasting brass and blood.

It wasn't Jim.

Her legs gave out, and she fell into a chair. Burying her face in her hands, she let her shoulders shake just once.

She should have realized it wasn't Jim. The victim was too skinny and short, and the sticky sweet scent of alcohol lay under the reek of blood and spilled intestines.

No time for this. I've got to save Jim.

Faith stood up and started for the door that lay across the darkened kitchen. If she didn't get moving, the next corpse really would be his.

And that wasn't going to happen, if Faith had to gut every vampire and rogue she could get her claws on.

Jim backed away, watching the rogues' confident pursuit. He couldn't afford to let them surround him.

To his left, he saw the blond wolf's attention shift toward Reynolds. That was all he needed. He lunged, delivering an open handed swat with claws bared, right across the man's muzzle. The rogue staggered back with a startled yelp.

Jim pivoted and kicked a clawed foot into the belly of the red-haired one standing beside the blonde. The kick landed, but the rogue raked his calf. He ignored the pain, spinning to avoid a grizzled were whose salt-and-pepper coat reminded him of Ayers. Claws tore his shoulder, and he spun to rake the owner's belly.

Above him, voices shouted in approval and blood lust. He threw a quick look upward.

The vampires stared down at him, avid hunger on their faces. It occurred to him that they didn't really care who bled, as long as somebody did.

"Fucker!" Reynolds roared, the instant before the Dire Wolf plowed into him like an offensive lineman sacking a quarterback. Jim went down with a *whoof*. The rogue drew back a hand.

Jim swung out, trying to block, but he was too slow. Claws punched into his belly with an explosion of pain. He kicked up and over anyway, rolling onto his shoulders to send the werewolf flying. Another rogue leaped for him, so he slashed his claws across his attacker's eyes. Blinded, the rogue stumbled, giving Jim a chance to scramble to his feet.

He curled an arm across his belly. Blood poured over his forearm with a rhythmic arterial pulse. Something red bulged through the crimson flow.

Fuck. That was a wound he couldn't ignore. He called the magic and transformed into wolf form. The Change was barely complete when he looked up to see a clawed fist coming right at his head.

Jim ducked. The wind of the swipe ruffled his fur as he leaped away. The rogue roared and shot after him.

He ran, tucking his tail tight, conscious of the blond-furred wolf that was gaining on him. Wait for it, wait . . . He called the magic.

It poured through him. Veteran of a thousand transformations, he didn't let the pain stop him, instead whirling to grab the rogue as the man reached for him. He let their momentum spin them around, and flung the rogue into the pit wall with all his strength. The man's head hit with a crunch. Blood splattered. *Well,* Jim thought, with vicious satisfaction, *he won't be getting back up.*

Fangs clamped into his shoulder. He roared as muscle tore in an explosion of agony. As Jim turned to batter at his attacker, another set of jaws clamped into the back of his neck. He felt himself being forced down on the ground.

Faith ran down the hallway toward the sound of screams and shouts. She thought one of those inhumanly deep voices was Jim's. Fear choked her, metallic with the taste of panic. If he died, there was really no point in . . .

"And where the hell do you think you're going?" Three uniformed cops stepped into her path, their eyes bright with vicious excitement.

One of them bared his teeth, obviously pissed. "You wrecked my cycle, you little bitch!"

"And you spat on your badge," Faith snarled back.

With a roaring chorus of fury, they charged.

Ingrained cop instinct cried out against what she was about to do. She ignored it and hit the lead vamp with every erg of her strength.

Her fist smashed into his head and his feet flew out from under him. His body crashed to the ground at her feet. She didn't look at what was left of his face. She didn't have to. She could feel the gore on her fist.

Faith didn't let it stop her as she pivoted to rake the second vamp across the chest with her talons. The third threw a roundhouse, and she ducked.

The second one, cursing in pain, drew his weapon. Faith flinched back, throwing up an arm as he fired. She felt the hot pain in her side and knew she'd been hit.

But she didn't go down.

Instead, she slapped out with one long arm and sent the gun flying. Snatching the vamp that had held it, she smashed him into the wall so hard plaster shattered, then heaved him into his partner. Both went down.

Faith didn't stop to finish them off. Jim didn't have that much time. Instead she leaped over their stunned bodies and flew down the corridor.

The hallway opened out into a ballroom, marbled in gleaming black and white tiles. A gang of uniformed vampires stood in a circle in the middle of the towering room, looking down and shouting like men at a football game.

Faith raced toward them . . .

Boom! The floor shook under her feet as something hot singed her fur. She ducked and spun.

Celestine stood just behind her, wearing a pissed-off expression and a great deal of leather, magic blazing around her hands. "I knew it was you when I heard that crash," the vampire witch growled. "You just don't have the sense to stay away." She hurled another energy blast. Faith ducked, and the spell splashed harmlessly against the column behind her.

From the center of the vampire's huddle, she heard a man bellow in pain and rage.

Jim!

Without hesitating, Faith flung herself straight into the gang of men. They saw her massive furred form flying toward them and dodged with startled shouts. She soared right past them—and into empty air.

With a startled yelp, she plunged into the pit.

NINETEEN

Faith hit the ground hard and rolled to blunt the impact. Even so, pain radiated savagely up her legs. She ignored it and surged to her feet.

Overhead, some vampire shouted a warning, and the rogues spun. Magic shimmered, and a big black wolf leaped from their midst—Jim.

Shit, she thought, *he must be hurt badly to risk changing to wolf form during a fight with that crowd.* One of the weres swiped at him, raking across his haunches. Jim bounded, barely avoiding capture.

He transformed, but as he did, she saw his magic twist and snake in a malformed surge. When he returned to Dire Wolf form, his face was twisted in a grimace of agony.

Something he'd said flashed through her mind—*if you Change too many times too close together, the magic can turn on you.*

Oh, God. He was cutting it too close.

* * *

Dammit, he knew it! There she was, rushing in to get herself killed for nothing.

With a roar of pure fury, Jim pivoted, grabbed the nearest werewolf by the muzzle and one shoulder, and jerked. The rogue's neck snapped like a green stick, and Jim let him fall.

"Taylor!" the heavyset rogue yelled, and drove his fist right at Jim's head.

Jim grabbed his wrist, opened his mouth, and crunched down on his hand, shattering the delicate bones. The rogue howled in pain and slapped him across the muzzle, raking his face with claws extended. Blood blinded him. Somebody grabbed him from behind in the same hold he'd used on Taylor and started trying to break his neck. Jim twisted, grabbed the man's arm, and heaved. The grizzled were went flying.

He looked around for Faith. To his horror, he saw Reynolds circling her as she pivoted with him, hot-eyed and wary.

Jim started toward them, but somebody slammed into his knees, taking him down hard. He kicked the heavyset were away just as Ayers landed on his chest. Clawed hands grabbed his throat and dug in.

He felt flesh tearing and drove both clawed hands for the other's gut. Blood spurted from his neck, but he ignored the pain and forced his talons deeper into fur and flesh. They started sinking into something slick.

With a screech, Ayers jerked away from him, transformed to wolf form, and scrambled away. Jim jumped up, meaning to grab the wolf and kill him before he had time to Change again.

But claws came out of nowhere, catching him across his wounded neck. He stumbled and went to one knee, as fanged jaws plunged toward his face.

Faith saw Jim stagger, and her heart stuffed its way into her throat. She had to get to him. She tried to dart around Reynolds.

The rogue stepped into her path, grabbed her, and slung her against the wall so hard, it drove the breath from her chest. "Uh, uh. You've got your own problems, bitch."

She recovered her balance and her breath enough to bare her teeth at him. "Traitor."

Ayers, a red-furred wolf, and the heavyset one she recognized as Young were attacking Jim from both sides. He couldn't last much longer, not with the blood pouring down his chest. He had to Change—but she wasn't sure he could without the magic turning on him.

The Spirit Link! Her eyes widened as she remembered the psychic bond he'd mentioned. He'd said they could just call the magic and Link. It was their only chance. But she had to get to him.

Reynolds started toward her, his jaws gaped, obviously expecting her to grapple.

Instead she feinted right and summoned her power. He saw it rise and dove for her, clawed hands outstretched, only to grab empty air as she leaped past in wolf form.

With a roar of rage, Reynolds wheeled to lunge after her.

Faith darted across the pit, saw Young blocking her way to Jim, and leaped, sinking her fangs into his hamstring. The big were howled and went down, grabbing for his thigh. She danced aside and plunged in. A red-furred were—Granger?—limped clear at her approach, but Ayers was bent over Jim as the two exchanged a flurry of blows. The chief's furry testicles hung between his spread thighs.

Faith sailed forward and sank her fangs right into them. The chief tried to jerk around, howling, tripped over her and fell, writhing in the dirt.

Bleeding from a dozen wounds, Jim rolled to his feet and aimed a clawed kick at Ayers. The chief ducked and scrambled off, transforming as he ran.

Swaying, obviously badly wounded, Jim stepped in front of Faith to provide cover while she transformed to Dire Wolf again.

"We've got to Spirit Link!" she panted, once she had

vocal chords. "It's the only way you're going to be able to transform!"

"Forget it." He didn't even look around, all his attention on their foes. "If you're Linked to me when I die, it'll kill you."

"If you die, I'm dead anyway!" she said savagely, watching grimly as the rogues regrouped. "I already thought you died once tonight, and it almost killed me then. It's the only chance we've got!"

"Fuck!" Ayers, Young, Granger, and Reynolds were edging around them, obviously preparing to charge. Jim grabbed her hand.

Faith licked her lips. "How do we . . . ?"

"Damned if I know. Just go!" He called the magic as she let her own surge. The pit lit up around them with a hot blue glow.

Having no idea of what to do or how to do it, Faith simply threw her consciousness toward his. For a moment, she touched him, felt the warm, solid strength of his mind.

And then the magic started to burn.

Startled, Faith screamed as Jim's body began to blaze hot and blue. *Shit!* Horror rolled over her. She sensed its match in him and knew what he was thinking.

He was losing it! He was going to die, and the rogue fire would destroy her, too.

Jim tried to force her consciousness from his as his body blazed brighter and brighter, the pain building to a searing burn. She felt him start to die.

No! You're going to live! Faith told him fiercely. *We're going to live!* Dragging in still more of the magic, she sent it streaming into him, picturing him as he was—handsome, stubborn Jim, the man she loved, the man she couldn't stand to live without.

The man she damned well wouldn't give up.

Even in the midst of his agony, she sensed his startled joy as he felt her love. Seizing her magic with his will, he drew it into his. Strengthened it. Together, they forced their mingled magic to obey. The fire began to cool, swirling around them, shaping itself into their Dire Wolf bodies.

Until at last it vanished, leaving them standing in the center of the pit on shaking legs, whole again.

Panting, they stared at one another, hardly daring to believe they'd survived after all.

"What the fuck was that?" Ayers demanded, his voice a bit too high.

Jim turned to bare his teeth. "Your curtain call."

As one, he and Faith bounded toward Ayers. She circled to the chief's left and went after him, forcing him to defend himself from her slashing claws as he retreated—right into Jim's waiting hands. As Faith turned to fend off Reynolds, he grabbed Ayers by the muzzle and whipped his other arm around the rogue's throat, jerking him violently off his feet. The werewolf flailed, raking Jim's face with his claws, ripping at his ears. Jim gritted his teeth and jerked, snapping Ayers's neck with a crack.

He dropped the chief's body and turned to meet Granger's furious charge. The red-furred were struck out at his eyes with his claws. Jim blocked, just as Faith, ducking Reynolds's roundhouse, suddenly spun in and rammed her clawed foot against the side of Granger's knee. The joint snapped. The rogue toppled with a howl of agony. Jim stepped forward and kicked like a football player going for a field goal, catching the rogue right under the chin. The force of the blow flipped him up and over to land on his head. His body toppled with a thud, neck unnaturally twisted.

Jim turned. Young and Reynolds had gone after Faith in a flurry of snapping teeth and ripping claws. Jim plowed into the heavyset were's side, knocking him into the wall. Young twisted, raking Jim's shoulders with his claws, trying to rip his neck with his teeth. Jim ducked his head, protecting himself, feeling Faith running up behind them through their Link. Before Young could get a grip, she dragged back his head and raked her claws across his throat. Yelping, he transformed to wolf form—and Jim broke his back.

Dropping the furry corpse, Jim turned just in time to sense Reynolds's fist hitting Faith through their Link. Her pain made him stagger, and he looked around to see the rogue smirking down at her. "Remember me?"

Jim leaped on him with a bellow. "Remember *me*, you son of a bitch?" They hit the ground together, clawing and biting.

Faith shook off the punch, rolled to her feet, and dove into the fray.

She and Jim went after the rogue without mercy, each feeling the other's intentions through their new psychic bond. Reynolds quickly realized the last place he wanted to be was in a close quarters fight with the two of them, so he tore himself free and raced off. They followed, grimly intent.

As Jim went for Reynolds's throat, forcing the rogue to back away, Faith raced around to his rear and hamstrung him with rake of her claws. He went down with a bellow, sending a last vicious kick into Jim's gut. Jim fell back, the wind knocked out of him.

Cursing, the rogue tried to regain his feet, realized his muscles wouldn't obey, and transformed to wolf to scuttle away. Faith pounced, in no mood to give the bastard any mercy. God knew he'd never had any for anyone else. A swipe of her claws sent him flying into the pit wall. She started to jump him, then thought better of it and held back, letting him transform again. Reynolds hadn't had to Change as often in as short a time as Jim, but he had to be pushing his limits by now.

To her disappointment, he didn't burn. Instead, he faced her in Dire Wolf form, panting, his eyes flicking to Jim's as the big man moved around to his left. "You really think you can win?"

Faith's grin was slow and nasty. "We're doing pretty well so far."

Jim just bared his fangs as they gathered themselves to charge. The rogue scuttled away from them both, fear in his eyes. He shot a look up at Celestine, who stood watching from the top of the pit. The rest of her vampires surrounded her, wearing identical expressions of hot anticipation.

Faith, following his gaze, saw the witch held an ornate gold cup in one hand. Was that the grail everybody was after?

"Celestine!" Reynolds called. "Help .me, dammit! They're cutting me apart!"

There was absolutely no pity on the vampire's face as she leaned over the pit, contempt in her eyes. "And you deserve nothing better. You had six-to-one odds on London, and he beat you all anyway." She smiled coldly, tauntingly, and toasted him with a mocking lift of the grail. "But you've done a really good job of feeding the rest of us. Thanks."

Reynolds stared up at her in growing fury. "You're just going to let them kill me?"

She shrugged. "Why not? Afterward, we'll kill them. Eight magical sacrifices are a lot better than two."

Oh, she is a bitch, Faith thought. She exchanged a worried look with Jim, realizing the vampire witch might be able to carry out her threat.

Reynolds stopped retreating to stare up at his former colleagues in helpless fury. "You're all just going to stand there and *watch*?"

"Well, Keith," one of them drawled. "You always were a bit of an asshole."

Sheer, blazing hate leaped in the werewolf's eyes as he returned his attention to his former mistress. "Remember when I told you a thirty-foot pit was too deep for a werewolf to jump out of?"

She lifted an arrogant brow. "Yes."

"I lied." Reynolds sprinted across the pit and threw himself at the edge. Catching the marble lip, he vaulted over it, slamming into the witch before she had time to scream.

The grail shot from her hands, revolved lazily, and hit the pit floor with a clang. Jim and Faith stared at the cup as it rolled across the ground, then dove for it simultaneously. As Jim scooped it up, a thunderous magical boom sounded, followed by a piercing female shriek.

The vampires howled. So did Reynolds.

Something plummeting over the lip of the pit, accompanied by Celestine's scream of fear and fury. The witch hit the ground with a meaty thud and a splatter of blood.

For a moment, Faith and Jim stared at the still body as the howls and screams increased in volume overhead. They exchanged a cautious glance and started toward the fallen witch.

"Get away!" The hiss was low and broken, but it stopped them in their tracks.

Celestine lifted her head. Her eyes glared wildly from a blood-smeared face. She peeled her lips back from her fangs as she fought to roll onto her side, freeing her right hand.

It was glowing.

"I'm going to heal myself," she snarled, "and them I'm gonna fuckin' kill you if it's the last fuckin' thing I do!"

"No," Faith growled, "not this time."

She didn't hesitate as she pounced on the vampire. Ignoring Celestine's clawing hands and the death spell they sent sizzling into her fur, Faith grabbed the witch's head and gave it a ruthless, efficient jerk. Something cracked, and Celestine went limp.

Faith let the body fall, and stepped back, swallowing hard.

She looked up to meet Jim's compassionate silver gaze. "You had no choice."

"Yeah." Faith straightened, feeling exhausted to the bone. "That's why I did it." Her attention fell on the grail he still cradled in one big hand. "Think there's any way we can destroy that thing? I'd love to get rid of the rest of these damned vampires without yet another battle to the death." She'd had about all of that she could stomach.

He frowned. "I think it takes some kind of magical spell. Just stomping on it won't do the job."

"Too bad." Faith bit her lip and looked upward, dreading the coming fight. "Damn, I wish we could do magic. A gate spell would come in really handy right now. We're going to have a hell of a time getting out of here."

He shrugged and tucked the grail in the curve of his arm like a football. "No time like the present."

Together, they backed up several paces, then ran for the other side of the pit and leaped.

But as they scrambled over the lip, a glowing sword blade blocked their way. Startled, they looked upward.

An armored knight stood there at the edge of the pit.

Before Jim could get a word out of his mouth, the knight lifted his sword and started to hack down right at their heads. His battle cry rang over the screams of the battling vampires. "For Avalon and for Merlin!"

"Shit." Jim pushed Faith aside and rolled in the opposite direction. As they scrambled to their feet and danced away from their furious armored attacker, they realized more than a dozen knights were locked in combat with the vampires. "Charlie's going to have a stroke."

Behind him, Faith saw a woman preparing to hurl a ball of energy at his head. "Stop!" she yelled, throwing up her hands in an *I'm unarmed* gesture. "We're the good guys!"

Jim lunged forward and grabbed the knight's wrists before he could bring the sword down on her head. "I'm Llyr Galatyn's brother-in-law!"

The warrior sneered and tried to jerk his wrists free of Jim's clawed fingers. "Prove it."

"Okay." Jim opened his free hand, revealing the cup he still held. "Llyr told me you guys are looking for this."

The knight's eyes went wide behind the slits in his visor. "Gwen?"

The woman stared, the spell she was about to cast winking out. "That's it! Arthur, it's the Black Grail!"

Arthur? Faith thought, startled. *King Arthur?*

Cautiously, Jim released the knight and offered him the cup. Giving him a wary look, Arthur took it.

As Jim and Faith watched and vampires battled around them, Arthur handed the Black Grail to his wife. With a flick of her delicate fingers, she opened a dimensional gate.

The four of them watched as the gate lifted into the air and rotated until it hung open and waiting over their heads.

Gwen began to chant, the words rising over the chaos of the raging battle. Her right hand began to glow as the spell took shape within it.

Faith caught her breath in wonder as the Maja tossed the Black Grail skyward and flung the energy blast at it with a final incomprehensible shout. The blast hit the grail with a silent, blinding burst of light.

Celestine's vampires froze, shouting in alarm, as if they'd finally sensed something. The cup began to glow, brighter and brighter until Faith was forced to shield her eyes.

Then the Black Grail exploded.

Spikes of power shot outward, slamming into the former cops, lighting them up until they blazed like stars, their mouths open in soundless screams. One by one, they vanished in a salvo of silent explosions.

Simultaneously, the energy spilled into the gate overhead in a flood of white-hot force. Distant screams of terror sounded, growing louder as more voices joined the rising death shriek.

Until it cut off.

Blinking, Jim and Faith looked at each other, each feeling the other's moment of stunned relief.

"Fuck you."

The werewolves and Magekind turned in surprise as a trembling furred figure rose from the seared floor beside the pit. Reynolds's feral eyes met theirs from the mask of red that was his face. He was covered in blood. With an involuntary start of pity, Faith realized the vampires had bitten him over and over.

"You haven't beaten me, you bastards," the were rasped. "I'm going to kick all your asses." He reached for the magic.

And screamed as he began to burn. Blazing, he staggered, clawing at the flames, shrieking in pain. For just a heartbeat, his gaze met Faith's in fear and pleading.

Then, mercifully, he vanished.

"What the fuck was that?" Arthur demanded, frowning at the empty space the rogue had occupied.

Jim sighed. "That's . . . a long story. And it's past time you heard it."

TWENTY

Charlie Myers *was* sitting in front of his TV in a wife-beater shirt and stripped boxers when Arthur Pendragon, King Llyr Galatyn, and Jim stepped through the dimensional gate.

The Dire Wolf chieftain gaped at them for a beat, a beefy, florid man with a receding hairline. Who had, Jim thought, entirely too much power for his intellect.

At last his stunned paralysis broke. *"You told him?"* Charlie roared at Jim in fury, leaping out of his easy chair, his face reddening.

"If you transform," Jim told him coldly, "I'm going to kick your ass."

"I'll help," Arthur drawled, resting one armored hand on Excalibur's hilt.

"And I will put you on a leash," Llyr snarled, moving to tower over Charlie. A tall, muscular Sidhe, he was dressed in a dark gray Armani suit that provided a stark contrast with his pale waterfall of hair. Something moved across his chest with the flap of wings and a lashing forked tail—the mark of the Dragon God, Cachamwri. Its agitated flight was an indicator of how pissed off Llyr really was.

Charlie's eyes flicked to the dragon, disconcerted, before he frowned and drew himself to what passed for his full height. His voice rang with self-righteous certainty. "Merlin himself—"

"Was my friend and ally," Llyr snapped back. "And he would have been appalled to see the Direkind sit back like cowards while we fight vampires you were designed to kill! I have lost three hundred warriors while you"—he curled a regal lip at the Bud on the arm of Charlie's recliner—"Sit around drinking beer."

"And I've lost a hell of a lot more people than that," Arthur growled. "There are another two thousand of Geirolf's vampires left. And *you*, by God, are going to help us find that last Black Grail and kill them!"

Unease flickered in Charlie's eyes. He took a step back, lifting his pudgy hands. "That's not our responsibility! Our job is keeping the Magekind in check." He shot Jim a glare that promised bloody retribution. "Which we can't do with everybody fucking *knowing* about us."

"We don't need to be kept in check!" Arthur roared back, in a fine royal rage.

"Merlin—"

"If they were going to lose control," Llyr interrupted, his icy rage a chilling counterpoint to Arthur's fury, "it would have been in the first two hundred years. It's been sixteen centuries—the danger is long past."

Charlie sneered. "You're just saying that because you married that bitch Diana, and—"

Llyr grabbed him by the throat and smashed him into the wall so hard the house shook. "One word," he hissed. "One more word, and *you die*!"

Charlie's eyes widened. Jim half expected him to transform, but he simply froze, obviously unable to move.

"I took an oath to Merlin to keep your secret," Llyr connued in that low, frigid whisper, "Do you think I would ave *married* one of you, knowing it would all come out, ad there been any need for secrecy any longer?" The mell of Sidhe magic rose, wild and deadly. "When I give n oath, I keep it." He bared his teeth. "So please believe ie when I tell you *it's time to come out of the kennel!*"

Jim's lips twitched to hear the king use Diana's favorite hrase.

Charlie threw a glare at Jim. "I guess we don't have a hoice, do we?"

Suddenly Jim had enough. "Give us a moment, gentle-ien, would you? Open another gate and go have a beer, or /hatever it is you drink."

Llyr and Arthur looked at him, then at Charlie. For a ioment, he thought one or the other would protest.

Then Llyr released Charlie and flicked his royal fingers. he two weres watched as he and Arthur stepped back irough the gate.

"You stupid fuck," Charlie snarled the second the gate /inked out. "I'm going to order your entire family sanc-oned."

"No, you're not." The magic poured into Jim in a hot, eady rush. It was stronger than it had ever been now that e was Linked with Faith, and he suspected his Dire Wolf orm was even bigger now.

A Dire Wolf again, he peeled his lips back from his :eth. "Change, Charlie. Come on. I dare you."

The chieftain took a step back as his eyes widened in larm. They both knew he couldn't take Jim in a fight. You wouldn't."

"Oh, wouldn't I?" He flexed his claws.

Charlie dropped his eyes.

"Pussy." Jim growled in disgust and called the magic gain. "Llyr's right," he said when he was human once iore. "Our secrecy has turned us into cowards. Arthur hould have been able to count on us as allies against those ionsters, instead of turning to the Sidhe."

"It wasn't our job!" But the Dire Wolf chieftain looked shamefaced even as he insisted.

"Yes, it was. It's past time we started pulling our own weight, and you know it. Call a meeting of the clans, Charlie. Tonight. We need to meet with Arthur and Llyr and decide how to kill the rest of these bastards."

Charlie stared at him. "The clans are going to blame me—and you, too."

"Not after Llyr and Arthur get through with them. Call the meeting, Charlie."

With a sigh, the chieftain picked up the phone.

Faith lay naked on a mound of pillows as the sun streamed down on her from the skylight overhead. A couple of feet away, Jim stood wearing only a pair of worn, paint-smeared jeans, a brush in one big hand as he worked at a huge canvas.

A week had passed since the showdown with Celestine and the vampires. There had been so many questions to answer, so many loose ends to tie up, they'd barely been able to steal any time together. And when they had, they hadn't done much talking.

"So how'd the latest meeting with the clans go?" she asked, enjoying the heat of the sunlight on her face.

There had been three clan conferences so far as the Direkind, Sidhe, and Magekind met to decide on a strategy for finding and destroying the last of Geirolf's vampires. The first had been the most personally nerve-racking, since for a while Faith had thought the gathered weres would kill her and Jim both before they had a chance to speak.

Luckily, Llyr had come to their defense with a combination of eloquence and terrifying power. Not even the Direkind, it seemed, wanted to piss off the Heir to Heroes.

Which also meant nobody was inclined to lay one hostile claw on Llyr's in-laws, the London clan.

Now Jim shrugged and leaned closer to the canvas, plyng his brush in tight, skillful strokes. "It was pretty ugly 'or the first hour or two—the Dire Wolf from Russia still sn't happy the Magekind knows our secret. But then Arthur and Llyr went to work on him, and he ended up on->oard. How'd your interview with the Atlanta chief go?"

"Surprisingly well. Turns out they fired Ron."

He looked over the edge of the canvas at her. "You're kidding!"

Faith smiled slightly. "A store camera caught him bang-ng his dispatcher in his patrol car."

Jim shook his head. "Hound."

"While they were both supposed to be on duty. She's gone, too."

"Revenge is sweet."

"And a little nutty. Met with that SLED agent and some->ody from the FBI yesterday, too." As the last surviving member of the Clarkston Police Department, Faith had known she'd face questions from South Carolina's State Law Enforcement Division.

Telling the truth was, obviously, out of the question for a number of reasons, chief among which was that nobody would believe it anyway.

Luckily, Faith had help developing a cover story from Guinevere and Llyr. The Magekind were old hands at stag-ng believable catastrophes to explain whatever they'd been engaged in.

In this case, they'd blown up Celestine's plantation and planted enough fake bodies to answer the question of where all those cops had gone.

After a short debate, everybody had agreed that reveal-ng the entire department had turned corrupt would do nothing but add to the agony of the cops' families.

Instead, Faith told investigators that Ayers and his offi-cers had discovered a member of a New York Satanic cult was in town, planning another terrorist attack. It had been a believable detail, since the cult in question was one of a number that had been in the news last year for a series of murders. Though the public didn't know it, the cult's killings had actually been sacrifices to Geirolf.

Faith explained that Ayers and the Clarkston cops had tried to launch an operation against the terrorist. She theorized that when they entered her hideout, Celestine detonated the fertilizer bomb she'd built, killing them all.

Again, believable. Celestine was already wanted in the murders of her entire family, after all.

Sheri Miller, her memories having been mercifully altered by Magekind magic, corroborated the story, as did several county dispatchers. She told investigators she'd tipped the cops off about Celestine's plans after she'd escaped an attempt to sacrifice her.

Faith explained that Ayers ordered her to protect the girl while the rest of the department staged its raid on Celestine's plantation. As a result, she'd escaped being caught in the blast.

Now, questions answered, Faith had finally joined Jim in Atlanta. She knew the investigation would probably go on for months, but the outcome wasn't really in doubt.

And if it ever was, either Llyr or some Maja would convince officials otherwise.

Jim straightened away from the canvas and rolled his powerful shoulders. "By the way, I got a call from Tony Shay's mother. She's invited us over for dinner on Friday. She wants to meet you." He smiled slightly. "So do my mom and dad. I thought we'd go see them on Sunday."

"Sure." Faith put a hand back and massaged the tight muscles in the base of her neck. She'd been posing for almost an hour. "Can we take a break? I'm feeling a little stiff."

Jim gave her a wicked smile. "Now that you mention it, so am I."

She returned that smile with one of her own. "Oh, really?"

Actually, she knew exactly how stiff he was—she could feel it through their Spirit Link. It teased her own need even higher.

Her posttransformation Burning Moon had ended, but her hunger for him seemed no cooler. Which was something of a relief, since in the back of her mind she'd wondered how much of their new love was a product of pheromones.

Turns out they could generate plenty of heat all by themselves.

Jim moved across the polished floor of the studio in a slow, seductive stride, his pale eyes heavy-lidded. Paint smeared his bare, muscular torso, and those faded jeans did little to hide his thick erection.

All afternoon, Faith had sensed his growing need through their Spirit Link. She strongly suspected he'd been fantasizing about just what he was going to do to her when they took a break. Only iron discipline had kept him working as long as he had—that and his determination to paint the portrait of her he'd apparently been dreaming of since they'd met.

Her heart pounding, Faith settled back on the peach silk covered studio bed. He'd sprinkled peach rose petals over her pale skin, and now they slid off her belly and fluttered down her breasts.

She looked down at the petals, then gave him a mischievous feline smile. "How are we ever going to get them arranged the same again?"

"I'll fake it," he said, and slid an arm around her to draw her up into his kiss.

Jim's mouth tasted like the honey and biscuits they'd had for breakfast, flavored with dark woods and wild magic. His hands felt warm and strong as he drew her against him, his tongue stroking slowly into her mouth. She opened for him, reaching up to cup the back of his dark head, savoring the wet slide of his kiss. One big hand tangled possessively in her unbound hair. Licking, sucking, they nibbled gently at each other's lips, tasting each other, savoring the sweet pleasure they felt.

With a low rumble of passion, Jim pressed into her, tumbling her backward on the slick silk. Faith laughed, a happy little bark of joy as he landed on top of her. "Why, hello there!" Purring, she wrapped her legs around his lean waist.

He smiled, the sunlight illuminating the pure, glowing silver of his eyes. "Hello, yourself." Cupping her cheek, he gazed into her face, content for the moment to simply look at her.

Faith traced her fingertips along the arrogant angle of his cheekbone, then down to his mouth. His lower lip felt like velvet, a bit damp from the kiss.

"You're beautiful," Jim breathed.

He meant it. She could sense the wonder in him, how the bright green of her eyes entranced him, how he loved the faint dimple on the left side of her lip, the stubborn line of her chin. Faith smiled at him and let herself feel her own delight in him—his tough, handsome face, his seductive mouth, that big, hard body. "I was thinking the same thing about you."

His lips quirked. "Sounds like we've got a mutual admiration society going here."

"Y'know—I think that's part of the whole 'hopelessly in love' thing."

"Good point." He rolled onto his side, the better to look down her slim, naked body. His fingers slid down to cup her breast, stroke the nipple, tease it to an aching point. Pleasure rose, slow and lazy. He played gently for a while, exploring down the length of her, testing the rise of her rib cage, the hollow of her navel.

Faith let her head fall back with a soft moan as the pleasure rose with every slow caress of his strong hands. When she finally looked down at herself to track the progress of those clever fingers, she found smears of cobalt and peach, emerald and crimson streaking her pale skin from his demanding touch. She glanced up to flash him a smile. "You've marked me."

He grinned, masculine satisfaction in his eyes. "Every chance I get."

"Maybe I should return the favor." Faith traced a fingertip through a dot of wet crimson on his chest, then drew a line of brilliant red across his cheek like war paint. Tilting her head, she considered the effect. "It suits you, my handsome warrior. My wild lover."

Jim inhaled sharply and kissed her again, suddenly ravenous, pushing her gently down on the bed. Long moments spun by as they kissed, sipping at one another's mouths in luscious exploration.

When he came up for air, it was only to switch his attention to her full breasts. Faith shuttered her eyes and simply floated in the silken sensations his lips and tongue created as he suckled and teased each nipple in turn. "Oh, God," she murmured, and eased her thighs apart.

He came down over her, still stroking her breasts, one hand sliding down between her thighs. She was slick and ready—no surprise, since just the sight of him at work with all that fierce concentration had turned her on.

Jim groaned at the sensation of her snug flesh gripping his fingers. He started working his way down her torso.

"No," Faith gasped, knowing what he intended. "I want to taste you, too."

Pale eyes flashed to hers and crinkled in a wicked smile. "You've talked me into it."

Eagerly, Faith sat up as he eased back to give her room. She reached for his zipper with a hand that shook ever so slightly with the intensity of their mutual need. Jim watched her fingers draw down the metal tab with hooded, hungry eyes. His hungry shaft pressed against the parting V, still contained by the white cotton of his briefs.

Watching her, he lifted his hips and let her slide jeans and underwear down his muscular legs.

At last his cock sprang free, so hard it stood more up than out, taut and aching with his need. Impatient, she tossed his jeans aside and held out her arms in welcome.

It was all the invitation he needed. With a hungry growl, Jim rolled her onto her back and straddled her, head down along her slender torso.

Faith caught her breath as his fingers spread her lips for his tongue. She looked up his cock, jutting just over her head as he knelt over her. Reaching up, she caught the thick shaft in one hand and dragged it down until she could run her tongue over its round, flushed head. It bucked longingly.

She swirled her tongue over and around the tight, warm flesh, then drew it into her mouth for a sucking pull, drawing so hard her cheeks hollowed. Jim's tormented groan rewarded her.

In turn, he attacked her clit with greedy licks and wicked little swirls. The pleasure soon had her rolling her hips against his face in longing thrusts. "God, that's good," she breathed.

"I was just thinking the same thing," he said, amusement in his voice, as he gently rocked his hips. The motion stroked his big cock between her fingers, silently begging for more.

So she gave it to him—nibbling gently on the crown of his cock, running her tongue along its underside until he panted and bucked.

And returned the favor, subjecting her to still more lush oral torture, dancing his tongue over her clit, tugging gently at her lips with his teeth, swirling his tongue around her most sensitive flesh until arousal burned through her in a sweet, fiery torrent.

Neither of them could take it for very long.

"Jim!" she gasped, begging.

"Yes . . ." He tore himself away from her, sweating, his eyes wild and bright as flung himself down and scooped her off the bed. Eagerly, she threw a leg over his hips and positioned herself. Strong hands wrapped around her waist, lifted her, impaled her on his cock in one luxurious plunge.

She hissed in pleasure, throwing her head back until her hair whipped the small of her back. He rolled his hips upward, urging her on.

Taking his cue, Faith started riding him, gasping each time the thick shaft plunged deep. Shuttering her eyes in blind delight, she ground down as he lunged up in deep, impatient thrusts that jammed delight into them both. He felt huge, filling her, rocking her, all surging strength and pleasure. Primeval and male and impossibly delicious.

Faith convulsed with a shout as a rolling orgasm stormed her nervous system, twisting and sparking like an electric line.

As she came, Jim stiffened and drove to his full length, roaring as he came. She felt him pour himself out in deep, heavy pulses.

At last they collapsed together, shaken and spent, their bodies still twitching from the ferocity of the pleasure storm.

Long moments passed as they lay panting together. Boneless, she clung to him and listened to his heart pound. "This feels so damn good," he groaned.

She smiled and rubbed her cheek against his. "I was just thinking the same thing. I could stay like this forever." Faith lifted her head and gave him an impish grin. "I love you so much, it's almost embarrassing."

Jim went suddenly still. She could feel what he was thinking. Scarred by past betrayals, she would have never said anything like that before. "I'm not afraid anymore," Faith told him simply. "You'd never hurt me."

"Not as long as I draw breath." Jim's arms tightened around her. "I love you more than I've ever loved anyone or anything."

And he did. She could feel it there in the depths of his soul, just as he felt her own love for him. He opened his mouth, but before he could ask the question, she grinned. "Yes."

"Hey!" Jim gave her a mock glare. "You're supposed to let me ask first. I've been practicing."

"I know. I heard you." She winked. "Dire Wolf ears."

"Yeah, well, you haven't heard this." He reached a hand under the pillow and drew out a small velvet box.

Faith stared at it. Suddenly the question he was trying to ask seemed a lot more serious.

With a thumb, he opened the lid, revealing an exquisite ruby set in a beautifully ornate gold band. "It was my grandmother's," he told her softly. "When I came back from my first transformation, she gave it to me to give to my wife."

Stunned, she looked up into his warm silver gaze.

"Faith Weston," Jim asked, "will you marry me?"

Her smile trembled. "How could I do anything else?"

Turn the page for a special preview of
Angela Knight's next novel

MASTER OF SWORDS

Coming October 2006 from Berkley Sensation!

Greenhaven, North Carolina

Lark McGuin took a bite of her dinner as her tension headache faded away. She was still a little shaky from last night's close call, but there was no better comfort food than her mother's fried chicken.

And no better accompaniment to that meal than the sounds of her family laughing, squabbling, and generally having a good time around her.

Her father was currently giving her niece a hard time. George McGuin was a tall, lanky man, with an angular face and big, square hands. There was more gray in his hair every time Lark saw him, but she did her best to ignore it. "Just remember," he told Kerry Rogers, "Twenty-one or sixty-one, you'll always be my baby."

Kerry gave him an affectionate grin. "Well, duh."

Lark's sister smiled at her daughter. "What Dad is trying to say is, just because you're legal, don't start hanging around in bars."

"And if you do, don't go picking up any strange men," added Lark dryly. *Look what happened to me.* She didn't regret that night, but it had certainly complicated her life.

"Oh, give me a break!" Kerry rolled her eyes. Petite, pretty, and dark haired, she looked just like her mother at that age. "How dumb do you think I am, anyway?"

"Men have a way of overcoming a woman's common sense." Robin grinned at her husband, a bluff, balding auto worker with broad shoulders and a perpetual grin. "Your daddy overcomes mine every chance he gets."

Larry Rogers smirked. "It's what I live for."

"Speaking of what we live for, isn't it time for the cake?" George lifted his bushy gray eyebrows hopefully at Lark's mother.

Sherry McGuin sighed. "I guess that's my cue." Plump and pretty, gray salting her once-dark hair, she'd been cooking for her granddaughter's birthday dinner all day.

"You stay in that chair," Lark told her firmly. "I'll get it." Wiping her mouth with her napkin, she rose and headed for the kitchen.

Like the rest of the house, it was a homey room, warm and welcoming. The chocolate cake sat on the butcher-block counter, topped by twenty-one unlit candles, guarded by a member of Sherry's collection of ceramic roosters.

Lark glanced around for the box of matches, but it was nowhere to be seen. Which meant she was in for fifteen minutes of pawing through drawers and cabinets to find it. Her mother kept a neat home, but organization had never been Sherry's strong suit.

Maybe . . . Lark shot a glance at the dining room door just as her niece drawled a protesting "Graaandaaaad!" Sounded like everyone's attention was still safely focused elsewhere.

She flicked her fingers with a quick mental chant, summoning a tiny burst of magic. Instantly the circle of twenty-one candles burst alight.

Much simpler.

With a satisfied smile, Lark picked the cake up and carried it into the dining room as she started to sing. "Happy birthday to you . . ."

onesville, Tennessee

Make a left," Kel said. Sir Gawain leaned into the turn, teering the big Harley Davidson Electra Glide down Henry Street with absent skill. Normally you couldn't neak up on a deaf man on an Electra Glide, since the massive bike's Twin Cam 88 engine roared like all the hounds of hell. Tonight, however, the motorcycle glided along as ilently as a ghost, Kel's magic having rendered it utterly ilent. Even its headlights were off. With his vampire night ision, Gawain didn't really need them anyway.

The Geirolfians might sense his approach magically, but here was no reason to give them any extra warning.

"This is it," Kel said. "Up ahead on the right."

There was only one building on the right, a big modern tructure with curving walls, most of which were stained lass. A towering spire thrust from its cream brick face. Gawain frowned at the cross that topped the spire as he brought the hog to a halt. "Kel, this is a church." He'd earned years ago how to speak so softly no one but his partner could hear him.

"Yeah, well, this is where the trail leads."

"They're planning to sacrifice that girl in a church? Most of Geirolf's crowd constructs underground temples or this kind of sick shit."

"Maybe they didn't want to spend the magic on building one."

"Or maybe they're the kind of assholes who like to desecrate churches." Gawain swung off the bike and drew the our-foot blade sheathed diagonally across his back.

"Gawain, they kidnapped a sixteen-year-old virgin to murder in an act of death magic," the sword said. "I'd say he asshole thing is pretty much a given."

"Good point." He grinned, slowly and viciously. "Guess we'll kill 'em slow, then."

"Sounds like a plan to me."

Gawain started up the sidewalk toward the double glass doors that looked as though they'd lead to the sanctuary. His black motorcycle leathers creaked faintly as he walked. He was acutely aware of the sound, every sense alert and singing with the rise of adrenaline.

"I think it's time for a wardrobe change," he told Kel in a low voice. "For this, I'm going to need something a little more substantial than cowhide."

"That's what I'm here for."

The faceplate of his motorcycle helmet began to glow and morph, reforming itself into the Dragon Helm Gawain had worn into combat most of his long life. At the same time, he felt his leathers transform, becoming even lighter and more flexible. "Thanks."

Though most of the Knights wore plate, the armor Kel created lay over Gawain's body in thousands of tiny magical scales that shifted with his every movement. The suit was as beautiful as it was otherworldly—a shimmering iridescent blue that reminded him of dragon scales. Despite its seeming delicacy, it could have stopped a tank blast.

Considering what he was going up against, Gawain needed all the protection he could get. He was a Magus—one of the vampire knights of Avalon—which meant he couldn't cast spells. The vamps he was hunting were the spawn of Geirolf, an alien demon that had created them as a perverted version of Merlin's knights. Like their late, unlamented master, they practiced death magic, drawing power from the life force of their victims.

Which was why they'd snatched sixteen-year-old Theresa Davis from the steps of the town library half an hour ago. It was a good thing Gawain was already in Jonesville hunting them, or Theresa wouldn't have a prayer. It was also damned lucky Kel could follow the

Geirolfians' magical trail, allowing Gawain to start tracking them as soon as he learned of her disappearance.

He paused at the church entrance, gathering himself, enjoying the furious thump of his own heart, the power that surged through his body. A feral grin spread across his face.

The grin disappeared when he heard a faint sound through the glass doors—a muffled female cry of pain. Over it rang an ugly shout of male laughter.

"Doors," Gawain snarled. Normally he'd kick them in, but the breaking glass would make hell's own racket. A shimmer of magic flung them wide, and he strode in, sword in hand.

Somebody was going to pay dearly for what they'd done to Theresa Davis.

Greenhaven, North Carolina

Kerry's gifts had been unwrapped and the dishes put away by the time Lark escaped out to the back porch. Settling into the wooden swing with a sigh, she gazed through the porch's surrounding screen at the moon rising over the trees.

Damn, it felt good to be back. Her parents had lived in the sprawling brick Colonial since she was ten years old. Though Lark had her own place now, this would always be home.

It was a pretty spring night, and lightning bugs circled the yard, flashing on and off like flying green Christmas tree bulbs. Frogs croaked in the darkness, calling out to mates or rivals as crickets chirped their backup vocals from the surrounding woods.

Lark let her head fall against the back of the swing and took a deep breath, inhaling the sweet, heavy scent of honeysuckle. Living in the tiny town of Greenhaven had its drawbacks, but spring nights weren't one of them.

Her sister stepped through the sliding glass door onto the porch, then closed it behind her. "Mind if I join you?"

" 'Course not." She took another deep breath as Robin slid into the seat beside her. "Smell that. Now *that's* magic. One deep breath and I'm a kid again, catching lightning bugs and roasting marshmallows. You can almost taste the s'mores."

Her sister sighed, settling back against the swing's wooden back. "And the hot dogs. Don't forget the hot dogs." A smile of quiet remembrance lit her face. Moonlight silvered her high cheekbones even as it hid the tiny spray of crowsfeet in the corner of her eyes.

At the thought of her sister's age, pain bit into Lark's chest. Her entire family was getting older. Second by second, they were leaving her, like sand castles succumbing to the tide.

She thrust away the depressing thought and pushed off with her foot, sending the swing rocking. For a moment, there was no sound except the metallic creak of its chains.

"You were quiet tonight."

Lark shrugged. "Work's been tough lately." Her sister was the only member of the family who knew what she did. What she was.

"Y'all still hunting bad guys?"

"Yeah." She pushed a little harder than she intended, and the swing groaned as it picked up speed. "Nasty bastards."

"Lark McGuin!" Robin affected a scandalized tone. "Momma would wash your mouth out with soap!"

"Not if she'd ever met any of them." Lark's smile faded. "I almost died last night." She winced, regretting the words the minute they left her mouth.

In the moonlight, shock slackened Robin's face. "But . . . I thought you said you're immortal!"

"No, I just don't age, which is not the same thing." She had to cast a glamor on herself whenever she went to visit the family, planting crow's feet around her eyes and gray in her hair. Otherwise they'd wonder why forty-two-year-old Lark looked the same age as twenty-one-year-old Kerry. "I an still get killed. It just takes a lot more to do it." And Geirolf's demonic creations were more than up to the task.

Robin studied her face anxiously. "So what happened?"

She shrugged. "A couple thousand bad guys invaded Avalon."

"On the other Earth?" Robin had struggled with the idea that there could be a mirror Earth in another universe, one where magic was as commonplace as gravity. It was Lark's true home now. "How did they get there?"

"Same way we do—they created a magical gate." Lark stared blindly at the moon, remembering the moment of stark terror when she'd seen thousands of enemy fanatics pouring into the central square of the Immortal City, chanting that chilling battle cry of theirs. *We live in Geirolf. Geirolf lives in us!* "One minute it's business as usual. The next, we're up to our backsides in magic-using vampires."

"What did you do?" Robin's eyes were so wide, the whites showed all around her irises.

"Fought. Fought like hell." Flexing her hand, she looked down at it. The flesh was as clean and pink as ever. Thanks to the Maja healer, there was no sign of the death magic that had seared her fingers black the night before. "I damned near lost anyway."

"Oh, God."

"Yeah." Unable to sit still any longer, Lark rose from the swing and began to pace, remembering those moments of terror. The spawn's twisted, wild-eyed face, black hair standing straight up on his head, too-white fangs shining as he snarled into her face. "The Geirolf vamp got me down, Robin. He burned the sword out of my hands, and he jumped on top of me. He had one fist in my hair. I was blasting him with everything I had, and it wasn't doing any good. He didn't seem to feel it at all." She blew out a breath and tried to shake off the memory. "He was about to tear out my throat when he disappeared."

Robin swallowed. "Where did he go?"

"Dead. Lady Guinevere destroyed the Black Grail that

had created this particular group of vamps, and the resulting blast killed all of them." Lark took a deep breath. "But if she'd been five minutes later . . ."

"Don't think about that."

She'd been trying not to dwell on the memory all day, but it kept sliding back into her consciousness, insidious as fog. "Easier said than done."

"But all that's over now." Robin studied her face anxiously. "Right? The vampires are dead. It's over?"

Lark shook her head. "No. There's another group of vamps. We don't know exactly how many, but estimates put them at least at a couple of thousand. Geirolf created three Black Grails to make his army, and we've destroyed two of them with a special spell. Each time we blew one up, the spell killed all the vamps that drank from it. If we can just destroy that last one, it'll wipe the final third out. But we've got to find it first."

"My God." Robin shook her head. "I knew you were worried about something, but I didn't realize it was this bad."

"I didn't want to tell you, but after last night . . ."

"Lark, don't go back." Robin rose from the swing and moved to take her hands. "Please. They don't need you. They've got plenty of witches . . ."

"Not as many as we had." Lark shook her head, remembering the funerals she'd been to in recent months. "We've lost so many people fighting these lunatics. We need every Maja and Magus we've got if we're going to beat them."

"*I don't care.*" Robin's grip tightened almost hard enough to hurt. "You're the only sister I have, Lark! I don't want to lose you!"

"You're not going to lose me." But the words didn't sound nearly as convincing as she'd like.

"Lark, I damn near did last night, and I didn't even know it! And what the hell would I tell Mom and Dad? 'Hey, there's this secret I've been keeping for twenty-one years. Lark picked up one of the Knights of the Round Table in a bar and turned into a witch, but we never told you because she had to save the world. But now some evil vampire ate her, and she's dead.' Boy, wouldn't that be a fun conversation?"

Lark rubbed her forehead with her free hand, feeling the first throb of a headache. "I shouldn't have said anything. It was stupid and self-indulgent."

"No, it wasn't. I've got a right to know." Robin tightened her grip on Lark's fingers until her knuckles went white. "And so do Mom and Dad. You've got to quit lying to them."

"What good would that do? They'd just worry. Exactly the way you're worrying now."

"So? That's what families do!" There were deep lines around her mouth that hadn't been there before.

"Dammit, I should have kept my trap shut. But I'm scared, and I just wanted . . ." Lark broke off, furious with herself. Well, she'd screwed this up royally, hadn't she? Par for the course.

And now she had to do something she hated.

Looking deeply into her sister's worried eyes, she shot the spell home. "I just wanted to tell you how much I love you."

Robin blinked. The fear drained from her gaze as the lines around her mouth smoothed away. "Well, of course you do, hon." She looked around, her face going blank with confusion. "What we were talking about? I seem to have lost track."

Lark leaned over and kissed her on the cheek. "Nothing important, honey. You get on back to your family now. I've got to return to Avalon."

Robin smiled and patted her hand. "You take care of yourself now."

Lark's smile felt tight. "I'll try."

Jonesville, Tennessee

Gawain shoved open the double doors of the sanctuary with a crash. The three Geirolfians at the other end of the room looked up with a chorus of snarls. They crouched around a slim, blond girl lying on the red carpeted floor in front of the altar. They'd stripped and gagged her, then bound her spreadeagle with a spell.

Three monsters dressed in red robes, surrounding the naked teen as one of them prepared to drive a dagger into her chest. She sobbed in terror.

"What are you doing here, hero?" One of them laughed, the sound oozing lust and triumph. "Want a piece?"

Gawain's temples began to pound. He broke into a run, a wordless roar of rage tearing from his mouth as he charged down the aisle.

Leers turned to startled fear. "What the fu—"

The one with the knife never finished his curse. Gawain sent his head flying with one swing of the dragon sword.

The other two leaped in opposite directions, cursing. Magical armor shimmered into being around them, swords filling their hands.

The vamp on the right barely got his weapon up before Gawain hit him. Steel clashed on steel with a force the knight felt all the way to the bone. He ignored it. All he wanted was the bastard's head.

Light and heat exploded in his face as the Geirolfian shot a magical blast at his head. The Dragon Helm protected him, sending the blast splashing harmlessly away. Gawain ignored it, hammering the sword against the demon's guard, trying to break through.

"Gawain, behind . . ."

He spun before Kel finished the warning, first parrying the third vampire's attack, then kicking him so viciously in the gut, the Geirolfian flew ten feet to crash into the pews.

Gawain whirled back in time to block the blade swinging at his head. Another stinging blast of magic. Kel countered it with a mystical surge of his own, sending the vampire stumbling back. Gawain saw his moment and swung his blade with all his vampire strength. The other tried to block, but he was too late. The sword took off his head at the jaw.

Boom! Gawain went flying as the last Geirolfian's magical blast knocked him off his feet. He rolled, gritting his teeth against the wave of cold as the death spell tried to take hold. Kel smothered it the instant before Gawain slid to a stop, panting, sprawled on his back.

"Geiroooooolf!" The third vampire leaped toward him, sword lifted to cleave him in two.

He rolled aside the instant before the Geirofian hit the ground, bringing his sword smashing down where Gawain's head had been. The blade crunched into the floor, sinking five inches into the carpeted wood.

Where it lodged fast.

The vampire's panicked gaze met Gawain's as he realized he couldn't draw his weapon free in time.

Gawain grinned.

One sword-swing later, his enemy's body and head toppled in two different directions.

He turned to scan the church. "Anybody else?"

"Evidently not," Kel told him.

The knight looked toward the altar. "Oh, shit." With her captors' deaths, the spell that had held the girl had collapsed. She was gone.

But not far. Gawain's vampire senses easily detected the frantic pound of her heart, the rasp of her breathing as she crouched behind the priest's massive wooden podium in a shuddering knot of terror.

Gawain sighed and murmured, "Give her something to wear, Kel, would you?"

Magic shimmered from behind the podium. The girl gasped and jumped to her feet, staring down at the jeans and T-shirt that had suddenly materialized over her body. Then she froze, her gaze flying to Gawain as she realized she'd given herself away.

He sheathed Kel in the scabbard that hung across his

back. She didn't look comforted. Probably the helm—
between its snarling muzzle and the dragon wings on either
side of his head, it made him look even more intimidating
than he normally did. Quickly, he pulled it off and tucked it
under one arm. Raising his empty hand, Gawain started
talking, keeping his tone low and soothing. She'd been
frightened more than enough already. "No, it's okay. It's
okay. I'm not going to hurt you. I'm here to help. You're
safe."

The girl looked like the child she was as she stared at
him, her blue eyes huge, her mouth trembling. A gamine
cap of honey blonde hair added to the terrified waif effect.
"Who are you?"

Gesturing at his shimmering scale armor, Gawain tried
for a joke. "Can't you tell? I'm the knight in shining armor." He took a step forward.

Theresa cringed, gripping the podium. "Stay away from
me!" Her gaze flicked to the nearest of the three corpses.
She started to shake harder. "Don't hurt me."

"I only hurt bad guys, Theresa. That's the first rule of
the knight in shining armor gig." Despite his careful smile,
she didn't look as if she trusted him as far as she could
throw him. He tried again. "Why don't we find a phone and
call your parents to come get you?"

Some of her frightened tension relaxed at the mention
of her family. "They took my cell phone."

"Yeah, but I'll bet there's an office." Spotting a door to
the left of the altar, he jerked a thumb at it. "Maybe there's
a phone through there."

Theresa brightened. "That's right! I . . . um . . . go to
this church. The pastor's office is down the hall on the
left."

"Want to show me the way?" He could have found it
himself, but she needed a little control over the situation.

"Ummm. Sure." Cautiously, the girl slipped down the
steps and ducked toward the door, half-turned as she kept
one wary eye on him. In her hurry, she almost stepped on

one of the corpses. Gawain winced as she cringed back from it. "What about . . . them?"

"Don't worry about it, sweet. Kel will clean it up."

"Thanks a lot."

She jumped and looked around wildly. "Who was that?"

He gestured at the sheathed blade. "Just my sword."

"Your sword?" Theresa's eyes widened as she stared at the long hilt extending past his shoulder. "What, does it have a computer?"

"A *computer*?" Kel made a huffing sound in his ear. "I'm magic, child."

She opened her mouth, probably to inform them there was no such thing, then evidently thought better of it. Instead she said, "Magic?"

Gawain looked at the hilt. Its quillions were shaped like uplifted wings and its pommel like a dragon's head. At the moment, Kel's tiny reptilian face looked distinctly disgusted. "It's actually a dragon. One of Kel's enemies turned him into a sword sixteen centuries ago. We've been partners ever since."

"That's one word for it," Kel said dryly.

"He's been trapped in a sword for sixteen hundred years?" Attention successfully diverted, Theresa pushed open the door and walked into the hallway ahead of him. "Man, that must suck!"

"Yeah," Kel agreed. "Speaking of sucking, you had a pretty rotten night."

She shuddered. "Yeah. I'm going to have nightmares for years."

"No, actually, you won't."

Gawain stepped forward to catch her sagging body just as the girl passed out, rendered unconscious by a wave of Kel's magic.

"She won't remember anything," the sword told him as he swept her into his arms. "The police will conclude she was knocked cold for most of it."

Gawain frowned as he lifted her into his arms and carried her down the hall in search of the office. "How are we going to explain what happened to the bad guys? A dozen witnesses saw her snatched."

"Simple," Kel said. "They got into an argument and shot each other."

"Kel, I beheaded them."

The dragon's tiny eyes flared hot white. "Not any more. Now the heads are reattached and they've got big bullet holes in a whole lot of places."

"That works."

"I thought so."

"So—what? Our girl runs to the church office to call 911 as soon as the bullets stop flying?"

The sword considered the idea. "Why not? She won't remember you at all."

"And here I always thought I was so memorable." He looked through a window in one of the hallway doors and spotted a desk and phone. Testing the doorknob one-handed while supporting Theresa with the other, he found it locked. Breaking the lock with a ruthless twist of his wrist, he shouldered his way through.

Carefully, Gawain put the girl down in the office chair. Stroking a gentle hand over her gleaming hair, he looked down at her a moment. "Take care of yourself, sweet." He turned and walked out of the office the moment before Kel's spell woke Theresa.

As he strode down the church corridor, he heard her pick up the phone. It felt good to save one for once. Unfortunately, there were plenty more victims where she came from.

And even more vampires to kill.

Jane's Warlord
by Angela Knight

The sexy debut novel from
the author of
Master of the Night

The next target of a time travelling killer,
crime reporter Jane Colby finds herself in the
hands of a warlord from the future sent to
protect her—and in his hands is just where
she wants to be.

"CHILLS, THRILLS...[A] SEXY TALE."
—EMMA HOLLY

0-425-19684-4

Available wherever books are sold or at
penguin.com

From the author of
Master of the Night

Master of the Moon
by Angela Knight

In the light of the moon,
a sexy paranormal world awakens.

Unknown to the citizens of her small town,
policewoman Diana London is a shape-shifting
werewolf on the track of a killer vampiress.
And through erotic dreams, Diana is drawn to
Llyr, king of the faeries.

"THE FUTURE BELONGS TO KNIGHT."
—EMMA HOLLY

0-425-20357-3

Available wherever books are sold or at
penguin.com

B866

Three novellas of bold erotic adventure by
USA Today bestselling author

Angela Knight

MERCENARIES
0-425-20616-5

Beautiful Trinity Yeager's mission: join Nathan
August's star-hopping team of mercenary soldiers.
With one condition: Trinity must prove her resilience
as a lover for him and his first officer, Sebastian Cole.
Trinity not only sees Nathan's bet. She raises it.

"A STAR IS BORN."
—*ROMANTIC TIMES*

"EXHILARATING...A NEW WRITING TALENT
HEADING FOR THE STARS."
—*MIDWEST BOOK REVIEW*

Available wherever books are sold or at penguin.com

B867